The Three Investigators
in

The Flaming Footprints

The Nervous Lion

The Singing Serpent

This *Three Investigators* Three-in-One
was first published in 1994 by Diamond Books,
77–85 Fulham Palace Road, Hammersmith,
London W6 8JB.

The Three Investigators
in

THE FLAMING
FOOTPRINTS

by M.V. Carey

Based on characters created by
Robert Arthur

The Mystery of the Flaming Footprints was first published
in the UK in a single volume in 1972 by
William Collins Sons & Co. Ltd.

A word from
Alfred Hitchcock

Since it is awkward to be introduced to someone you
already know, those of you who are acquainted with
The Three Investigators may skip this introduction and
proceed directly to Chapter One, where the fun begins.

If you have not yet met Jupiter Jones, Pete Crenshaw,
and Bob Andrews, however, a smattering of background
information on this remarkable trio may be in order.

Any discussion of The Three Investigators begins
with Jupiter Jones, the plump and brainy lad who has
no hesitation in admitting that he is the leader of the
group—First Investigator and, according to some
individuals, chief troublemaker. Jupiter is assisted in
his endeavours by Pete Crenshaw, an athletic boy with a
prudent desire to avoid danger. This desire is frequently
thwarted when Jupiter Jones has a case to solve. The
third member of the team is Bob Andrews, a quiet,
studious type whose part-time job in the library gives
The Three Investigators quick and expert access to
information on almost any subject.

All of these lads reside in Rocky Beach, a small town
on the shore of the Pacific Ocean, not too far from
Hollywood. Bob Andrews and Pete Crenshaw live with
their parents, but Jupiter Jones, who was orphaned
when he was very young, makes his home with his aunt
and uncle. He assists them in the care and management
of The Jones Salvage Yard, the most well-organized
junk operation on the entire Pacific Coast.

One must admit that Jupiter occasionally neglects his

duties at the salvage yard when there are more exciting things to claim his attention—such as the lonely Potter whom you will encounter shortly, and the bewildered visitors who come to Rocky Beach anticipating a pleasant summer, only to find themselves living in a house which is haunted by a barefooted ghost.

Or is it haunted by something even more sinister?

Of one thing you can be certain, Jupiter Jones and his chums will find out.

So much for the introductions. On with the adventure!

ALFRED HITCHCOCK

I

The Potter Appears–and Disappears

JUPITER JONES heard the truck turn off the Coast
Highway. There was no mistaking it. It was The
Potter.

Jupe had been raking the white gravel drive of The
Jones Salvage Yard. Now he stopped and listened.
"He's coming this way," announced Jupiter.

Aunt Mathilda was nearby, watering the geraniums
she had planted along the edge of the drive. She turned
the nozzle of the hose, cutting off the flow of water, and
looked down the short street towards the highway.
"Now why on earth?" she wondered.

The Potter's ancient truck wheezed up the very slight
grade between the Coast Highway and The Jones
Salvage Yard. "He'll never make it," said Aunt
Mathilda.

Jupiter grinned. The man who was known in Rocky
Beach simply as The Potter was a source of some
anxiety to his Aunt Mathilda. Every Saturday morning,
The Potter drove his battered old truck into town to
pick up his supplies and groceries for the week. Often
Aunt Mathilda had been present when the truck
coughed and spluttered its way into the parking lot
outside the Rocky Beach Supermarket. Always Aunt
Mathilda predicted that the ancient vehicle would never
be able to groan and puff back up the highway. Always
Aunt Mathilda was wrong.

This Saturday was no exception. The truck topped the little slope with steam spouting from the radiator. The Potter waved and swung round the corner and into the salvage yard. Jupe jumped to get his stocky self out of the way, and the truck veered past him and stopped with a tired gasp just inside the gate of the yard.

"Jupiter, my boy!" shouted The Potter. "How are you? And Mrs Jones! My, you're looking radiant this June morning!"

The Potter fairly bounced out of the cab of his truck, his spotless white robe swirling around him.

Aunt Mathilda could never decide whether or not she approved of The Potter. It was true that he was one of the most skilled craftsmen on the West Coast. People came from as far south as San Diego and as far north as Santa Barbara to buy the pots and jars and vases that he fashioned so beautifully. Aunt Mathilda admired fine craftsmanship. Still, she believed firmly that all male human beings should wear trousers once they had graduated from the romper stage.

The Potter's flowing robes disturbed her sense of things as they should be. So did The Potter's long, gleaming white hair and his neatly combed beard, to say nothing of the ceramic medallion that dangled from a leather thong about his neck. The design on the medallion was a scarlet eagle with two heads. In Aunt Mathilda's opinion, one head per eagle was the right number. The two-headed bird was only another of The Potter's strange whims.

Now Aunt Mathilda looked down at the man's feet with open disapproval. As always, The Potter was barefooted. "You'll step on a nail!" warned Aunt Mathilda.

The Potter only laughed. "I never step on nails, Mrs Jones," he told her. "You know that. But I could do with some help from you folks today. I am expecting—"

The Potter stopped suddenly and stared at the cabin which served as office for the salvage yard. "What," demanded The Potter, "is that?"

"Mr Potter," said Aunt Mathilda, "do you mean you haven't seen it? It's months old." She lifted a picture frame down from the office wall and offered it to The Potter for his examination. Under the glass was a series of brightly coloured photographs with captions. They had obviously been taken from a magazine. There was one of the front of The Jones Salvage Yard. In the picture, Uncle Titus posed proudly before the wooden fence which surrounded his yard. Artists of Rocky Beach had decorated the fence with a painting of a sailing ship struggling through a stormy, green ocean. In the photograph, one could clearly see a curious painted fish which thrust its head above the waves to watch the ship.

Beneath the photograph of the salvage yard was a picture of Mr Dingler, who made silver jewellery in a small shop in Rocky Beach, and one of Hans Jorgenson painting a seascape. And there was one of The Potter himself. The photographer had snapped an excellent close-up of the old man as he emerged from the market, his beard gleaming in the sunlight, his two-headed eagle showing clearly against the white of his robe— and a very ordinary, everyday bag of groceries clutched in one arm. The caption beneath The Potter's photograph pointed out that the residents of Rocky Beach were not disturbed if some of the more artistic citizens took to wearing eccentric garb.

"Surely you knew about it," said Aunt Mathilda.

11

"It's from *Westways* magazine. You remember, they did a story on the artists in the beach towns?"

The Potter frowned. "I didn't know," he said. "I remember one day there was a young man with a camera. I didn't pay much attention. We get so many tourists and they all seem to have cameras. If only . . ."

"If only what, Mr Potter?" asked Aunt Mathilda.

"Nothing," said The Potter. "It can't be helped now." He turned away from Aunt Mathilda and her treasured photograph and put a hand on Jupe's shoulder. "Jupiter," he said, "I'd like to look through your merchandise. I'm expecting company, and I'm afraid my guests may find my house a little . . . well, a little bare."

"Expecting company?" echoed Aunt Mathilda. "My gracious to heavens!"

In spite of his cheerful, outgoing ways, The Potter had never been known to have a close friend. Jupiter knew that his aunt was wondering mightily who might be coming to visit the old man. However, she refrained from questioning him and simply ordered Jupiter to show him around. "Your Uncle Titus won't be back from Los Angeles for more than an hour," she said, and hurried away to turn off the hose at the tap.

Jupe was only too happy to show The Potter around. Aunt Mathilda might have her doubts about the old man, but Jupe liked him. "Live and let live" seemed to be his motto, and Jupe thought it was no one's business but The Potter's if he enjoyed bare feet and white robes.

"Now first," said The Potter, "I'll need a couple of bedsteads."

"Yes, sir," said Jupe.

The Jones Salvage Yard was an extremely well-organized operation. It would be hard to imagine any

12

other kind with Aunt Mathilda Jones on the scene. Jupe led The Potter to the shed where used furniture was sheltered from any dampness which might creep in from the ocean. There were desks, tables, chairs and bedsteads. Some of them were broken or marred by years of use and misuse. There were also pieces which had been refinished or painted by Jupe, his Uncle Titus, and Hans and Konrad, the two Bavarian brothers who helped in the yard.

The Potter examined the bedsteads stacked against one wall of the shack. He had purchased new mattresses and springs, he told Jupe, but to his mind springs and a mattress had a very temporary look unless a good solid bedstead was holding them up.

Jupe's curiosity began to get the upper hand. "Are you expecting your company to stay for a long time, Mr Potter?" he asked.

"I am not sure, Jupiter," said The Potter. "We will have to see. Now what do you think about that brass bed with the scrollwork on the top?"

Jupe was doubtful. "It's very old-fashioned," he told The Potter.

"So am I," announced The Potter. "Who knows? My company may like me that way." He picked up the end of the bed and gave it a good shake. "Nice and heavy," he remarked. "They don't make them that way these days. How much?"

Jupe was puzzled. The bed was from an old house in the Hollywood hills. Uncle Titus had bought it just the week before. Jupe had no idea what his uncle planned to ask for it.

"Never mind," said The Potter. "I don't have to know this minute. Put it aside and I'll speak to your uncle when he gets back."

13

The Potter looked around. "I'll need a second bedstead," he told Jupe. "One for a boy about your age. What would you choose, Jupiter, if you were buying a new bed?"

Jupe didn't hesitate. He hauled out a white wooden bedstead with a bookcase built into it. "If the boy likes to read in bed, this would be perfect," he told The Potter. "The wood is not the best, but Hans sanded it down and painted it. I imagine it looks better now than when it was new."

The Potter was delighted. "Fine! Just fine! And if the boy doesn't read in bed, he can keep his collection on the bookshelf."

"Collection?" questioned Jupe.

"He *must* have a collection," The Potter countered. "Don't all boys collect things? Seashells or stamps or rocks or bottle caps or something?"

Jupe was about to announce that he did not. Then he thought of Headquarters, the old mobile home trailer concealed behind a cunningly arranged pile of junk at the back of the yard. In truth, Jupiter Jones did have a collection. He had a collection of cases solved by The Three Investigators. The records were all in the trailer, neatly preserved in file folders.

"Yes, Mr Potter, I guess all boys have collections," he said. "Will there be anything else this morning?"

With the question of bedsteads settled, The Potter could not decide what came next. "I have so little in my house," he confessed. "I suppose two more chairs would be in order."

"How many chairs do you have now, Mr Potter?" asked Jupe gently.

"One," said The Potter. "I have never needed more

14

than one before, and I try not to clutter up my life with things I don't need."

Jupe silently selected two straight chairs from the pile on the right side of the shack and put them down in front of The Potter.

"A table?" asked Jupiter Jones.

The Potter shook his head. "I have a table. Now, Jupiter, there is that thing called television. I understand that it's extremely popular. My guests might like to have a television, and perhaps you could—"

"No, Mr Potter," interrupted Jupe. "By the time a set reaches us, we can usually salvage only a few spare parts. If you wish to have a television set, why not buy a new one?"

The Potter looked doubtful.

"New sets are guaranteed," Jupe pointed out. "If they are defective, you can return them to the dealer and have them repaired."

"I see. Well, no doubt you are right, Jupiter. We can make do at first with the beds and the extra chairs. After that—"

The Potter stopped. Outside, in the salvage yard, a car horn was blowing violently and repeatedly.

Jupe stepped to the door of the furniture shack. The Potter followed. Parked in the drive, close to The Potter's battered truck, was a gleaming black Cadillac. The horn blared again, and the driver of the car got out, stared around impatiently, then started for the door of the office.

Jupe hurried forward. "Can I help you?" he called.

The man stopped and waited for Jupe and The Potter to come to him. He had, thought Jupiter, a shuttered expression, like one who is used to keeping his thoughts to himself. He was tall and lean and not very old, though a frosting of silver showed here and there in his dark, curling hair.

"Yes, sir?" said Jupe. "You wanted something?"

"I am looking for Hilltop House," said the man. "I seem to have taken the wrong turn off the highway." The man spoke the very precise English of the well-educated European.

"It's a mile north," Jupe told him. "Go back to the highway and turn right. Drive until you see The Potter's place. The lane to Hilltop House is just beyond that. You can't miss it. There's a wooden gate with a padlock."

The man nodded a curt thanks and got back into the car. Then, for the first time, Jupe was aware that there was a second person in the Cadillac. A rather thickset man had been sitting motionless in the back seat. Now he leaned forward to touch the driver's shoulder and say something in a language which Jupe could not understand. The second man seemed neither young nor old nor anywhere in between. He looked ageless. It took Jupe a moment to realize that this was because he was completely bald. Even his eyebrows were gone—if he had ever had eyebrows. And his skin was tanned to the point where it looked like fine leather.

The ageless one glanced at Jupe, then turned his dark, slightly-angled eyes to The Potter, who had been standing quietly beside Jupe. The Potter made an odd little hissing sound. Jupe looked at him. He was standing with his head to one side, as if he were listening intently. His right hand had come up to grip the medallion which hung around his neck.

The ageless man in the car leaned back in his seat. The driver shifted the gear stick smoothly into reverse and backed out of the drive. Across the street from the salvage yard, Aunt Mathilda emerged from the house in time to see the Cadillac sweep by and speed back down to the highway.

The Potter touched Jupiter's arm. "My boy," he said, "would you go and ask your aunt if I may have a glass of water? I feel a little dizzy all of a sudden."

The Potter sat down on a pile of lumber. He did look ill.

"I'll get it right away, Mr Potter," promised Jupe. He hurried across the street.

"Who were those men?" asked Aunt Mathilda.

"They were looking for Hilltop House," said Jupiter. He went into the kitchen, took out the bottle of water that Aunt Mathilda always kept in the refrigerator, and poured a glass for The Potter.

"How peculiar," said Aunt Mathilda. "No one's lived at Hilltop House for years."

"I know," said Jupe. He hurried out with the water. But by the time he got back to the salvage yard, The Potter had disappeared.

2

The Searcher

THE Potter's decrepit truck was still in the drive when Uncle Titus and Hans returned from Los Angeles. They had a load of rusted garden furniture in the back of the salvage-yard truck. Uncle Titus struggled to manoeuvre his load past The Potter's vehicle, then exploded from the cab of his truck. "What is that thing doing in the middle of the drive?" Uncle Titus demanded.

"The Potter left it when he disappeared," said Jupe.

"When he what?"

"He disappeared," repeated Jupiter.

Uncle Titus sat down on the running board of the truck. "Jupiter, people do not simply disappear."

"The Potter did," said Jupe. "He stopped to buy some furniture to accommodate his expected guests. When he said he was feeling dizzy, I went across to the house and got him a glass of water. While I was gone, he disappeared."

Uncle Titus pulled at his moustache. "Guests?" he said. "The Potter? Disappeared? Disappeared where?"

"It is not difficult to trace the movements of a barefooted man," Jupe told his uncle. "He went out through the gate and down the street. Aunt Mathilda had been watering, and he got his feet wet. At the corner, he turned up towards Coldwell Hill. There are several clear footprints in the dust on the path that leads

18

up the hill. Unfortunately, he left the path about fifty yards up and struck off to the north. I found no sign of him after that. The terrain is too rocky to show footprints."

Uncle Titus heaved himself up off the running board. "Well!" he said. He tugged at his moustache and eyed The Potter's truck. "Let's move this wreck out of the drive. We won't do any business with it blocking the way. Let us also pray that The Potter returns soon to claim it."

Uncle Titus made four vain attempts to start The Potter's truck, but the temperamental old engine refused to turn over for him.

"Don't tell *me* machines can't think," declared Uncle Titus. "I wager that The Potter is the only one in creation who can coax any life into this thing."

He climbed down from the truck and motioned Jupe into the driver's seat. Then, with Jupe steering, he and Hans pushed until the truck was safely parked in an empty space next to the office.

Aunt Mathilda had hurried across the road from the house to watch. "I'm going to put The Potter's groceries in our deep freeze," she decided. "If his things stand out in the sun, they'll spoil. I can't imagine what possesses that man. Jupiter, did he say when his guests were coming?"

"No, he didn't."

Aunt Mathilda took a bag of groceries from the back of the truck. "Jupiter, I think you should take your bike and ride up to The Potter's," she said. "Perhaps he'll be there. Or perhaps his company has come. If they're there, Jupiter, bring them back with you. It would be awful to come for a visit and find an empty house."

Jupiter had been about to suggest a trip to The

Potter's himself. He grinned and hurried to get his bike.

"And don't dillydally!" Aunt Mathilda called after him. "There's work to be done!"

At that, Jupiter laughed out loud. He pedalled up the highway, keeping well to the right to avoid the cars speeding north, and concluded that The Potter's young guest, if he had arrived, would doubtless be a junior helper in The Jones Salvage Yard before the day was over. Aunt Mathilda knew exactly what to do with boys who were Jupiter's age. Aunt Mathilda put them to work.

The road curved at Evanston Point, and The Potter's house, stark white against the green-black of the California hills, leaped to meet the eye. Jupiter stopped pedalling and coasted. The Potter's place had been an elegant residence once. Now it struck Jupe simply as a brave house, flaunting its Victorian gingerbread on that lonely stretch of coastline.

Jupiter stopped at The Potter's gate. A small sign on the fence proclaimed that The Potter's shop was closed, but that The Potter would return shortly. Jupiter wondered whether he was even now inside the big white house, unwilling to cope with the usual run of Saturday morning customers. He had certainly looked ill when Jupiter had gone to fetch the water.

Jupiter leaned his bike against the fence and went in through the gate. The Potter's front garden was paved with flagstones and crowded with tables on which were displayed huge ceramic pieces—large urns, big plaques decorated with flowers or fruit, gigantic vases on which birds hovered in constant, motionless flight.

"Mr Potter?" called Jupe.

There was no answer. The tall, narrow windows of the old house looked blank. The shed where The Potter kept his supplies was locked and silent. Across the road, parked on the shoulder above the beach, was a dusty tan Ford. There was no one in the car. The owner, no doubt, was on the beach below either surfing or fishing.

The lane which led from the highway up the mountain to Hilltop House was only a few feet beyond The Potter's yard. Jupiter saw that the gate was open. Hilltop House itself was not visible from The Potter's, but Jupe could see the stone wall which supported its terrace. Someone was standing, leaning over that wall. At this distance, Jupe could not tell whether it was the driver of the Cadillac—the man with the dark, curly hair—or his strangely ageless passenger.

Jupe walked quickly past the displays on the wooden tables and up two little steps which were guarded by a pair of urns. The urns were almost as tall as Jupiter himself. A band of double-headed eagles, similar to the eagle on The Potter's medallion, encircled each urn. The eyes glared white in the birds' heads, and the beaks were open as if they screamed defiance at one another.

The wooden porch creaked slightly under Jupe's feet. "Mr Potter?" he called. "Are you here?"

There was no answer. Jupe frowned. The front door stood slightly open. The Potter, Jupe knew, did not worry greatly about the things in the front garden. They were large and couldn't be carried off easily. But Jupe also knew that everything else The Potter owned was kept securely under lock and key. If the front door was open, The Potter had to be at home.

But when Jupe stepped in through the door, the hall was empty—or as empty as a hall can be when it is lined, floor to high ceiling, with shelves, and when the shelves are crowded with platters, cups, plates, sugar-bowls and cream pitchers, little vases, and colourful small dishes. The things gleamed, dustless and in perfect order, each one placed so that it would look its very best.

" Mr Potter ?" Jupe was shouting now.

There was no sound, except for the refrigerator which Jupe could hear clicking and humming away in the kitchen. Jupiter looked at the stairs, wondering whether or not he should venture up to the first floor. The Potter might have returned and crept up to bed. He might have fainted.

Then Jupe heard a tiny sound. Something in the house had stirred. To Jupe's left, as he stood in the hall, was a closed door. It was, Jupe knew, The Potter's office. The sound had come from there.

" Mr Potter ?" Jupiter rapped at the door.

No one answered. Jupiter put his hand on the door-knob. It turned easily, and the door swung open before Jupe. Except for the roll-top desk in the corner, and the shelves piled high with ledgers and invoice forms, the office was empty. Jupiter went slowly into the room. The Potter did quite a brisk mail-order business. Jupiter saw stacks of price lists, a pile of order forms and a box of envelopes perched on the edge of one shelf.

Then Jupiter saw something which made him catch his breath. The Potter's desk had been forced open. There were fresh scratches on the wood and on the lock which usually secured the desk's roll top. One drawer was open and empty, and file folders were spilled across the top.

Someone had been searching The Potter's office.

Jupe started to turn towards the door. Suddenly he felt hands on his shoulders. A foot was thrust between his ankles, and he was shoved, floundering, towards the corner of the room. His head struck the edge of a shelf and he fell, a cascade of papers fluttering down on top of him.

Jupiter was barely aware that a door slammed and a key turned in a lock. Footsteps pounded away across the porch.

Jupe managed to sit up. He waited a moment, afraid that he might be sick. When he was sure that his breakfast would remain where he had put it and that his wits were fairly steady, he got up and stumbled to the window. The Potter's front garden was unoccupied. The searcher, whoever he was, had escaped.

3

The Potter's Family

THERE should be a law, thought Jupiter, about telephones. Even eccentric potters should be required to have one.

On the other hand, even if The Potter had had a telephone, it would have been of little use by this time. Whoever had ransacked the office was probably a mile away by now.

Jupiter yanked at the doorknob. The door didn't budge. Jupe went down on one knee and looked through the old-fashioned keyhole. The door had been locked from the outside, and the key was still in the lock. Jupe went to The Potter's desk, found a letter opener, and set to work on the lock.

He could, of course, have gone out through the window, but he preferred not to do that. Jupiter Jones had a well-developed sense of his own dignity. Besides, he knew it would look highly suspicious if anyone on the road outside saw him climbing through a window.

Jupe was prodding at the lock when he heard more footsteps on the porch outside. He froze.

"Grandfather!" shouted someone.

The doorbell rasped rustily in the kitchen.

"Grandfather! It's us!"

Someone knocked on the door.

Jupiter abandoned his efforts with the lock and went

to the window. He unlocked it, threw it open, and leaned out. A fair-haired boy stood on the porch, eagerly hammering at the door. Behind him was a youngish woman, her short blonde hair looking untidy and windblown. She held sunglasses in one hand and had an over-stuffed brown leather bag slung over her arm.

"Good morning!" said Jupiter Jones.

The woman and the boy stared at him and did not answer.

Jupiter, who had not planned to climb out of the window, now very sensibly did just that. He had nothing to lose.

"I was locked in," he explained shortly. He went back into the house through the front door, turned the key in the office door, and threw the door open.

After a slight hesitation, the woman and the boy trailed into the house after Jupiter.

"Someone was searching the office, and I was locked in," he said.

Jupiter surveyed the boy. He was just about Jupe's age. "You must be The Potter's guests," Jupiter announced.

"I am ... uh ... but, who are you, anyway?" demanded the boy. "And where's my grandfather?"

"Grandfather?" echoed Jupiter. He looked around for a chair. There was none, so he sat on the stairs.

"Mr Alexander Potter!" snapped the boy. "This is his house, isn't it? I asked at the filling station in Rocky Beach, and they said . . ."

Jupe put his elbows on his knees and rested his chin in his hands. His head hurt. "Grandfather?" he said again. "You mean, The Potter has a grandson?"

Jupiter couldn't have been more surprised if someone

had told him that The Potter kept a trained dinosaur in his basement.

The woman put on her sunglasses, decided that it was too dark in the hall, and took the glasses off again. She had a nice face, Jupiter decided. "I don't know where The Potter is," Jupe confessed. "I saw him this morning, but he isn't here now."

"Is that why you were climbing through the window?" demanded the woman. "Tom," she said to the boy, "call the police!"

The boy named Tom looked around, bewildered.

"There's a public telephone on the highway," said Jupiter politely, "just outside the garden."

"You mean my father doesn't have a phone?" demanded the woman.

"If your father is The Potter," said Jupe, "he does not have a telephone."

"Tom!" The woman fumbled in her purse.

"You go and call, Mum," said Tom. "I'll stay here and watch this fellow!"

"I have no intention of leaving," Jupiter assured them.

The woman went, slowly at first, then running down the path towards the highway.

"So The Potter is your grandfather!" said Jupe.

The boy named Tom glared at him. "What's so weird about it?" he demanded. "Everybody's got a grandfather."

"True," admitted Jupiter. "However, everyone does not have a grandson, and The Potter is . . . well, he's an unusual person."

"I know. He's an artist." Tom stared around at the shelves of ceramics. "He sends us stuff all the time," he told Jupiter.

Jupiter digested this in silence. How long, he wondered, had The Potter been in Rocky Beach? Twenty years, at least, according to Aunt Mathilda. Certainly he had been well established long before Aunt Mathilda and Uncle Titus had opened The Jones Salvage Yard. The distracted young woman could be his daughter. But, in that case, where had she been all this time? And why had The Potter never spoken of her?

The young woman returned, stuffing a purse back into her handbag. "There'll be a police car right here," she announced.

"Good," said Jupiter Jones.

"And you'll have some explaining to do!" she told Jupiter.

"I'll be glad to explain, Mrs . . . Mrs . . ."

"Dobson," said the woman.

Jupiter got to his feet. "I am Jupiter Jones, Mrs Dobson," he said.

"How do you do," she said, in spite of herself.

"Not too well at the moment," confessed Jupiter. "You see, I came here looking for The Potter, and someone knocked me down and locked me in his office."

Mrs Dobson's expression indicated that she did not think this a likely story. The wail of a police siren sounded on the highway.

"Rocky Beach doesn't have too many emergencies," said Jupiter calmly. "I am sure Chief Reynolds's men are happy to have a chance to use their siren."

"You're too much!" snorted Tom Dobson.

The siren faltered and died outside the house. Through the open front door, Jupiter saw a black-and-white patrol car come to a stop. Two officers leaped out and hurried up the path.

Jupiter sat down again on the stairs, and young

27

Mrs Dobson—her first name was Eloise—introduced herself to the policemen in an absolute avalanche of words. She had, she said, driven all the way from Belleview, Illinois, to visit her father, Mr Alexander Potter. Mr Potter was not at home at the moment, and she had found this . . . this juvenile delinquent climbing out of a window. She pointed an accusing finger at Jupe, and suggested that the police might wish to search him.

Officer Haines had lived in Rocky Beach all his life, and Sergeant McDermott had just celebrated his fifteenth year on the force. Both men knew Jupiter Jones. Both men were also well acquainted with The Potter. Sergeant McDermott made several brief notations on a pad he carried, then said to Eloise Dobson, "Are you prepared to prove that you're The Potter's daughter?"

Mrs Dobson's face went red, then white. "I beg your pardon?" she cried.

"I said, are you prepared—"

"I heard you the first time!"

"Well, ma'am, if you'll just explain—"

"Explain what? I told you, we came and found this . . . this cat-thief. . . ."

Sergeant McDermott sighed. "Jupiter Jones may be a pain in the neck," he admitted, "but he doesn't steal things." He favoured Jupe with a resigned stare. "What happened, Jones?" he asked. "What were you doing here?"

"Shall I begin at the beginning?" asked Jupiter.

"We've got all day," said McDermott.

So Jupiter began at the beginning. He told of the appearance of The Potter at the salvage yard, and of the purchase of furniture for the expected guests.

Sergeant McDermott nodded at that, and Officer Haines went into the kitchen and brought out the chair, so that Mrs Dobson could sit down.

Jupe then reported that The Potter had simply walked away from the salvage yard, leaving his truck behind, and had taken to the hills behind Rocky Beach. "I came up to see if he had returned home," said Jupe. "The front door was open and I came in. I did not find The Potter, but someone was hiding in the office. He must have been standing behind the door. When I went in and saw that The Potter's desk had been forced open, whoever it was tripped me from behind and shoved me down. He then ran out and locked the door behind him. Thus it became necessary for me to climb out through the window when Mrs Dobson and her son appeared and rang the bell."

Sergeant McDermott waited a moment, then said, "Huh!"

"The Potter's office has been searched," Jupe insisted. "You will see that his papers are upset."

McDermott stepped to the office door and looked in at the files spread on the desk, and at the desk drawer sagging open.

"The Potter is extremely orderly," Jupe pointed out. "He would never leave his office in that condition."

McDermott turned back to the group in the hall. "We'll get the fingerprint man up here," he announced. "In the meantime, Mrs Dobson—"

At which, Eloise Dobson burst into tears.

"Hey, Mum!" The boy named Tom moved close and put a hand on her arm. "Hey, Mum, don't!"

"Well, he *is* my father!" sobbed Mrs Dobson. "I don't care! He is, and we drove all the way to see him and we

29

didn't even stop at the Grand Canyon because I wanted
. . . because I can't even remember . . ."

"Mum!" pleaded Tom Dobson.

Mrs Dobson dug into her bag for a handkerchief.
"Well, I didn't expect I'd have to prove it!" she cried.
"I didn't know you needed a birth certificate to get into
Rocky Beach!"

"Now, Mrs Dobson!" Sergeant McDermott folded
his notebook and put it into his pocket. "Under the
circumstances, it might be best if you and your son did
not remain here."

"But Alexander Potter *is* my father!"

"That may be," conceded the sergeant, "but it looks
as if he's decided to make himself scarce—at least for
the moment. And it appears that someone has entered
the house illegally. I'm sure that The . . . that Mr Potter
will show up, sooner or later, and explain things. But in
the meantime, you and the boy would be safer if you
stayed in the village. There's the Seabreeze Inn, and
it's very nice and—"

"Aunt Mathilda would be glad to have you," put in
Jupiter.

Mrs Dobson ignored him. She sniffled and dabbed at
her eyes, her hands shaking.

"Besides," said McDermott, "the fingerprint man
will be here, and we don't want anything disturbed."

"Where is this Seabreeze Inn?" asked Mrs Dobson.

"Down the road a mile and a half to the village,"
said McDermott. "You'll see the sign."

Mrs Dobson got up and put on her sunglasses.

"Chief Reynolds may want to talk to you later," said
McDermott. "I'll tell him he can find you at the inn."

Mrs Dobson began to cry again. Young Tom hurried
her out of the house and down the path to the road,

where she got behind the wheel of a blue convertible with Illinois licence plates.

"Now I've seen everything!" said Sergeant McDermott. "The Potter's daughter!"

"If she *is* The Potter's daughter," said Officer Haines.

"Why would she pretend?" said McDermott. "The Potter's a real kook, and he's got nothing anybody wants."

"He must have something," said Jupiter Jones, "or why would someone go to the trouble to search his office?"

4

Too Many Newcomers

JUPITER refused Haines's offer of a ride back to Rocky Beach. " I've got my bike," he told the policeman. " And I'm okay."

Haines squinted at the bruise on Jupe's forehead. " You sure?" he asked.

" I'm sure. It's just a bump." Jupiter started down the path.

" Well, watch it, Jones!" McDermott called after him from the house. " You keep poking your nose in where it doesn't belong, you'll get it cut off one of these days. And stick close to home, you hear? The chief will probably want to talk to you, too."

Jupiter waved, picked up his bicycle, and stood waiting for a break in the traffic so that he could cross the highway. The tan Ford which Jupe had noticed earlier was still parked on the shoulder above the beach. The traffic slackened, and Jupe raced across the road with his bicycle. He stood beside the car and looked down at the beach. The tide was going out, leaving broad stretches of wet sand. Coming up the path towards him was the most magnificent fisherman Jupe had ever seen. He had on a sparkling white turtleneck shirt and, over it, a spotless pale blue jacket with a crest on the pocket. The jacket exactly matched his pale blue duck trousers and these, in turn, blended beautifully with his blue sneakers. He wore a yachting cap so immaculate it might have been taken off the shelf at the sporting goods store only yesterday.

"Hello, there!" said the man, as he came abreast of Jupe. Jupe saw a thin, tanned face, oversized sunglasses, and a grey moustache, waxed so that the ends pointed out and up towards the man's ears.

The man's fishing tackle and creel were as perfect, as gleaming bright as the rest of him.

"Any luck?" asked Jupiter Jones.

"No. They're not biting today." The man opened the boot of the dusty Ford and began to stow his gear. "Maybe I'm not using the right bait. I'm new at this."

Jupiter had already guessed that. Most fishermen, he knew, looked like refugees from the Salvation Army store.

The man looked across at the patrol car parked in front of The Potter's house. "Excitement?" he asked.

"A little," said Jupiter. "A housebreaker, probably."

"How dull." The lid of the boot thumped closed.

The man unlocked the car door on the driver's side. "Isn't that the shop of the very famous Potter?" he said. Jupe nodded.

"He a friend of yours?" asked the fisherman. "You live around here?"

"Yes, I live around here. I know him. Everybody in town knows The Potter."

"Hm. I should think so. Does beautiful work, I understand." Behind the sunglasses, the eyes went over Jupe from head to toe. "Nasty bump you've got there."

"I fell," said Jupe shortly.

"I see. Can I give you a lift anywhere?"

"No, thank you," said Jupiter.

"No? Well, you're right. Never take rides from a stranger, eh?" The man laughed as if he had just said something terribly funny, then started his car, backed on to the highway, waved at Jupe, and drove off.

Jupe rode back to the salvage yard. He did not, however, go in through the main gates. Instead he continued on down the length of the wonderfully painted fence until he came to the curious fish poking its head up from the sea to watch the ship sailing through the furious storm. Jupiter got off his bike and pressed on the eye of the fish. Two boards swung up, and Jupe pushed his bicycle ahead of him into the salvage yard.

This was Green Gate Number One. In all, there were four secret entrances to The Jones Salvage Yard—and Aunt Mathilda Jones was unaware of the existence of any of them. Jupiter, emerging in the corner of the junkyard by his outdoor workshop, could hear Aunt Mathilda. She was evidently out behind the furniture shed, applying herself to cleaning up the recently purchased garden furniture. And she was urging Hans, with some vigour, to do likewise. She could not see Jupiter because he had cleverly arranged the piles of junk in front of his workshop to block the view. Jupe grinned, propped his bike against an old printing press, pulled aside a cast-iron grate which leaned against a workbench behind the printing press, and bent to crawl into Tunnel Two.

Tunnel Two was a length of corrugated iron pipe. It was padded inside with odd scraps of carpeting, and it led to a trapdoor in the trailer which was Headquarters for The Three Investigators. Jupe crawled the length of Tunnel Two, climbed up through the trapdoor, and reached for the telephone on the desk in the trailer.

The telephone was another improvement in The

Jones Salvage Yard of which Aunt Mathilda was unaware. Jupiter and his friends, Bob Andrews and Pete Crenshaw, paid for it with money they earned working in the salvage yard, and with occasional fees The Three Investigators collected for solving a case.

Now Jupiter dialled Pete's number. Pete answered after only two rings. "Hey, Jupe!" Pete seemed delighted to hear from Jupiter. "Surf'll be up this afternoon. What do you say we take our boards and—"

"I doubt that I will have an opportunity to do any surfing today," said Jupiter dourly.

"Oh? You mean your aunt's on the warpath?"

"Uncle Titus acquired several pieces of garden furniture today," said Jupiter. "They are badly rusted, and Aunt Mathilda is now directing Hans on the removal of rust and old paint. I am certain that when she sees me, I shall join Hans."

Pete, who was accustomed to Jupiter's precise method of speech, simply wished him happy paint-removal.

"That is not why I called," Jupiter informed him. "Can you come to Headquarters tonight at nine?"

Pete could and would.

"Red Gate Rover," said Jupiter simply, and hung up.

He then dialled Bob Andrews' home. Mrs Andrews answered. Bob was at his part-time job at the Rocky Beach Public Library.

"May I leave a message, Mrs Andrews?" asked Jupe.

"Of course, Jupiter, but I'd better get a pencil and write it down. You boys never seem to say anything in plain English."

Jupiter did not comment on this. He waited while Mrs Andrews found a pencil and a piece of paper, and then said, "Red Gate Rover at nine."

"Red Gate Rover at nine," repeated Mrs Andrews.

"Whatever that may mean. All right, Jupiter, I'll tell him when he gets home."

Jupiter thanked her, hung up, and retreated out of Headquarters and back down Tunnel Two. He opened Green Gate One, pushed his bike on to the street, and rode up to the gravel drive of The Jones Salvage Yard.

Aunt Mathilda was waiting beside the office, stained rubber gloves on her hands. "I was about to send the police after you," she announced. "What happened?"

"The Potter wasn't there," Jupe told her. "His company came, though."

"They did? Why didn't you bring them back with you? Jupiter, I told you to invite them!"

Jupiter parked his bicycle next to the office. "They are not sure whether or not I am Jack the Ripper," he told his aunt. "They have gone to the Seabreeze Inn. One of them is a lady named Dobson who says she is The Potter's daughter, and the other is her son Tom."

"The Potter's daughter? Jupiter, that's ridiculous. The Potter never had a daughter!"

"Are you sure?" asked Jupe.

"Well, of course. He never mentioned ... he never ... Jupiter, why should they think you're Jack the Ripper?"

Jupiter explained, as briefly as he could, about the intruder in The Potter's office. "They think I broke into the house," he finished.

"The very idea!" Aunt Mathilda bristled with indignation. "And look at your head. Jupiter, go in the house this minute. I'll get you an ice pack."

"Aunt Mathilda, it's all right, really."

"It is not all right. In the house. Now! Go!"

Jupiter went.

Aunt Mathilda brought him an ice pack. Also a

36

peanut-butter sandwich and a glass of milk. By dinner time she had decided that his bump on the head was no worse than any one of a hundred other bumps he had survived. She clattered through the dinner dishes, left Jupiter to dry and put away, and went to wash her hair.

Uncle Titus gratefully went to sleep in front of the television set, and when Jupiter tiptoed out of the house, his big moustache was vibrating softly to the rhythm of his snores.

Jupiter crossed the street and circled round to the back of the salvage yard. The yard's back fence was as fancifully decorated as the front fence. The painting depicted the great San Francisco fire of 1906, with terrified people fleeing from burning buildings. In the foreground of the scene, a little dog sat watching the excitement. One of his eyes was a knot in the wooden board. Jupiter deftly picked the knot out of the board, reached through the hole to undo a catch, and three boards swung open. This was Red Gate Rover. Inside, a sign with a black arrow pointed the way to "Office." Jupiter followed the direction of the arrow, crept under a pile of lumber, and came out into a corridor with junk piled high on every side. He made his way along the corridor until he came to several heavy planks which formed the roof of Door Four. He had only to get under these, crawl a few feet, and push on a panel—and he was in Headquarters.

Eight forty-five. He waited, reviewing the events of the day in his mind. At ten to nine Bob Andrews wriggled into the trailer. Pete Crenshaw put in his appearance promptly at nine.

"Do The Three Investigators have another client?" asked Pete brightly. He looked at the bruise on Jupe's forehead. "Like you, maybe?"

"Possibly," said Jupiter Jones. "Today The Potter disappeared."

"I heard about that," said Bob. "Your Aunt Mathilda sent Hans down to the market to pick up some stuff. He met my mother. Just walked away and left his truck here?"

Jupiter nodded. "That is exactly what he did. The truck is still parked beside the office. The Potter disappeared, and a number of other people appeared."

"Such as that woman who checked into the Seabreeze Inn after you got bonked on the bean?" questioned Pete.

"Rocky Beach is indeed a small town," murmured Jupiter.

"I met Officer Haines," Pete explained. "She claims she's The Potter's daughter. If she is, that kid with her must be his grandson. Crazy! That Potter's a funny old guy. You'd sure never suspect he had a daughter."

"He must have been young once," said Jupiter. "But Mrs Dobson and her son are not the only newcomers in Rocky Beach. There are two men at Hilltop House."

"Hilltop House?" Pete straightened up. "Has somebody moved into Hilltop House? That place is a wreck!"

"Someone at least visited there today," said Jupiter. "It was an interesting coincidence that they stopped at the salvage yard this morning to ask directions. The Potter was there at the time, which may also be an interesting coincidence. They saw him, and he saw them. And Hilltop House directly overlooks The Potter's shop."

"Did he know them?" asked Bob.

Jupe pulled at his lip, trying to recall every detail of the scene. "I could not say with any certainty that he did, or that they knew him. The driver, who seemed to be European, asked for directions, and the passenger—

an odd-looking person with a completely bald head—became somewhat excited. They talked together for a moment in a foreign language. The Potter stood there, holding on to that medallion he always wears. After they left, he said he felt ill. I went to get him some water, and he disappeared."

"He was okay when he came into the yard?" asked Bob.

"Very okay," confirmed Jupiter. "He was expecting company, and he seemed pleased. But after the men came and asked about Hilltop House—"

"He disappeared!" said Bob.

"Yes. He walked away. Now I wonder, was he only holding that medallion out of habit, the way one would twist a button perhaps, or was he trying to cover it up?"

"It's an eagle, isn't it?" asked Bob.

"An eagle with two heads," said Jupiter. "It could be a design The Potter made up, or it could be something more—a symbol that meant something to the men in the car."

"Like a signal?" asked Pete.

"Or a crest," decided Bob. "Europeans are big on crests, and they have all kinds of things on them, like lions and unicorns and falcons and such."

"Can you check it out?" Jupiter asked. "Do you remember what it looked like?"

Bob nodded. "There's a new book on heraldry in at the library. If I see that double-headed eagle again, I'll recognize it."

"Good." Jupiter turned to Pete. "You're friendly with Mr Holtzer?" he asked.

"The real estate man? I mow his lawn once in a while, when he doesn't feel like doing it himself. Why?"

"He has the only real estate agency in Rocky Beach," said Jupiter. "If someone has moved into Hilltop House, he will know it. He may also know who and why."

"He probably won't want his lawn mowed tomorrow," said Pete, "but he's open on Sunday. I'll drop in and see him."

"Fine," said Jupiter. "I believe that Aunt Mathilda wishes to go to the Seabreeze Inn tomorrow. She will be a one-woman welcoming committee for Mrs Dobson and her son. I will accompany her, and will also keep an eye out for an amateur fisherman in a tan Ford."

"Another newcomer?" said Bob.

Jupiter shrugged. "Perhaps. Or perhaps he only came down from Los Angeles for the day. If he is staying in Rocky Beach, and if Hilltop House has been rented, we know that we have five new people in town in one day— and one of them may have broken into The Potter's house."

5

The Flaming Footprints

"WEAR your white shirt, Jupiter," ordered Aunt Mathilda, "and your blue blazer."

"It's too hot for a blazer," said Jupe.

"Wear it anyway," said Aunt Mathilda. "I want you to look respectable when we call on Mrs Dobson."

Jupiter sighed and buttoned the starched white shirt almost to the neck. The top button was impossible. He would have choked if he'd tried it. He shrugged himself into his blue blazer.

"Are you ready?" he asked his aunt.

Aunt Mathilda smoothed down a tweed skirt which was so sturdy that it almost prickled and threw a tan cardigan around her shoulders. "How do I look?"

"Most respectable," Jupiter assured her.

"I certainly hope so," said Aunt Mathilda, and they went downstairs and out through the living room. Uncle Titus had voted himself out of the welcoming party for the Dobsons. He was taking his Sunday afternoon nap on the sofa.

A fresh breeze had sprung up to blow away the morning fog, and the sun sparkled on the ocean as Aunt Mathilda and Jupiter walked down to the highway and then turned south. There were few people on the sidewalks in the business district of Rocky Beach, but there was a solid procession of cars edging through the town. Jupiter and his aunt passed the Rocky Beach

Bakery and the delicatessen, and came to the pedestrian crossing opposite the Seabreeze Inn.

"Miss Hopper does keep the inn very nicely," said Aunt Mathilda. She stepped on to the crossing and directed a no-nonsense glare at the radiator of an oncoming Buick. The driver of the Buick, properly cowed, applied his brakes, and Aunt Mathilda ploughed on across the road with Jupiter hurrying in her wake.

Aunt Mathilda strode into the office of the Seabreeze Inn and rang the little bell on Miss Hopper's registration desk.

A door behind the desk opened. "Mrs Jones!" cried Miss Hopper. She emerged, tucking in a stray wisp of white hair. She carried with her a distinct odour of roasting chicken. "Jupiter, nice to see you."

"I understand that Mrs Dobson and her son are staying with you," said Aunt Mathilda, getting right to the point.

"Oh yes, poor dear thing. What a state she was in when she checked in yesterday. And then Chief Reynolds came to see her, right here in the inn! Imagine!"

Miss Hopper appreciated Chief Reynolds's service to the citizens of Rocky Beach, but it was plain that she did not care to have the police invade her little inn.

Aunt Mathilda made a clucking sound to indicate that she understood Miss Hopper's position. She asked again for Mrs Dobson, and was directed to the little terrace behind the inn. "She and the boy are there, and that nice Mr Farrier is trying to cheer them up," said Miss Hopper.

"Mr Farrier?" echoed Jupiter.

"One of my guests," explained Miss Hopper. "Charming person. Seems to take a real interest in Mrs Dobson. It's nice, don't you think? Nowadays, people don't seem

42

to care about one another. Of course, Mrs Dobson's a very pretty young woman."

"That always helps," said Aunt Mathilda.

She and Jupiter went out of the office and walked back along the verandah of the inn, past numbered doors and blue-shuttered windows, to the little terrace that looked out over the beach to the ocean.

Young Mrs Dobson and her son were sitting at a small round table on the terrace. With them was the jaunty, moustached fisherman whom Jupiter had met on the highway the day before. If possible, he was more magnificent than he had been when Jupe first saw him. His jacket and his duck trousers were a sparkling, crackling white. His yachting cap was pushed back on his head, so that a lock of iron-grey hair showed. He was telling Mrs Dobson of the wonders of Hollywood, and offering to be her guide should she wish to take a little tour. From the glazed look in Mrs Dobson's eyes, he had been at it for some time.

He had not, decided Jupiter, cheered Mrs Dobson up. He was only boring her to death. Eloise Dobson looked profoundly grateful at the sight of Jupe escorting his aunt on to the terrace.

"Hi!" shouted young Tom Dobson, who leaped up to get another couple of chairs.

"Mrs Dobson," Jupiter began, "my aunt and I—"

Aunt Mathilda firmly took the introductions into her own hands. "I am Mrs Titus Jones," she informed Mrs Dobson. "Jupiter's aunt. I have come to assure you that Jupiter would never, under any circumstances, break into Mr Potter's residence."

Tom Dobson placed a chair at the table and Aunt Mathilda sat down.

Eloise Dobson smiled a tired smile. "I'm sure he

wouldn't," she said. "Sorry I flew out at you like a rusty shutter yesterday, Jupiter. I was just tired, I guess, and nervous. We'd driven straight through from Arizona, and I hadn't seen my father since I was a baby." She turned the paper cup on the table. "I guess you could say I've never seen him. You don't remember much that happened when you were three. I wasn't sure what to expect, and then when we arrived and found you climbing out the window, I thought—well, I thought you'd broken in."

"Naturally," said Jupiter. He sat down, and young Tom hurried off to the soft drink machine with a handful of dimes.

"And then the police behaved so strangely, and no one seemed to believe I am who I am," continued Mrs Dobson. "And Father disappearing the way he did. I didn't sleep a lot last night, I can tell you."

Mr Farrier murmured, "I should think not, my dear." He made a move as if to take Mrs Dobson's hand. She quickly put it under the table. "This is Mr Farrier," she said, not quite looking at him. "Mr Farrier, Mrs Jones—and Jupiter Jones."

"Jupiter Jones and I have met," said Farrier heartily. "How's the head, young friend?"

"Very well, thank you," answered Jupiter.

"Have to be careful about falls," said Farrier. "I remember the time I was in Cairo—"

"Never been there!" snapped Aunt Mathilda, who did not want this intruder running off with the conversation.

Mr Farrier closed his mouth.

"Mrs Dobson, what do you plan to do now?" Aunt Mathilda asked.

Mrs Dobson sighed. "I'm certainly not going to go

back to Belleview without finding out what happened," she said bravely. "Luckily, I have a letter from my father telling me that I am welcome here for the summer—if I insist on coming. It isn't the warmest invitation I ever had, but it *is* an invitation. I showed it to Chief Reynolds this morning. It's on Father's own headed paper, so he knows I'm telling the truth. He has a man on guard at the house, but he says the fingerprint men are through there, and if we want to move in, he won't try to stop us. But I don't think he likes the idea."

"Are you going to do it?" asked Aunt Mathilda.

"I think so. The trip's been expensive, and we can't stay here at the inn for nothing, and Tom's going to start clucking if he eats one more piece of fried chicken at a roadside restaurant. Mrs Jones, why can't the chief send a search party into the hills to find my father?"

Jupiter stirred. "It wouldn't be practical, Mrs Dobson," he said. "Obviously The Potter disappeared because he wanted to disappear, and there are a thousand places in those hills where he could hide out. Even in his bare feet, he could—"

"Bare feet?" said Eloise Dobson.

There was a short, unhappy silence. Then Aunt Mathilda said, "You didn't know?"

"Know what? Did he leave his shoes behind, or what?"

"The Potter never wears shoes," said Aunt Mathilda.

"You're joking!"

"I am sorry," said Aunt Mathilda, and she was. "He does not wear shoes. He goes about in his bare feet and a white robe." Aunt Mathilda stopped, not wishing to add to Mrs Dobson's distress. Then she decided she might as well complete the description. "He has long white hair and rather a full beard."

45

Young Tom Dobson had returned with drinks for Aunt Mathilda and Jupiter. "Sounds like the prophet Elijah," he decided.

"In other words," said Mrs Dobson, "my father is the town eccentric."

"He's only one of many," Jupiter assured her. "Rocky Beach has its full share of eccentrics."

"I see." There was a paper straw on the table. Mrs Dobson picked it up and began folding it into waxy pleats. "No wonder he never sent pictures of himself. He was probably nervous about my coming. I don't think he liked the idea a lot, but I did want to see him. So I suppose, when the time actually came, he got scared and lit out. Well, he's not going to get away with it. I'm his daughter and I'm here and I'm going to stay, and he darn well better show up."

"You tell 'em, Mum!" applauded young Tom.

"So there's no sense in wasting time," said Eloise Dobson. "Tom, you go and tell Miss Hopper we're checking out this afternoon. And call that police chief. He'll have to notify his guard to let us into the house."

"Are you sure you are doing the wise thing?" asked Jupiter. "I didn't break into The Potter's yesterday, but someone did. I have a bump on the head to prove it."

Eloise Dobson stood up. "I intend to be careful," she told Jupe. "And anyone who comes snooping around had better be careful, too. I don't believe in guns, but I'm handy with a baseball bat, and I brought one with me."

Aunt Mathilda regarded her with open admiration. "How clever. I wouldn't have thought of it."

Jupiter wanted to laugh out loud. His Aunt Mathilda wouldn't need a baseball bat. If they had an intruder at

The Jones Salvage Yard, Aunt Mathilda would probably swat him with a second-hand bureau.

Aunt Mathilda now surged to her feet. "If you are going to move into The Potter's house today, you'll need your furniture," she said. "He stopped at our salvage yard yesterday and selected a bedstead for you and one for your son—and a couple of other things. Jupiter and I will attend to it. We'll meet you at the house in half an hour. Will that be time enough?"

"Plenty of time," said Mrs Dobson. "You're very kind. I hate to trouble you."

"Not at all," said Aunt Mathilda. "Come, Jupiter." She started down the verandah towards the street, and then remembered something. She turned back towards the terrace. "Good afternoon, Mr Farrier," she called.

Jupiter and Aunt Mathilda were halfway back to the salvage yard before Jupe allowed himself to laugh out loud. "I wonder whether that guy Farrier has ever been so completely ignored," he said to his aunt. "You ran over him like a Sherman tank."

"Silly ass!" snapped Aunt Mathilda. "I am sure he was bothering that poor girl. . . . Men!"

Aunt Mathilda stormed into the house to rouse Uncle Titus from his Sunday afternoon stupor. Uncle Titus, in turn, called Hans and Konrad, and in fifteen minutes the salvage-yard truck was loaded with the bedsteads selected by The Potter, the two straight chairs, plus two small chests of drawers which Aunt Mathilda herself hauled from the furniture shed. "She'll need something to unpack her things into," said Aunt Mathilda.

Hans and Jupiter gathered up The Potter's groceries, and then Aunt Mathilda, Hans, and Jupe squeezed into the cab of the truck and headed up the highway towards The Potter's house.

The blue convertible with the Illinois plates was standing near the shed where The Potter kept his supplies when Aunt Mathilda drove the truck in off the main road. Young Tom Dobson was carrying two suitcases into the house, and Mrs Dobson stood on the porch, the wind ruffling her short hair.

"Everything all right?" called Aunt Mathilda.

"Well, fingerprint powder is grey, in case you were wondering," said Eloise Dobson. "And it's all over the place. It'll clean up, I suppose. But outside of about six zillion dishes, this place is bare as a barn."

"The Potter did not believe in encumbering himself with possessions," Jupiter explained.

Eloise Dobson shot him a curious glance. "Do you always talk like that?" she asked.

"Jupiter reads a great deal," explained Aunt Mathilda, and she went around to the back of the truck to supervise the unloading of the furniture.

Jupiter, struggling with the heavy brass headboard, saw two men stroll down the lane from Hilltop House. They were the two visitors of the day before—the thin, dark-haired man and the heavier, bald person. Both were wearing neat business suits and black hats. They glanced at the activity in The Potter's yard, then crossed the main road and disappeared down the path to the beach.

Tom Dobson came around to give Jupe a hand. "Who are they?" he asked. "Neighbours?"

"I'm not sure," said Jupiter. "They're new in town."

Tom got hold of one side of the headboard and Jupiter hefted the other. "Funny outfits for beach-walking," said Tom.

"Not everybody dresses the part," said Jupiter, thinking of the magnificently costumed Mr Farrier.

48

Tom and Jupiter staggered into the house with the headboard and up the stairs, and Jupiter saw that Eloise Dobson had spoken the truth. The Potter's house was barer than most barns. There were four bedrooms on the first floor, and a bath with an old-fashioned tub set high on claw legs. In one bedroom was a narrow bunk bed, neatly made up and covered with a white spread. The Potter also had a small bedside table, a lamp, an alarm clock and a little three-drawer chest painted white. That was all. The other three rooms were immaculate, but completely empty.

"You want this one, Mum?" called Tom, poking his head into the front room.

"Doesn't matter," said Mrs Dobson.

"It's got a fireplace," said Tom. "And wow, look at that wild thing!"

Tom and Jupiter leaned the headboard against the wall and looked at that wild thing. It was a ceramic plaque, fully five feet across. It was set into the wall above the fireplace.

"The double-headed eagle!" said Jupiter Jones.

Tom cocked his head to one side and examined the scarlet bird, screeching from both pointed beaks. "Old friend of yours?" he asked Jupiter.

"Possibly an old friend of your grandfather's," said Jupiter. "He always wore a medallion with that design on it. It must have meant something special to him. There are rows of double-headed eagles on those two big urns by the front steps. Did you notice them?"

"I was busy," said Tom. "We had a bed to move." Aunt Mathilda's footsteps were heavy on the stairs. "I hope that man thought to get enough sheets," worried Aunt Mathilda. "Jupiter, did you see mattresses anywhere?"

"They're in the back room," called Tom. "Brand new. Still have the paper round them."

"Thank goodness," declared Aunt Mathilda. She yanked open doors until she found the linen closet, and there were the sheets, also new, the mattresses and blankets. And two new pillows still encased in plastic.

Aunt Mathilda threw open one of the front windows. "Hans!" she called.

"Coming!" Hans was making his way up the front steps, the footboard of the brass bed balanced on his head.

"That will be a stinker to put up," said Tom Dobson.

It was. It took the combined efforts of Tom, Jupiter and Hans to get the big bed firmly erect on its four legs. Then springs and mattress were carried in from the back room and put in place, and Aunt Mathilda began unfolding sheets.

"Oh, the groceries!" she said suddenly. "They're still in the back of the truck."

"Groceries?" said Mrs Dobson. "Mrs Jones, you shouldn't have done that."

"I didn't," Aunt Mathilda informed her. "Your father bought enough food to take Sherman's Army clear to the sea. I had it in my freezer so that it wouldn't spoil."

Eloise Dobson looked perplexed. "Father certainly seems prepared for us. So why did he run off? . . . Well, I'll get the groceries," she said quickly, and went out of the room and down the stairs.

"Jupiter, give her a hand," ordered Aunt Mathilda.

Jupiter was halfway down the stairs when Mrs Dobson came in, brown paper bags in her arms. "We won't go hungry, anyway," she announced, and marched towards the kitchen.

Jupiter was close behind her when she suddenly

stopped dead. Her arms went limp, and the bags thumped to the floor.

Then Eloise Dobson screamed.

Jupiter pushed her to one side and stared past her into the kitchen. Near the pantry door, three weird, eerie green flames leaped and flickered.

"What is it?" Aunt Mathilda and Tom thundered down the stairs. Hans came behind them.

Jupiter and Mrs Dobson were immobile, staring at those tongues of ghostly green fire.

"Gracious to heavens!" gasped Aunt Mathilda.

The flames sputtered and sank, then died, leaving not a wisp of smoke.

"What the heck?" said Tom Dobson.

Jupiter, Hans and Tom shoved forward into the kitchen. For almost a minute they looked at the linoleum—at the places where the flames had danced. Then Hans said it. "The Potter! He came back! He came back to haunt the house!"

"Impossible!" said Jupiter Jones.

But he could not deny that there, charred into the linoleum, were three footprints—and they were the prints of naked feet.

6

The Investigators Have a Client

HANS was immediately sent to the telephone box on the main road to summon the police, who appeared within minutes and searched the house from attic to cellar and found nothing—nothing but the strange, charred footprints in the kitchen.

Officer Haines sniffed at the footprints, measured them, dug a few bits of burned linoleum out of the floor and put them into an envelope. He gave Jupiter a cool look. "If you know anything about this, and you're holding out on us—" he began.

"Ridiculous!" snapped Aunt Mathilda. "How could Jupiter know anything we don't know? He has been with me all day, and he was just going downstairs to help Mrs Dobson with the groceries when those—those footprints appeared."

"Okay. Okay," said the officer. "Only he has this habit, Mrs Jones. He's always around when trouble happens."

Haines put the envelope with the burned bits of linoleum in his pocket. "If I were you, Mrs Dobson," he said, "I'd get out of here and go back to the inn."

Eloise Dobson sat down and began to cry, and Aunt Mathilda angrily ran water into a kettle and set about making a heartening cup of tea. Aunt Mathilda believed there were few crises in life which could not be eased by a good hot cup of tea.

The police departed for headquarters. Tom and Jupiter went quietly out into the big front yard and sat on the steps between the two huge urns.

"I'm almost ready to think Hans was right," said Tom. "Suppose my grandfather is dead, and . . ."

"I do not believe in ghosts," said Jupiter firmly. "What's more, I don't think you believe in them, either. And The Potter made great preparations for your visit. Why should he return and frighten your mother that way?"

"I'm scared, too," Tom admitted, "and if my grandfather isn't dead, where is he?"

"The last we knew, he was up in the hills," said Jupiter.

"But why?" demanded Tom.

"That may depend on a great many things," Jupiter said. "How much do you really know about your grandfather?"

"Not much," admitted young Tom. "Just what I've heard my mother say. And she doesn't know much herself. One thing, his name wasn't always Potter."

"Oh?" said Jupiter. "I have always wondered about that. It seemed too coincidental."

"He came to the United States a long time ago," Tom said. "About 1931 or so. He was a Ukrainian and he had a name that was so full of c's and z's that nobody could pronounce it. He was taking ceramics at a night school in New York when he met my grandmother, and she didn't want to be Mrs . . . Mrs . . . well, whatever it was, so he changed his name to Potter."

"Your grandmother was a New Yorker?" asked Jupiter.

"Not really," said Tom. "She was born in Belleview, just like us. She went to New York to design clothes or

53

something. Then she met this Alexander Whosis and she married him. I don't suppose he wore a long white robe in those days. She wouldn't have gone for that. She was pretty square."

"You remember her?"

"A little. She died a long time ago. I was only a kid. Pneumonia. From what I've heard, in the family you know, she and my grandfather didn't hit it off from the beginning. He was real good at ceramics, and he had a little shop, but she said he was awfully nervous, and had three locks on every door. And she said she could not stand the continual smell of wet clay. So when my mother was going to be born, she came back to Belleview, and she stayed."

"She never returned to her husband?"

"Nope. I think he came to see her once, when my mother was a baby, but she never went back to him."

Jupiter pulled at his lip and thought of The Potter, so alone in his house by the sea.

"He never gave up on her," said young Tom. "He sent money every month—for my mother, you know. And when my folks were married, he sent them a terrific tea set. And he never stopped writing. Even after my grandmother died, he wrote to my mother. Still does."

"And your father?" asked Jupiter.

"Oh, he's a great guy," said Tom happily. "He runs the hardware store in Belleview. He didn't exactly go into fits of joy when Mum decided to come out here and see Grandfather, but she argued him round to it."

"I don't suppose you know why your grandfather came to California," said Jupiter.

"The weather, I suppose," said Tom. "Isn't that why most people come?"

"There are other reasons," Jupiter told him. His eyes were on the path to the beach. The two dark-clad men came floundering up the path, crossed the main road, and started to walk up the lane to Hilltop House.

Jupiter stood up and leaned against one of the urns, tracing the pattern of the screaming scarlet eagles with a forefinger. "An interesting series of puzzles," he remarked. "First, why did The Potter choose to disappear? Second, who searched his office yesterday? Also, who, or what, caused those flaming footprints in the kitchen? And why? And isn't it curious that no one in Rocky Beach even knew you existed?"

"But if he was a hermit?" said young Tom. "I mean, a guy who only has one chair in his house isn't exactly running a social club."

"Hermit or no hermit," said Jupiter Jones, "he was also a grandfather. A number of Aunt Mathilda's friends are grandparents, and they're always showing off snapshots of their grandchildren. The Potter never, never did that. He never even mentioned you or your mother to anyone."

Tom hunched forward and hugged his knees. "Makes you feel invisible," he declared. "This thing's like some kind of a bad dream. I'd say we ought to hightail it out of here and get back home, only . . ."

"Only, if you did that, you'd never know the answer, would you?" said Jupiter. "I would suggest that you employ a firm of private investigators."

"Hey, we couldn't do that!" protested Tom. "We aren't wracked in poverty, but we aren't exactly rolling in the green stuff either. Private investigators cost money."

"You'll find this firm very reasonable," said Jupiter. He took a card out of his pocket and handed it to Tom.

It was an oversized business card, and it read:

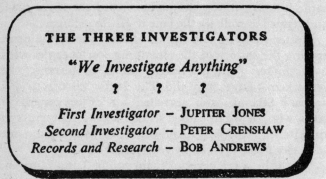

THE THREE INVESTIGATORS

"We Investigate Anything"

?   ?   ?

First Investigator – JUPITER JONES
Second Investigator – PETER CRENSHAW
Records and Research – BOB ANDREWS

Tom read the card and smiled a wry smile. "You're putting me on," he said.

"I am quite serious," Jupiter told him. "Our record is very impressive."

"Why the question marks?" asked Tom.

"I knew you would ask that," said Jupiter. "The question mark is the universal symbol of something unknown. The three question marks stand for The Three Investigators, and we are prepared to solve any mystery which may be brought to us. You might say that the question marks are our trademark."

Tom folded the card and tucked it into his shirt pocket. "Okay," he said. "So if The Three Investigators take on the case of the missing grandfather, what then?"

"First," said Jupiter, "I suggest that any agreement between us remains between us. Your mother is already somewhat upset. She might, quite unwittingly, disturb any arrangements we might make."

Tom nodded. "Grown-ups do gum things up," he said.

"Second, Officer Haines is right. I think it unwise that you and your mother remain in this house alone."

"You mean you want us to go back to the Seabreeze Inn?"

"It will depend upon your mother, of course," said Jupiter. "However, if you remain here, you would probably be more comfortable if one of the investigators stayed in the house with you."

"I don't know about Mum," said Tom, "but I'd be a darn sight happier."

"It's settled then," said Jupiter. "I'll talk it over with Bob and Pete."

"Jupiter!" Aunt Mathilda bustled out of the house. "We have finished putting up the other bed. I must say, you could have been a little more helpful."

"Sorry, Aunt Mathilda. Tom and I got to talking."

Aunt Mathilda sniffed. "I have been trying to persuade Mrs Dobson to return to the inn, but she insists that she will remain here. She has the ridiculous idea that her father will show up at any moment."

"Perhaps he will," said Jupiter. "This is his home."

Mrs Dobson came out, looking pale but somewhat braver after her cup of tea.

"Well, my dear," said Aunt Mathilda, "if there's nothing more we can do for you, we'll be going. If you get frightened, just call. And do be careful."

Eloise promised that she would be most careful, and that they would lock the house securely.

"They'll have to get a locksmith, you know," said Aunt Mathilda as she, Jupiter, and Hans drove down the road towards Rocky Beach. "They can lock the doors from the inside, but they can't unlock them from

57

the outside. That crazy Potter must have all the keys with him. And they should have a telephone put in. It's simply madness for them to be there without a telephone."

Jupe agreed. When they reached the salvage yard, he slipped away and crawled through Tunnel Two to call Pete Crenshaw and Bob Andrews.

"The Three Investigators have a client," he told Pete, "and this time, it is not Jupiter Jones!"

7

A Royal Tragedy

IT was after five when The Three Investigators met in their trailer Headquarters. Jupiter reported briefly on the Dobsons' move to The Potter's house, and on the flaming footprints which had appeared in the kitchen.

"Good grief!" exclaimed Pete. "You don't suppose The Potter died, and is coming back to haunt the place?"

"That is what Hans suggested," said Jupiter. "But those footprints were not made by The Potter. At least, they were not The Potter's footprints. The Potter has gone barefoot for many years. You may have noticed that his feet have spread. The footprints were small; they might be the prints of a short man, or of a woman."

"Mrs Dobson?" said Pete.

"She would not have had time to manage it," said Jupiter. "She went down the stairs and out to the truck to get the groceries. I followed immediately. She had already collected the groceries and was about to enter the kitchen when she saw the flames. I was right behind her. Also, why would she do such a thing? And how was it accomplished?"

"The men from Hilltop House?" suggested Pete.

"A possibility," said Jupiter. "They came down to the beach as we started moving the Dobsons in. We have no

59

assurance that they stayed on the beach. They could have walked in through the front door, which was open, set the footprints on fire in some manner, and slipped out the back way and down to the beach again. Pete, what were you able to find out about Hilltop House?"

Pete took a small notebook out of his pocket. "Mr Holtzer has never been so happy," he told the others. "I stopped in his office today to see if he wanted his lawn mowed—which he doesn't—and I didn't even have to ask any questions. He's had Hilltop House on his books for about fifteen years, and it's such a mouldering ruin that he's never been able to sell it or rent it or even give it away, and then along comes this man who decides it is the one and only house in Rocky Beach, and he has to have it. Took a year's lease and paid three months in advance. Mr Holtzer had the lease out on his desk—I think he was working out his commission— so I got a look at the new tenant's name."

"Which is?"

"Mr Ilyan Demetrieff," said Pete. "Or maybe it's Demetrioff. I was looking at it upside down, and Mr Holtzer needs to clean his typewriter. Anyhow, Demetrieff, or Demetrioff, listed his previous address as 2901 Wilshire Boulevard, Los Angeles."

Bob reached for the Central Telephone Directory which was on top of a file cabinet, leafed through, then shook his head. "He's not listed."

"Lots of people aren't," said Jupiter. "We can check the address later and see what we can find out about Mr Demetrieff." Jupiter pulled at his lower lip. "I wish we knew more about the double-headed eagle. I think that may be very important. It appears not only on The Potter's medallion, and on those two urns in his yard, but there is an immense plaque in one of his bedrooms with the design. It seems to have fascinated The Potter."

Bob Andrews grinned. "On that we've been lucky," he told Jupiter.

"What do you mean?"

"We don't have to wait for the library to open tomorrow," said Bob. "My father bought a coffee-table book."

"A what?" said Pete.

"A coffee-table book—one of those big picture books they're always advertising by mail. Dad's got a weakness for them." Bob had been sitting with a cardboard package at his feet. Now, smiling proudly, he put the package on the desk and opened it. Jupiter and Pete saw a handsome volume with a glossy jacket. *Royal Riches*, read the title. *A photographic study of the crown jewels of Europe, with commentary by E. P. Farnsworth.*

"Isn't that the British crown?" said Jupiter, looking at the magnificent object which decorated the cover. It had been photographed at close range, resting on a scarlet velvet cloth.

"One of them," said Bob. "The British have a couple of crowns, plus so many sceptres and orbs and maces and swords you wouldn't believe it. The guys who did this book covered a lot of territory. They've got photographs of the British crown jewels, plus the crown of Charlemagne, which is in Austria, and the crown of St Stephen of Hungary. Also something called the Lombard crown, which is made out of iron. There's a little bit on Russia, and the Russians went in for eagles in a big way, but I think the eagle we want is this one."

Bob had paged through past the middle of the book. He pushed the volume across the desk to Jupe. "The imperial crown of Lapathia," he said.

Pete bent over Jupe's shoulder to stare. "Yeah!" he exclaimed.

The imperial crown of Lapathia looked more like a helmet than a crown—but a helmet of gold, solidly encrusted with blue stones. At the top, four bands of gold encircled a huge ruby, and above this gem was an eagle—a scarlet eagle with two heads. The brilliant wings were spread wide, and the heads looked to right and to left, diamond eyes glittering, beaks open in fierce, warlike defiance.

"It certainly looks very much like The Potter's eagle," said Jupiter.

"The commentary is on the next page," said Bob.

Jupe turned the page and began to read aloud:

" 'The imperial crown of Lapathia was fashioned by the artisan Boris Kerenov in approximately 1543. Kerenov based his design for the crown on the helmet worn by Duke Federic Azimov in the battle of Karlon. Azimov's victory at Karlon brought to an end the civil wars which had devastated the tiny country of Lapathia. After their defeat by Azimov's army, the barons of the south each took a solemn oath that the peace of Lapathia would not again be broken. The following year, Duke Federic called the nobles to meet in the fortress of Madanhoff, and there he declared himself king of Lapathia. The nobles, isolated in the fortress and cut off from their own armies, bowed to the wishes of Duke Federic and pledged their allegiance to him as sovereign ruler. One dissenter, Ivan the Bold, refused to take the oath of allegiance. Legend has it that this proud warrior was executed in the main hall of Madanhoff, and his head was impaled on a spear and displayed on the battlements of the fortress.

" 'The coronation of Federic I of Lapathia took place

in the chapel at Madanhoff in 1544. The crown, designed and executed by Kerenov, remained in the possession of the Azimov family for almost 400 years, and was last used in the coronation of William IV in 1913. Following the overthrow of the Azimov dynasty in 1925, the crown was declared the property of the people of Lapathia. It is now on display in the National Museum at Madanhoff, the capital city which grew up around the site of Duke Federic's ancient stronghold.

" 'The Azimov crown, solid gold and set with lapis lazuli, is surmounted by a huge ruby said to have been the possession of Ivan the Bold, whose estates were forfeited to Federic Azimov after his execution. The two-headed eagle atop the ruby is the family device of the Azimovs. Kerenov fashioned it of enamel on gold. The eyes are diamonds, each weighing more than two carats.' "

Jupiter stopped reading and turned back to examine the photograph of the crown again.

"That's one way to get to the top," said Pete. "Kill off the opposition."

"Swiping the poor guy's ruby and sticking it in the crown was a nasty touch," said Bob.

"They played rough back in those days," said Jupiter.

"They played rough in 1925, too," said Bob. He had his notebook out. "I looked up Lapathia in the encyclopedia. Believe it or not, it's still there."

"You mean none of the big powers gobbled it up?" said Jupe.

"No. It is now the Republic of Lapathia, area 73 square miles, with a population of about 20,000 people. The major industry is cheese. There is a standing army of 350 men, 35 of whom are generals."

"That's one general for every ten soldiers," exclaimed Pete.

"Well, you can't say they lack direction," laughed Jupe. "What else?"

"The National Assembly of Lapathia is the governing body, and is made up of the 35 generals plus one representative from each of the departments or provinces. There are ten provinces, so I guess we know how the voting goes."

"The generals run the country," said Jupiter.

"They also elect the president," said Bob.

"But what about the Azimovs?" asked Pete.

"Aha! They are *not* still there. I said they played rough in 1925. William IV—you remember, he was the last one to wear the crown—decided that the royal treasury was getting low. He had married a Lapathian lady—she was a cousin, actually, so she was an Azimov, too—and she had very expensive tastes. She liked diamond bracelets and Paris gowns and she also had four children, each of whom had to have his own tutor and his own carriage and his own horses. King William ran into debt, so he put a tax on every pound of cheese that came out of the Lapathian dairies. Naturally, the Lapathians were unhappy, and the generals saw their chance. They waited until King William's birthday, when all of the Azimovs would be gathered in the capital, and they marched into the palace and told William he wasn't going to be king any more."

"What happened then?" asked Jupiter.

"Probably much the same thing that happened to old Ivan the Bold," said Bob. "The official account is that His Majesty became distraught and jumped off a balcony."

"Someone shoved him!" declared Pete, horrified.

"It seems likely," said Bob. "The rest of the family became so upset that they did away with themselves in various ways. The queen is supposed to have taken poison."

"You mean the people believed that?" cried Pete.

"With all those generals around, who was going to argue?" Bob retorted. "Also, the generals immediately removed the tax on cheese, which helped. The royal palace became the National Museum, and the crown jewels were donated to the people, so everybody could enjoy them."

"And no one could wear them," put in Jupiter. "A fantastic story. On the other hand, a tax on tea had a great deal to do with our American Revolution, so perhaps it isn't so fantastic. And are there no Azimovs left?"

"I'll double-check it at the library tomorrow," promised Bob. "According to the encyclopedia, the family became extinct when King William jumped off that balcony."

Jupe brooded. "Tom Dobson said his grandfather came from Ukrainia. Suppose Tom is wrong? The Potter and that Azimov eagle seem to be old friends. I wonder if he could have had anything to do with that royal family."

"Or with the revolutionary generals," added Bob.

Pete shivered. "Whole families do not commit suicide," he said. "Remember what happened to the Romanovs in Russia."

"They were massacred," said Jupe.

"Right. And if The Potter had any part in that, I don't want to know him any better than I do already."

8

Worthington Comes Through

"I AM sure," said Jupiter Jones firmly, "that whatever may have happened in the past, Tom Dobson and his mother know only that The Potter makes beautiful ceramics and that he is missing. Also that somebody or something left flaming footprints in his kitchen this afternoon. Mrs Dobson is extremely upset, and Tom is not at all happy about the situation. I suggested to Tom that one of The Three Investigators might spend the night with the Dobsons. They will feel safer, and one of us will be on the scene if something unusual occurs. There is another line of inquiry I would like to follow up with Bob. Pete, could you call your mother and—"

"Not me!" cried Pete. "Listen, Jupe, somebody could burn that house down with those flaming footprints! And the windows upstairs are awfully high. If you got shoved out of one of them, you might not recover."

"You won't be alone," Jupiter reminded him.

"King William wasn't alone, either."

"Well, if you won't, you won't," said Jupiter Jones. "I had hoped, though . . ."

Pete scowled savagely. "All right! All right! I'll do it. I get all the dangerous assignments." And he picked up the telephone and dialled his home.

"Mum?" he said. "I'm with Jupiter. Can I stay over tonight?"

The boys waited.

"Yeah, all night," said Pete. "We're looking for something. It's a medallion. It's lost."

The telephone made worried noises.

"Jupe says his aunt won't mind," said Pete. And, "Yes, I'll be home early in the morning." And, "Yes, I know I'm supposed to cut the grass tomorrow."

Finally, "Okay, Mum. Thanks. See you." And Pete hung up.

"Beautiful!" said Bob.

"And quite true," announced Jupiter. "We are looking for a lost medallion—the one The Potter wears."

Then, at Jupiter's request, Bob called his mother and received permission to stay for supper at the Jones's.

"Jupiter!" Aunt Mathilda's voice carried clearly through the air vent in the top of the trailer. "Jupiter Jones! Where are you?"

"Just in time!" said Jupe. The boys hurried out as fast as they could through Tunnel Two, brushed off their knees, and emerged from Jupiter's outdoor workshop.

"I declare to Betsy!" exclaimed Aunt Mathilda, who stood near the office of the salvage yard. "I don't know what you boys do, pottering in that workshop all the time. Jupiter, supper's ready."

"Aunt Mathilda," said Jupe, "can Pete and Bob stay and . . ."

"Yes, they can stay and eat with us," said Aunt Mathilda. "We're only having pancakes and sausages, but there's plenty for everyone."

Pete and Bob thanked her and accepted the invitation.

"Call your folks," ordered Aunt Mathilda. "You can use the phone in the office. And lock up after yourselves. Five minutes, and I want you boys ready to eat."

She crossed the street to the house.

"Do you suppose she's a mind reader?" said Pete.

"I hope not," declared Jupiter fervently.

Five minutes later the boys were at the table in the Jones's dining room, devouring pancakes and sizzling sausages, and listening to Uncle Titus tell of the old days, when Rocky Beach was only a wide spot in the road.

After supper, the boys leaped to help Aunt Mathilda clear away and do the dishes. When they had finished, and the sink was scoured to perfection, they made for the door.

"Where to now?" demanded Aunt Mathilda.

"We aren't quite finished with our job," Jupe explained.

"Well, don't be too late," warned Aunt Mathilda. "And don't leave the light on in the workshop. And remember to lock the gate again."

Jupiter promised that they would obey all instructions, and they escaped across the street, where Pete collected his bicycle.

"How will Tom Dobson know it's me?" Pete asked.

"Just tell him," Jupiter advised. "He has one of our cards."

"Okay." Pete wheeled out of the yard and started for the highway.

"Now to check on that Mr Demetrieff who rented Hilltop House," Jupiter decided. "I think Worthington could help us there."

Some time before, Jupiter Jones had won a prize in a contest sponsored by the Rent-'n-Ride Auto Rental Company. The prize had been the use of a gold-plated Rolls-Royce and a chauffeur for thirty days. Worthington, the very proper English chauffeur who had driven Jupiter and his friends in the course of many of their investigations, had become a rather enthusiastic amateur sleuth himself, and always took an interest in the boys' cases.

Bob looked at his wristwatch. It was well past seven. "We can't ask Worthington to come out here this late," he said. "Not on a Sunday night."

"It won't be necessary to ask him to come here," said Jupiter. "Worthington lives in the Wilshire district. Unless he's terribly occupied with something, he could go and look at that address in Wilshire. Perhaps that would give us some clue to Mr Demetrieff."

Bob agreed that this was worth a try, and the two boys crawled through Tunnel Two and back into Headquarters, where Jupiter consulted his little telephone list and called Worthington's number.

"Master Jupiter?" Worthington sounded very pleased to hear Jupe's voice on the telephone. "How are you, sir?"

Jupiter assured Worthington that he was very well.

"I am afraid that the Rolls-Royce isn't available tonight," said Worthington ruefully. "There is a big party in Beverly Hills. Perkins took the car over."

"We didn't want the car tonight, Worthington," said Jupe. "I was only wondering if you would have time to do a small favour for The Three Investigators."

"I was busily engaged," said Worthington. "I was playing solitaire—and losing. The interruption is most welcome. What can I do for you?"

"We are attempting to get information on a Mr Ilyan Demetrieff," Jupiter told him. He spelled the name for Worthington. "Possibly, it is Demetrioff, with an 'o,'" he told the chauffeur. "We are not positive. However, he has given his address as 2901 Wilshire Boulevard. We would like to know if Mr Demetrieff has, in fact, recently lived at this address. Also, it would be interesting to know what kind of place 2901 Wilshire is."

"It's practically around the corner from me," said Worthington. "I shall stroll over and ring the bell."

"That's fine, Worthington," said Jupiter. "And what will you say if someone opens the door?"

Worthington scarcely hesitated. "I shall inform them that I am chairman of the Volunteer Committee for the Beautification of Wilshire Boulevard," said Worthington. "I shall ask their opinion of putting potted shrubs along the sidewalks. If they are receptive to the idea, I can ask them to join the committee."

"Wonderful, Worthington!" cried Jupiter.

Worthington promised to call Headquarters within half an hour, and hung up briskly.

"There are times when I think we should take Worthington into our agency," laughed Jupiter after he reported the chauffeur's plan to Bob.

"He considers himself a member already," said Bob. "What do you think he'll find at that Wilshire address?"

"Possibly nothing," admitted Jupiter. "An empty house, or perhaps an apartment with no tenant. But at least he'll be able to tell us something about the neighbourhood. I like the idea of a Volunteer Committee for the Beautification of Wilshire Boulevard. We could join the committee and ring doorbells in Mr Demetrieff's area, and perhaps glean some information on him."

"City people never know their neighbours," said Bob.

"Sometimes they know more than one thinks." Jupiter put his hands behind his head and leaned back in his chair. "Suppose it is a neighbourhood of elderly people," he said. "Elderly people are home all day. They look out of their windows. They watch what is going

70

on. I wonder how many crimes have been solved because some little old lady who slept lightly got up in the middle of the night to see who was making a noise on the street?"

Bob grinned. "Remind me to be careful when I go past Miss Hopper's."

"I think she doesn't miss a great deal," conceded Jupiter. He opened the book on the crown jewels which Bob had brought with him and stared at the photograph of the Azimov crown. "It is beautiful, in a barbaric way," he said. "I suppose it was typical of old Duke Federic to have it made in the shape of a helmet."

"He must have been a real charmer," said Bob. He shuddered. "Executing Ivan the Bold was bad enough. He didn't have to stick his head up on the castle wall."

"They did things like that in those days," said Jupe. "It was supposed to serve as an example, and I am sure it did. The Azimovs survived for 400 years afterwards."

The telephone rang.

"That can't be the Wilshire Boulevard Beautification Committee already," exclaimed Bob. "He wouldn't have had time to do his stuff."

But it was Worthington. "I am sorry, Master Jupiter," the chauffeur reported, "but no one lives at 2901 Wilshire Boulevard. It is a small business building, and at this hour it is locked."

"Oh," said Jupiter.

"However, there was a light in the outer lobby, and I could read the building directory," Worthington announced brightly. "I made a list of the companies occupying the building. They are the Acme Photostat Service, a Dr H. H. Carmichael, the Jensen Secretarial Bureau, the Lapathian Board of Trade, Sherman Editorial—"

"Wait a minute!" cried Jupiter. "What was that last?"

"Sherman Editorial Bureau," said Worthington.

"No, the one before that? Did you say Lapathian—?"

"Lapathian Board of Trade," said Worthington.

"Worthington," declared Jupiter, "I think you have told us exactly what we want to know."

"I have?" Worthington sounded astonished. "There was no Mr Demetrieff listed," he reminded Jupiter.

"Well, if you were to ask for him at the Lapathian Board of Trade," said Jupiter, "they might tell you that he's vacationing in Rocky Beach. Then again, they might not. Thanks, Worthington. And good night."

Jupiter put down the telephone. "Our new tenant at Hilltop House hails from the Lapathian Board of Trade," he told Bob. He looked again at the picture of the crown. "The scarlet eagle was the device of Lapathia, and a favourite symbol with The Potter. And a man from the Lapathian Board of Trade leases a house overlooking The Potter's shop. This suggests a number of interesting possibilities."

"Like The Potter is really a Lapathian?" said Bob.

"Also, that we might pay a visit to Hilltop House, tonight," said Jupe firmly.

9

Hilltop House

BOB and Jupe slipped out of The Jones Salvage Yard through Red Gate Rover and hurried towards the place where a hiking trail meandered in a series of switchbacks to the top of Coldwell Hill.

"We could take the coward's way out," said Bob, looking up towards the top of the hill. "We could take our bikes up to The Potter's and leave them there and walk up the lane to Hilltop House."

"That would scarcely be the coward's way out," said Jupiter. "We do not know what brought those two men to Hilltop House. I would prefer to approach the place without being seen. It is unlikely that they are watching the path, but they might easily spot us if we attempted to walk up their lane from the main road."

"You're right," admitted Bob. He turned to look back towards the sea. The sun had already disappeared behind a bank of fog that lurked offshore. "It'll be dark before we can get back here."

"We should have no difficulty," said Jupiter Jones. "The moon will be up shortly."

"You checked the almanac?" asked Bob.

"I checked the almanac."

"Silly of me to ask," said Bob, and he started up the trail. Jupiter followed more slowly, panting as the going got steep, and stopping now and then to rest. But after ten minutes he had his second wind and climbed more easily. "Here it is," said Bob finally.

He turned and held out a hand to Jupe to help him up on to the trail that ran along the crest of the hill. "It'll be a cinch from here," he said. "We'll be on a downgrade all the way to Hilltop House."

Jupe stood for a few seconds, looking north along the trail. It was almost dark and the moon was not yet up. Still, the road—almost eight feet of bare earth scraped clear of growth—looked like a tawny ribbon stretching along the top of the range of hills. The scrub oak that crowded close to its sandy surface seemed black and menacing in the fading light.

"What do you expect to find tonight?" questioned Bob.

"Most certainly the two strangers who stopped at the salvage yard," said Jupiter. "One of them, we assume, is Mr Demetrieff of the Lapathian Board of Trade. The other could be almost anyone. It will be interesting to see how they are amusing themselves at Hilltop House."

Jupiter began to walk, and Bob stepped briskly along beside him. The moon edged up beyond the hills, silvering the road and throwing deep black shadows beside the boys. There was little conversation until the hulking, dark mass of Hilltop House came into sight ahead and to their left. The upper storeys of the place were dark, but a light gleamed faintly in one of the lower rooms.

"I explored that house once," said Bob. "I think that light is in what used to be the library."

"Windows could use a cleaning," murmured Jupiter, "and that does not look like an electric lamp."

"No. More like a lantern or a paraffin lamp. Well, give them a chance. They just moved in yesterday."

A little stream bed ran down the hill from the trail and curved past Hilltop House. It was summer-dry now, and the boys stepped into it silently, feeling step by step for any loose pebbles which might slide and send them tumbling. They almost crawled for the last fifty feet before the bed turned and ran beside the retaining wall that held the driveway of Hilltop House firm.

Jupiter pulled himself up over the retaining wall and on to a paved apron at the rear of the house. The big Cadillac stood outside a triple garage. Jupiter walked once around the car, saw that it was empty, and decided to ignore it.

The windows that looked out on to the rear area were black. There was a door with a pane of glass set into the upper half, and it was locked. "Kitchen," decided Jupiter.

"The servants' quarters are upstairs," said Bob.

"They have hardly had time to acquire servants," said Jupiter. "I suggest we proceed directly to the library."

"Jupe! You're not planning on going inside?" Bob's voice came in a horrified whisper.

"I think not," said Jupe. "It might lead to unnecessary unpleasantness. We can go round the house and look into the library window."

"Okay," said Bob. "Just so long as we stay outside. If anything goes wrong, we can run like crazy."

Jupiter didn't answer this. He led the way around past the dark kitchen to the lighted windows of the library. There was a narrow, paved path which made the going easy. The shrubbery that had once decorated the side of the house had long since withered away from neglect and lack of water.

The library windows, as Jupiter had pointed out,

could have used a good cleaning. The boys knelt and peered in over the sill and saw, mistily, the two strangers who had stopped at the salvage yard the day before. Two bunk beds had been set up in the huge room. Cans and paper plates and paper napkins were heaped helter-skelter on shelves which had once held books. There was a fire roaring away in the fireplace, and the younger man—the driver of the Cadillac—knelt in front of the flames and toasted a hot dog on a long piece of wire. The ageless, hairless man sat in a folding chair at a card table. He had the air of a man waiting in a restaurant for the waiter to serve his dinner.

Bob and Jupe watched the younger man turn the hot dog on the improvised spit. Then the bald man made an impatient movement, got up, and walked away through the wide arch into a darkened room beyond the library. He was gone for some minutes, and when he returned the hot dog was ready. The younger man inserted it clumsily into a roll, put it on a paper plate, and placed it before the bald man.

Jupiter could hardly suppress a chuckle at the expression of the bald one as he confronted his hot dog. He had seen Aunt Mathilda look like that once when a Danish friend in Rocky Beach had served cold eels and scrambled eggs at a dinner party.

The boys backed away from the window and returned to the rear of the house.

Bob leaned on the Cadillac. "Now we know what they're doing," he said. "That's the untidiest camp-out I ever saw."

"There has to be more to it than that," declared Jupiter. "No one would rent a mansion—however aged—so that they could sleep on bunks and toast hot

76

dogs in the library. Where did that bald man go when he walked through the archway?"

"The living room's on the ocean side of the house," said Bob.

"And the terrace," Jupiter reminded him. "Come on."

Bob followed Jupiter to the corner of the house. The terrace adjoined the drive, and extended all the way across the front of the place. It was almost fifteen feet wide, made of smoothly poured cement and edged with a stone wall more than three feet high.

"There's something set up there," whispered Jupiter. "An instrument of some kind, on a tripod."

"A telescope?" said Bob.

"Probably. Listen!"

A man's voice came to them where they stood. Jupiter pressed himself close to the house, watching. The younger man came out of the house on to the moonlit terrace, crossed to the instrument on the tripod, looked into it, then called out something. He looked again and laughed, then made another remark. Jupiter frowned. The cadence of the speech was peculiar. There was almost a singsong quality to what the man said.

Then a second, deeper voice was heard. It was a voice which sounded immensely tired. The bald man stepped out on to the terrace, came to the tripod and bent to peer into it. He said a word or two, shrugged, and returned to the house. The younger man hurried after him, speaking rapidly and urgently.

"Not French," said Jupiter when they had gone.

"Or German," said Bob, who had had a year of that language.

"I wonder," said Jupiter, "what Lapathian sounds like."

77

"I wonder," said Bob, "what they were looking at."

"That, at least, we can find out," said Jupiter. He stepped quickly and noiselessly from the drive on to the terrace and stole forward to the instrument on its tripod. As Bob had guessed, the thing was a telescope. Jupiter bent, careful not to touch the instrument, and looked through the lens.

He saw the back windows of The Potter's house. The bedrooms were brightly lighted, and he could clearly see Pete sitting on a bed, talking with young Tom Dobson. There was a checker board between the two boys. Tom jumped one of Pete's men, and Pete made a wry face and pondered his next move. Mrs Dobson came into the room carrying a tray on which there were three cups. Cocoa, Jupiter assumed.

Jupiter stepped away from the telescope and returned to the driveway. "We now know how they are amusing themselves," he told Bob. "They are spying on The Potter's house."

"About what you expected," said Bob. "Let's get out of here, Jupe. Those two give me the willies."

"Yes. And there is nothing more to be learned at the moment," said Jupiter Jones.

The boys passed the Cadillac and headed for the retaining wall to let themselves down again into the dry steam bed.

"It's closer here, I think," said Bob, cutting across an open patch of ground which might once have been a kitchen garden.

And with that, Bob suddenly shouted, threw up his arms, and dropped out of sight.

10

Caught!

"Bob, are you hurt?"

Jupiter knelt beside the hole which had appeared in the earth. Below, in what seemed to be some sort of cellar, Jupe could barely see Bob getting to his knees.

"Blast!" said Bob.

"Are you hurt?"

Bob stood up and hunched his shoulders. "No, I don't think so."

Jupiter stretched full length on the ground and reached one hand towards Bob. "Here!" he said.

Bob grasped the hand, put one foot on a shelf and tried to climb out of the hole. Wood splintered under his feet and he fell back, almost taking Jupe with him.

"Blast!" he said again, and then he froze, caught by the sudden beam of a very powerful torch.

"Do not move!" said the younger of the two tenants of Hilltop House.

Jupiter did not move, and Bob remained where he was, sitting on bare earth at the bottom of the hole, staring up past rotted, splintered planks.

"Exactly what are you doing here?" demanded the younger resident of Hilltop House.

Only Jupiter Jones could manage an air of superiority while stretched full-length on the ground. "At this precise moment," he said, "I was endeavouring to get my friend out of this hole. Please assist me, so that we can ascertain as quickly as possible whether he is injured."

"Why you impudent—!" began the younger man.

This outburst was interrupted by a deep chuckle. "Peace, Demetrieff," said the older, bald person. He knelt, surprisingly agile for one who was not slender, and reached towards Bob. "Can you take my hand?" he asked Bob. "We do not have a ladder on the premises."

Bob stood up and stretched, and in a second the bald man had hauled him up through the jagged hole and set him upon his feet. "Now how does it go?" he asked. "No bones broken, eh? Good. Nasty things, broken bones. I remember the time my horse fell on me. It was two months before I could ride again. It is painful when one must lie still and do nothing." The bald one paused, then added in a cold voice, "Naturally, I shot the horse."

Bob swallowed, and Jupiter felt goose bumps come up on his arms.

"Klas Kaluk is not noted for his patience with bunglers," said the younger man.

Jupiter stood up slowly, brushing dust from his clothes.

"Klas Kaluk?" he echoed.

"You would say General Kaluk," the younger man informed him. Jupiter was suddenly aware that the younger man held a gun as well as a torch.

"General Kaluk." Jupiter nodded to the bald one, then turned back to the man with the gun. "And you are Mr Demetrieff," he said.

"How did you know that?" demanded Demetrieff.

"General Kaluk called you by name," said Jupiter.

The general chuckled again. "You have a quick ear, my plump friend," he told Jupiter. "Boys with quick ears interest me. They hear many things. Shall we go into the house and discuss what you may have heard tonight?"

"Hey, Jupe," said Bob quickly. "Hey, we don't really want to. I mean, I'm okay, and we can go now and . . ."

The man named Demetrieff made a quick motion with his gun and Bob fell silent.

"It would be most inadvisable for us to leave this gaping hole in your yard," said Jupiter. "Some other member of the Chaparral Walking Club might cut across this way and fall in. Would you be liable, Mr Demetrieff, or would it be General Kaluk?"

Again the bald general laughed. "You have a nimble set of wits, my friend," he told Jupiter. "I believe, however, that the owners of this house would be liable. However, as I said, broken bones are unpleasant things. Demetrieff, there are some planks behind the stable."

"I think it's a garage," ventured Bob.

"No matter. Get them and put them over the hole." The older man looked down through the gap at broken shelves and earth floor. "It seems that we have an extension to the foundation of this building which projects out under the garden. A wine cellar, I should think."

Demetrieff hauled a pair of damp and dirty planks from behind the garage and dropped them hastily into place across the hole.

"That should take care of the matter, at least for the moment," said General Kaluk. "Now we shall go into the house and you will tell me about this Chaparral Walking Club of yours. You will also tell me your names, and why you chose to walk across this piece of property."

"We would be delighted," said Jupiter.

The man named Demetrieff gestured towards the

kitchen door, and General Kaluk led the way. Jupe and Bob trailed after the general. They went through a dusty and disused kitchen to the library, where the general sat easily in the folding chair next to the card table and ordered Jupiter and Bob to sit on one of the folding beds in the room.

"We cannot offer you lavish hospitality," said the general. His bald head gleamed in the light from the fireplace. "A glass of hot tea, perhaps?"

Jupiter shook his head. "Thank you, sir. I don't drink tea."

"Me, neither," said Bob.

"Oh, yes," said the general. "I forget. There is some custom about American children, is there not? No tea or coffee—or wine. You drink milk, do you?"

Jupiter admitted it.

"Well, we have no milk," said the general. Demetrieff stood to one side, a little behind the general.

"Demetrieff, have you heard of this Chaparral Walking Club?" asked the general.

"Never," said Demetrieff.

"It's a local thing," said Jupiter quickly. "Walking in the chaparral is more pleasant by day, but sometimes hikers try the paths on fine nights like this. You can hear the animals stirring in the underbrush as you pass. Sometimes, if you stand still for a long time, you can see the animals. I saw a deer once, and several times a skunk has crossed the road in front of me."

"Fascinating," said the man named Demetrieff. "And I suppose you also watch birds."

"Not at night," declared Jupiter truthfully. "You do hear an owl occasionally, but you never see one. In the daytime, the chaparral is alive with birds, but—"

The general held up one hand. "A moment," he said.

"Chaparral. This is a new word. Will you explain to me, please, what it is?"

"It's a community of growing things," said Jupiter. "The plants you see on this hillside are all part of the chaparral community—they are dwarfed trees and shrubs—the scrub oak and juniper and the sage, and at higher elevations the manzanita. They are extremely hardy plants which can survive on very little rainfall. California is one of the few areas where chaparral exists, so there is great interest in the plants."

Bob sat silently and marvelled at Jupiter's almost total recall of an article on chaparral that had appeared in a recent issue of *Nature* magazine. Total recall, Bob knew, was not uncommon among actors who had to remember lines, and Jupiter had once been a child actor.

On went Jupiter Jones, and on and on, describing the smell of chaparral in the spring, after the rains. He was telling how it held the hillsides firm when General Kaluk suddenly lifted one hand.

"Enough," said the general. "I share your admiration for chaparral. Courageous plants, if plants can be said to have courage. Now, if you please, we will get to the point. Your names?"

"Jupiter Jones," said Jupe.

"Bob Andrews," said Bob.

"Very well. And now you will tell me what you were doing in my garden."

"It's a shortcut," said Jupe truthfully. "We hiked up the trail from Rocky Beach and cut across. We can get down to the main road on your lane."

"The lane is private property."

"Yes, sir. We know. But Hilltop House has been empty for many years, and people have become accustomed to using the lane when they hike."

"They will have to become unaccustomed," declared the general. "I think, Jupiter Jones, that I have met you before."

"We didn't actually meet," said Jupe. "Mr Demetrieff talked to me yesterday when you took the wrong turn off the road."

"Ah, yes. And with you was an elderly man with a beard. Who is he?"

"We call him The Potter," said Jupiter. "I believe that is his real name—Alexander Potter."

"He is a friend of yours?" asked the general.

"I know him," admitted Jupiter. "Everyone in Rocky Beach knows The Potter."

The general nodded. "I believe I have heard of him." He turned towards Demetrieff, and firelight gleamed on his tanned skin. Jupiter saw a fine tracery of wrinkles on his cheeks. Kaluk was not ageless; he was old.

"Demetrieff," said the general, "did you not tell me there was a famed craftsman here who made pots?"

"And other things," put in Bob.

"I would enjoy very much meeting him," said the general. It was not exactly a question, and yet the general paused as if he were waiting for a reply.

Neither Jupiter nor Bob said anything.

"It is his shop at the bottom of my hill," said the general at last.

"It is his shop," said Jupiter.

"And he has guests," the general went on. "A young woman and a boy. Unless I make a mistake, you helped them today when they arrived at the shop."

"That's right," said Jupiter.

"A neighbourly thing to do, no doubt," said the general. "You know those people?"

"No, sir," said Jupiter. "They're friends of Mr Potter from someplace in the Midwest."

"Friends," said the general. "How pleasant to have friends. One would think this man who makes pots—and other things—would be present to greet his friends."

"He's . . . uh . . . rather eccentric."

"One gathers this. Yes, I would like very much to meet him. In fact, I must insist upon it."

The general suddenly sat straight, gripping the arms of his chair. "Where is he?" he demanded.

"Huh?" said Bob.

"You heard me. Where is the man you call The Potter?"

"We don't know," Jupiter said.

"That is impossible!" said the general. A flush of colour rose to his leathery cheeks. "He was with you yesterday. Today you helped his friends when they arrived at his house. You know where he is!"

"No, sir," said Jupiter. "We have no idea where he went after he left the salvage yard yesterday."

"He sent you here!" The accusation was curt.

"No!" cried Bob.

"Do not tell me fairy tales about wandering in the chaparral!" shouted the general. He beckoned to his associate. "Demetrieff! Your gun, if you please!"

The man handed the weapon to the general.

"You know what to do," said Kaluk harshly.

Demetrieff nodded and began to unbuckle his belt.

"Hey, wait a minute!" shouted Bob.

"You will remain seated," said General Kaluk. "Demetrieff, take the fat one who talks so well. I want to hear him talk more."

Demetrieff went around behind the bunk on which

85

Jupe and Bob were seated. Jupiter felt the leather of the belt settle around his head.

"Now you will tell me about The Potter," said the general. "Where is he?"

The belt tightened on Jupiter's head.

"I don't know," said Jupiter.

"He simply walked away from your . . . your salvage yard and was not seen again?" The general was almost sneering.

"That's what happened."

The belt tightened some more.

"And he was expecting guests—these friends you speak of—these friends to whom you were so helpful."

"That's right."

"And your police have done nothing?" demanded Kaluk. "They have not looked for this man who walked away?"

"It's a free country," said Jupiter. "If The Potter chooses to walk away, he is entitled to do so."

"A free country?" The general blinked and ran a hand over his hairless chin. "Yes. Yes, I have heard that before. He said nothing to you? You swear it?"

"He said nothing," declared Jupiter. He stared straight at the general, unblinking.

"I see." The general stood up and walked to Jupiter. He looked at him for half a minute, then sighed. "Very well, Demetrieff. We will let them go. He is telling the truth."

The younger man protested. "It's mad! Too much of a coincidence!"

The general shrugged. "A pair of children, curious as all children are curious. They know nothing."

The belt was removed from Jupiter's head. Bob, who

had not realized that he was holding his breath, let out a great gasp of relief.

"We should call your excellent police, who do not look for people," snapped Demetrieff. "We should tell them that you have broken the law. You have trespassed on this property."

"You talk about breaking the law!" exclaimed Bob. "If we told what happened here tonight . . ."

"You will not tell," said the general. "What really happened tonight? I asked about a famous artisan, and you informed me that you did not know his whereabouts. What could be more natural? The man has achieved some fame. He has been written about in your periodicals. As for this—"the general tossed the gun in his hand—"as for this, Mr Demetrieff has a permit for the gun, and you *were* trespassing. Nothing has occurred. We are being generous. You may go now, and do not return."

Bob was up instantly, pulling Jupiter along with him.

"You will find it convenient to use the lane," said the general. "And remember, we will be watching you go."

The boys did not speak until they were away from the house and hurrying down the drive that led from Hilltop House to the highway.

"Never again!" exclaimed Bob.

Jupiter looked up and back at the stone buttress of the terrace. Demetrieff and the general stood there, plain in the moonlight, motionless and watching.

"Malignant pair," said Jupiter. "I have a distinct feeling that General Kaluk has presided over other inquisitions."

"If you mean he's used to giving the third degree to people, I couldn't agree more," said Bob. "Nice that you have an honest face."

"It was even nicer to be able to tell the truth," said Jupiter.

"Yeah! You did that, didn't you?"

"I tried. One can consider one's daughter a friend from the Midwest."

The road curved then, and Hilltop House was lost to sight behind a clump of brush on the boys' left. And then, from lower on the hill, there was a muffled sound and a flash of flame. Something, or some things, whizzed over Bob's head and spattered into the brush.

"Get down!" cried Jupiter.

Bob dropped on his face, Jupe beside him. The two waited, not daring to move. There was a crackling in the underbrush off to the right. Then there was quiet, except for the scolding of some night bird.

"Buckshot?" wondered Bob.

"I think so," Jupiter decided. He got to his hands and knees and crawled forward until they had rounded yet another turn in the lane. Bob followed him. When they had gone perhaps fifty yards in this fashion, both boys leaped up and sprinted for the main road.

The gate at the bottom of the drive was closed. They did not pause to see whether the lock was in place. Jupe climbed over and Bob hurdled the barrier in one leap. The two raced down the road to The Potter's gate and burst through that, stopping only when they had reached the shelter of The Potter's front porch.

"That shot!" gasped Jupiter. "It couldn't have come from Hilltop House. Demetrieff and the general were standing on the terrace there as we came around the bend in the road." He stopped to let his breathing quiet. Then, "Someone was waiting on the hill with a gun. Bob, there's a third man involved!"

11

The Ghost Returns

JUPITER JONES had his hand on the doorbell of The Potter's house when a window upstairs was thrown open and Eloise Dobson's voice called out.

"Who's there?" Mrs Dobson demanded.

Jupiter stepped back away from the door and out from under the roof of the porch. "It's Jupiter Jones, Mrs Dobson. And Bob Andrews is with me."

"Oh," she said. "Just a second."

The window slammed shut. An instant later, Jupe and Bob heard locks turning and bolts being drawn back. The door opened and Pete looked out.

"What's up?" he demanded.

"Let us in, and keep calm," said Jupiter in a low voice.

"I am calm. What's the matter?"

Jupe and Bob stepped into the hall. "I don't want to alarm Mrs Dobson unnecessarily," said Jupiter quickly, "but the men at Hilltop House—"

Jupiter broke off when Mrs Dobson appeared at the top of the stairs and started down. "Did you hear a loud bang a minute ago, Jupiter?" she asked. "Like a shot?"

"It was only a backfire on the road," said Jupiter quickly. "Mrs Dobson, you haven't met our friend, Bob Andrews."

"How do you do, Mrs Dobson," said Bob.

Mrs Dobson smiled and came the rest of the way

down the stairs. "I'm glad to meet you, Bob," she said. "What brings you two here so late?"

Tom Dobson came down the stairs carrying a tray piled with empty cups. "Hey, Jupe!" he said.

Again Jupiter introduced Bob.

"Aha!" said Tom. "The Third Investigator!"

"The what?" said Mrs Dobson.

"Nothing, Mum," said Tom. "It's just a joke. Kind of."

"Hm!" Mrs Dobson looked at her son in the searching manner peculiar to mothers. "We can do without jokes right now," she said. "What are you boys up to? It's not that I don't appreciate your trouble. It's very nice to have Pete spend the night with us, but let's not have any secrets, huh?"

"I'm sorry, Mrs Dobson," said Jupiter. "Bob and I hadn't planned to come here tonight. However, we went hiking along the path at the top of the hill, and we could not help but notice the men at Hilltop House."

Bob choked.

Jupiter continued calmly. "Hilltop House is the big place almost directly behind this house, but up near the crest of the hill. Two new tenants moved into the place yesterday, and from their terrace they can look directly into the back bedrooms in this house. The thought came to us that you would wish to know of this, so that you can keep the window blinds down."

"Oh, that's just great!" Mrs Dobson sat down on the stairs. "Makes the day perfect. First we get flaming footprints, then that nut from the inn, and now a couple of Peeping Toms."

"Nut from the inn?" questioned Bob. "What nut, from what inn?"

"Guy named Farrier," answered Pete. "He popped up

90

about half an hour ago, said he wanted to see if Mrs Dobson and Tom got moved in okay, and was there anything he could do for them?"

"The jolly fisherman," said Jupiter.

"Too jolly for words," said Mrs Dobson. "For some reason, he gives me the creeps. Why's he trying so hard? He smiles so much my face aches just watching him, and he's always so darned . . . so darned . . ."

"Splendid?" said Jupiter.

"I guess you could say splendid." Mrs Dobson put her chin in her hands and rested her elbows on her knees. "He looks like . . . well, like one of those dummies in a department store. I don't think he sweats. Anyhow, he tried to invite himself in for coffee. I told him I was planning to lie down with a cold cloth on my head, and he took the hint and went away."

"He was driving?" said Jupiter.

"Well, sure," Pete put in. "An old tan Ford. He went on up the road."

"Hm," said Jupiter. "No reason why he shouldn't take a drive along the ocean. Well, we had better get home. See you tomorrow, Mrs Dobson."

"Goodnight, boys," said Mrs Dobson. She took the tray of dirty cups from Tom and headed for the kitchen.

Jupiter quickly filled in Tom and Pete on the full events at Hilltop House and the subsequent gunshot. He warned them again about keeping the blinds down. After Jupe and Bob went out, they could hear the sound of locks being locked and bolts being bolted.

"I think I am extremely pleased that The Potter equipped his house so well with locks," said Jupiter.

The boys began the walk back to Rocky Beach on the shoulder of the road.

"Do you think Pete and the Dobsons are in any real danger?" wondered Bob.

"No," said Jupiter. "No, I think not. The men at Hilltop House may be curious about them, but we know now that they are really interested in The Potter. And they are aware that The Potter is not at home."

"What about the guy on the hill?" said Bob. "You know, the one who took a shot at us."

"We were the ones who were threatened," said Jupiter. "It does not appear that he menaced the Dobsons in any way. It is interesting that Mr Farrier has been so persistent in his attentions to Mrs Dobson. She has certainly not encouraged him, and Aunt Mathilda was positively rude to him this afternoon. Most people do not intrude when they are clearly unwelcome. That tan Ford is also interesting."

"There must be a million of those around," said Bob. "Why is it interesting?"

"Because it doesn't match the rest of the man," explained Jupiter. "As Mrs Dobson agreed, he is quite splendid in his appearance. One would expect him to drive something more elegant—a foreign sports car, perhaps. And although he seems meticulous about his own appearance, he has not even troubled to have his car washed."

The lights of Rocky Beach gleamed ahead, and the boys walked faster, suddenly fearful that Aunt Mathilda might be looking for them. The Jones house was quiet, however, when the boys reached it. Jupiter peered in through the window to see his Uncle Titus still napping contentedly as an old movie unfolded on the TV screen.

"Come over with me, and we'll close the yard up for the night," said Jupiter to Bob.

The boys went across and in through the big iron

gates. The light burned brightly in Jupiter's outdoor workshop. As Jupiter reached to turn it off, a red light over the printing press flashed furiously off and on. This was the signal that the telephone in Headquarters was ringing.

"At this hour?" exclaimed Bob. "Now who—?"

"Pete!" said Jupiter. "It could only be Pete." He tore aside the grating that covered Tunnel Two. In seconds he and Bob were inside Headquarters and Jupiter had snatched up the telephone.

"Come back!" Pete's voice sounded thin and shaky coming over the wire. "It's happened again!"

"More footprints?" said Jupiter tersely.

"Three of them, on the stairs," said Pete, "I put them out. There's a funny smell. Also, Mrs Dobson is having hysterics."

"We'll be right there," promised Jupiter.

He hung up the telephone.

"Another set of flaming footprints," he told Bob. "On the stairs, this time. Also, Pete reports that Mrs Dobson is having hysterics, which is not surprising."

"Back we go?" questioned Bob.

"Back we go," said Jupiter.

The boys hurried out through Tunnel Two and were just locking the gate of the salvage yard when Aunt Mathilda opened the door of the Jones house. "What are you boys doing over there all this time?" she called.

"Just sorting things out," Jupiter called back. He turned away from the gate and ran across to his aunt. "We thought we might ride up and see how Mrs Dobson and Tom are getting along," he said. "Do you mind?"

"I do," said Aunt Mathilda. "It's too late to go

93

visiting. And Jupiter, you know I don't like to have you on that busy road after dark."

"The bikes have lights," Jupiter pointed out, "and we'll be careful. Mrs Dobson was so upset this afternoon, we thought we might just check in on her and see if she's settled comfortably."

"Well . . . all right, Jupiter. But you boys be careful." She stopped suddenly. "Where's Pete?" she asked.

"He left," said Jupiter shortly.

"All right. Well, if you're going, hurry. It's not getting any earlier. And remember—be careful!"

"We'll remember," promised Jupiter.

With the bicycles, the return trip to The Potter's house took only minutes. Bob and Jupiter pounded on the front door and called, and Pete let them in.

"Did you search the house?" Jupiter asked.

"By myself?" said Pete. "You crazy? Besides, I've been busy. I had a set of burning footprints to put out, and a trip to the telephone on the main road to call you guys, and Mrs Dobson is going out of her head."

Indeed, Mrs Dobson was not herself. Bob and Jupiter followed Pete upstairs to the big front bedroom where the brass bed had been put up. Mrs Dobson was stretched out on the bed, face down, and sobbing bitterly. Young Tom Dobson sat beside her, patting her shoulder and looking highly nervous.

Bob slipped into the bathroom, turned on the cold water tap, and soaked a washcloth.

"There it goes again!" cried Mrs Dobson.

"There what goes?" asked Jupiter.

"It stopped," said Mrs Dobson. "The water was running someplace."

"I did that, Mrs Dobson." Bob came in, carrying the wet cloth. "I thought you might use this."

"Oh." She took the cloth and dabbed at her face.

"Just after you left," Pete explained, "we could hear water running in the pipes, but every tap in the house was turned off. Then, we were all about to turn in, and there was this sound downstairs, like a thud. Mrs Dobson came out to see what was up, and there were three little fires on the stairs. I smothered them with a blanket, and we've got another set of footprints."

Jupiter and Bob returned to the stairs to examine the charred marks.

"Exactly like the ones in the kitchen," said Jupiter. He touched one, then sniffed his fingertips. "Peculiar odour. Chemicals of some type."

"So what does that get us?" demanded Pete. "We've got a ghost with a Ph.D. in chemistry?"

"It is probably too late," said Jupiter, "but I suggest that we search the house."

"Jupe, nobody could have got in here," insisted Pete. "This place is locked up tighter than the vault at the Bank of America."

Jupiter insisted, however, and the house was searched from cellar to attic. Except for the Dobsons, The Three Investigators, and a vast amount of ceramic art, the place was empty.

"I want to go home," said Eloise Dobson.

"We'll go, Mum," promised Tom. "We'll go in the morning, okay?"

"What's the matter with right now?" asked Mrs Dobson.

"You're tired, Mum."

"You think I could sleep in this place?" demanded Mrs Dobson.

"Would you feel safer if we all stayed tonight?" asked Jupiter Jones.

Eloise Dobson shivered and stretched out on the brass bed, kicking at the footboard with her stocking feet. "I'd feel safer," she admitted. "Do you suppose we could ask the fire department up for the night, too?"

"Let's hope we don't need them," said Jupiter.

"Try to rest, huh, Mum?" Tom had padded out to the linen closet for an extra blanket. He covered his mother, who was still wearing the blouse and skirt she had had on that afternoon.

"I ought to get up and get undressed," said Mrs Dobson wearily. She didn't, however. She put one arm up to cover her eyes. "Don't turn out the light," she said.

"I won't," said Tom.

"And don't go away," she murmured.

"I'll stay right here," said Tom.

Mrs Dobson said nothing more. She had dropped into an exhausted slumber.

The boys tiptoed out to the landing. "I'll get another blanket and sleep on the floor in Mum's room," said Tom softly. "Will you guys really stay all night?"

"I can telephone Aunt Mathilda," announced Jupiter. "I will inform her that your mother is feeling rather upset and wishes company. And perhaps she can call Mrs Andrews."

"I'll call my mother," said Bob. "I can just tell her I'm staying over with you."

"Maybe we should call the police," said Tom.

"So far that has done no good," Jupiter told him. "Lock the door after us when we go to the call box."

"Don't worry," said Pete.

"I'll rap three times when we come back," said Jupiter. "Then I'll wait, and rap three more times."

"Got you." Pete unlocked and unbolted the door and

Jupiter and Bob slipped out into the night, crossed The Potter's yard, and went into the call box on the main road.

Aunt Mathilda was more than concerned when she learned that Mrs Dobson was upset and wanted company. Jupiter did not mention the second set of flaming footprints to her. He spent the better part of his three minutes persuading her not to rouse Uncle Titus and have him come with the truck to collect the Dobsons and remove them bodily to the security and comfort of the Jones house. "Mrs Dobson's asleep now," Jupiter said finally. "She only said she'd feel safer if we all stayed in the house with her."

"There aren't enough beds," argued Aunt Mathilda.

"We'll make do," said Jupiter. "It'll be all right."

Aunt Mathilda finally subsided and Jupiter gave the telephone to Bob, who simply received permission from his mother to spend the night with Jupiter.

The boys went back to The Potter's house, rapped the agreed-upon raps, and were admitted by Pete.

As Aunt Mathilda had pointed out, there were not enough beds to go around—not even with Tom Dobson sleeping on the floor in his mother's room. Pete did not see this as an obstacle. One of them, he decided, should be on watch at all times. Two would sleep. They could take turns. Bob and Jupiter both felt that sentinel duty might be an excellent idea, and Jupe volunteered for the first watch—which was to be for three hours. Bob disappeared into The Potter's bedroom, to stretch out on The Potter's narrow, immaculate bunk bed. Pete vanished into the room which had been prepared for Tom.

Jupe stationed himself in the hall at the head of the stairs. He sat down on the floor, leaned back against the

97

wall, and stared speculatively at the charred marks on the steps—the marks of bare feet. He sniffed at his own fingers. The chemical smell which he had noticed when he first touched the footprints was gone. Doubtless some extremely volatile mixture had been used to create the flames. Jupe wondered idly what it had been, then decided that the substance itself wasn't important. What was important was that someone had come into a locked and double-locked house to create the eerie and terrifying effect. How had it been done? And by whom?

Of one thing Jupiter Jones was sure. No ghost was playing a devilish prank. Jupiter Jones refused to believe in ghosts.

12

The Secret Library

Jupiter awakened in Tom Dobson's bed and heard a determined clanking and slamming and clattering from the kitchen below. He groaned slightly, turned over, and looked at his watch. It was after seven.

"You awake?" Bob Andrews was looking in through the doorway.

"I am now." Jupiter got up slowly.

"Mrs Dobson's furious," reported Bob. "She's down cooking breakfast."

"That's good. I could use breakfast. What's she furious about? Last night she only wanted to go home."

"Not this morning. This morning she's ready to take the town of Rocky Beach apart. Wonderful what a good night's sleep will do for a person. Come on down. You'll enjoy it. Reminds me of your Aunt Mathilda in one of her more active moods."

Jupiter chuckled, went into the bathroom and splashed some water on his face, put on his shoes—which were all he had bothered to remove the night before—and followed Bob down to the kitchen. Pete and Tom were already sitting there watching as Eloise Dobson dealt with bacon and eggs. She was relieving herself of numerous opinions about The Potter, the house, the flaming footprints, and the ingratitude of a father who disappeared when his only daughter had taken the trouble to drive almost all the way across the country to see him.

"And don't think I'm going to let him get away with it," said Mrs Dobson. "I'm not. I'm going down to the police station this morning and file a missing persons report on him, and then they'll have to look for him."

"Will that do any good, Mrs Dobson?" Jupiter questioned. "If The Potter is missing because he wishes to be missing, it's difficult to see—"

"I don't wish him to be missing," interrupted Mrs Dobson. She set a platter of fried eggs and bacon on the table. "I am his daughter and he is my father and he'd better get used to it. And that police chief of yours had darn well better do something about those footprints, too. That has to be a crime."

"Arson, I imagine," said Bob.

"Call it whatever you like. It's got to stop. Now you boys eat. I'm going to town."

"You didn't have any breakfast," protested Tom.

"Who needs it?" snapped his mother. "Eat. Go ahead. And stay put, for Pete's sake. I'll be right back."

She snatched up her bag, which had been laid on top of the refrigerator, rummaged for car keys, then strode down the hall and out the door. A second later, the boys heard the engine of the blue convertible.

"Mum kind of gets a second wind," said Tom, a little embarrassed.

"Good eggs," said Jupiter. He had served himself and was eating on his feet, leaning against the doorway. "I think we'd better do the dishes before she gets back."

"Your years with Aunt Mathilda have given you a sound sense of psychology," Bob said.

"Your mother is, of course, quite justified in being

angry with your grandfather," Jupiter told young Tom. "However, I don't believe The Potter wanted to hurt her. He never wanted to hurt anybody. A lonely person, but very gentle, I think." Jupiter put down his plate in the sink and remembered again the men in the Cadillac and their confrontation with The Potter. He remembered The Potter standing in the driveway of the salvage yard, holding his medallion with his hand.

"The double-headed eagle," said Jupiter. "Tom, you said your grandfather sometimes sent you things which he had made. Did he ever send anything with a double-headed eagle?"

Tom thought a minute, then shook his head. "Mum likes birds," he told Jupiter. "He sent things with birds on them, mostly, but just regular birds—robins and bluebirds. No freaks like that plaque upstairs."

"But he wore the eagle on the medallion," said Jupiter, "and he used it when he designed that plaque—and a plaque for an empty room, incidentally. Now why would he go to the trouble to make a huge thing like that and install it in an empty room?"

Jupiter wiped his hands on a tea towel and started for the stairs. The other boys instantly abandoned their breakfasts and followed him up and into the room which had been occupied by Mrs Dobson.

The crimson eagle glared at them from above the mantel.

Jupiter felt around the edges of the plaque. "It seems to be cemented into place," he said.

Tom Dobson ducked back into his own room and returned with a nail file. "Try this," he said.

Jupe pried at the edges of the ceramic piece. "No. It's up there to stay," he announced. "I think The Potter

101

must have replastered the wall above the fireplace and put the plaque right into the plaster."

Jupe stepped back and looked up at the screaming bird. "What a job that must have been. It's a very large piece."

"Everybody's got to have a hobby," said Tom.

"Wait!" said Jupiter. "It isn't cast all in one piece. We need something to stand on."

Pete darted down to the kitchen and came back with one of the chairs. Jupiter stood on it and reached up towards the right head of the eagle. "That eye isn't the same as the other," he said. "It was cast separately." Jupiter pressed on the white porcelain of the eagle's eye. It gave under his fingers, and the boys heard a faint click. The entire wall above the mantel moved slightly.

"A secret door," said Jupiter. "Somehow, that makes sense." He stepped down from the chair, took hold of the ornate moulding that edged the wall panel and tugged. The panel swung out on well-oiled hinges.

The boys crowded close to look into a compartment that was almost six inches deep. There were four shelves between the mantel and the ceiling, and they were piled with papers. Jupiter lifted one out.

"Why, they're only old copies of the Belleview *Register and Tribune*!" exclaimed Tom. He took the paper from Jupiter's hands and glanced through it. "This is the one that has the story about me," he said.

"How'd you make the news?" asked Bob.

"I won an essay contest," said Tom.

Jupiter had unfolded another paper—a much older one. "Your mother's wedding announcement," he said.

There were more—stories about the birth of young Tom, and about the death of his grandmother. There was a story on the grand opening of the Dobson

102

Hardware Store, and one about a speech Tom's father had given on Veter an's Day. All the doings of the Dobsons had been chronicled in the papers, and The Potter had saved every one.

"A secret library," said Pete, "and you and your mother were the big secrets."

"Sure makes you feel appreciated," said young Tom.

"He was most reticent," said Jupiter. "No one even knew you existed. Odd. What is even more odd is the fact that there is nothing about The Potter himself in this secret library."

"Should there be?" said Pete. "He didn't like getting his name in the papers. Not that I could ever recall."

"True. And yet the men at Hilltop House yesterday mentioned that accounts of his artistry had appeared in periodicals. When accounts of your artistry appear in periodicals, the normal thing to do is to save the periodicals. Right?"

"Right," said Bob.

"So we can assume one of two things," said Jupiter. "Either The Potter does not have even the normal amount of vanity, or there were no accounts in periodicals—except for the photo spread in *Westways*. And The Potter did not even know of that until Saturday. He was not pleased when he did see it."

"Meaning?" asked Tom Dobson.

"Meaning that The Potter wanted to keep your existence a secret—and the last thing in the world he wanted for himself was acclaim. Perhaps he had very good reasons. Tom, we do not know why, but we learned last night that the two men who have rented Hilltop House are most interested in your grandfather. They appeared in Rocky Beach almost two months after the *Westways* spread came out with your grandfather's photograph. Does this suggest anything to you?"

"It suggests that Grandpa may have been on the run," said Tom. "But from what?"

"Do you know anything about Lapathia?" asked Jupiter.

"Never heard of it. What is it?"

"It's a country—a small European country, where a political assassination took place many years ago."

Tom shrugged. "According to Grandma, my grandfather was from the Ukraine," he said.

"Have you ever heard the name Azimov?" asked Jupiter.

"Nope."

"That could not have been your grandfather's name before he changed it to Potter?"

"No. He had a very long name. Very long. You couldn't pronounce it."

Jupiter stood, pulling at his lip.

"He went to a lot of trouble to hide a bunch of old newspapers," said Tom. "He could have done it much easier, if it was all that important. He could have stuck them in a file with some old bills—you know, like 'The Purloined Letter' by Edgar Allan Poe."

Pete put a hand to the heavy plaque. "That would have made more sense," he said. "A thing like this in an empty room is bound to attract attention, if you're looking for attention."

"And he wasn't," said Jupiter. "It was the last thing in the world he wanted."

Jupiter bent to examine the fireplace beneath the mantel. It was spotless. Obviously no one had ever lighted a fire in it. Jupe went down on his knees and peered inside, looking up. "There is no chimney," he announced. "The fireplace is a sham."

"Probably The Potter built it himself," guessed Bob.

"In that case, why is this little trap here?" said Jupiter. He lifted a small metal flap which had been built into the floor of the fireplace. "When you have a real fireplace, you have one of these to sweep the ashes out. Why put one in a false fireplace, where there will never be ashes?"

Jupiter squeezed his hand into the opening in the brick floor of the fireplace. He touched paper. "There's something here!" he cried. "An envelope!" He edged it up and out, and let the little metal trap clank shut.

It was a brown manila envelope sealed with a large blob of red wax.

"The other secret library behind the plaque was a decoy," Jupiter decided. He held up the envelope. "I think the real secret is here. Well, Tom, what do we do now? It belongs to your grandfather, and he is missing and you are our client. What do we do?"

"We open it," said Tom without hesitation.

"I was hoping you'd say that," murmured Bob.

Jupiter broke the seal on the envelope.

"Well?" said Tom.

Jupiter took out a single sheet of heavy parchment which had been folded three times. He unfolded it with great care.

"Well, what is it?" asked Tom.

Jupiter frowned. "I don't know. A certificate of some kind. It looks like a diploma or a degree, except that it's not big enough."

The boys crowded around Jupiter. "What kind of language is that?" asked Pete.

Bob shook his head. "Beats me," he said. "I never saw anything like it before."

Jupiter went to the window and held the hand-lettered document close to his eyes. "I can only recognize two things," he announced after a few moments. "One is the seal at the bottom. It is our old friend, the two-headed eagle. The other is a name—it's Kerenov. Someone at some time conferred some honour on one Alexis Kerenov. Have you ever heard that name, Tom?"

"No," said Tom. "It couldn't have been Grandfather. Like I said, his name was real, real long."

"You recall the name, Bob, don't you?" said Jupiter.

"You bet I do," said Bob. "Kerenov was the artisan who created the crown for old Federic Azimov."

Tom stared from one of them to the other. "Federic Azimov? Who's he?"

"He was the first king of Lapathia," Jupiter told him. "He lived 400 years ago."

Tom Dobson stared at the Investigators. "But what would that have to do with my grandfather?" he asked.

"We don't know," said Jupiter, "but we intend to find out."

13

The Odd Eagle

JUPITER JONES piled the copies of the Belleview newspaper neatly on the shelves in the compartment above the fireplace and swung the panel closed.

"Your mother will be back any minute," Jupiter said, "and I imagine Chief Reynolds will be with her. I have a strong feeling that we would be doing your grandfather a disservice if we turned the document we found over to the chief. The Three Investigators are following up certain lines of inquiry having to do with Lapathia and the royal family of the Azimovs. Do you agree, Tom, that we should be allowed to continue these until we have real evidence to present to the police?"

Tom scratched his head in bewilderment. "Wherever you are, you're way ahead of me," he said. "Okay. You keep the paper—for the time being. What about those newspapers behind the plaque?"

"It is possible that the police will discover the secret compartment," said Jupiter. "If so, there can be no harm done. I believe that is what the compartment was built for—to draw attention away from the real secret."

"I sure hope I get to meet my grandfather before all this is over," said Tom. "He must be a character."

"It will be an interesting experience," Jupiter promised him.

Bob looked out of the window. "Here comes Mrs Dobson now," he reported.

"Chief Reynolds with her?" asked Jupe.

"There's a squad car right behind her," said Bob.

"Omigosh! The dishes!" cried Pete.

"Indeed," said Jupiter Jones, and the boys dashed down the stairs. By the time Mrs Dobson had parked and crossed the yard to the front door, Jupiter was running hot water into the sink, Tom was frantically scraping plates, and Bob stood by with a towel.

"Oh, how nice!" said Mrs Dobson when she saw the activity in the kitchen.

"Delicious breakfast, Mrs Dobson," said Pete.

Chief Reynolds, followed by Officer Haines, stalked into the kitchen after Mrs Dobson. He ignored the other boys and focused his wrath on Jupiter. "Why didn't you call me last night?" he demanded.

"Mrs Potter was upset," said Jupiter.

"And since when are you a member of the Ladies Aid Society?" demanded the chief. "Jupiter Jones, one of these days, you are going to get your fat head knocked clean off."

"Yes, sir," agreed Jupe.

"Flaming footprints!" snorted the chief. He turned to Haines. "Search the house," he ordered.

"We did that, Chief," Jupiter reported. "There wasn't anyone here."

"You mind if we do it our way?" said the chief.

"No, sir."

"And get out, will you?" said the irate police chief. "Go on. Go and play baseball, or whatever it is normal kids do."

The boys fled to the yard.

"Is he always that grumpy?" Tom asked.

"Only when Jupe doesn't let him in on things," said Bob.

"That figures." Tom sat down on the steps between the two huge urns which were banded with double-headed eagles.

Jupiter frowned at one of the urns.

"What's your problem?" said Bob.

"One of these eagles has only one head," said Jupiter, puzzled.

The boys crowded round the urn. It was true. One of the birds in the bright band which decorated the piece was missing a head—the right-hand head. It looked like an ordinary, one-headed creature gazing off to the left.

"Interesting," said Jupiter.

Bob circled the other vase, examining the band of eagles. "All of these have two heads," he reported.

"Maybe my grandfather made a mistake," said Tom.

"The Potter does not make mistakes such as this," said Jupiter. "His designs are always perfect. If he intended to put a band of double-headed eagles on this urn, he would have done so."

"It could be another decoy," said Bob, "like that secret compartment in the bedroom. Is there anything in it?"

Jupiter tried to lift the top off the urn. It did not budge. He tried to unscrew it, and it did not unscrew. He examined the sides of the piece, and the pedestal, which was cemented in place on the steps. He pressed on the single-headed eagle, as he had pressed on the eye embedded in the plaque. Nothing gave way.

"Really a decoy," he murmured. "It was never intended to be opened."

Chief Reynolds came out on to the porch. "If I didn't know better," he announced to anyone who cared to listen, "I'd say the place *was* haunted."

"It is mysterious," Jupiter agreed. He went on to tell

the chief of the strange chemical odour he had detected on the newly burned footprints.

"Was it anything you recognized?" asked the chief. "Paraffin? Anything like that?"

"No," said Jupiter. "It was entirely unfamiliar—a sharp, acid smell."

"Hm," said the chief. "The lab has samples of the charred linoleum. Maybe they can find out something. You boys have anything else you can tell me about this thing?"

The Three Investigators looked at one another, and then at Tom Dobson. "No, sir," said Tom.

"Then you can leave," said the chief, rather curtly.

"Right," agreed Bob. "I have to go home and change my clothes and get to the library."

Jupiter made for his bicycle. "Aunt Mathilda will be wondering," he said.

The Three Investigators waved a hasty good-bye to Tom Dobson and started down the highway towards Rocky Beach. At the intersection near The Jones Salvage Yard, Jupiter pulled his bike to the kerb. The other two boys also stopped.

"I wonder if the jolly fisherman is connected with the disturbances," said Jupiter.

"He's just a creep," declared Pete.

"Perhaps," said Jupiter. "However, he has a way of being around just before things happen—or just after. He was parked across from The Potter's when the house was searched and I was knocked down. He attempted to call on Mrs Dobson last evening, not long before the second set of flaming footprints appeared. He could have been the man who shot at us from the hillside. We are sure the two men at Hilltop House didn't do that."

"But why would he?"

" Who knows?" said Jupe. " Perhaps he is a confederate of the men at Hilltop House. If we could solve the secret of The Potter, we might know many things." Jupe reached into his pocket and took out the document he had discovered in the dummy fireplace. "Here." He handed it to Bob. "Is there any possibility that you could identify the language on this parchment, or perhaps even translate it?"

" I'm willing to bet it's in Lapathian," said Bob. " I'll do what I can."

" Good. And also, if we could find out more about the Azimovs it could be helpful. The name Kerenov on that document is most provocative."

" The crown-maker? Right. I'll try." Bob pocketed the envelope and rode on.

" What time is it?" Pete asked nervously. " My mum will be having a fit."

" It's only nine," said Jupiter. " Will she be so worried? I thought we might pay a visit to Miss Hopper."

" At the Seabreeze Inn? What's she got to do with it?"

" Not a thing. She is, however, the landlady of that jolly fisherman, and she usually takes an acute interest in the welfare of her guests."

" Okay," said Pete. " Let's see her. But let's not be all day about it. I want to get home before Mum starts phoning your Aunt Mathilda."

" That would be wise," Jupiter conceded.

The boys found Miss Hopper in the lobby of the Seabreeze Inn, in worried consultation with Marie, the maid.

" It can't be helped," Miss Hopper was saying. " You'll just have to skip 113 and come back to it after lunch."

" Serve him right if I skipped it altogether," snapped

Marie, and she banged out of the lobby pushing her cart with cleaning utensils in front of her.

"Something wrong, Miss Hopper?" asked Jupiter.

"Oh, Jupiter. And Pete. Good morning. It's nothing important, really. It's only that Mr Farrier has a 'Do Not Disturb' sign on his door and Marie can't get in to do his room. It always upsets her when she can't follow her regular routine."

Miss Hopper hesitated for a moment, then said with a touch of slyness, "I heard Mr Farrier come in last night. Well, actually it was this morning. Three o'clock."

"That's interesting," said Jupiter. "Most fishermen are early morning people."

"I have always understood that," said Miss Hopper. "Mr Farrier was so attentive to young Mrs Dobson yesterday, I wondered if he might not be helping her get settled."

"Until three in the morning?" exclaimed Pete.

"No, Miss Hopper," said Jupiter. "We have just come from The Potter's, and Mr Farrier did not spend the evening with Mrs Dobson."

"Now where do you suppose the man could have been until that hour?" wondered Miss Hopper. "Well, it is his own concern, I am súre. And how is poor, dear Mrs Dobson this morning? I saw her drive by earlier."

"She is reasonably well, under the circumstances. She came into town to file an official report with Chief Reynolds. She wants her father found." Jupiter had no hesitation about confiding this much to Miss Hopper, who always found things out anyway.

"Most proper," said Miss Hopper. "What a strange thing for The Potter to do—going off that way without a word to anyone. But then, he has always been a strange man."

"That's for sure," said Pete.

"Well, we must be going, Miss Hopper," said Jupiter. "We only thought you would like to know that Mrs Dobson and her son are settled in at The Potter's house. You always take such an interest in your guests."

"How nice of you, Jupiter," said Miss Hopper.

"And I hope Mr Farrier wakes up before lunch."

"It would make Marie happy," said Miss Hopper. "Poor man. One shouldn't be too hard on him. He has such dreadful luck!"

"Oh?" prompted Jupiter.

"Yes. He's been here four days just for the fishing, and he hasn't caught a thing."

"Terribly frustrating," said Jupiter, and he and Pete took their leave of Miss Hopper.

"Now where do you go at three in the morning in Rocky Beach?" asked Pete, once they were outside.

"Several places occur to me," said Jupiter. "One could, of course, try fishing by moonlight. Or perhaps one could be waiting on a hillside with a gun. Or one might amuse oneself by frightening people with flaming footprints."

"I might buy that last," said Pete, "if there was any way he could have got into that house. Jupe, all the downstairs windows are locked, and most of them are painted shut. There are two locks and a bolt on the front door and one regular lock and a dead-bolt lock on the back. He couldn't have got in."

"Someone did," Jupiter pointed out.

"For my money, only one person could," said Pete. "The Potter would be the only one with the keys."

"Which brings us back to the question of why?" Jupe reminded him.

"Maybe he doesn't like house guests," said Pete.

"You know that's ridiculous," said Jupiter.

"The alternative is even sillier," said Pete. "He's gone off and kicked the bucket someplace, and then come back to haunt the house." And with that, Pete mounted his bicycle and pedalled away towards his home.

Jupiter returned to The Jones Salvage Yard to confront an anxious Aunt Mathilda and a concerned Uncle Titus.

"How is Mrs Dobson?" was Aunt Mathilda's first question.

"She's better this morning," Jupiter reported. "Last night she was extremely emotional—not to say hysterical."

"Why?" asked Uncle Titus.

"There was a second set of those flaming footprints," said Jupiter. "On the stairs, this time."

"Merciful gracious to heavens!" cried Aunt Mathilda. "And she still insisted on staying in that house?"

"Aunt Mathilda, I do not believe she was in any condition to move last night," said Jupiter.

"Jupiter, you should have told me," scolded Aunt Mathilda. She turned to her husband. "Titus Andronicus Jones!"

Uncle Titus always paid strict attention when he was addressed by all three of his names. "Yes, Mathilda," he said.

"Get the truck," said Aunt Mathilda. "We must go up there and persuade that poor, misguided child to get out of that terrible house before something happens to her."

Uncle Titus started for the truck.

"As for you, Jupiter," said Aunt Mathilda severely, "I am very much annoyed with you. You take too much upon yourself. What you need is some work to do to keep you out of mischief."

Jupiter didn't answer this. Aunt Mathilda was an ardent advocate of work even when there was no mischief afoot.

"There are those marble garden ornaments your uncle brought from that ruined house in Beverly Hills," said Aunt Mathilda. "They are absolutely filthy. You know where the bucket is, and the soap."

"Yes, Aunt Mathilda," said Jupiter.

"And plenty of elbow grease!" ordered his aunt.

Aunt Mathilda and Uncle Titus clattered away in the truck. Jupiter cleared a space in the back of the salvage yard and set to work with hot soapy water on the marble figures and the garden urns. The things were coated with years of soil and grit and mould. Jupiter scrubbed away, cleaning the face of a chubby cherub who held up an apple. Hans found him there.

"I see your aunt been talking to you," said Hans, eyeing the scrubbing brush and the bucket.

Jupiter nodded, wiped off the marble cherub, and turned to a bulging urn with grapes clustered on its sides.

"Where is everybody?" Hans wanted to know. "I been over to house, and nobody there. Nobody in office, either."

"Aunt Mathilda and Uncle Titus have gone up to The Potter's house to see Mrs Dobson," reported Jupiter.

"Huh!" snorted Hans. "I don't go to that place—not for a million dollars. That place is haunted. That crazy Potter, he's walking round up there in his bare feet. You saw it. I saw it."

Jupiter sat back on his heels. "We saw the footprints," he reminded Hans. "We did not see The Potter."

115

"Who else could it be?" demanded Hans.

Jupiter didn't answer. He stared at the urn, which was an ungainly piece, and he thought of The Potter, who made such handsome things. "The urns on The Potter's porch are much better than this one," said Jupiter.

"Yah! Yah! His stuff's good. But he was crazy anyway."

"No, I don't think so," said Jupiter. "But I wonder why one of the eagles on that urn has only one head."

"Nothing wrong with one head on eagle," declared Hans.

"True. Except that The Potter seemed to prefer them with two," answered Jupiter Jones.

14

The Jolly Fisherman

IT was noon before Aunt Mathilda and Uncle Titus returned to the salvage yard with the information that Eloise Dobson was the most stubborn creature on the face of the earth. In spite of Chief Reynolds' urging and Aunt Mathilda's considerable powers of persuasion, Mrs Dobson had firmly, and rather angrily, announced that no one was going to drive her out of her father's house.

"She was ready enough to go last night," said Jupiter.

"Then you should have seen that she left," snapped Aunt Mathilda, and she stormed across the street to the house to make lunch.

Jupiter rinsed the last of the marble pieces with the hose and went in to take a shower. After lunch, he returned to the salvage yard. His aunt had neglected to issue any instructions for the afternoon, so Jupiter made his way to Headquarters through Tunnel Two, and then escaped unseen from the salvage yard through Red Gate Rover. He then hurried down to the Rocky Beach Police Department.

Jupiter found Chief Reynolds brooding behind his desk.

"Anything on your mind, Jones?" asked the chief.

"There is a man staying at the Seabreeze Inn who has been rather over-attentive to Mrs Dobson," said Jupiter.

"In that department," said the chief, "I think Mrs Dobson can take care of herself."

"That is not what concerns me," said Jupiter. "He has led Miss Hopper to believe that he is here to fish. However, he does not catch anything."

"So? He's got rotten luck."

"That is certainly possible, but his car was parked across from The Potter's house on Saturday when I was attacked in The Potter's office. Also, he attempted to visit Mrs Dobson last evening not long before that second set of flaming footprints appeared in the house. And then, there are his clothes."

"What about his clothes?"

"They are all brand new, so far as I can judge," said Jupiter. "It is almost as if he were costumed for a part in a film. The clothes, incidentally, do not match the car he drives. That is old and somewhat battered. It is a tan Ford. Perhaps you might wish to wire to Sacramento to see how the car is registered. The man calls himself Farrier."

"He may just do that because it's his name," said the chief. "Look, Jones, I know you think you're the greatest thing since Sherlock Holmes, but I wish you'd knock off this business of snooping around where you're not wanted. And I've got real problems. That Mrs Dobson seems to expect me to produce her missing father—if he *is* her father—by nightfall, if not sooner. With my overwhelming staff of eight men, I am to go out and scour the Pacific Coast Range and find a man who doesn't want to be found. I am also expected to figure out how somebody got into a locked house and set the stairs on fire."

"Have you had any report from the lab on the charred linoleum?" asked Jupiter.

"When I do, you may be the last to know," said Chief Reynolds. "Now go away and let me have my headache in peace."

"You don't plan to wire Sacramento?" Jupiter persisted.

"No, I don't. And if you go bothering that Farrier guy, I will personally have you declared a public nuisance."

"Very well," said Jupiter. He left the chief's office and proceeded with all due speed to the Seabreeze Inn. He noted with satisfaction that the tan Ford was not in the parking area. Miss Hopper, he knew, was addicted to afternoon naps and might well be dozing peacefully in her own apartment. With the exception of a stray guest or two, that left only Marie the maid to be reckoned with.

The lobby of the Seabreeze Inn was deserted, and the door behind the desk was closed. Jupiter tiptoed around the desk. Miss Hopper was an extremely meticulous innkeeper, and Jupiter knew her very well. He found the spare key to room 113 where he knew it would be—in its properly numbered slot in the bottom drawer of Miss Hopper's desk. Jupiter extracted the key without making a sound, put the key in his pocket, and strolled out on to the verandah. Marie was nowhere to be seen, and there were no guests lounging on the terrace which overlooked the beach.

Jupiter put his hands in his pockets and sauntered along the verandah. When he reached the door of room 113, he stopped and waited, listening. No one stirred anywhere in the inn.

"Mr Farrier?" he called, knocking softly. Mr Farrier did not answer.

With great care, Jupiter slid the key into the lock, opened the door, and stepped into the room.

"Mr Farrier?" he said again softly.

But the room was empty—empty and tidy. Marie had had time to make up the bed and vacuum the carpet.

Jupiter eased the door shut and set to work. The dressing-table drawers were empty, and so were the desk drawers. Mr Farrier had not troubled to unpack his handsome suitcases—except for several crisp and sporty jackets which hung in the wardrobe along with half a dozen spotless turtleneck shirts and several pairs of cleanly creased blue duck slacks. Jupiter felt the pockets of these garments, but they were empty.

Next, Jupe turned his attention to the suitcases. There were two. One stood open on a little bench at the foot of the bed. It contained about what one would expect a suitcase to contain—pyjamas, socks, a pair of sneakers which looked as if they had never been worn, underwear, and, wadded at the bottom of the bag, a few pieces of clothing in need of laundering.

The second suitcase stood on the floor next to the bench. It was closed, but when Jupe tried it he discovered that it was not locked. There were more clothes—all new, and bearing the labels of various Los Angeles men's shops. One shirt still had the price tag attached, and Jupiter almost gasped when he saw how much it had cost.

Jupiter's probing fingers touched paper in the bottom of the suitcase. He lifted the clothes out, careful not to disarrange anything, and stared at a piece of folded newspaper. It was the classified section of the *Los Angeles Times*. An item in the "Personal" column was circled. It read: "Nicholas. I am waiting. Write Alexis at P.O. Box 213, Rocky Beach, Ca."

Jupiter lifted the paper out. There was another sheet of newsprint beneath it. This was part of the classified section of the *New York Daily News*, and an identical advertisement appeared there. There was also a copy of the *Chicago Tribune*, with the same notice. Jupiter glanced at the dates on the newspapers. They were all the April 21 editions of that year.

Jupiter frowned, put the *Chicago Tribune* back where he had found it, placed the *Daily News* back on top of that, and the Los Angeles newspaper on top of that. He then replaced the clothing in the suitcase, closed the case, and put it down again on the floor.

Whatever the jaunty fisherman had come for, Jupiter Jones decided, it had little or nothing to do with fish.

Jupiter quickly inspected the bathroom—which contained only shaving gear and clean towels—and was on his way to the door when he heard brisk footsteps on the verandah outside. A key rattled in the lock of room 113.

Jupe looked around wildly, decided that he would not be able to squeeze himself under the bed, and dodged into the wardrobe. He took shelter behind one of Mr Farrier's clean jackets and held his breath.

Jupe heard Farrier come into the room. The man was humming a tuneless hum. He crossed to the bed, stopped there for a moment or two, and then went on into the bathroom. The bathroom door closed and Jupiter heard water running in the basin.

Jupiter slipped out of the closet and sped on his toes towards the door. He had it open in a second. The water continued noisily running in the bathroom Jupiter backed out on to the verandah, pulling the door closed as he went. The instant before it shut completely, he saw that Mr Farrier had dropped something on the bed. The supposedly jolly fisherman had a gun!

15

Jupe Has a Plan

PETE had finished mowing the lawn and was mixing a lemonade when the telephone rang.

"Pete?" said Jupiter Jones. "Can you come to Headquarters right after supper?"

"I can if it isn't going to be another all-night thing," said Pete. "Mum's not going to go for that twice in a row."

"It won't be an all-night thing," promised Jupiter. "I have some new and interesting information which may help our client. I have left a message for Bob. Perhaps, when he returns from the library, he will also have helpful information for us."

"That we can use," said Pete.

Jupiter's hopes were well-founded. When Bob appeared at Headquarters that evening, he was almost staggering under the weight of two large books which had pieces of paper tucked in to mark various pages.

"A Lapathian dictionary," said Bob brightly. "Lapathian-English, that is. You wouldn't believe how hard they are to come by. We had to arrange a special loan from the big library in Los Angeles. My father picked the books up on his way home from work. The second one is a complete history of Lapathia."

"Great!" exclaimed Pete.

"Have you been able to decipher the document we found at The Potter's?" asked Jupe.

"Most of it. The rest we can guess," said Bob. "Thank heavens Lapathian isn't like Russian. They use a regular alphabet. If I had to translate from some other kind of writing, I think I'd just go shoot myself."

"What is the document?" Jupiter asked.

Bob took the folded parchment from between the pages of the dictionary and put it down on the desk. Next to it he put a piece of paper on which he had worked out, in pencil and with many erasures and crossings out, the message of the parchment.

"It goes kind of like this," said Bob. " 'Know all men that on this day, the 25th of August of the year 1920, Alexis Kerenov, having attained his majority and having sworn fealty to his monarch, is named Duke of Malenbad and to his care and conscience are entrusted the crown and sceptre of Lapathia, he to guard them with his body against all enemies for the peace of the monarch.' "

Bob looked up. "That's about it," he said. "There's the seal with the eagle, and there's a signature, but you can't read it. People are sloppy about signatures."

"And the more important they are," said Jupiter, "the sloppier they tend to get. Could it be Azimov?"

Bob shrugged. "It could be anything," he said. "It probably is Azimov, or some variation, because the Kerenov family turned out to be big wheels in Lapathia. Boris Kerenov didn't just fade away and disappear. He hung around and was ever so helpful." Bob opened the second book he had brought to a place which he had previously marked with paper. "This book's indexed," he said happily, "so we don't have to wade all the way through. Boris Kerenov, who made the crown for old Duke Federic, then advised Federic when Federic decided to be king. He helped Federic lay out the streets round

123

the castle at Madanhoff, and he superintended things when the castle itself was enlarged. He figured that kings need sceptres, so he designed and made the sceptre of the Azimovs. Federic was duly grateful and named him Duke of Malenbad. Malenbad, by one of those interesting coincidences, happened to be the duchy which had formerly been ruled by Ivan the Bold."

"Wait a second," interrupted Pete. "Let's keep track of the cast here. Ivan the Bold. Wasn't he the guy who stood up to Duke Federic and wouldn't swear the oath of loyalty? And he got very dead as a result."

"And his head was stuck up on the castle at Madanhoff. He's the one. Kerenov got Ivan's ruby for the imperial crown, and he got Ivan's estates for his very own, and he got himself named a duke and also keeper of the royal jewels—which makes sense since he made them—and he got very, very rich and the Kerenovs stayed that way from that day on. This book is full of Kerenovs. All the first sons of the first sons became Dukes of Malenbad, and also keepers of the crown and sceptre."

Bob turned to another part of the book. "The Kerenovs are almost more interesting than the Azimovs," he said. "They lived for a while in old Ivan's castle at Malenbad, but along about 300 years ago they abandoned the castle and moved to the capital at Madanhoff, and you're going to love the reason why."

"Why are we going to love it?" asked Jupiter.

"It's so pat, I can't believe it," said Bob. "It seems there was a bit of trouble at Malenbad. One of the Kerenov daughters—her name was Olga—was accused of practising witchcraft."

"Wasn't that tricky?" asked Pete. "I mean, wouldn't it be kind of dangerous to accuse the duke's daughter of being a witch?"

"Not as tricky as you might think," said Bob. "It was one of those hysteria things, much like the epidemic of supposed witchcraft at Salem, and everybody was accusing everybody. The girl had had the bad fortune to fall out with her father because she wanted to marry the local innkeeper, and he did not approve. Besides, he was accused himself. He was worried about his own skin, and he had to call on the then-ruling Azimov to come to his defence. So the girl was burned at the stake."

"Oh, wow!" said Pete.

"Burned?" Jupiter came to rigid attention. "And then the Kerenovs left their castle at Malenbad?"

"Yes. You see, after she was burned, the girl—or I guess you could say her ghost—kept coming back to the castle and tramping around and leaving . . ."

"Flaming footprints!" cried Jupiter.

"Right!" said Bob. "So the castle was deserted, and is now a ruin, and the Kerenovs stayed on in the capital until that revolution we know about in 1925, when they disappeared. There isn't another mention of them in the entire book."

The Three Investigators sat in silence for a moment, digesting this information.

"I will hazard a guess—a very well-informed guess, thanks to Bob—at what Mr Alexander Potter's real name is," said Jupiter at last.

"If you guess that it's Alexis Kerenov, I'm with you," said Bob

"But Tom said it was a long name," protested Pete. "It had lots of c's and z's in it."

"No doubt he was not using his real name when he met Tom's grandmother," surmised Jupiter. "And remember her description of him?"

"He smelled like wet clay?" said Pete.

"Yes. And he was extremely nervous and had three locks on every door. To this day he is a great believer in locks. The Potter is a man with a secret, and he is also a man trying to send a message."

"What?" asked Bob.

Jupiter quickly recounted his adventure of the afternoon. He told of the search of the jolly fisherman's room, and of the gun, and also of the newspapers with identical advertisements in the classified columns. "A New York paper, a *Los Angeles Times* and the *Chicago Tribune*," he said. "All published on the same date—April 21. All begging Nicholas to write to Alexis at a post office box in Rocky Beach."

"Nicholas?" echoed Bob.

"Your index got a Nicholas we can use?" asked Pete.

"Nicholas was the name of the oldest son of William IV of Lapathia," said Bob. He turned several more pages in his book and shoved the volume around so that the other two boys could see the last photograph ever taken of the royal family of Lapathia. There was His Majesty, William IV, his extravagant wife, and four sons, ranging from a tall young man who stood directly behind His Majesty to a boy who was about ten. "The one right behind the king is Grand Duke Nicholas," said Bob.

"And William IV was the one who fell off the balcony," said Jupiter. "According to the account in the encyclopedia, the queen took poison. What happened to Nicholas?"

"He is said to have hanged himself."

"And the other children?"

"The two middle boys also hanged themselves, according to the generals who engineered the takeover.

126

The little one accidentally fell in his bath and was drowned."

"Hm!" Jupe pulled at his lip. "Let us suppose, just for the sake of argument, that the Grand Duke Nicholas did not hang himself. How old would he be today?"

"Over seventy," said Bob.

"How old would you think The Potter is?"

"Well, somewhere around there. Jupe, you don't think The Potter could really be the Grand Duke?"

"No, I do not. I think he is Alexis Kerenov, who vanished on the day the Azimov family was destroyed. What day was that, by the way?"

Bob consulted his book. "April 21, 1925."

"And on April 21 of this year, someone named Alexis, who we suspect is The Potter, inserted an advertisement in newspapers in widely separate parts of the country imploring someone named Nicholas to communicate with him. The advertisement would seem to have drawn Mr Farrier, who is really no fisherman at all, to Rocky Beach. He could not possibly be Nicholas Azimov. He is too young."

"Perhaps the same advertisement got those two nuts from Lapathia here," said Bob. "By the way, there's a bit on General Kaluk. He was in at the kill, and he has been one of the ruling generals of Lapathia ever since. There's a picture of him on page 433."

Jupe turned the leaves to page 433. "The caption indicates that the general was 23 when this was taken in 1926," he said. "He hasn't changed a great deal. He didn't have any hair then, either. I wonder if he's naturally bald or if he shaves his head. That would be a novel way to prevent the appearance of ageing. You shave your head and your eyebrows, and nothing will ever go grey."

"Should work fine, if you don't sag too much," declared Pete.

"He most certainly has not sagged," said Jupiter. "He would be about the same age as the Grand Duke Nicholas—if the Grand Duke Nicholas is still alive—and as The Potter. I don't think, however, that it was the advertisement which brought him to Rocky Beach. I think it was that photo spread in *Westways*. Demetrieff is evidently a resident of Los Angeles, since the Lapathian Board of Trade maintains an office there. Remember, Kaluk said that The Potter had been written up in our periodicals. So far as I know, *Westways* is the only periodical which has ever published a photograph of The Potter. Demetrieff could have seen it, and the eagle medallion, and informed his superiors in Lapathia."

"And in comes the general."

"Yes. A thoroughly distasteful person. However, all this speculation does not bring us any closer to helping our client, Tom Dobson. It seems clear that someone who knows the family history of the Kerenovs, and the tale of the flaming footprints in the haunted castle, is trying to frighten Mrs Dobson and Tom out of the house. There can be only one reason for this. They believe that there is something of value in the house. Now, Mrs Dobson knows nothing of the Kerenovs and she has a remarkable stubborn streak, so she refuses to move. If we can persuade Mrs Dobson and Tom to leave the place and return to the Seabreeze Inn—or perhaps even go into Los Angeles—we may see some action more significant than flaming footprints."

"Like baiting a trap," said Pete.

"Yes, except that in this case, the trap must be empty. Mrs Dobson and Tom cannot be in the house. The two men at Hilltop House have not made a move since she arrived, and the man who calls himself Farrier has done nothing more effective than to attempt to have coffee with Mrs Dobson. And of course The Potter remains among the missing."

"So we get Mrs Dobson to move out, and then we watch," said Pete.

"That's right. We will have to be very careful."

"You will have to be very persuasive," said Pete. "There are times when Mrs Dobson reminds me of your Aunt Mathilda."

16

The Trap is Sprung

IT was well after seven when The Three Investigators reached The Potter's house. Pete pounded on the front door and Jupiter called out to identify himself.

Young Tom Dobson opened the door. "Your timing is perfect," he said. "Come on in."

The Investigators trailed after Tom to the kitchen, where Mrs Dobson sat in one of the straight chairs and watched a pair of green flames flicker and die out on the linoleum near the cellar door.

"You know," she said, without much emotion, "this sort of thing loses its shock value after a while."

"Where were you when it happened?" asked Jupiter.

"Upstairs," said Mrs Dobson. "Something went 'bang' and Tom came down to see what, and there were some more of these nice, cheering footprints."

"Want to search the house?" Tom Dobson invited. "I was about to do that when you guys showed up."

"I doubt that we would learn anything new," said Jupe.

"We've already searched it," put in Pete. "And so have Chief Reynolds's men."

"Have you had any news from the chief, incidentally?" Jupiter asked.

"Not a word," said Eloise Dobson.

"Mrs Dobson," said Jupe, getting quickly to the main

purpose of his visit, "we think you should leave here—and the sooner the better."

"I will not!" said Mrs Dobson. "I came to see my father, and I am going no place until I do see him."

"The Seabreeze Inn isn't far," suggested Bob gently.

"Aunt Mathilda would be glad to put you up for a night or two," offered Jupiter.

"You wouldn't have to leave Rocky Beach," urged Pete. "Just leave this house."

Mrs Dobson glared at the three of them. "What's up with you three?" she demanded.

"Hasn't it occurred to you that someone is trying to frighten you out of here?" said Jupiter.

"Of course it has occurred to me. I would have to be the world's champion dimwit for it not to occur to me. Well, I don't scare that easy."

"We believe that the person who is creating the flaming footprints is not simply a trickster," said Jupiter. "Whoever he is, he knows a great deal about your father, and about your father's family history. He knows more than you do—although he cannot suspect how little you really have been told. It is our theory that he wants a clear field. He wants to search this house without interruption. We suggest that you give him the opportunity. Move out now, while it is still light. Give him a chance to see that you are going. Then drive down to Rocky Beach and remain there. Pete, Bob, and I will watch to see what takes place after you leave."

"You can't mean that!" cried Mrs Dobson.

"We do," said Jupiter.

"You want me to clear out and let this oddball who's been running around making flaming footprints come romping through my father's house?"

"I think that is the only way we will ever discover the

purpose behind all of this—your father's disappearance, the search of the house which occurred the day you arrived, the flaming footprints—everything."

Eloise Dobson frowned up at Jupiter. "Chief Reynolds told me about you," she said. "And you, too, Bob. And Pete. He said, if I remember correctly, that your talent for stirring up trouble is only exceeded by your knack for figuring things out."

"A mixed compliment," said Jupiter.

"All right." Mrs Dobson stood up. "Tom and I pack and move out, with all the fuss possible. Then you boys hide someplace and watch the house. I'll go along with you partway. We'll even leave the door open so that the nut—whoever he is—can get in. Although he doesn't seem to have had any trouble doing that so far, and whenever he wants to. But unless the guy is really hung up on ceramics, I don't see what he expects to find. This place is full of nothing."

"Perhaps it is not," said Jupiter. "We will see."

"One thing," said Mrs Dobson. "I would like to know what this big, dark secret is that is hidden on my father's family tree."

"Mrs Dobson, we really do not have time to explain," said Jupiter. "It will be dark in half an hour. Please, let's hurry and get you moved out!"

"Okay. But there's another thing."

"Yes?" asked Jupiter.

"The minute Tom and I get into town, I'm going straight to that police chief and tell him what you're doing," announced Mrs Dobson. "If somebody starts to play rough, you're going to need help."

The Three Investigators paused. Then, "That might be a wise idea," said Jupiter.

132

"Hey, Jupe, it will wreck everything if a police car comes roaring up here!" protested Pete.

"I am sure Mrs Dobson will be able to persuade Chief Reynolds not to come roaring," said Jupiter. "We will ride partway back to Rocky Beach on our bikes," he told Mrs Dobson. "When we are out of sight of the house, we will stop, conceal the bicycles in the undergrowth beside the road, and return here. The scrub growth on the hillside is especially thick right now. No one on the road will see us, and we will not be seen from Hilltop House, either. Tell Chief Reynolds that we will be keeping watch from just beyond the oleander hedge behind the house."

"Say, can we move now?" pleaded Bob. There was a note of urgency in his voice. "It's getting dark!"

"Come on, Tom," said Mrs Dobson.

The two went up the stairs, two steps at a time, and The Three Investigators, waiting in the kitchen, heard drawers open and close and wardrobe doors bang and suitcases thump on to the floor.

In four minutes Eloise Dobson came swiftly down the stairs carrying a square cosmetic case and a small suitcase. Tom followed her with two larger bags.

"A record!" Jupiter applauded. "Did you bring everything—toothbrushes—everything?"

"Everything," said Mrs Dobson. "But it's going to be a mess when I unpack."

"That can always be straightened out later," said Jupiter. He took the small suitcase from Mrs Dobson, and Pete relieved Tom of one of the bigger bags. Jupe looked round. "Let's go," he said.

They started down the hall towards the front door. As they passed the office, Mrs Dobson suddenly stopped. "Wait!" she cried. "Tom, get the box!"

"What box?" asked Pete.

"I went through my father's things," said Mrs Dobson. Her tone was a bit defiant. "I wasn't snooping. I just was wondering—you know—and I found a box with some personal things in it. Nothing important. A picture of my mother and father taken on their wedding day, and a bunch of letters from my mother and some from me, and—Jupiter, I don't want anybody pawing through that stuff."

"I understand, Mrs Dobson," said Jupiter. He took the second suitcase from Tom Dobson, and Tom ducked into The Potter's office and emerged with a cardboard box about a foot square. "My grandfather seems to have saved everything," he said.

Pete got the front door open, and the procession filed out past the two urns towards Mrs Dobson's car, which stood near The Potter's supply shack.

Jupiter raised his voice. "I'm sorry you've decided to leave, Mrs Dobson," he said.

"Huh?" said Eloise Dobson.

"Act frightened," whispered Jupiter.

"Oh!" said Mrs Dobson. Then she raised her voice. She became almost shrill. "Jupiter Jones, if you think I'm going to hang around here while somebody burns the house down around my ears, you're crazy."

She put her cosmetic case down on the ground beside the car and opened the boot.

"So far as I'm concerned," she announced, for all the world to hear, "I wish I'd never had a father. I wish I'd been born an orphan."

Mrs Dobson energetically hurled suitcases into the boot of the car. "And if I never see Rocky Beach—or this house—again, it will be soon enough for me! Tom, give me that box!"

Tom handed the box of old letters to his mother, and she started to cram it into the car. Suddenly, "Hold it!" said a voice from beside the Potter's shack.

The Three Investigators and the Dobsons turned. There, in the dense, golden light of the sunset, stood the jaunty fisherman, holding a gun.

"Everybody just stand quietly," said Farrier. "Don't move and you won't get hurt." The fisherman trained his gun on Eloise Dobson.

"I think," said Pete, "that something went wrong with our schedule."

"Give me the box," ordered Farrier. "Better still, open the box and dump it out on the ground."

"It's only some old letters to my grandfather," said Tom Dobson.

"Open it!" snapped Farrier. "I want to see."

"Don't argue with the man," advised Jupiter.

Tom sighed, hauled the square carton out of the boot, opened and upended it. A mass of envelopes slid out into a heap on the ground.

"It *was* filled with letters!" exclaimed the jaunty fisherman. He sounded genuinely surprised.

"You were expecting a diamond tiara or something?" asked Tom Dobson.

The man called Farrier took one step forward. "What do you—?" he began. Then he checked himself. "The suitcases," he ordered. "Take them back into the house. I think they're too small, but we'll see."

Eloise Dobson knelt and scooped the letters into the cardboard carton, while the boys removed the suitcases from the boot of the blue convertible. Then the Dobsons and The Three Investigators marched back into The Potter's house, with Mr Farrier and his gun bringing up the rear.

In the hallway, Eloise Dobson fumed as the boys were forced to empty her suitcases out on to the floor. Young Tom's bag was also opened, and its contents spread out for the inspection of the insolent Mr Farrier.

"So you didn't find it," said Farrier at last. "I was sure, when I saw that cardboard box. . . ."

"Find what, for heaven's sake?" demanded Mrs Dobson.

"You don't know?" said Farrier. His voice was very smooth. "No, you really don't know. Just as well. In fact, my dear, charming Mrs Dobson, it's just as well if you never find out. Now, everybody down in the cellar!"

"I will not!" cried Eloise Dobson.

"Yes, Mrs Dobson, you will," said Farrier. "I have already searched the cellar. The walls are solid brick, the floors are cement, undisturbed for decades. It will make an excellent resting place for you while I finish my business. You see, there are no windows in that cellar."

"It was *you* who searched the house on Saturday," accused Jupiter.

"Unfortunately, I did not have time to finish," said Farrier. "I found only one treasure on that occasion." Farrier took a huge bunch of keys from his pocket.

"The Potter's keys," said Jupiter.

"The second set, I assume," smirked Farrier. "It was thoughtful of him to leave them in his desk. All right, everybody. Move!"

The Dobsons and the Investigators moved, down the hall and through the kitchen and then into the cellar. Mrs Dobson stopped only long enough to click the light switch at the top of the stairs before she went down into the bare, brick-walled place.

"You shouldn't be too uncomfortable here," said Farrier from the top of the stairs. "And no doubt someone will miss you before long and come looking for you."

With that, the jaunty fisherman closed the cellar door on them. A key turned in the lock, then was removed. The bolt on the door slid into place.

"I wish my grandfather hadn't been such a fanatic about locks," mourned young Tom.

"Oh, I don't know," said Jupiter Jones. He sat down on the cellar stairs and looked around. "It is not the ideal place in which to spend protracted periods of time, but it is far more comfortable than being tied up. I am sure that our guess was correct, and that the man who calls himself Farrier will now search the house thoroughly. It must have been that carton full of letters that did it. When he saw that, he decided that we had found what he is looking for. Our trap has been sprung."

"Yes, it has," said Pete bitterly, "only we're the ones who got caught."

17

The Other Watchers

THE Dobsons and The Three Investigators arranged themselves as comfortably as possible on the cellar stairs and listened as, above them, the bogus fisherman searched The Potter's house.

Drawers in the kitchen were pulled open. Cupboard doors banged. Footsteps hurried into the pantry and cans tumbled to the floor. Walls were knocked.

They heard Farrier retreat from the kitchen and go down the hall to The Potter's office. There was a heavy, wrenching sound, and a thud that shook dust down around their ears. "He's knocked over the filing cabinet," Pete decided.

The Potter's ancient desk was moved, screeching a protest against the bare boards of the floors. Then again there came the sounds of walls being thumped.

"Did the police find The Potter's secret library?" Jupiter asked Tom.

"No, they didn't," Tom reported.

"You boys have been holding out on me," declared Eloise Dobson. "What secret library?"

"It's nothing, Mum," said Tom. "Just a bunch of old newspapers behind that eagle plaque in your room."

"Now why would anyone hide a bunch of old newspapers?" asked Mrs Dobson.

"To give a searcher something to find," said Jupiter.

There was a crash from overhead.

"Oh, dear!" said Mrs Dobson. "That must be the big vase in the hall."

"A pity," said Jupiter.

Farrier's footsteps crossed the hall and sounded heavily on the stairs.

"He must be the one who planted all those flaming footprints!" decided Mrs Dobson suddenly.

"Undoubtedly," said Jupiter. "He had the keys, and could come and go as he pleased. He would have used the back door, I am sure, since the front door had a slide bolt."

"And the footsteps . . ." began Tom.

Jupiter held up his hand suddenly. "Listen."

They were silent. After a moment, "I don't hear anything," whispered Tom Dobson.

"Someone came up on to the back porch," said Jupiter. "They tried the door and then went down again."

"Oh, good!" said Eloise Dobson. "Let's yell!"

"Please don't, Mrs Dobson," said Bob earnestly. "You see, there isn't only this Farrier creep. There's these two real sinister types up at Hilltop House."

"The Peeping Toms?" said Mrs Dobson.

"I am afraid they are more sinister than that," Jupiter informed her. "They rented Hilltop House for a definite reason—because it overlooked this house."

Jupiter motioned for silence. There were footsteps in the hall above.

"Farrier forgot to lock the front door," whispered Pete.

"This may get more interesting." Jupiter got up and went to the top of the cellar stairs, where he pressed his ear against the door. He heard, very faintly, a murmur of voices. He held up two fingers, to indicate that two more searchers were among them.

The two men came down the hallway almost as far as the kitchen, then went back again. There were more footsteps on the stairs above. Then a shout, and a sharp crack.

"That was a shot!" said Jupiter.

There was no more shouting, but rumbling voices came muffled to the Dobsons and the Investigators as they waited in the cellar. There were more footsteps on the stairs. Someone stumbled. Then the searchers came into the kitchen and a chair scraped.

"You will sit quietly, and you will not move," said the voice of General Kaluk.

Jupiter backed a step or two away from the cellar door.

The door swung open, and the bulky figure of the Lapathian general filled the doorway.

"So?" said the general. "My young friend Jones. And Master Andrews. You will come up, please, all of you."

The Three Investigators and the Dobsons came up into the kitchen. The ceiling light was on, and Eloise Dobson gasped at the sight of Farrier, the jaunty fisherman, sitting in one of The Potter's straight chairs, pressing a handkerchief against his right wrist. A splash of red showed on his smart white jacket.

"The sight of blood upsets Madame?" asked General Kaluk. "Do not be alarmed. The man is not badly hurt." He placed a chair for Mrs Dobson and indicated that she should sit down. "I do not approve of violence unless it is necessary," he told her. "I fired upon this intruder only to prevent his firing upon me."

Mrs Dobson sat down. "I think we should call the police," she said shakily. "There's a call box on the highway. Tom, why don't you—"

General Kaluk waved her to silence, and the younger

140

Lapathian, Demetrieff, went to stand in the kitchen doorway. He held a gun—an efficient-looking revolver.

"I think, Madame, that we may dismiss this person as being of no importance," said General Kaluk, nodding towards the wretched Farrier. "I was not aware that he was in the area, or I would have taken steps to see that he did not annoy you."

"You sound like old friends," prompted Jupiter. "Or should I say old enemies?"

The general laughed a short, ugly laugh. "Enemies? This creature is not important enough to be an enemy. He is a criminal—an ordinary criminal. A thief!" The general placed a chair for himself and sat down. "You see, Madame, it is my business to know these things. Among my other duties in Lapathia, I supervise the national police. There is a dossier on this person. He calls himself many names—Smith, Farrier, Taliaferro— it is all the same. He steals jewels. You will agree, Madame, that this is a wicked thing to do?"

"Dreadful!" said Eloise Dobson quickly. "But . . . but there are no jewels in this house. What did he . . . why are you here?"

"We saw from our terrace, Madame, that this wicked person seemed to be interfering with you and my young friends, so naturally we came to your assistance."

"Oh, thank you!" said Mrs Dobson. She bounced up from her chair. "Thank you so much. Now we can call the police and—"

"All in good time, Madame. You will please sit down."

Mrs Dobson sat down.

"I have neglected to introduce myself," said the general. "I am Klas Kaluk. And you, Madame?"

"I am Eloise Dobson. Mrs Thomas Dobson. And this is my son, Tom."

"And you are a friend of Alexis Kerenov?"

Mrs Dobson shook her head. "Never heard of him."

"He is called The Potter," said General Kaluk.

"Of course Mrs Dobson's a friend of Mr Potter," said Jupiter quickly. "From the Midwest. I told you that."

The general scowled at Jupiter. "Allow Madame to answer for herself, if you please," he ordered. He turned back to Mrs Dobson. "You are a friend of the man who is known as The Potter?"

Eloise Dobson looked aside. She had the wary look of an unskilled swimmer who suddenly finds herself in deep water. "Yes," she said softly, and her face coloured.

General Kaluk smiled. "I think Madame is not telling me the whole truth," he said. "Bear in mind, if you please, that I am an expert at this sort of game. Now, perhaps Madame would care to tell me how she met the person known as Mr Potter?"

"Well," said Mrs Dobson, "by . . . by letter. You see, we wrote, and . . ."

"The Potter does a big mail-order business!" said Pete quickly.

"Yeah!" said Bob. "And he mailed stuff to Mrs Dobson, and she wrote and one thing led to another and—"

"Stop that!" the general shouted to Bob. "What nonsense. Do you expect me to believe that? This woman writes letters to an old man who makes pots, and what they have to write to one another is so interesting that she comes to this small village and moves into his house—and on that day he vanishes? I am not a fool!"

"Don't shout!" cried Eloise Dobson. She was shouting

142

herself. "You have some nerve, barging in here! And I don't care if this Farrier swiped the royal crown of England. We need to get a doctor for him. He's . . . he's bleeding all over the floor!"

The general glanced at Farrier, and at two drops of blood which had dripped on the floor. "Madame is too soft-hearted," he said to Mrs Dobson. "We will attend to Mr Farrier when we are ready. Now, you will tell me how you became acquainted with Mr Potter."

"Well, it's none of your darn business!" cried Mrs Dobson. "But if you have to know—"

"Mrs Dobson, I wouldn't," pleaded Jupiter.

"He's my father!" finished Mrs Dobson triumphantly. "He's my father, and this is his house and you have no business here. And don't you dare—"

The general threw back his head and laughed heartily.

"It isn't funny," snapped Mrs Dobson.

"Oh, but it is!" chortled the general. He looked up at the younger Lapathian who stood in the doorway. "Demetrieff, we have a real prize. We have the daughter of Alexis Kerenov!"

The general leaned towards Mrs Dobson. "Now, you will tell me what I wish to learn. Then we will attend to Mr Farrier, who is such a worry to you."

"What is it that you wish to learn?" asked Mrs Dobson.

"There is a certain piece of property—a thing of great value—which belongs to my people," said the general. "You know that to which I refer?"

Eloise Dobson shook her head.

"She doesn't know," said Jupiter Jones urgently. "She doesn't know anything—nothing about Lapathia—nothing at all!"

143

"Hold your tongue!" snapped the general. "Madame Dobson, I am waiting!"

"I don't know," said Eloise. "Jupiter is right. I don't know anything. I never heard of any Alexis Kerenov. My father is Alexander Potter!"

"And he did not entrust you with the secret?" demanded the general.

"Secret? What secret?" cried Mrs Dobson.

"Ridiculous!" snorted the general. "He must have told you. It was his duty. And you will tell me—now!"

"But I don't know anything!" cried Mrs Dobson.

"Demetrieff!" shouted the general, losing his iron control. "She will talk!"

Demetrieff started towards Mrs Dobson.

"Hey!" yelled Tom. "Don't you touch my mother!"

Demetrieff shoved Tom roughly aside.

"Into the cellar with them!" ordered General Kaluk. "All of them, except this obstinate woman!"

"No you don't!" yelled Pete. He and Bob launched themselves at the younger man, Pete going for Demetrieff's gun and Bob headed in a beautiful tackle at the man's legs.

Demetrieff went down with a loud grunt, and the gun blasted harmlessly towards the ceiling.

That shot was followed by a second thunderous roar. The back door had burst open and The Potter stood there, an ancient and somewhat rusty shotgun in his hand.

"Don't move!" shouted The Potter.

Jupiter froze halfway between the cellar door and the chair where General Kaluk sat. The general remained where he was, and Pete and Bob sprawled on the floor on top of the fallen Demetrieff.

"Grandfather?" said Tom Dobson.

"Good evening, Tom," said The Potter. "Eloise, my dear, I am sorry about all this."

General Kaluk started to get up. The shotgun which The Potter held instantly swung in his direction. "Do not move, Kaluk," said The Potter. "There is a second shell in this gun, and it would give me great pleasure to discharge it right in your face."

The general sat down again.

"Jupiter, my boy!" said The Potter. "Will you please collect the guns? From the general's friend on the floor, of course, and I am sure the general has one someplace. The general has always been fond of guns."

"Yes, sir, Mr Potter," said Jupiter. "I mean, Mr Kerenov."

18

The Bargain

No one spoke until Jupiter Jones had taken Demetrieff's revolver, and had searched General Kaluk and relieved him of Farrier's blunt automatic and a smaller, but still deadly, pistol.

"Lock the guns in the pantry, Jupiter, and bring me the key," said The Potter.

Jupiter did so. The Potter tucked the key into a pocket hidden somewhere in his robe and allowed himself to relax a bit, leaning against a cupboard.

Only then did Eloise Dobson begin to cry.

"Now, now, my dear," said The Potter. "It is all over. I have been watching these scoundrels the entire time. I would never have let them touch a hair of your head."

Mrs Dobson got up and went to The Potter. He handed his shotgun to Jupiter and put his arms round her. "I know, I know," he said. He laughed and held her away from him, so that she could not help but see his hair, his beard, and the robe, now soiled and stained. "Yes, I am a shock to you, eh?" he said. "No one has a father like Alexander Potter."

Mrs Dobson nodded, then shook her head, then burst into new tears.

General Kaluk said something in that strange, sing-song language which Jupiter and Bob had heard at Hilltop House.

"I must ask you to speak English," said The Potter to

him. "It is so many years since I heard my mother tongue that I am no longer proficient in it."

"Astonishing!" exclaimed the general.

"And who is that?" said The Potter, indicating the unfortunate Mr Farrier, who still crouched in his chair, holding his injured wrist.

"A person of no importance," said the general. "A common thief."

"His name is Mr Farrier, Grandfather," said Tom Dobson. "Jupe thinks he's the one who's been trying to scare us out of the house."

"Scare you? How?"

"On three separate occasions," said Jupiter Jones, "flaming footprints have appeared in the house. You will notice three footprints near the pantry and two near the cellar door. There is a third set on the stairs."

"Ho-ha!" said The Potter. "Flaming footprints? I see you've done your homework, Mr Farrier, and learned about our family ghost. Jupiter, why is the man bleeding?"

"General Kaluk shot him," said Jupe.

"I see. And do I understand correctly that this person has been entering the house and trying to frighten my family?"

"You'll never prove it," growled Farrier.

"He has your extra set of keys," said Jupiter.

"I believe we should summon Chief Reynolds," announced The Potter. "My dear Eloise, I had no idea. I was so concerned lest Kaluk might do you some harm, that I neglected to keep a proper watch on my own house."

The general looked at The Potter with some awe. "Do I understand correctly, Alexis, that *you* have been watching *me*?"

"I have been watching you, and you have been watching my daughter."

"May I ask, old friend, where you have been these three days?"

"There is a loft in the garage at Hilltop House," said The Potter simply. "The garage doors are locked, but there is a window on the north side."

"I see," said the general. "I fear I am getting careless in my old age."

"Exceedingly," said The Potter. "And now, Jupiter, let us call Chief Reynolds and have these people removed from my house."

"One moment, Alexis," said the general. "There is the matter of some jewels which were removed from their rightful owners many years ago."

"The rightful owners are the Azimovs," countered The Potter. "It is my duty to safeguard those jewels."

"The rightful owners are the people of Lapathia," said the general. "The Azimovs are gone!"

"You lie!" flared The Potter. "Nicholas did not die in the palace at Madanhoff. We fled together. We were to meet in America. It was arranged. I had a way to send a message to him. I have been waiting."

"Poor Alexis," said the general. "You have waited a lifetime, and for nothing. Nicholas did not even reach the railroad station. He was recognized." The general reached into an inside pocket and produced a photograph. He handed it to The Potter.

The Potter looked at the thing for almost a minute. Then, "Murderer!" he said to the Lapathian general.

The general took back the photograph. "It was not my choice," he told The Potter. "His Highness was my friend, remember?"

"And so you use your friends?" asked The Potter.

"It could not be helped," said the general. "There may be a justice in it. We cannot say. The Azimovs began in blood, they ended in blood. But Alexis, they did end. And what of you? You have spent a lifetime waiting. Waiting behind locked doors. Hiding behind a beard, and the robe of an eccentric. Living without your family. You did not see your daughter grow up, I assume?"

The Potter shook his head.

"For a crown," said the general. "All of this you have done for a crown which no one can wear."

"What do you want?" asked The Potter at last.

"I wish to take it back with me to Madanhoff," said the general. "It will be put into the National Museum there. That is where it belongs. That is where the people wish to see it. It is what the generals promised them so long ago."

"That promise was a mockery!" cried The Potter.

"I know. I know. I myself did not approve, but Lubaski insisted, and once the gesture had been made, we had to go on with it. Anything else would have shaken the faith of the people."

"Liars!" stormed The Potter. "Murderers! How dare you talk about the faith of the people?"

"I am an old man now, Alexis," said the general, "and you are old, too. And the people of Lapathia are happy—I promise you, they are happy. How much love was there for the Azimovs? And now the Azimovs are gone. What will you accomplish if you refuse me? Would you make yourself a thief? I cannot believe it. You have the crown. You swore you would always have it. That is why I came. Give it to me, Alexis, and let us part friends."

"Never friends," said The Potter.

"Then let us at least not part enemies," pleaded the general. "Let us consider what will be the greater good for all. And let us forget the price we have both paid."

The Potter was silent.

"You cannot claim it for yourself," said the general. "Alexis, you have no choice. There is no place it can go but to Madanhoff. And think, what would be the consequences to yourself if it were known that it is in your possession? And what would be the consequences to Lapathia? I do not know, but I can imagine—distrust, unrest, perhaps a revolution. Would you wish another revolution, Alexis?"

The Potter shuddered. "Very well, I will get it for you."

"It is here now?" asked General Kaluk.

"It is here," said The Potter. "Just a moment."

"Mr Potter?" said Jupiter Jones.

"Yes, Jupiter?"

"Shall I get it?" asked Jupe. "It's in the urn, isn't it?"

"You are a clever boy, Jupiter. It is in the urn. Will you get it?"

Jupe left the room and was gone for perhaps a minute, during which time no one spoke. When Jupiter returned he was carrying a bulky bundle. Layers of soft cloth had been wrapped around an object which Jupiter put down on the table.

"You can open it," said The Potter.

General Kaluk nodded agreement. "I am sure you are curious," he said.

Jupiter undid the wrappings and folded back the cloth. There, exposed on The Potter's kitchen table, was a magnificent crown of gold and lapis lazuli, surmounted by a huge ruby, with a crimson eagle screaming from both sharp enamelled beaks.

"The imperial crown of Lapathia!" exclaimed Bob.

"But . . . but I thought that was in the museum at Madanhoff!" said Pete.

The general stood up and looked at the marvellous object almost with reverence. "The one at Madanhoff is a copy," he said. "It is a clever copy, although it was executed without the help of a Kerenov. I suppose there were a few experts, like this . . . this Farrier person . . . who may have guessed at the truth, but the secret has been kept well. The crown is always under glass, of course, and the barriers which protect it are set well back from the case. No one can look too closely at it. Not too long ago a photographer even received permission to include it in his book. He was an expert on photography, not jewels, so we granted his request."

The general began to restore the wrappings to the crown. "The secret will still be kept," he said, "but the crown in Madanhoff will be the real one."

"How can you be so sure your secret will be kept," said the surly Farrier. "You've only got a score or so of witnesses here."

"Who would believe you?" said the general. "You may talk all you wish."

He took the crown and held out his hand to The Potter. The Potter turned away.

"Very well, Alexis," said the general. "We will not meet again. I wish you happiness."

And the general went out, followed by the slim and unsmiling Mr Demetrieff.

"Jupiter," said The Potter, "I think that now you may summon the police."

It Would Make a Great Movie

A WEEK later Mr Alfred Hitchcock, the famous motion-picture director, sat in his office and leafed through the notes which Bob had compiled on The Potter and his wonderful secret.

"So the crown was hidden in the urn," said Mr Hitchcock, "outside The Potter's shop, where hundreds of people came and went every week. That scoundrel Farrier must have passed it a dozen times while he was working so hard to frighten Mrs Dobson away."

"He told us that he tried to open the urn," said Jupiter Jones. "Of course, he did most of his mischief at night, so he didn't have time or light to examine the urn with care and notice the single-headed eagle looking to the left. The top of the urn came off when you turned it clockwise—to the left. All ordinary containers open the other way. That is the signal which The Potter and the Grand Duke agreed upon when they fled from the palace. If anything happened to The Potter, the Grand Duke Nicholas was to look for a single-headed eagle among a group of the double-headed eagles of Lapathia, and that eagle would be the clue to the whereabouts of the crown."

"And was The Potter planning to take up ceramics even before the revolution in Lapathia?" asked Mr Hitchcock.

"No," said Bob, who was perched in a chair next to

Jupiter Jones. "He became a potter because he had to make a living, but he could have found a number of ways of creating eagles. He could have painted them, or stencilled them on a wall, or . . . or . . ."

"There's always embroidery," put in Pete, who occupied the chair on Jupiter's left side.

"I am sure a scarlet eagle would be most effective in cross-stitch," said Mr Hitchcock. "Now about this Farrier—your report states that he was arrested by Chief Reynolds on charges of unlawful entry and malicious mischief. I should not think they could hold him long. Will he keep the secret of the crown, do you suppose?"

"He has everything to gain and nothing to lose by keeping his mouth shut," said Jupiter Jones. "Unlawful entry and malicious mischief are minor charges compared to attempted grand larceny. He's in jail in Rocky Beach now, pondering on his sins—which are more numerous than we suspected at first. All those elegant clothes were purchased with a credit card which he found in a wallet that someone had dropped on the street. I am not certain what the charge is for unauthorized use of a credit card, but I should think forgery would enter into it."

"At least," agreed Mr Hitchcock.

"His car was so shabby," said Jupiter. "It bothered me. It didn't match. He's not even going to be able to pay Miss Hopper for the room he occupied at the Seabreeze Inn. The Potter says he feels responsible, so he's taking care of that bill."

"Most generous," said Mr Hitchcock.

"Chief Reynolds found the stuff Farrier used to create the flaming footprints in the boot of Farrier's car, which was parked up the highway out of sight of the house," said Bob. "Whatever it was, he says we'll never know. He thinks it's a good idea not to spread some kinds of information around."

"The man is not without imagination."

"Farrier? No. He has quite a record, and has done time in some of the best prisons. He used to be a crack jewel thief. According to Chief Reynolds, he got too well known. Police everywhere started putting tails on him the second he showed up in any town. Cramped his style. He's been trying to make a living running a little hobby shop in Los Angeles."

"So it was the article in *Westways* which brought him to Rocky Beach?" said Mr Hitchcock.

"No," said Jupiter Jones. "He told us how he got his first clue to the whereabouts of the crown while we were waiting for Chief Reynolds to come and collect him. He always reads the personal ads in the *Los Angeles Times*. He suspected, as did a number of experts on such things, that the crown on display at Madanhoff was an imitation. He had done some research on the history of Lapathia, and knew about the disappearance of Alexis Kerenov, who was the hereditary guardian of the crown. When he saw the advertisement in the *Times*, with the names Alexis and Nicholas, he remembered the Grand Duke Nicholas who was supposed to have hanged himself during the revolution, and he wondered if it might not have something to do with the crown. He went to the trouble of buying papers from Chicago and New York on a hunch—and he found identical advertisements in them. Then he came to Rocky Beach on a quick visit, and wandered into The Potter's shop one bright afternoon, and . . ."

"And saw the medallion with the eagle," finished Mr Hitchcock. "That is one thing I do not understand.

Why did Kerenov insist on wearing that medallion?"

"He admits it was foolish," said Jupiter. "He felt lonely, peihaps, and it may have reminded him of better times. Also, he felt there was little chance of anyone from Lapathia appearing in Rocky Beach unless they were summoned, and his advertisement—which he placed annually in all the major papers in the United States—was addressed to Nicholas. He felt only Nicholas would understand it. It was part of the agreement which they made when they fled together from the palace at Madanhoff. They would separate and both try to make their way to the United States. Alexis would advertise once a year, on the anniversary of the revolution, until Nicholas found him. And if anything happened to Alexis before Nicholas found him, Nicholas could always examine the files of back editions of various newspapers and would, at least, know in which town Alexis had settled. Then he was to look for the odd eagle with the single head."

"An involved scheme," said Mr Hitchcock, "and one that left a great deal to chance. However, I suppose they did not have a great deal of time to work out anything more practical with a revolution going on around them. So for a lifetime Alexis waited."

"And Nicholas never escaped."

"What was the photograph which the Lapathian general showed The Potter?" asked Mr Hitchcock.

"He wouldn't tel. us," said Pete. "Something gruesome."

"And proving that Nicholas was dead, no doubt," added Jupiter.

"It must have been a great shock to The Potter," said Mr Hitchcock. "On the other hand, he must have begun to suspect that his vigil was in vain. So many years had passed."

"I guess he hoped right to the end that Nicholas would show up, and the Azimovs would be restored to their throne," said Bob.

"In which case," chuckled Pete, "The Potter would be the Duke of Malenbad, and Mrs Thomas Dobson of Belleview, Illinois, would eventually get to be a duchess. I wonder how Mrs Dobson would enjoy being a duchess."

"Has she forgiven her father?" asked Mr Hitchcock.

"Yes," said Bob. "She's still there, and she's helping him in the shop. She and young Tom will stay until the end of summer."

"And the Lapathians have departed?"

"They left the minute they got their hands on the crown," Jupiter reported. "We have to rely on guess-work with the men from Lapathia. We can only assume that the *Westways* article led them to The Potter. I think that they rented Hilltop House planning to wage some sort of war of nerves on The Potter. It upset them greatly when he disappeared and a young woman and a boy moved into his house. But they kept watching and waiting until they saw Farrier make his move, out there in The Potter's yard, and then they came scrambling down that hill to make sure nobody got the crown before they did.

"General Kaluk, I am sure, was sent to Rocky Beach because he had once known Alexis Kerenov, and might be better able to recognize him than Demetrieff, who never knew him personally. And he did recognize him, in spite of all the beard and the white hair. The Potter had not changed that much, and Kaluk had changed scarcely at all."

"It would make a great movie, don't you think, Mr Hitchcock?" asked Pete. "I mean, flaming footprints and a family ghost and an innocent daught r who doesn't know what the score is, and stolen jewels!"

"It has some points to recommend it," said Mr Hitchcock. "There are still one or two things you have not explained in your report, however. The sound of water running in the pipes in The Potter's house when all the taps were off."

"That was The Potter using the outside tap," said Jupiter. "He could not hide out in that old garage without water, and since the Lapath ans never left Hilltop House, he couldn't get water there. He had to come to his own house at night. He did not want to reveal himself to Mrs Dobson, however, because he felt that the less she knew, the better off she would be. The Lapathians could not see him at the tap, even in the moonlight, because of the thick hedge of oleanders behind the house. It was for that reason that they could not see Farrier, who entered and left by the back door."

"How did Farrier get into the house to get the keys?" asked Mr Hitchcock.

"That was ironical," said Jupiter Jones. "The Potter was apparently so preoccupied with preparations or the Dobsons that for once he neglected to lock up tight. Mr Farrier claimed he had no trouble getting in the front door—only had to pick one lock. He told Chief Reynolds he was just curious about the house, and that later, when Mrs Dobson snubbed him, he grew angry and tried to frighten her with the flaming footprints."

"And the police chief of Rocky Beach believed him?" said Mr Hitchcock, with some astonishment.

"Not at all, but no one has come up with a better story, so he has to take what he can get."

"One other detail," said Mr Hitchcock. "You were fired upon when you came down from Hilltop House. Was that Farrier?"

"No," said Bob. "The Potter again. He apologized. He wanted to scare us off, since he felt the men at Hilltop House were dangerous. He had had that shotgun stored in the shack where he kept supplies, so he had no trouble getting his hands on it when he wanted it."

"What do you think?" insisted Pete. "Wouldn't it make a great movie?"

Mr Hitchcock sniffed. "No love interest."

"Oh!" Pete subsided.

"However," said Mr Hitchcock, "Alexis Kerenov, the Duke of Malenbad, has been reunited with his daughter, so at least we do have a happy ending."

"She's a great cook," said Jupiter. "The Potter's putting on weight. And he went into Los Angeles and bought a suit of clothes and some shoes. He's going back to Belleview with Mrs Dobson in the autumn to meet his son-in-law, and he doesn't want his daughter's friends to think he's . . ."

"A nut," put in Pete.

"Eccentric," said Jupe. He paused. "Which he certainly is."

The Three Investigators
in

THE NERVOUS LION

by Nick West

Based on characters created by
Robert Arthur

The Mystery of the Nervous Lion was first published
in the UK in a single volume in 1972 by
William Collins Sons & Co. Ltd.

A Few Words from Alfred Hitchcock

GREETINGS and salutations! It is a pleasure to have you join me for another adventure with that remarkable trio of lads who call themselves The Three Investigators. This time a nervous lion leads them into a tangled web of mystery and excitement.

I imagine that you have already met The Three Investigators and know that they are Jupiter Jones, Bob Andrews, and Pete Crenshaw, all of Rocky Beach, California, a small community on the shores of the Pacific not far from Hollywood. But just in case this is your first meeting with the three, let me add that they make their Headquarters in a mobile home trailer cleverly hidden from sight in The Jones Salvage Yard. This fabulous junkyard is owned by Jupiter's aunt and uncle, for whom the trio works to earn spending money when they are not busy with their investigations.

Enough of introductions. On with the case! Our lion is growing nervous!

ALFRED HITCHCOCK

7

1

Empty Cages

JUPITER JONES turned his head at the sound of a horn and groaned. "Oh, no! Here comes my Uncle Titus with a lorryload for the yard. You know what that means—work!"

Pete Crenshaw and Bob Andrews followed Jupiter's despairing look. Coming through the big iron gates of The Jones Salvage Yard was a small lorry. Konrad, one of the two Bavarian yard helpers, was driving. Titus Jones, a small man with an enormous moustache, sat beside him.

As the lorry stopped, Mr Jones hopped off. Jupiter and his friends could see that the truck was filled with a lot of rusty pipes and other odds and ends. Some of the junk appeared to be broken cages.

Jupiter's Aunt Mathilda, who had been sitting in her wrought-iron garden chair outside the office cabin, leaped to her feet.

"Titus Jones!" she yelled. "Have you gone out of your senses? How do you expect to sell a lorry-load of pipes and iron bars?"

"No problem, my dear," Titus Jones said, unruffled. He knew from past experience that

9

almost everything that interested him eventually sold to a buyer. And usually at a tidy profit. "Some of these bars come with cages."

"Cages?" his wife repeated. She came closer, squinting into the lorry. "You'd need some especially large canaries for those cages, Titus Jones."

"These are animal cages, woman," her husband declared. "Or rather, they used to be. I'll leave it to Jupiter and his friends here. Take a look, Jupiter. Could we put them to some use?"

Jupiter looked over the lot. "Well," he answered slowly, "they could be repaired, I suppose. New bars added, roofs put on, the cage floors mended, everything painted. We could do it, all right, but then what?"

"Then what?" his uncle roared. "Why then we'd have animal cages ready for them when they need them, wouldn't we?"

"When who needs them, Uncle Titus?" asked Jupiter.

"Why, the circus, my boy," his uncle replied. "Circus comes to town every year, don't it? Well, then, next time they come, we'll be ready in case they need some good solid cages for their brutes."

Jupe shrugged. "I guess so," he said doubtfully.

"You guess so!" his uncle roared. "Don't forget I spent my early years travelling with a circus. I guess I ought to know what they'd be looking for, wouldn't you say?"

Jupiter smiled. "Yes, Uncle Titus." He had

forgotten how proud his uncle was of his past association with the big top.

"Fine!" Titus said. "Hans! Konrad! Get this stuff off the lorry. Stack the cages separately so that we can get to work on them soon."

Konrad's brother, Hans, appeared from the back of the yard, and the Bavarian helpers began unloading the lorry. Uncle Titus got his pipe out, searched his pockets for a match, and slowly began puffing.

"Those cages," he began. "Got 'em for a song out in the valley. Found them with a lot of old junked cars. Feller didn't see much need for cages and such, so I bought the lot cheap. I'll be heading back in a while to try again. Just might be another load there."

He walked away puffing contentedly on his briar. Jupiter and his friends idly watched him go. Mrs Jones had a better idea of how the boys should pass their time.

"Jupiter!" she called. "Those iron bars and railings on the lorry should be stacked together. Perhaps we can sell them at a bargain price for the lot."

"Right, Aunt Mathilda," Jupe said. The stocky boy scrambled awkwardly up into the lorry with Pete and Bob. "Okay, fellows," he said. "You heard the order."

Pete Crenshaw stared down at the pile of rusty rails and bars. "It sure beats me, Jupe, where your uncle ever finds this junk. But what puzzles me even more is how he ever manages to sell it."

Jupiter grinned. "Uncle Titus has always been lucky that way, Pete. He's brought in stuff you'd swear nobody in the world would ever want, and sells it the very next day. So if he says he can sell these pipes, I believe it."

Bob put in, "Well, anyway, we get paid for working. And we can use the money. We need some new equipment for Headquarters."

Headquarters was a damaged mobile home trailer that Mr Jones had given to Jupiter to use as a meeting place for his friends. It was over at one side of the salvage yard, hidden by junk the boys had piled round it. Close by was Jupe's workshop section, fitted out with various tools and a printing press.

Inside Headquarters, the boys had equipped a tiny office with telephone, desk, tape recorder, and filing cabinets. There was also a small lab and a darkroom for developing pictures. Most of the equipment had been rebuilt by Jupe and his friends from junk that had come into The Jones Salvage Yard.

Bob, Pete, and Jupiter had started a puzzle-solving club originally, which they later turned into a junior detective firm called The Three Investigators. Although they had started the club in fun, they had solved several genuine mysteries that had come their way and had decided to pursue detective work more seriously.

Peter Crenshaw, the strongest member of the trio, now looked unhappily at the large pile of pipes remaining after the two big Bavarian helpers had unloaded the cages. "Okay," he said reluctantly, "might as well get started." He dragged out several long bars and hoisted them to his shoulder. "Where do you want them stacked, Jupe?" he asked, staggering under the heavy load.

Jupe pointed out an area near a shed. "We'll stack them in a pile there, Pete."

Pete grunted and backed off with his load. Jupe and Bob then took turns feeding the bars to Pete on return trips. Work progressed rapidly and soon the pile in the lorry was down to one.

Rubbing his hands, Pete stepped up. "All right, Jupe," he said, "I'll take that last little one now."

Jupe leaned forward to hand the bar over, and hesitated. He felt the weight of the bar again. "We'd better set this aside. It's just the size I've been looking for."

Bob looked puzzled. "For what? You starting your own junkyard now?"

"It just happens to be shorter than the rest," said Jupe. "We can use it for a slide bolt inside our headquarters door. For security reasons."

"Security?" Bob asked.

Jupe reddened. "I'm getting tired of crawling through our tunnel into Headquarters. There's got to be an easier way of doing things. I thought we might unlock the door."

Pete and Bob smiled at this roundabout explanation. The truth was that Jupiter was a little too fat to enjoy using their secret tunnel all the time.

Jumping off the lorry, Jupe walked over to Headquarters and the junk surrounding the trailer. "Maybe Uncle Titus won't need it," he said. "Or we can work off the price."

Pete wiped sweat from his brow. "I think we already did that. If you ask me, we did a good day's work in an hour."

"Okay, Jupe," Bob said. "Now what—?"

At that moment the red light mounted over their printing press blinked!

"A phone call!" Pete cried. "Maybe it's somebody wanting a mystery solved."

"I hope so," Jupe said excitedly. "We haven't had any to investigate in a long time."

Quickly they pushed aside the iron grillwork beside the printing press. Crawling through the box behind it, they entered Tunnel Two. This was a large corrugated pipe leading to a trap door in the floor of the hidden trailer. The boys rushed through on their hands and knees and surfaced in the small office of Headquarters.

Jupiter snatched up the ringing telephone.

"Jupiter Jones speaking," he said.

"One moment, please." A woman's voice could be heard clearly through the loudspeaker attachment Jupe had rigged up. "Mr Alfred Hitchcock is calling."

The three boys exchanged surprised and happy grins. As a rule, they found an exciting mystery waiting for them whenever Mr Hitchcock called.

"Hello there!" the famous director boomed. "Is this young Jupiter?"

"Yes, Mr Hitchcock," Jupe said.

"I hope you and your friends are not too busy just now. I have a friend who is in need of help, and I think you three lads are just the ones to solve his problem."

"We'd like to try, sir," Jupe said. "Can you give us an idea of your friend's problem?"

"Certainly," Mr Hitchcock said. "If you boys can arrange to be at my office tomorrow morning, I shall be happy to tell you all about it."

2

A Case in Lion Territory

SOME time ago, Jupiter and his friends had won the use of an antique Rolls-Royce, complete with chauffeur, in a contest. Their prize time eventually ran out, but then they helped a youthful client to gain an enormous inheritance. The grateful client arranged for the boys to have the use of the Rolls whenever needed. It had proved invaluable to them as investigators. Distances in southern California are vast, and it is difficult to cover them except by car.

Now Jupiter leaned forward and tapped the shoulder of the tall, English chauffeur, Worthington. "This will be fine, Worthington," he said. "Wait here. We won't be too long with Mr Hitchcock."

"Very good, Master Jones," Worthington replied. He guided the old, box-like automobile to a careful stop. Then he got out and held the door open for the boys. "I trust Mr Hitchcock has an interesting mission for you young gentlemen."

"We hope so, too, Worthington," Bob said. "Things have been kind of dull lately. We could use some excitement."

He quickly joined Jupe and Pete as they entered the Hollywood studio building where Mr Hitchcock had his office.

Alfred Hitchcock motioned them to seats in front of his big desk. He pushed some business correspondence aside and looked at the boys thoughtfully. Then casually he asked, "How comfortable are you lads with wild animals?"

Opposite him, The Three Investigators looked startled.

Jupiter cleared his throat. "It all depends on what kind of animals, sir, and the proximity involved. Given a reasonable distance between them and us and a measure of protection, I would say we are all quite at ease with them, and interested in their behaviour and habits."

"Jupe means we like them," Pete said. "It just goes against his nature to say something simple."

"Why, Mr Hitchcock?" asked Bob. "Is this about a mystery?"

"Perhaps," Mr Hitchcock said slowly. "And if not indeed a mystery, certainly a case that merits investigation. The wild animals I mentioned are part of the background where certain mysterious happenings are taking place."

Alfred Hitchcock paused. "Have you lads heard of a place called Jungle Land?"

"That's over in the valley near Chatwick," Bob replied. "It's some kind of wild-animal farm with lions and other animals roaming around. It's supposed to be a tourist attraction, I think."

"Yes," Alfred Hitchcock said. "The owner, Jim Hall, is an old friend. Lately he's run into a problem and I thought at once of you boys and your investigative talents."

"What's Mr Hall's problem exactly, sir?" asked Jupiter.

"It would appear he has a nervous lion," Mr Hitchcock said.

The boys looked at each other wide-eyed.

"To continue," Mr Hitchcock said. "Jungle Land is indeed open to the public. In addition, various movie companies at times rent the use of its premises. Its terrain and vegetation are suggestive of Western and African locales. Occasionally Jim Hall rents his animals. Some of them are wild, but several have been brought up gently and trained by Jim.

"Jim Hall's favourite lion is a remarkable example of his way with animals. This lion has been featured in many commercials for TV and has been used in films. It has always been a great attraction at Jungle Land and a good financial asset to Jim Hall."

"You mean, until now," Jupe said. "Your friend's lion is nervous and now he can't depend on it. That's his problem, isn't it?"

Alfred Hitchcock gave Jupiter a penetrating stare. "As usual, my astute young friend, your powers of deduction are equal to the task at hand. A film unit has rented the farm now to shoot sequences for a jungle film. Naturally Jim Hall cannot afford any accidents that might interfere with the film's speedy and successful completion. If anything were to go wrong, it would be ruinous to his entire operation."

"And we're supposed to go there and solve the mystery of the nervous lion," Jupe said. "Is that it?"

"Precisely," intoned Mr. Hitchcock. "Quickly and quietly. Without fuss or fanfare. And I need hardly add, without further disturbing the already unsettled lion."

Pete Crenshaw licked his lips. "How close do we have to get to this crazy cat?"

Alfred Hitchcock smiled affably. "Closeness is its own definition, young Peter. You will all be on the Jungle Land premises. Jim Hall's lion is there. And while ordinarily it might be considered reasonably safe to be in the lion's vicinity, I must warn you the situation has changed. A nervous lion—any nervous animal—can be dangerous."

The Three Investigators gulped.

"You can tell your friend Jim Hall not to

worry," said Bob. "His lion won't be the only nervous one there anymore."

"That's right," Pete added. "I'm not even there yet and I'm nervous already."

Mr Hitchcock turned to Jupiter. "Any further comment, young Jupiter, before I call my friend to say you lads are willing to undertake the assignment?"

Jupe shook his head. "No comment. But it might be a good idea to ask Mr Hall to put in a word for us with his lion!"

Mr Hitchcock smiled and picked up his phone. "I shall convey your message. And I shall expect a full report from you soon. Good-bye and good luck."

The Three Investigators waved and walked out wondering what kind of luck they could expect dealing with a nervous lion!

3

Welcome to Jungle Land

IT was past noon when The Three Investigators careered down the last steep grade of a narrow back road. Rolling mountains encircled the valley, which was a scant thirty minutes from Rocky

Beach. Jupiter's Uncle Titus had sent Konrad on a pickup job in nearby Chatwick and had allowed the boys to go along for their appointment in Jungle Land.

"Slow down, Konrad," Jupe ordered. "That's the place."

"Hokay, Jupe." The big Bavarian braked the small lorry to a jolting stop outside the main gate. The entrance sign read:

WELCOME TO JUNGLE LAND!
ADMISSION ONE DOLLAR, CHILDREN FIFTY CENTS

As the boys got out, they heard strange hooting and chattering cries. In the distance a loud trumpeting sound echoed in the hills. As if in answer to this challenge, there came a deep, rumbling roar that sent chills down their spines.

Konrad gestured to the gate. "You fellers going in there?" he asked. "You better watch it. I think I hear lions."

"There's nothing to worry about, Konrad," Bob said. "Mr Hitchcock wouldn't have sent us on this job if he thought it was really dangerous."

"We just have to look into something for the owner," Jupe said. "This is a safe tourist attraction."

Konrad shrugged. "Hokay," he said. "If you say it's safe, hokay. But better take care all the same. I be back for you a little later."

He waved and wheeled the lorry back to the main road. Soon the lorry was out of sight.

Jupe looked at his friends. "Well, what are we waiting for?"

Pete pointed to a small sign posted at the gate:

CLOSED TODAY

"I wondered why there wasn't anyone around," he said.

"It might be because the movie company is inside shooting," said Jupe.

Bob peered inside. "Shouldn't Mr Hall be here to meet us?"

Jupe nodded. "I expected him. But maybe he's busy with other things inside."

"Like his nervous lion," Pete said. "Maybe he's having a hard time convincing him we're not here for his dinner."

Jupe pressed on the gate. It opened to his touch.

"It's not locked," he said cheerfully. "That's either so the movie people can get in and out—or for us. Let's go."

The gate creaked shut behind them as they stepped inside. From beyond the trees, they heard chattering sounds punctuated by harsh screeches.

"Monkeys and birds," Jupe observed. "Harmless creatures."

"We'll find out soon enough," Bob said in a low voice.

The entrance road was narrow and twisting, bordered on either side by trees and thick foliage. Large curling vines looped down from trees.

"Looks like a jungle, all right," Pete observed.

The others nodded. As they advanced slowly, they cast suspicious glances at the dense undergrowth on either side, wondering what strange creature might be crouching there waiting to spring. The odd sounds beyond continued, and again they heard the dull, reverberating roar.

They stopped at a signpost at a fork in the road.

" 'Western Village and Ghost Town,' " Bob read on the sign pointing left. "What does the other say?"

Jupe was looking up at it quizzically. "To the animals," he said.

They turned right at the fork. After a few hundred yards, Pete pointed ahead. "There's a house. Maybe Mr Hall has his office there."

"It looks like a bunkhouse," Jupe said as they drew closer. "There's a corral behind it."

Suddenly there was a loud, ear-piercing scream. The boys froze, and then, as if with a single mind, dived into the shrubbery for cover.

Hidden behind the thick trunk of a barrel palm, Pete peered across the dirt road at the bunkhouse. Jupe and Bob, crouched behind a bush, also looked out anxiously. They waited for more sounds, their hearts beating fast. But now the thick jungle was silent.

"Jupe," Pete whispered. "What was that?"

Jupe shook his head. "I'm not sure. Maybe a cheetah."

"It could have been a monkey," Bob whispered.

They stayed in the shrubbery, waiting.

"Good grief!" Pete said hoarsely. "We came here

22

to find out about a nervous lion. Nobody said anything about nervous monkeys or cheetahs!"

"We've got to expect the animals here will be making some kind of sounds," Jupe said. "It's only natural. Whatever that was, it's quiet now. Let's get to the house and find out what's happening."

The others hesitated as Jupe started forward, moving slowly and warily. Then they joined him.

"Anyway, that sound came from way up ahead," Pete muttered.

"Where the wild animals are locked up tight—I hope," Bob added.

"Come on," Jupe urged. "We're almost there."

The bunkhouse was old and needed paint. Pails and feedbins were scattered carelessly at the side. Tracks from many vehicles had carved deep ruts in the road. The corral fence sagged.

The old house stood silent, as if waiting for them.

"Now what?" Pete asked in a low voice.

Jupe stepped on to the low, slatted porch. There was a determined expression on his face. "We knock on the door," he said flatly, "and tell Mr Hall we're here."

He rapped vigorously. There was no response. "Mr Hall!" Jupiter called loudly.

Bob scratched his head. "Guess he's not home."

Pete held up his hand warningly. "Hold it!" he whispered. "I hear something."

They all heard it then. A low, muttering sound in an odd cadence. The sound came closer, approaching from the rear of the house. They could hear the crunching of footsteps on gravel. They drew back, eyes wide.

Suddenly it came at them, darting forward in an erratic line, head bobbing angrily. Yellow legs dug fiercely into the ground.

The Three Investigators stared.

4

Stalking a Lion

JUPITER JONES was the first to recover his voice. "Careful now!" he cautioned. "We don't want to be scared off by a mad rooster!"

"Gosh!" Pete said sheepishly. "Is that all it is?"

Bob let out a relieved sigh. "I never would have believed it!"

He looked down at the clucking black fowl that had sounded so ominous only a moment before, and laughed.

"Shoo, bird!" he yelled, waving his arms.

Startled, the cock lifted its black wings. Making angry sounds, it scuttled across the road, its high, red comb bobbing.

The boys all laughed.

"There's proof of how the mind can deceive

you," Jupe said. "We were intimidated by the jungle growth and the sounds of wild animals. We all expected something dangerous to be coming at us. We were conditioned for it."

He started for the door again.

"Hey, look over there, Jupe," Bob said.

The other boys followed Bob's pointing finger. In the shadows of the thick jungle, they caught a sudden movement. A figure in khaki stepped from behind a tree.

"Mr Hall!" Jupe yelled.

The man waited as the boys ran towards him.

"Hi," Pete said. "We've been looking for you."

The man looked at the boys questioningly. He was stocky and deep-chested, his faded safari shirt open at the throat. His light blue eyes contrasted vividly with the deep tan of his face. His nose was long and dented to one side. On his head was an old Aussie campaign hat, its wide brim folded over one ear.

As the boys came closer, he made an impatient movement with his hand. Something glinted.

Jupe and his friends stared down at the long, broad-bladed machete the man held carelessly at his side.

Jupiter spoke quickly. "We're The Three Investigators, Mr Hall. Didn't Mr Hitchcock tell you we were coming?"

The man blinked and looked surprised. "Oh, yes. Hitchcock. You say you're the three investigators?"

"That's right, Mr Hall," Jupe said. He reached

into his pocket and produced a business card on which was printed:

```
┌─────────────────────────────────────────┐
│                                           │
│        THE THREE INVESTIGATORS            │
│                                           │
│        "We Investigate Anything"          │
│                                           │
│             ?      ?      ?               │
│                                           │
│     First Investigator – JUPITER JONES    │
│     Second Investigator – PETER CRENSHAW  │
│     Records and Research – BOB ANDREWS    │
│                                           │
└─────────────────────────────────────────┘
```

"I'm Jupiter Jones. These are my partners, Pete Crenshaw and Bob Andrews."

"Nice to meet you, boys." He took the card and studied it. "What are the question marks for?"

"The question marks stand for things unknown," Jupiter explained. "For questions unanswered, riddles, enigmas. It's our business to answer those questions, unravel the riddles, and find solutions for the enigmas. That's why we're here. Mr Hitchcock told us about the trouble you're having with your nervous lion."

"Oh, he did?"

"Actually, he merely mentioned your lion was nervous. I imagine he expected you to fill in the details."

The stocky man nodded, and slipped the card into his shirt pocket. He frowned and squinted into the distance. There was a trumpeting sound, almost immediately followed by an answering roar.

"Well," he said smiling. "If you're feeling up to it, we can go out and have a look at him."

"That's what we're here for," said Jupe.

"Fine. Let's get moving then."

Turning abruptly, he skirted the bunkhouse and followed a faint trail through the jungle. The boys fell into step behind him.

"Perhaps you can fill us in on the way, Mr Hall," Jupe said, dodging a thick vine.

The long machete flashed in the air. The vine parted as if it were paper. "What d'ya want to know?" the man asked, resuming his rapid pace.

Jupe struggled to stay close behind. "Well, for example, all we know is that your lion is nervous. That's—well—rather unusual for a lion, isn't it?"

The man nodded, walking fast and slashing at the undergrowth looming in their path. "Not usual, at all. Know anything about lions?"

Jupiter gulped. "No, sir. That's why we'd like to know. It's curious, isn't it? I mean, this is a new development, isn't it?"

"Yep," the man said shortly. He held up his hand for silence. There were faint chattering sounds. Then came a booming roar. The man smiled. "Just up ahead," he said. "That's him out there." He cocked his head at Jupiter. "I'll leave it to you. Does he sound nervous?"

"I—I don't know. It sounds like—well, a normal lion roar." Jupe was determined to let Mr Hall know he wasn't the least bit nervous himself.

"That's right," the man said. He stopped for a moment, swishing his machete at the tall grass surrounding them. "Y'see, the lion is not a nervous animal, at all."

"But—" Jupe started, perplexed.

The man nodded. "Unless," he said, "unless somebody or something is making him that way. How does that strike you?"

The boys, together now, nodded.

"Sure, but what?" Bob asked.

The man shifted his position suddenly. "Don't move," he whispered. "Something out there."

Before they realised it, he had disappeared into the tall grass. They heard his footsteps, the swish of grass, and then suddenly nothing at all.

Somewhere overhead a bird screeched and they jumped nervously.

"Relax, fellows," Pete said. "That was only a bird."

"Only a bird!" Bob repeated. "Some bird! It sounded like a vulture."

The boys waited for several minutes. Jupe glanced at his watch. "I've a funny feeling that vulture is trying to tell us something," he said.

"Oh, come on, Jupe," Bob protested. "Tell us what?"

Jupe's face was pale. He licked his lips. "I have the feeling that Mr Hall isn't coming back. I think he's arranged some kind of test for us—to see how we react to the danger of the jungle."

"But why, Jupe?" asked Pete. "What would his

reason be? We're here to help him, aren't we? He knows that."

Jupe listened for a moment before answering. Strange calls came from high in the trees. Then once again they heard a deep, menacing roar.

Jupiter inclined his head in the direction of the last frightening sound. "I don't know what Mr Hall's reason can be. But I know that lion out there sounds a lot closer than before. He seems to be coming this way. I think that's what the vulture is telling us—that we're the prey! They usually circle a dead or soon-to-be-dead animal. In this case, us!"

Pete and Bob stared at Jupe. They knew he wasn't apt to joke in serious circumstances. Instinctively the three boys moved closer together.

They listened tensely.

They heard the swish of grass. Then footfalls, soft and stealthy.

Holding their breath, they edged closer to a large tree.

Then, almost directly behind them, they heard a blood-chilling sound—*the roar of the lion!*

5

Dangerous Game

"QUICK!" Jupe whispered urgently. "Up this tree! It's our only chance!"

In an instant the three had scrambled up a smoothboled gum tree. They huddled breathlessly in its fork barely ten feet from the ground, looking intently at the waist-high grass beyond.

Pete pointed towards a thick cluster of growth. "I—I just saw some grass bend there. You hear it? Something is moving—"

He blinked at a soft call, a whistle from the high grass. Then to the amazement of all three, a young boy stepped out of the brush, peering cautiously about.

"Hey!" Bob called. "Up here!"

The boy whirled. In the same motion, he swung a rifle upward. "Who are you?" he demanded.

"F-friends," Bob gasped weakly. "Put down that gun."

"We've been invited here," Pete added. "We're The Three Investigators."

"We're waiting for Mr Hall to come back," Jupe put in. "He left us waiting while he went out there to investigate something."

The boy swung the rifle down. "Come down out of there," he said.

Cautiously the three slid down the trunk. Jupe pointed into the grass. "We heard a lion out there a little while ago. We thought we'd be safer up in the tree."

The boy smiled. He appeared to be about their age. "That was George," he said.

Pete gulped. "George? The lion's name is George?"

The boy nodded. "You don't have to be afraid of George. He's friendly."

A deep roar came from the high grass. It sounded terrifyingly close.

The Three Investigators stiffened.

"Y-you call that roar friendly?" Pete asked.

"I suppose you've got to get used to it first. But that's George—and he wouldn't harm anybody."

A twig snapped sharply. Bob paled. "What makes you so sure?"

"I work here," he boy answered, smiling. "I see George every day. By the way, my name's Mike Hall."

"We're glad to meet you, Mike," said Jupe. He introduced himself and his companions. Then, "I'm not sure we appreciate your father's sense of humour."

Mike Hall looked surprised.

"Bringing us out here and then deserting us with a lion close by," Pete burst in heatedly. "That's no joke."

"That's probably why he's in trouble here,"

Bob added. "You can lose a lot of people trying to help you if you play games like that."

The youth looked at the three angry investigators, puzzled. "I don't understand. First, I'm Jim Hall's nephew, not his son. Second, Jim wouldn't have left you here with the lion. We've all been looking for him—George got out somehow, and we forgot you were coming, in the excitement. I've heard George roaring and been trying to catch up with him."

Jupe listened to this explanation calmly. "I'm sorry, Mike. We're telling the truth. Mr Hall led us out here and then abandoned us. The lion roared out there, and he told us to wait. He disappeared into the grass—and—well, we've had a long wait—and a worried one!"

Mike shook his head stubbornly. "There must be some mistake. That couldn't have been Jim. I've been with him all day and I just left him. You must have met somebody else. What did he look like?"

Bob described the stocky man with the Aussie campaign hat. "We called him Mr Hall and he didn't deny it," he added.

"He carried a long machete," Pete said, "and knew how to use it. He also knew his way around. He cut his way right to this spot to show us the lion."

Jupe added, "I suppose we can't blame you for sticking up for your uncle, Mike, but—"

"I'm not," Mike interrupted angrily. "That man you described was Hank Morton. He used to work here as an animal trainer and handler."

He stared out at the high grass, listening intently. "What I don't understand is how he got here. My Uncle Jim fired him."

"Fired him?" Jupe asked. "What for?"

"He was cruel to the animals, for one thing," Mike said. "My Uncle Jim won't stand for that. For another, he's mean—a troublemaker. He drinks a lot. When he's in that condition, he doesn't know what he's doing."

"Perhaps," Jupe said thoughtfully. "But if that was Hank Morton who brought us out here, he wasn't the least bit drunk. He was cold sober—and knew exactly what he was doing."

"But why?" Bob asked. "Why did he do it? What was his idea—marooning us out here?"

"I don't know," Mike Hall said. "Perhaps—" His eyes gleamed. "Did you tell him anything—about why you're here?"

Jupe clapped his head ruefully. "That's it! We told him Alfred Hitchcock sent us to see him about his nervous lion. I recall now that he looked surprised at first."

"I can think of a reason," Pete said. "He was trying to get even with Jim Hall for firing him. We just happened along conveniently."

"But why us?" asked Bob. "We've got nothing to do with Jim Hall and his getting fired."

"The nervous lion," Jupe reminded. "The case we're on and the reason we're here. Perhaps he didn't want us to find out why that lion is nervous."

33

"That could be it," young Mike Hall said. "And Hank Morton probably let George get loose, too. George couldn't have got out by himself."

"Well," said Jupe. "When we see your uncle, he might have a better explanation. I suggest we start back now, Mike, and have a talk with him."

"I don't think we can do that right now," Bob said quietly.

Jupe looked at Bob, surprised. "Why not? What's wrong with that idea?"

Bob's voice was low and shaking. "It's—right behind you, fellows. A great big lion just came out of the brush. Maybe it's George—but he sure doesn't look friendly!"

Mike turned around. "It's George, all right. But he knows me. Just don't make any sudden movements, fellows. I'll handle him."

The boys watched uneasily as Mike took a step forward. He lifted one hand, carefully extending it palm up. "All right, George. Easy now, fellow. Nice boy, George."

His reassuring voice was answered by a snarl. Slowly and menacingly a massive, thick-maned lion advanced. Its head was down and its huge yellow eyes were narrowed. It turned its big head to one side and snarled again. Less than ten feet away it halted. The huge jaws opened, exposing long, frightening fangs.

Then, with a deep roar rumbling in its throat, the lion came forward again.

The Three Investigators stared at it helplessly, unable to move, their throats tight with fear.

34

Mike was speaking again. "Easy, George," he said quietly. "Easy, boy. You know me, fellow. Easy now. Nice and easy."

The huge, tawny beast flicked its tail. A low rumble came rolling like thunder. It came forward another step.

Young Mike shook his head. "Something's wrong, fellows. George knows me. But he isn't acting his usual friendly way."

Slowly, the boy backed away.

The lion came on.

6

A Narrow Escape

THE Three Investigators stood rooted to the ground as inch by inch young Mike Hall retreated before the advancing lion. His voice was still low and friendly but the lion ignored it.

Jupiter Jones was as paralysed with fear as his companions. But his brain was still active. He was puzzled by the lion's behaviour towards somebody it knew. It gave no sign that it recognised young Mike Hall.

Suddenly Jupe discovered what was wrong. He tried to keep his voice low and not attract the lion's attention.

"Look at his left foreleg, Mike," he said. "He's wounded!"

Mike looked quickly at the lion's leg. It was covered by a thick film of blood.

"No wonder George isn't obeying," said Mike softly. "I'm afraid I've got bad news for you guys. A hurt animal is dangerous. I don't know if I can handle him."

"You've got a rifle," Bob whispered. "Maybe you ought to shoot."

"This is only a .22 calibre. It wouldn't do more than tickle George. It might make him even madder. I just carry it for emergencies, for firing a warning shot."

The lion took another step forward. The huge beast winced as the bloody leg took its weight. Its mouth opened in a twisting snarl.

The Three Investigators inched backward to the gum tree. Mike saw their movement and shook his head.

"Don't try it, fellows," he cautioned. "He'd be on you before you got one leg up."

"Okay, Mike," said Jupe. "But why not fire a warning shot? Wouldn't that scare George off?"

Mike smiled grimly. "Not a chance. He's got his head down. That means his mind is made up and nothing is going to change it." He bit his lip. "I just wish my Uncle Jim was here."

A soft whistle trilled from the high grass. Abruptly a tall, bronzed man stepped out.

"You've got your wish, Mike," he said dryly.

"Now nobody moves, nobody talks except me, understand?"

The man stepped lithely forward. "Now, Georgie, what's going on here?" he asked pleasantly.

The words were spoken in a light, conversational tone. They had their effect. The lion turned its head towards the man. Its long tail flicked. Then, cocking its head, it opened its jaws and roared.

The tall man nodded. "I see," he said softly. "You're hurt. Is that it?"

Then to the amazement of the boys, he strode up to the lion and took its huge head in his hands.

"Come on, George," he said. "Let's have a look at it."

The lion opened its jaws again. The expected roar became a moaning sound instead. Slowly it extended its bleeding leg.

"Oh, it's your leg, is it?" asked Jim Hall. "Okay, old fellow, take it easy. I'll take care of it for you."

He removed a handkerchief from his pocket and bent to one knee. Deftly, he bandaged the wound, his face dangerously close to the lion's jaws.

The lion stood patiently as Jim Hall knotted the handkerchief. The man rose. He rubbed the lion's ears and twisted his mane. Then, affectionately, he pounded the beast's shoulders.

"There you are, George—almost as good as new."

Smiling, he turned away. The lion's voice rumbled in its thick throat. Its muscles quivered.

Then suddenly there was a quick, blurring yellow movement. Instantly Jim Hall was down, the lion upon him.

"Look out!" Pete cried.

The Three Investigators looked on in horror as the man writhed under the weight of the big jungle cat.

Jupe turned to Mike Hall. The boy was watching calmly, a slight smile on his lips. Jupe couldn't understand. "Do something!" he shouted.

"Use your gun, Mike!" Bob yelled.

Mike Hall lifted his hand. "It's nothing to worry about, fellows. They're only playing. George was brought up by Jim and loves him."

"But—" Jupe started to say. His eyes bugged out as he saw the huge lion thrown aside by Jim Hall. With a ferocious snarling sound, it lashed back, wrapping its forelegs around the man's shoulders. It opened its jaws wide, its large teeth inches from the man's face.

Unbelievably, Jim Hall laughed!

He braced to confront the snarling lion, and as he was knocked aside, pounded its ribs and yanked at the long mane. The animal moaned and flicked its long tail. Then to the utter bewilderment of the boys, it rolled over on its back, a strange sound coming from its throat.

"He's purring!" Bob exclaimed.

Jim Hall sat up and dusted himself off. "Whew!" he said in mock dismay. "That cat's a lot heavier than he thinks! It was easier when George was a cub."

Jupiter sighed his relief. He turned to Mike. "That just about scared me out of my wits. Do they always play that rough?"

"It scared me too when I first saw them at it," Mike admitted. "But I'm used to it now. George is so well-trained, he acts like a big overgrown puppy. You can see how good-natured he really is, now."

Jupe narrowed his eyes. "But Mr Hitchcock said—" He turned to the tall man stroking the lion's chest. "Mr Hall, we're The Three Investigators. Alfred Hitchcock told us you were having trouble, that your lion was nervous for some reason."

"That's right, son," Jim Hall said. "Take what happened here. Ol' George never acted that way before. He knows Mike and never should have come on that mean and ornery. I've brought him up, so naturally he listens to me, but lately he hasn't been dependable, at all."

"Maybe we can find out why," Jupe offered. "That wound on his leg, for example. Does that strike you as an accident?"

"What do you mean?"

"It looked like a slashing cut," Jupe said. "Something that could have been made by a long, sharp instrument—a machete, for instance."

The man nodded. "Yes. But—"

"When we arrived, we mistook another man for you, sir. He led us out here and he was wielding a machete—"

"It was Hank Morton," Mike interrupted. "Jupe

39

described him to me. He must have let George loose."

Jim Hall's jaw set grimly. "Hank Morton was here? When I fired him, I warned him not to come back." He looked at his lion, puzzled. "*Somebody* let George out. It might have been Hank. You say he brought you out here?"

"Yes," Bob put in. "Then he left us and went off into the high grass, telling us to wait."

"If he used to handle your lion, maybe he was able to get close enough to wound him with that machete, and make him mad enough to go for *us*," Pete said.

"If he did," Jim Hall said angrily, "that will be Hank Morton's last trick. Because if I don't catch up with him for that, *George will!*"

He tugged at the lion's ears affectionately. "Come on, boy. We're going to have Doc Dawson take a look at you."

Mike answered Jupe's inquiring look. "Doc Dawson is our veterinarian. An animal doctor. He takes care of George and all our other animals here."

Jim Hall led his lion off through the jungle. "Come along, boys. I'll fill you in on what's been happening when we get back to the house. Alfred Hitchcock said you fellows were pretty good at unravelling mysteries. Maybe you can spot what's wrong. Because sure as shooting, something is going on around here that I can't figure out."

7

The Trouble with George

"HERE we are."

Jim Hall stopped at a small covered van parked on a side road. He dropped the tail-board, urged George up, then fastened it in place.

"Come on," Mike said to Jupe and his friends. "We'll sit up front with Jim."

The Jungle Land owner got behind the wheel and started the vehicle. As he backed and turned the van round, Jupe leaned forward.

"How did George get out, Mr Hall? Where do you usually keep him—in his own compound?"

Jim Hall shook his head. "He stays in our house —with Mike and me. I don't know how he got out unless Hank Morton saw me leave. He could have let him out then. George was used to him being around so that would have been no problem. Once George was out, he could have wandered anywhere. That's what had me worried," he added, his lips tightening.

He followed the narrow, winding road up a hill and swung up a gravel drive leading to a large white house.

"Here we are," he announced. "Run inside and call Doc Dawson, will you, Mike?"

As Mike jumped off, Jupiter looked around in surprise. "Is this where you live? We thought that first one we came to—the bunkhouse—"

"That's for show," Jim Hall answered, smiling. "People come to Jungle Land for a lot of reasons. It's an animal farm and ranch, and we throw in a bit of the old Wild West for them, too. Sometimes we use the place for filming movies. One is being shot right now, matter of fact—a jungle picture."

"So Mr Hitchcock told us," Jupe said. "He led us to believe that was your concern at the moment, your lion not being trustworthy while a movie was being made here."

"Correct," Hall said. "George happens to be rented out, too, for the production. If he forgets he's supposed to be gentle and doesn't respond to my commands, Jay Eastland might lose a valuable leading man."

"Who's Jay Eastland?" Bob asked.

"That name sounds familiar," Pete said. "My dad does special effects for film companies. I'm sure I've heard him mention Jay Eastland's name."

Jim Hall said, "Eastland is a very important film producer and director—at least, he thinks he is."

He turned to unfasten the tail-board of the van. Mike Hall, who had just come out of the house, whistled and pointed to an approaching cloud of dust.

"Here comes trouble, Uncle Jim," he called.

Jim Hall looked up, his brow darkening.

42

"Trouble is right—here it comes in the person of Mr Eastland himself."

The cloud of dust cleared to reveal a station wagon. In a few seconds it pulled up and stopped. A short, beefy, bald-headed man hopped out of the back seat. He advanced with jerky steps, his face flushed and angry.

"Hall," he shouted, "I'm holding you to the terms of our contract."

Jim Hall looked down at the perspiring director. "I don't know what you're talking about, Eastland. What's up?"

Eastland shook his fist at the animal owner. "That contract states no danger to myself or my people, remember? I guess you have a good explanation for what's happened?"

Jim Hall's eyebrows flew up. "My contract and agreement stand," he said coldly. "What happened?"

"Rock Randall's been hurt," Eastland yelled. "One of your animals got loose and attacked him —that's what happened!"

"That's impossible!" Hall said firmly.

The angry visitor pointed accusingly at the big lion in the rear of the van.

"There's all the proof I need, right there! Your pet lion! I happen to know he was loose and roaming around an hour ago. I'd like to hear you deny it!"

"You're right, Eastland. George was loose for a time. But that's no proof he attacked Randall. I can't believe it."

"You'll believe it when you see him," Eastland sneered.

"Is he hurt badly?" asked Hall quickly.

Eastland shrugged. "Let's say that being attacked by a bad-tempered lion doesn't do anybody any good."

Jim Hall's lips tightened. "Now, hold on there. We still don't know for certain George did it."

"Who else could do a job like that? Wait till you see—"

"I'm going to do that right now," Jim Hall snapped. "Just as soon as I lock George in the house."

As he lowered the tail-board, a horn sounded. A small old lorry came bouncing around the turn.

"It's Doc Dawson," Mike Hall whispered to the boys.

The driver braked to a skidding halt and jumped out. He was tall and thin. Under his grizzled moustache jutted the stub of an unlit cigar. He hurried towards the group with long strides, carrying a black leather medical bag.

The visitor stopped as he saw the lion in the van. Ignoring Eastland, he addressed Jim Hall in a gruff voice. "Got here as fast as I could, Jim, after Mike's call. What's that about George being hurt?"

"Flesh wound on his leg, Doc," Jim answered. "Somebody let George out while Mike and I were away. We rounded him up north of the bunk-house."

"It looks like somebody cut him with a knife or machete, Doc," Mike Hall put in.

44

The angular vet turned to Mike, frowning. "Who could have done that to old George? I'd better have a look. Hold him steady for me, will you, Jim?"

The vet leaned forward as Jim Hall held the lion's mane. "Let's have a look, Georgie, boy," the vet said softly.

He slipped off the handkerchief bandage and lifted the lion's leg. The animal whimpered.

"Come on, George," the vet said. "I won't hurt you. Been taking care of you since you were a baby."

After a cursory glance, Dawson dropped the leg. "Superficial cut, Jim, but nasty. I'd better take him back to the dispensary for a better look. We don't want to risk an infection."

"Right," Jim Hall said. "You're going with Doc Dawson, George," he informed the lion, guiding him down the slanted tail-board.

As the vet started for his truck, the irate film producer stepped in his way. "What's going on?" he bellowed. "Where you taking that lion? We hired him for the movie. He starts work tomorrow morning at eight sharp."

Doc Dawson stopped to light his stub of cigar and blew smoke in Eastland's face. "That lion will be ready to work when I say he is. His leg may be better by tomorrow morning, and then again it may not. My job is to keep George healthy. I don't care two cents for your crummy movie. Now get out of my way, mister, or I'll walk right over you!"

Jupe and his companions quietly watched the drama. At the sudden vehemence in the vet's voice, Eastland paled and backed off. Dawson opened the rear door of his truck. Jim Hall brought George forward, patted the lion's flank, and raised his hand.

"Up you go, Georgie."

Obediently, the lion leaped into the truck. Hall closed the door and Dawson drove off. The lion pressed against the open-mesh sides of the truck, looking sad, a whimpering sound in its throat.

Eastland stepped forward again. "I'm telling you now, Hall, that lion better be ready," he threatened. "Now do you want to see what he did to Rock Randall, or not?"

Without a word, Jim Hall followed the film producer into his station wagon. He waved to Mike as the driver spun the long car around, calling as he caught Jupe's eye, "Sorry, fellows— I'll see you later."

Jupe watched thoughtfully until the station wagon disappeared into the jungle. "That sounds like a bad scene, if it's true," he said.

"If what's true?" Mike Hall snapped. "My Uncle Jim's story or Mr Eastland's?"

Jupe shrugged. "I'm not disputing your uncle's word, Mike. But you have to admit he looked worried."

"I'm sorry, Jupe," Mike said, his voice breaking. "I didn't mean to flare up at you. But anything that concerns my uncle, concerns me, too. I—well, I'm living with him because my parents were killed in a car accident. He's my father's brother, and my only family now—except for Cal."

"Cal?" asked Bob.

"Who's he?" Pete put in.

"Cal Hall is my other uncle. He's a big game hunter and explorer in Africa," Mike explained. "He sends Jim animals for Jungle Land. If Jim gets them young enough, like with George, he can train them easily. He puts the others on exhibit here and hopes to train them all some day. But it's a lot harder to do once they're full grown."

"How come Jay Eastland acts so nasty?" Pete asked. "What's he got against your Uncle Jim?"

"Nothing I know of," Mike said. "He's worried about his movie getting done on schedule. And before he leased Jungle Land, he wanted an agreement it would be safe working here, with the animals around. Jim guaranteed it would."

"What happens if your uncle guessed wrong—and there's an accident?" Bob asked.

"Jim would lose a lot of money. He had to put up a bond of fifty thousand dollars as a guarantee. He signed over Jungle Land as security for the bond. So he could lose everything. He's losing money already because tourists aren't allowed in when we rent out for a movie. They might disrupt things."

Jupiter listened carefully. "I assume, though, that your uncle will make a considerable amount of money if the movie goes through on schedule, without any accidents. Correct?"

"Yes," Mike admitted. "I don't know the exact

amount but it's so much a day. And George gets paid five hundred dollars when he works. Trained animals are rented for a lot of money—just like movie stars."

"Has George had any accidents before?" asked Jupe. "Has he ever attacked anybody?"

"No," Mike said. "Never. He's a very gentle animal and well-trained. That is—" he bit his lip "—until lately, anyway. Recently he's been acting up."

Bob, in charge of Records and Research, had his little memo book open. "We still have no information about that," he said. "How has George been acting? What's he doing now that he didn't do before? Maybe that might give us a hint, Mike, about what's making him nervous."

"Well, he's not himself. He's on edge. He stays in the house with us but lately he hasn't slept well. Almost every night, he's up and growling, walking around, trying to get out. Jim can't get him to go back to sleep, and he doesn't take orders as he used to. He's getting so hard to handle now I'm afraid he's not the good-natured, well-trained animal he used to be."

"It could be something outside is exciting him," Jupe said. "Are any animals here allowed to roam loose at night?"

Mike shook his head. "We have deer in a compound but they can't get out. We have horses that are used in a lot of Westerns. They're kept in a corral. We've got two elephants down by the lake but they're in their own compound, too, and stay there. We've got raccoons, monkeys, birds, dogs, chickens, and a lot of other animals—but they're all penned up at night and accounted for."

"Nevertheless," Jupe said, "something or somebody is making George nervous."

"Nervous enough, maybe, to attack that actor, Rock Randall," said Pete. "Though maybe he asked for it. I remember hearing he's a pretty nasty guy."

"He'd have to be pretty stupid as well as nasty to start up with George," Bob said. "George didn't look too friendly and gentle when we ran into him. Maybe it was because he got that cut on his leg. Maybe not."

"We can't say anything for sure yet, fellows," Jupe said. "We can't blame George for Randall's accident until Jim comes back and tells us what happened. Maybe it was another kind of accident. One that none of the animals here were—"

Mike clapped his hands suddenly. "The gorilla!" he cried.

"What gorilla?" Pete asked.

"Do you have a gorilla here, too?" Bob said.

"Not yet—but we're expecting one. Part of a new shipment from my Uncle Cal. Maybe it got here already, and got loose—and attacked Rock Randall!"

Jupe held his hand up. "Assuming it already got here how could it escape? Wouldn't it be in a locked cage?"

Mike nodded. "You're right. I'm acting as nervous as George, myself. Jim didn't say anything about the gorilla arriving, and he'd know. Besides, if it was here, there's no way it could get out of its cage unless—unless—"

"Unless what, Mike?" asked Bob.

The young boy licked his lips. "Unless somebody who didn't like my Uncle Jim opened its cage and let it out!"

8

A Tough Customer

IT was still early afternoon and The Three Investigators were on their way back to The Jones Salvage Yard with Konrad. Their time had run out before Jim Hall returned. The boys left Mike with the promise that they would return at the earliest opportunity.

Konrad, already waiting for them outside the Jungle Land gate, looked relieved when they came out. "You look hokay," he said. "I guess maybe you get along all right with that lion inside."

"He sounds a lot tougher than he is, Konrad," Jupe said. "We'll see what happens next time."

The big Bavarian shook his head dubiously. "You coming back here again? You push your luck too much maybe, Jupe."

Jupe smiled. "I don't think so, Konrad. At least, I hope not. Anyway, we're involved in a mystery and we'll have to keep coming back until it's solved."

Konrad only shook his head again and started the lorry, remaining gloomily silent on the trip home.

The boys resumed their conversation.

"We have one possible suspect anyway," Bob said. "Hank Morton. He has a motive for letting George out—to get even for being fired. I'd suspect Jay Eastland, too, but what could his motive be? I don't see that he gains anything by delaying his movie. Usually they try to get them done on time, don't they, Pete?"

"Sure," Pete replied. "I've heard it from my dad often. Film companies have a limited budget and a tight schedule, as a rule. Especially so when they're working on location, like Mr Eastland is now at Jungle Land. What do you think, Jupe?"

"I'm not certain yet what to think," their stocky leader said slowly. "It could be an act of revenge on Hank Morton's part. Or something to do with Jim Hall's putting up his whole operation as security for his animals' good behaviour while the movie is being shot. He stands to lose an awful lot if anything goes wrong. Too much, if you ask me."

"Anyway, that's not what we came out for," Pete said. "It was because of a nervous lion, remember? Nothing anybody's said so far deals with that. We still don't know what's making George nervous."

"That's true," Jupe admitted. "And for all we know, the lion getting out of the house and then being wounded could have been purely accidental. He could have jumped out of a window, or the wind might have blown a door open. He could have cut his leg any number of ways. His nervousness is something else."

"Maybe what they need there is a good animal psychologist instead of a vet," said Bob.

Konrad interrupted their speculations by announcing their arrival at the salvage yard with a warning blast of his horn.

Jupe looked up surprised. "Thanks, Konrad. You made good time."

"I go back that way again for more pickup stuff tomorrow," Konrad said. "In case you fellows still got business with that lion."

"Swell, Konrad," said Jupe. "I'll let you know if we're going."

The boys jumped out of the cab as Konrad continued to the far end of the junkyard. Jupe started towards Headquarters, then stopped abruptly, an astonished look on his face.

"They're gone!" he cried.

"What's gone?" Pete asked.

"The bars!" Jupe exclaimed. "That whole stack we unloaded from the lorry yesterday morning. All gone! Uncle Titus must have made a fast deal."

Bob scratched his head, puzzled. "Who would

want to buy a lorryload of rusty iron bars?"

Jupe shrugged. "I don't know. But it's the kind of luck my uncle always has."

Bob looked over Jupe's shoulder and groaned. "Uh-oh! Here comes your aunt, Jupe. She's got that look in her eye that means work!"

Jupiter turned to face his aunt. "Were you looking for us, Aunt Mathilda?"

"Indeed I was," his aunt said. "Where were you boys? A customer came and bought up all those iron bars, and there wasn't a soul around to help him load them."

Jupiter explained that Uncle Titus had given them permission to ride with Konrad on his trip to Chatwick. "Wasn't Hans around?" he asked.

"Indeed he wasn't," his aunt replied. "He was off again with your uncle to pick up some more of those bars. Apparently he's found a place that has plenty of them cheap."

Jupe smiled. "All right, Aunt Mathilda. We'll try to be around if that customer returns for more of the same."

"I wouldn't be at all surprised if he did," his aunt said. "So mind you are here tomorrow." As she turned to go, she added over her shoulder, "And by the way, I've fixed up a stack of sandwiches. They're in the office. You and your friends might be hungry."

As the boys started happily off towards the office cabin, Mathilda Jones added, "And when you've finished, Jupiter, you'll have to mind the office. I have to go downtown to do some shopping now. Titus should be back soon."

"All right, Aunt Mathilda," Jupe said.

"Konrad is driving me in the small lorry," Mrs Jones said. "Now mind you don't leave, and don't miss any sales, Jupiter."

"I won't. Don't worry."

Mrs Jones nodded and walked away.

Inside the small office, the boys found piles of sandwiches wrapped in wax paper and several bottles of root beer and orange pop.

"Too bad, Jupe, about having to work to-morrow," Pete said, wolfing down a thick sand-wich. "I was ready to go back to Jungle Land and have Mike show us around."

"We'd have some news then," Bob said, "about what happened to Rock Randall. If George really did it, they're in big trouble."

Jupe looked glum. "We still have a lot of work ahead of us at Jungle Land. We don't know the terrain at all yet. And there are far too many possibilities of what might be going on at night. Mike stated that George became nervous and restless at that time. So we'll have to check that out." He scowled. "Animals tend to become restless before an approaching storm. But Mike didn't mention the weather. Far as I can recall, it's been pretty good the past month. If not that, then who or what could be making the lion nervous? It's still a complete mystery."

"Why did Hank Morton pretend to be Jim Hall and bring us out to where George was?" asked

54

Bob. "If you ask me, that's a mystery, too. What did he have against us?"

"I don't know," answered Jupe. "But notice another curious thing. George was roaring before we got to him. It's possible that Hank Morton did not inflict that wound. No," he concluded, shaking his head, "I'm afraid next time we go back we'll have to keep our eyes and ears open. We have to learn a lot more than we know."

Pete noticed a movement out the window. "Uh-oh, Jupe—I think you have a customer. Somebody just came in. Didn't your aunt tell you not to miss any sales?"

A dark saloon had pulled into the salvage yard. A light-haired man was looking around the neatly arranged junk. He walked quickly around the piles, lifting objects off the top to peer behind and below. Seeming unsatisfied, he wiped dust from his hands and turned to the door of the office.

Jupe was standing there waiting. Bob and Pete were behind him, ready to help.

The customer was thin and broad-shouldered, wearing a business suit and a bow tie. His eyes were a very pale blue and his face had a curious, hatchet-like shape, wide at the cheekbones and tapering abruptly to a narrow, pointed chin. When he spoke, his voice had the toughness of a man used to giving orders.

"I'm looking for some iron bars," he said. He looked at Jupe questioningly. "Is the owner around?"

"No, sir," Jupe replied. "But I work here. I'm

sorry, but we don't have any more iron bars. We just sold the whole stack of them."

"What? When was this—who bought them?"

"Earlier today, I guess. I don't know who purchased them, sir."

"Why not?" the man demanded. "Don't you people keep records of your sales here?"

"Only of money received," Jupiter said. "Whoever bought those iron bars loaded and transported them himself. So we have no record of delivery. In a junkyard business like this, people generally just come in, pick what they want, and take it home with them."

"I see," the man said. He looked around again, disappointed.

"My Uncle Titus, the owner, is out now," Jupe said. "He might be hauling back some more iron bars. If you care to leave your name and address, he could get in touch with you."

"That's a thought," the man said. His eyes kept darting about the junk piled in the yard. "But so far as you know, there's not a single bar available now, big or small. Is that right?"

"Yes, sir," Jupe said. "I'm sorry. Maybe if you told me what you wanted them for, I might be able to find something else here you could use as a substitute."

The man shook his head. "I'm not interested in any substitutes." He suddenly pointed, his voice loud and triumphant. "What's that over there? What are you trying to do, kid—hold out on me?"

Jupe looked in the direction in which the man

was pointing. "Those are animal cages," he said.

"I know they are," the man said nastily. "But they have bars, don't they?"

Jupe shrugged. "Some do and some don't. We have to repair those cages, replace the missing bars, rebuild and repaint the tops and bottoms, you see, and—"

"Never mind all that," the man said impatiently. "I'm just interested in buying the iron bars. As many as I can get. How much?"

He took a thick wallet out and started to leaf through a number of notes.

Jupiter blinked. "You want the bars? Not the cages?"

"That's right, genius. How much?"

Jupe frowned. He remembered his uncle's plans to fix up the cages for the circus. Jupiter never questioned what his uncle wanted, nor his reasons.

"I'm sorry," he said. "Those bars aren't for sale. We need them to complete the cages so they can be sold to the circus."

The man grinned. "Okay," he said. "That's fine. That's just what I want—circus cages. I'll take them as is, and fix them up myself. How much?"

Again he riffled the thick pile of notes impatiently.

"Do you work for a circus?" Jupe asked.

"What's the difference?" the man snapped. "I want circus cages, and you got them. How much kid? C'mon. I'm in a hurry."

Jupe looked speculatively at the cages. There were four of them, all in extremely poor condition.

57

"That would be one thousand dollars," he said sleepily.

The man's fingers tightened on his wallet. "A thousand dollars for that junk? Are you kidding? Take a look at them—they're falling apart!"

Jupe heard Bob and Pete clear their throats nervously behind him. He looked again at the cages, then very deliberately at the man. "That would be one thousand dollars apiece," he said distinctly. "Four thousand dollars for all four."

The hatchet-faced man stared at Jupiter and slowly replaced his wallet in his pocket. "Maybe you shouldn't be left alone to run a business, kid. I can get new cages for that kind of money."

Jupe shrugged. Having been a child actor when he was very young, he appreciated the scene he was playing now. "Perhaps you can, sir. I've no idea what the current market price is for new circus cages. If you should care to drop back when my uncle is here, perhaps he might give you a more satisfactory price."

The visitor shook his head impatiently. "I don't have time for that, kid." He brought a note out of his pocket and offered it. "Here's twenty dollars for the lot. Take it or leave it. My guess is your uncle bought the whole lot for five dollars. That's all junk, kid." He waved the twenty-dollar note under Jupe's nose. "Well, what do you say? Twenty dollars?"

Jupiter sucked in his breath, hesitating. He knew the man was right. The bars as well as the cages were practically worthless. But he had learned to trust his instincts.

"Sorry," he said, turning away. "No deal."

He saw the man's hand dart to his pocket. For a long moment, Jupe held his breath, wondering if he had made a mistake.

9

More Trouble

THE hatchet-faced man's voice was cold and threatening. "All right, kid—have it your way. I'll be back!"

The man quickly got into his car, started his engine, and roared out of the salvage yard.

Jupe slumped, blowing out his cheeks in a long, relieved sigh.

"Good grief!" Bob exclaimed. "What was that all about?"

"A thousand dollars for each of those crummy cages?" Pete asked sarcastically. "I bet that man was right—that your uncle didn't pay more than five dollars for the lot—including the loose bars and pipes that we stacked."

Jupe nodded, feeling deflated. "I know," he said. "Uncle Titus hardly ever pays more than five dollars for anything."

"Then why did you ask so much?" Bob demanded. "That was a tough-looking customer. He wasn't happy when he left."

"I know." Jupe started to explain. "I—I had a hunch something was wrong, that's all. I'm not sure why. I felt he wanted those bars too much. So I just stepped up the price to find out how much they really were worth to him."

"Well, you found out," Pete said. "Twenty dollars. And when your uncle finds out you turned down that much money, I'll bet he blows his top."

Jupe looked up and sighed. "We'll find out soon enough. Here comes Uncle Titus now!"

The large pickup truck rolled into the yard with Hans behind the wheel. As Titus Jones got down from the cab, Jupe noticed that the truck was empty.

"What happened, Uncle Titus?"

His uncle tugged at his long walrus moustache. "Seems as if there's been a run on iron bars lately. Guess I got to the place too late. Every last one of them was gone."

Jupe cleared his throat. "Aunt Mathilda already sold that batch you bought yesterday. And we just had another customer looking for some, too."

"That so?" his uncle asked. He dug out his pipe and lit it. "Well, no mind. We'll get some more in some day."

Jupe moved his feet uneasily. "This customer wanted to buy those last few bars, the ones for the cages. He was willing to buy them with or without the cages."

60

His uncle looked at him. "Buy the bars without the cages? How much did he offer?"

"Twenty dollars," Jupe replied, swallowing hard.

"Twenty dollars?" Titus thought about it. "What did you tell him?"

"I said it wasn't enough. That we didn't want to sell the bars alone. That we were planning to fix up the cages to sell to the circus."

Titus Jones rocked back and forth, blowing smoke. "How much did you ask him for the cages?"

Jupe took another deep breath. "A thousand dollars," he said, waiting for the explosion. The only response was more smoke as Titus Jones puffed silently away. "A thousand dollars apiece," Jupe added slowly. "Four thousand for the lot."

His uncle removed the pipe from his mouth. As Jupe waited for the expected tongue-lashing, a car swung into the yard. It came to a quick, jarring stop near them. A man stepped out.

"That's him," Jupe said.

The hatchet-faced man walked up. "You the owner of this junkyard?" he demanded.

"I am," Mr Jones said.

"My name's Olsen." The visitor jabbed his finger in Jupe's direction. "Fine help you leave when you're away. I tried to buy some of your old junk bars and this kid tried to scalp me."

"That so?" Mr Jones asked in a matter-of-fact voice. "Sorry to hear about it, mister."

The man grinned. "I thought you would be."

He took out his wallet and extracted a twenty-dollar note. "I offered him twenty dollars for those bars over on that pile and he turned me down flat."

Titus Jones inclined his head towards the pile the man indicated. "Aint no bars there, mister. Just some old animal cages."

"I know," Mr Olsen said impatiently. "But I don't need the cages. Just the bars." He extended the money to Titus Jones. "Here you are—twenty dollars. Is it a deal?"

Titus Jones relit his pipe and puffed hard to get it going properly. Jupe waited. The man stirred restlessly.

"Sorry, mister," Titus said at last. "But my nephew here told you the truth. Those bars you're talking about there are for animal cages. When we get 'em fixed up nice and proper, I figure on selling them to the circus for their animals."

Jupe stared at his uncle. Pete and Bob stood open-mouthed.

Mr Olsen scowled. "Okay—animals cages. Do you know what he wanted for the four of them? Four thousand dollars! He asked a thousand dollars apiece!"

"Well," Titus said, "the boy's young, and he did make a mistake quoting the price."

"I thought so," the man said, smiling with satisfaction.

"The price is six thousand dollars," Titus Jones said. "That would come to fifteen hundred dollars apiece."

The visitor stared. Titus Jones put his pipe in his mouth, puffed, and rocked on his heels. Once more Jupe held his breath, waiting for Mr Olsen to explode.

At that moment Hans walked up. "Anything else I can do, boss?" he asked Mr Jones. "I still got time to do some cleaning up."

Mr Olsen looked at the hulking figure of the yard helper. His cold eyes flickered. Then he snarled. "Forget it, mister. I've got better use for my money."

Jupiter watched the saloon roar out of the yard. He felt like hugging his uncle.

A few minutes later, The Three Investigators were crawling through the big pipe leading to Headquarters. As soon as they were inside, Jupe squinted into the See-All periscope, which let him see over the piles of junk outside the trailer.

"All clear," he reported. "Mr Olsen hasn't returned."

"Gosh!" Bob exclaimed. "You could have knocked me over with a feather when your Uncle Titus backed you up."

"Six thousand dollars!" Pete said. "And I thought that *you* were off your rocker!"

Jupiter nodded. "I don't blame you, Second. But Uncle Titus has an affection for the circus that goes far beyond his usual desire to do business and make a reasonable profit."

"What beats me," Bob said, "is why everyone wants to buy bars all of a sudden?"

"You should have asked your Aunt Mathilda who the other buyer was—the one who bought up the whole lot," Pete said to Jupe.

Jupe was about to reply when the telephone rang.

"Hello, Jupiter Jones speaking."

They could all hear the incoming voice through the loudspeaker attachment. "Hi, Jupe. This is Mike Hall. How would you fellows like to come back to our place again tonight?"

"I don't know if we can get away, Mike," Jupe said. "Why—is anything wrong at Jungle Land?"

"Not exactly," Mike said. "I just thought you'd like to see the gorilla. He just arrived."

"Swell," Jupe said. "Is he a big one?"

Mike laughed. "Big enough. Of course, he'll keep, but our big problem is still with George. And I hope you remember that he gets nervous after dark."

"We haven't forgotten, Mike. As a matter of fact, we were discussing that same point—that we don't know yet what goes on there after dark."

"Well, here's your chance to find out," Mike said cheerfully.

"All right, Mike. We'll try to get permission, and then it'll be just the matter of arranging transport."

"Great," Mike said. "I can meet you at the gate. You coming by pickup truck again?"

"I don't think so," Jupe replied. "This time I believe we'll be using the Rolls."

There was a gasp. "You have a Rolls-Royce?"

Mike asked. Then he began to laugh loudly.

"Ask him what's so funny," Bob said.

"I heard that," Mike said. "It's funny because Mr Jay Eastland acts like such a big shot, you know. And that's the car he drives to impress people."

Jupe consulted his watch. "We'll be there about nine, Mike, after dinner. As soon as I call Worthington."

"Worthington? Who's he?"

"Our chauffeur."

There was loud laughter from the other end. "Wow!" Mike managed to say finally. "Okay, see you later."

Jupiter replaced the phone. "I guess I should have explained to Mike we don't actually own the Rolls and Worthington."

"It's better this way," Bob put in. "At least we cheered him up. The way things are going at Jungle Land, he needs a laugh."

Promptly at nine o'clock that evening, the gleaming old Rolls-Royce rolled up to the main gate at Jungle Land.

Jupe peered out of the window. "I thought Mike said he would meet us here."

There was an overhead light illuminating the gate area. Beyond that, Jungle Land was dark. Palm leaves rustled in the night breeze. From the distance came strange chattering sounds.

Pete jumped out and opened the gate. As the Rolls passed through, he closed it again and got back into the car. "I'm glad Worthington is driving us in," he said. "This place is kind of scary at night."

Following Pete's unerring sense of direction, Worthington threaded his way through several junctions and side roads. As he was about to turn up the road leading to the big white house on the hill, Pete touched the dignified chauffeur's shoulder. "Hold it a second, Worthington."

Jupe raised his eyebrows. "What's up, Pete?"

"I thought I heard shouting up ahead—and some other noises."

They waited, concentrating on listening. Soon they all heard sounds in the undergrowth. Then they heard the faraway wail of a siren.

Bob pointed into the dark. "Look! Searchlights!"

As their eyes watched the blue arcs of light sweeping the skies, they became aware of crashing sounds directly ahead of them. They heard the rasp of heavy breathing. In the next instant, a figure broke out of the jungle. The headlights of the Rolls picked him out clearly as he ran across the road.

His eyes were wide and staring. Sweat glistened on the dirt-streaked face under the old Aussie campaign hat. There was no mistaking the man caught for a brief moment in the bright headlights.

"Hank Morton!" Bob exclaimed.

"Running wild through the woods—and looking mighty scared," added Pete. "I wonder what he's been up to now."

66

The panting man plunged into the thick jungle on the other side and disappeared. The crashing sounds of his flight gradually diminished.

They heard angry cries up ahead, and saw the beams of bobbing torches.

"It looks like some kind of trouble," Bob said, peering out.

"Let's see what's going on," Jupe cried.

In a moment the boys were scrambling out and running. A voice called out.

"Jupiter! Bob! Pete!'

Jupe turned, peering uncertainly into the darkness.

A torch signalled. "Over here. It's me—Mike."

He directed them with the torch until they were together. Jupe noticed Mike was breathing hard. Behind him, dim figures were walking slowly through the jungle, swinging torches from side to side, and then up towards the trees. A few men were holding rifles.

Jupe caught his breath as he took in the eerie scene. "What's going on?" he asked. "Did George break out again?"

"It's not George this time," Mike said breathlessly. "It's a lot more trouble than that."

"What happened?" asked Bob. "Some of those men have rifles. Are they looking for Hank Morton?"

"Who?"

"Hank Morton," Pete said. "We just saw him running scared. He broke out of the jungle below the hill and ran across the road."

"So that's it!" Mike Hall said grimly. "I knew it!"

"Knew what, Mike?" Bob demanded. "What's going on here?"

"The gorilla I told you about," Mike began. "He broke out of his cage and escaped!"

"When?" Pete demanded. "You mean there's a wild gorilla running loose here?"

"It happened a little while ago, right after Doc Dawson brought George home this evening."

"A wild gorilla and a lion," Jupiter said thoughtfully. "I don't know much about how those two species get along, Mike. Would a gorilla be that frightened at the presence of a lion that he would break out of his cage?"

Mike shrugged. "Jim knows more about that than I do. But after what you told me, I'm not at all sure he did break out of his cage."

"What do you mean, Mike?" asked Pete.

"I mean somebody could have let him out. Somebody who hated my Uncle Jim bad enough to pull a stunt like that. You said yourselves you saw him running through the woods.

"Unless I'm dead wrong, it was Hank Morton who let him out!" he said bitterly.

10

In the Dark

JUPE shook his head. "Hank Morton could have been running through the woods for any number of reasons. That's not proof that he let your gorilla escape. Perhaps if we could see its cage, we might find some clues."

"Okay, you fellows are the investigators," said Mike. "Maybe you'll discover something." He led them up the hill. "Say, where's that Rolls-Royce you said you were coming in?"

"Down at the foot of the hill," said Bob. "Worthington is used to us. He'll just wait until we show up again."

Mike chuckled and brought the boys to a clearing at the side of the house. Lights blazed in every room, lighting up the nearby area. Mike pointed and The Three Investigators found themselves staring at a large, empty cage.

"The shipment arrived not long after you left this afternoon. There were two cages this time and—"

"Two cages?" Jupe asked.

A snarling, spitting sound behind him made him whirl in fright. Bob and Pete flinched.

"Gosh!" Bob gasped. "What was that?"

Mike directed his flashlight to the far end of the house. "I guess I should have warned you first. Take a look! Isn't that a beauty?"

The boys looked in awe at the sinister creature caged barely twenty feet from them. As they slowly approached, it snarled again.

"It's a black panther," Mike said. "How do you like it?"

Gleaming yellow eyes stared unwinkingly at them from behind thick iron bars. As they took another cautious step forward, the panther hissed. Its mouth opened, showing long, white pointed fangs. Hastily, the boys stepped backward.

Bob gulped. "I like him fine. Just so long as he stays locked up in that cage."

"Wow!" Pete exclaimed. "Look at those muscles! If you ask me, that panther looks a lot tougher than old George."

As if acting in support of Pete's observation, the beast snarled and lunged at the bars with a frightening thud. The boys retreated another step, watching the black animal warily.

"It would be a pretty good fight, at that, Pete—lion against panther," Mike said. "Panthers, this kind, are really leopards. They strike like lightning. They've got terrible raking claws as well as sharp teeth. But don't let George fool you with his dumb, gentle act. He's still a lion—a good-sized one at that—over four hundred pounds—and he's simply too big and powerful for the panther. No panther ever beat a lion yet, that I ever heard of. It would take a tiger to do it."

The boys stared in silence at the animal pacing restlessly in its cage. "I kind of agree with Pete," Bob said finally. "This baby looks real mean and tough. What do you think, Jupe?" He looked around. "Jupe?"

The First Investigator was spotted by the cage the gorilla had escaped from. He motioned them over.

"What's up, Jupe?" asked Bob.

"This cage has been tampered with, fellows," Jupe announced. "While I'm not certain that Hank Morton was responsible for the gorilla getting out, somebody was!"

"How can you tell?" asked Pete.

Jupe pointed dramatically to the side of the cage. "See there? One bar has been removed. The adjoining two are bent. The bars are set approximately six inches apart. I think whoever removed the bar gave the gorilla his chance. He bent the other two far enough apart to slip out. You said he was a big one? How big?"

"He wasn't full size, but big enough," Mike said. "About our size." He shook his head as they appraised each other. "Don't let the size fool you. He's twice as powerful as a grown man."

"Where did he come from?" Jupe asked.

"Rwanda, in Central Africa. We were expecting a young gorilla from there. We've been waiting a long time. Uncle Cal went through all the mountain gorilla terrain—Rwanda, the Congo, and Uganda. He finally wrote to us from Rwanda that he had a gorilla, but he was having trouble getting it out of the country. Gorillas are on the endangered species list—there aren't very many of them left—and only zoos and scientists can get export permits for them. It took Uncle Cal a while to convince the authorities that Jungle Land was a kind of zoo."

"Gee," said Pete. "Wouldn't it have been easier to just get another kind of gorilla?"

"Well, there are lowland gorillas, but there's an embargo on them, too. I'm not even sure which species Uncle Cal finally sent us."

"It was a young male mountain gorilla," said a voice from the darkness. Jim Hall stepped out of the shadows and nodded to the boys.

"Have you found him yet?" Mike asked.

Jim Hall shook his head. His face was tired and dust-stained. "I just heard he's been seen up by the canyon. I wanted to check back here again before heading out."

"What happened with Mr Eastland?" Jupe asked. "Did George really attack Rock Randall?"

Jim Hall laughed harshly. "That was hogwash. It seems Randall got into a fight with somebody and got thrown around on some rocks on the movie set. He was beat up and bloody, and it did look as if George might have mauled him. But a doctor looked him over and said no animal could have made those marks. So we're clear of that mess, and now we have another. I'm glad you're back tonight, boys. You can see for yourselves that Alfred Hitchcock wasn't exaggerating when he told you something's wrong at Jungle Land."

72

There were shouts in the distance, and Jim Hall made an impatient gesture. "Sorry, boys, but I've got to get moving and trap that gorilla before something happens."

"I guess he'd be pretty dangerous to run up against," Pete ventured.

"He might be frightened now by all the racket out there. But if you happen to run into him, don't worry. Just get out of his way."

Bob blinked. "What? Meet a gorilla face to face and not worry? How do you manage that?"

Hall laughed. "I'll tell you something about gorillas. It applies to a lot of wild animals generally. Gorillas almost never behave aggressively. Oh, they bluff a lot, and scream and charge—that's how they frighten away any animal that seems threatening. But mostly gorillas are peaceful animals that mind their own business. They graze in the same area as elephants, for example, and although they eat the same food, there's no problem."

"What happens?" asked Bob.

The tall man shrugged. "Mutual disregard," he said. He glanced at his watch. A horn sounded. "That'll be Doc." He waved and walked away.

A moment later he passed, driving an open jeep. The thin, moustached man sitting next to him was holding a rifle.

Mike smiled. "It figures good old Doc Dawson would be around to help. He's crazy about animals."

Pete turned to look at the jeep carrying the two

73

men off. They looked prepared for action.

"If he likes animals all that much, why is he holding a rifle?"

"That's a stun gun," Mike said. "It shoots a tranquilliser dart—not bullets. Whatever is hit is only knocked out temporarily, Pete—not really hurt."

"Jim Hall and the search party should be able to find the gorilla," said Jupiter. "I suggest we look around now while we have the opportunity. Perhaps we can learn what's behind these animal escapes. First there was George, and now the gorilla."

"Well, George seems okay now," Mike said. "He's in the house sleeping off the tetanus and tranquilliser shots Doc Dawson gave him. Doc cleaned up the wound and George will be able to face the camera tomorrow and earn a day's pay for us."

Jupiter was looking round. "Does George have a cage, too?"

"No, we got rid of George's cage over a month ago," said Mike. "He sleeps in the house with Jim and me. He has his own room but he prefers to share Jim's."

Jupe glanced up at the lighted house. "You said somebody must have let him out before. Couldn't it happen again?"

Mike put his hand in his pocket and produced a key. "This time the house is locked. Only Jim and I have keys."

Jupe pondered. "You've told us, Mike, that

George becomes nervous and restless at night. I suggest we walk round to see if we can't uncover some reason for his nervousness. We should explore the area closest to the house to begin with."

"Swell," Mike said. "As you can see, the house is set in a clearing on this knoll. Over there's a shed for tools and firewood. It could be a garage but Jim parks outside here. The road at the foot of the drive leads north and runs into other roads."

He led the boys around the area. The night was quiet after the earlier excitement. The moon was now up, and the sky was cloudless.

Jupe nodded as if satisfied when they completed their circuit of the house. They returned to the cage area. The gorilla cage remained empty. The panther in the other lay quietly, switching its long tail and watching them balefully.

The Three Investigators followed Mike down the hill into the jungle. "I'll explain Jungle Land as we go along. Then the next time you come, you'll know your way around here without me."

"How big is Jungle Land?" asked Bob. "It seems with so much land to cover, you'd never know what's going on."

"It's about a hundred acres, and diamond-shaped. That's a lot maybe, but we've never had any trouble keeping track of things before."

"Where is the Jay Eastland movie being shot?" Pete asked.

"North of here, about a five-minute ride," Mike

said. "We're heading due east now, towards our closest border fence."

The trail descended steeply through brush, rocks and fissures. Faint patches of moonlight showed between trees.

"Where's the canyon your uncle said the gorilla was seen at?" asked Bob. "He seemed to be heading north, too."

"He was, but he'll cut left on another road. The canyon is north-west, about fifteen minutes away. Just below it, we have several acres that look like the African veldt, grassy and flat. We have the elephants there, contained by a moat, so they can't get out. But you can hear them trumpeting." He grinned. "I like that sound."

"I like it better myself now," said Pete, "knowing they can't get out."

Mike continued to describe Jungle Land as they went on downhill. "At the far west end opposite us is the built-up tourist section. Our main attraction used to be the jungle and animals, but a lot of folks seem to prefer the Wild West. So we have a frontier town, a mock graveyard, a ghost town, and a stagecoach ride for the kids. We keep the horses pretty near that area.

"In the southern part is the entrance where you come in, and lots of jungle. In the central part is the lake and then above that, where Eastland is, more jungle. At the northern end are mountains, with one high precipice. It's been used for a lot of movies where the hero has to dive off a cliff. Doc Dawson has his dispensary up that way."

There was an outburst of chattering cries and hoots. The boys stopped and looked at their guide.

"Those are monkeys and owls," Mike explained. "We've also got a snakehouse in the north-east section but the snakes don't make any noise. We keep them farthest away because they're the hardest to find in case they ever get away. We've a good collection of sidewinders—they're rattle-snakes—and a water moccasin and a good-sized king snake."

Jupe was peering intently back through the trees. "How far are we from your house now, Mike?"

"About five hundred yards. There's a fence down the end of this slope here—"

"Wait!" Pete whispered. "What's that?"

They all heard it then. A slow, dull, crunching sound echoing with a measured beat. The Three Investigators looked at each other. The crunching sound became louder, seeming to come closer. Prickly chills ran down their spines. Then they heard a new sound. It started as a low whine and began to rise on a shrill, insistent note.

"I don't like that," Pete said hoarsely. "Maybe we ought to be getting back—"

Jupiter's eyes were wide with fear, too, but they were also puzzled. "That sound—" he started to say. "It—it's—"

As he groped for words, the shrill, whining noise ascended to a full-noted shriek. The screeching seemed to be all around, engulfing them.

EEEE—ooo—EEEEE! EEE—ooo—EEEEE!

77

Bob yelled, "I'm getting out of here!"

With one mind, The Three Investigators wheeled and ran.

"Wait!" Mike called.

They turned to stare in utter amazement.

Mike Hall was laughing.

"It's nothing to worry about," he called. "That's only the *metal shredder!*"

II

Steps into Terror

THE shrill, wailing sound slowly fell until it became a low, whistling note.

"Metal shredder?" Jupiter repeated dumbly.

Mike was pointing ahead through some trees. "Yes, Jupe. Over the fence, the other side of our property. There's a salvage yard—steel and scrap iron. It's full of scrapped cars and other junk."

"What does the metal shredder do—besides scare people?" Bob asked.

"It's a new recycling process to salvage precious metal," Mike said. "Part of the new ecology drive. The cars used to be just pounded down and sold as scrap iron and steel. But now they have this new device—some kind of claw with a computer-selector-processing operation. It shreds the cars into little bits. The metal is separated from the other material, and then the more precious metals, like copper, are separated from the iron and steel."

"Whew!" Pete exclaimed weakly. "Is that all? It sounded like all the gorillas in town were holding a convention!"

Jupe was plucking at his lower lip. He glanced at his wristwatch.

"It is now nine thirty," he stated. "Does George usually become nervous and restless about this time, Mike?"

Mike shrugged. "Sometimes sooner or later. I don't know exactly what time—except that it's always after it gets dark."

"Always at night? Never during the day?"

"Never," Mike said firmly. "But I'm not counting this afternoon. George wasn't nervous then—just acting mean. I'd say because he was hurt."

"What's your idea, Jupe?" Bob asked. "That the sound of the metal shredder made George nervous?"

"Animals are more sensitive to sounds than humans," Jupe said. "Perhaps George is reacting to that high whine of the metal shredder."

"But he'd hear it all the time then," Pete put in. "Not just at night."

"A good point. Second," said Jupe, "does this metal-shredding process operate during the day, too, Mike?"

"Sometimes," Mike said. "Off and on again. I

don't pay much attention to the sound any more. It isn't nearly as loud up by our house."

"Hmmm," Jupe said. "How long has that machine been in operation?"

"It's kind of new, Jupe. The scrap yard has been here a long time, a number of years. And the wrecking part of it, also. But offhand my guess is they haven't been using this metal shredder more than a month."

"A month," Jupe repeated. "And how long has George been acting nervous and restless?"

"Since about two or three months ago," Mike said. "I remember it started just before the rainy season when Jim decided to bring George inside the house for good."

Jupiter scowled, puzzled.

"Don't forget, he didn't act up every night," Mike added. "He was restless at times, then seemed to be all right. But the last week or so, he's been getting much worse, and it's been regular since."

"So he was nervous before the metal shredder came in," Bob said.

Jupe looked thoughtful. "It would seem that George isn't used to being cooped up indoors at night. That might account for his actions. The metal shredder could be a factor, or perhaps not. There could be different reasons."

"Maybe it's working in the movie that's making him nervous," Pete suggested, grinning. "A lot of actors get nervous at night trying to memorise their lines for the next day's shooting."

Jupiter snapped his fingers. "A humorous

suggestion but nevertheless a possibility, Pete."
He turned to Mike. "How long have Jay Eastland
and his crew been working at Jungle Land?"

"They've been around here about two months,"
Mike said. "But a lot of that time was spent
checking the locations, getting the setups planned
for the shooting scenes, the right backgrounds,
and so forth. They didn't move in completely and
start shooting until two weeks ago."

"Do they shoot at night, too?" Jupe asked.

"Sometimes."

Jupe frowned. "You said their set is about five
minutes away from your house. Would their
mikes pick up the sound of the metal shredder?"

"It's possible," Mike admitted. "I don't know.
Mr Eastland hasn't complained."

"He might not have to do his sound work at
Jungle Land," said Pete, drawing on information
he'd picked up from his father. "Sometimes the
sound is dubbed in later—even the actors' voices."

Jupe nodded. "What about the actors and work
crew? Do they live here, too?"

"Most of them go home at night," Mike said.
"The motorway is near here and most of them
don't live too far away—Westwood, Hollywood,
West Los Angeles—it's only a half-hour ride."

"What about Mr Eastland?" Jupe asked. "Does
he stay here?"

"He can. He has his own trailer out there, and
one apiece for the two stars, Rock Randall and Sue
Stone. Uncle Jim rented them all of Jungle Land
so they can stay if they want to. The gate is open

and they come and go as they please. I don't check and neither does Jim."

"But they could be here," Jupe said stubbornly. "They could be snooping around your house at night and making George nervous."

"Why would they be doing that, Jupe?" asked Bob.

"I can't think of any sensible reason, Bob," he said. "All I say is the possibility exists."

"Let's get on with the tour, fellows," said Mike. "Come on down to the fence and then we'll circle around to the other side of the house."

As the boys approached the fence, the strange sounds from the scrap yard began again. The rhythmical crunching, grinding noises ebbed and then the wailing sound started. This time the boys were expecting the almost human shriek of the mechanism and remained calm.

"Happy metal shredding!" Bob said, holding his ears. "I'm surprised *all* your animals aren't nervous wrecks!"

Jupe looked at the fence gleaming in the moonlight. Metal stakes were pegged into the ground several yards apart, supporting a netting of wire links.

"Does this fence run all the way along your property line, Mike?" he asked.

"Yes," Mike said. "It continues north past the salvage yard. Then there's a big drainage ditch behind it which runs parallel the rest of the way. The fence is six feet high all the way, like it is here, and is strong enough to keep practically all our animals from escaping if they should happen to get loose."

The boys continued north along the fence and then began to cut back up the hill through trees and tall grass. Suddenly Pete stopped.

"What's up, Pete?" Bob said.

The tall boy pointed unsteadily ahead.

"Did you hear that?" Pete whispered.

The sounds from the salvage yard had ceased for the moment, and the boys all stood still, listening hard.

"Where, Pete?" asked Jupe. "What is it?"

Pete pointed again. "There."

They heard a rustling sound in the tall grass and then heavy breathing.

"*There!*" Pete whispered hoarsely again.

The others followed the line of his keen sight. As they stared into the jungle darkness, they saw a shadowy movement.

They froze, scarcely daring to breathe.

Something moved from behind a tree.

It came forward, moving in a peculiar way. Then they saw the dark head, swaying between hunched, shaggy shoulders.

Jim Hall had told them they would be in no particular danger. Somehow they could not believe it as the panting gorilla came closer!

12

Noises in the Night

JUPITER recovered his senses first.

"Run!" the stocky leader of The Three Investigators shouted. "Ramble and scramble!"

The three turned and ran. Mike hesitated, torn between flight and duty. He stared a moment longer at the oncoming gorilla. Red-rimmed eyes glowered at him from beneath the shaggy, beetling brows.

Jupe, glancing back, saw the situation. "Run, Mike! He might be dangerous now!"

The creature raised its long arms and bared yellow teeth. Mike, with a sharp intake of breath, wavered, then broke and ran to join the others.

The gorilla pounded its chest, veered, and disappeared into the high grass.

"Where'd he go?" Bob called.

"He's in the grass. I think we scared him off," cried Mike. "Come on—I think we'd better head for the house."

Warily they circled the area, their hearts pounding. They were nearly at the crest of the incline when suddenly the grass parted in front of them. Too late, they saw the shaggy creature step out.

The boys stood frozen with fear. The hulking creature raised its heavy arms and opened its mouth. A strange sound issued from its throat.

"Hit the ground!" a voice called sharply.

As the boys dived to the side, they heard a dull, thudding sound. They looked up to see Jim Hall and the vet with his stun gun raised.

The gorilla swayed, a puzzled look on its dark face. Then it moaned and toppled heavily to the ground.

"You boys all right?" Hall asked. They nodded dumbly, still shaken. "Nice shooting, Doc," he said.

The vet nodded without changing expression. He walked up quickly and stood over the fallen gorilla as it feebly moved its limbs.

"He's not hurt," he told the boys as they crowded round. "It just takes a few seconds for the tranquillising drug to take effect. Then he'll have a nice long sleep and we'll be able to get him back to his cage."

"Looks like we circled back in time," Jim Hall said, frowning. "Somebody sent us off on a wild goose chase to the canyon for nothing. He could have been hiding in the trees here all the time."

"Who told you the gorilla was in the canyon?" Jupe asked.

"Jay Eastland," Hall said tersely.

Doc Dawson leaned over the inert simian. "He's out already, Jim. Give me a hand and we can lug him to the car."

Hall stooped and deftly roped the gorilla. He

and Doc dragged the unconscious animal off. The boys followed as the two men hoisted it into the rear of the open jeep.

"Where are you taking him now, Mr Hall?" Jupe asked.

"Back to his cage. Let's hope he stays put this time."

"Uncle Jim," Mike put in, "Jupe noticed that one of the cage bars was missing. The ones next to it were bent, so that's how he got out."

Hall glanced keenly at Jupiter. "That's how it happened, all right. Sure looks like somebody is trying to sabotage us, doesn't it?"

"It would appear so, sir. But now I'm wondering how you can put the gorilla back into that cage and expect him to stay there."

"That's easy," Hall said. "There's a man at work now replacing the missing bar and straightening the bent ones."

The jeep nosed out along the trail and Jupiter and the others followed at a dogtrot. Workmen were busy at the gorilla's cage when they arrived at the house.

A large man with close-cropped hair turned to face them. His arms were thick and muscular, one of them heavily tattooed. He held a long hammer in one hamlike hand.

"She's all set now," he said to Jim Hall. He glanced at Doc Dawson. "Got him already? That was fast work, Doc."

Jim Hall strode forward to the cage and the burly helper stepped aside. Hall put his weight against the cage bars, gripping them tightly and jerking his body from side to side.

"Okay. That ought to hold him, Bo. Thanks." He turned to the jeep. "Better give us a hand here with Kong."

"Sure thing," the man said, tossing down his hammer.

"Hold it a second!" Doc Dawson said. "I want to check out that cage myself. I've got enough to do without running around day and night looking for lost animals."

The helper shrugged and grinned. "Sure, Doc. You want us to lock you up inside and then see if you can get out?"

"Very funny, Jenkins," Dawson snapped.

He came forward and picked up the heavy hammer. He slowly tapped each bar on the empty cage. He bent forward attentively as if he were listening for a flaw in the metal. Then he grabbed the bars in his strong, weatherbeaten hands, tugging and twisting, applying pressure from all sides.

"Satisfied?" Bo Jenkins asked.

"Seems okay," Doc Dawson growled. "Those bars stand up to me all right, but then I don't have the strength of a gorilla." He looked at Bo Jenkins coldly. "Reckon you don't either, Bo. But if you're taking Hank Morton's place here, you can't afford to make any mistakes!"

Jim Hall turned to Doc Dawson. "Bo is working out fine, Doc. You're the one who told me he could take Hank Morton's place and do a good job, and I'm satisfied so far. Why needle him?"

"Just want him to be on his toes, that's all," Dawson said gruffly. "We don't want any more accidents around here." He stepped back to look at the empty gorilla cage again, and shook his head. "Darned if I can figure out how that bar got removed. I'd better check the panther's cage too."

Carrying the hammer, he walked abruptly to the cage opposite. The black cat leaped to its feet, hissing and snarling. The vet walked around the cage striking each of the bars in turn.

"He appears to be checking for a metal fault," Jupe said to his friends. "I've heard of something called metal fatigue. Airplane parts are checked for that periodically."

"With a hammer?" Bob asked.

Jupe shrugged. "Maybe Doc Dawson has his own method of detection. After all, he spends a lot of time with caged animals."

After several ringing blows, Doc Dawson stepped back and nodded as if satisfied. "Okay, Jim," he said. "Far as I can tell, the bars check out with equal resistance. No cracks or fissures, and they're all securely in place. I guess you can put the gorilla back in now."

Jim Hall signalled the work crew, who lifted the still-slumbering gorilla into its cage. Hall slipped the ropes off, swung the cage door shut, and padlocked it.

Doc Dawson stepped into his jeep. "Looks like you're all set now, Jim. I've got a sick horse to look after at the corral. If you need me again, just holler."

"Let's hope I don't, for a while, Doc. Thanks again for your help."

"Put it on the bill!" Dawson yelled. He waved and drove off.

Bob nudged Jupiter. "More fun coming," he whispered. "Here comes Jay Eastland."

The long station wagon roared up and the fat, bald-headed producer jumped out. Hall's lips tightened.

Eastland strode up quickly and peered into the gorilla cage. "So you got him finally, eh? Sure took you long enough, Hall. You had my crew scared out of their wits!"

"Yes, we got him," Jim Hall said slowly. "We might have caught up with him sooner, but somebody gave us a wrong tip. It turned out he wasn't in the canyon area at all but right around here, down by the fence."

The producer shrugged. "So what? I heard he was seen near the canyon and passed the word on to you." His voice rose. "How do you expect me to shoot a movie if you can't keep your wild animals under lock and key? My actors are worried sick that any moment they're going to be attacked by another one you let get away!"

"I'm sorry, Eastland," Hall said quietly. "We've had a few accidents, but nothing serious has happened. Everything's fine now and under control. You can tell your actors not to worry. Go on back and shoot your movie and leave us alone. You're only getting my animals stirred up and excited."

Eastland's face turned a mottled red. He backed up a few steps and shook his fist. "Don't tell me what to do, Hall. I've rented this place and—"

Suddenly there was an ear-splitting snarl from behind him. Eastland turned in alarm. The black panther leaped forward, and Eastland screamed in terror as the big cat crashed against its cage bars and fell back snarling.

The producer looked ill. His face was white and his eyes rolled. Then he noticed Jupiter and his friends watching.

"What are these kids doing here?" he barked. "What are you running—a sideshow?"

"They're here at my invitation, Eastland," said Jim Hall. "They've a job to do for me here. Now, is anything else bothering you?"

Eastland glowered. His chest rose and fell quickly. "Just make sure your animals don't get loose again, or you'll be sorry!"

Head down, he stamped away.

As the station wagon roared off, Jupe looked after it, puzzled. "That man certainly doesn't act like a movie producer, Pete. He acts—well—very unstable!"

Pete smiled. "He's what they call a 'quickie' producer in the trade, Jupe. They're hustlers, only interested in grinding out something fast and getting their money back even faster. If you ask me, Mr Eastland has money problems. So what he does is holler and bully and bluster."

"Speaking of noise," said Jupe, "we haven't heard the metal shredder for a while. Let's go back to the fence. I want to have another look round down there before we leave."

"I'd go with you, Jupe, but I've a lot of chores to do around here yet," Mike said. "I'll have to say good night."

Jupe glanced at his watch. "We'll have a quick look. And we'll try to come back tomorrow to continue our investigation."

With that, the stocky boy headed away from the house into the darkness. Pete and Bob shrugged and slowly followed.

"Here goes," Bob said. "We're off to test the sound barrier again. Remind me next time to bring along earmuffs."

"Remind me next time to stay home," Pete said. "I've had enough excitement tonight with that gorilla chasing us."

They walked down the slope and soon caught up with Jupiter. He was crouching behind a tree near the bottom.

"What—" began Pete, stopping when Jupe held up his hand.

Putting his finger to his lips, Jupe motioned them towards him. Quietly they stooped and scuttled over.

The metal shredder was quiet, but something else wasn't. They heard a dull thud, then a clanking noise. Then a crackling sound.

"In the salvage yard," Jupe whispered. "There's a man there. Tell me if he looks familiar."

Pete and Bob peered intently through the fence into the moonlit yard. Suddenly there was a flare as a man struck a match and held it to a cigarette. His sharp features were clearly seen.

"Hatchet-Face!" Pete whispered. "The man who came to the junkyard!"

"That's him, all right," Bob whispered. "He said his name was Olsen, didn't he? What's he doing here?"

"Listen," Jupe said.

They heard a crackling, sputtering sound.

The hatchet-faced man hunched over. Something dark glittered in his hand. His lips moved.

Again there was the sputtering sound.

"Walkie-talkie," Jupe said. "Hatchet-face is transmitting!"

13

Pursued!

"COME on," said Jupiter, "I want to hear this."

He pointed diagonally ahead to a clump of eucalyptus trees right by the fence. Their low-hanging branches would give good cover if the boys could get under them unobserved. Cautiously Jupiter wriggled forward, practically on his stomach. Pete and Bob slithered after him. Soon they were safely under the trees, enveloped by darkness and the oily, medicinal smell of the eucalyptus leaves. The boys peered out and found themselves staring at Olsen barely twenty feet away.

A metallic sputter came from Olsen's walkie-talkie. He bent to speak into it, and this time the boys could hear him clearly.

"Come on over this way," Hatchet-Face ordered.

His walkie-talkie crackled. "Okay," came the answer.

A dark figure was making his way slowly across the huge, disorderly pile of scrap. He held a walkie-talkie, too, with its long antenna extended.

The hatchet-faced man spoke. "Any luck yet, Dobbsie?"

The other shook his head as he slowly advanced, peering closely at the scrap metal under his feet. "Not a thing," he said, his voice filtering through Olsen's walkie-talkie.

"Stay with it," Hatchet-Face said. "It could be buried."

Olsen stooped and tossed an old mudguard aside. It fell with a dull clank. He repeated the action with a bumper and a radiator grill, scrutinised the area closely, and shook his head.

The other man drew closer, also lifting and discarding objects in his path. At last he came close enough to join Olsen. He was dressed like Olsen, in a dark business suit.

Both men pushed down their walkie-talkie antennas. "It's like looking for a needle in a haystack," the other man complained wearily.

"I know," Hatchet-Face said. "But we can't take the risk of losing it now. It's too big a haul to let get away."

"What about the other place?"

"The junkyard? Probably clean, but we'll have to keep an eye on it. The fat kid may be wise to something. We'll get back to him later."

Jupe and his companions exchanged glances. He was the only fat kid they knew of connected with a junkyard. Jupe swallowed. He didn't like being called fat. And he liked even less the threat in Olsen's last words.

The other grinned. His face was square and pale, centred by a flat, mashed nose under little beady eyes. "What about the two new ones Hall just got in? Shouldn't we go for those?"

Olsen shook his head. He reached into his pocket for a scrap of paper and looked closely at it. "Not yet. It would be too risky and our birds might fly away." He tapped the paper. "The information we got from Dora's alarm spells it out for us. DOX ROX NOX EX REX BOX. Six X's. It could be the cable code or else they're talking about six hundred K's. That's about half a million dollars, Dobbsie—not bad, at all. That's a lot of rocks."

The beady-eyed man shrugged. "Sure it is, and we might blow the whole deal by waiting. Why don't we just move in on him?"

Hatchet-Face replaced the paper in his pocket. "We wait," he said firmly. "He'll give us an opening. Somebody got careless tonight. If we can find the rocks first, we'll wrap them both up."

"Okay. You're running the show."

"You bet. I'm going up now to find out if Eastland has his finger in this. He's desperate for money and maybe he let the gorilla out for his own reasons. Remember, he'd have Hall on the hook for fifty grand if anything were to happen."

The other grinned and smacked his fists together. "I'd like a crack at Eastland. He ran me off the set."

Hatchet-Face laughed. "He won't bother me. Okay, Dobbsie, we check tomorrow same time."

Olsen waved abruptly and turned away. The other moved off in the opposite direction, across the salvage yard.

Pete nudged Jupe and pointed along the wire fence. The section towards which Olsen was heading had been tampered with. Where earlier it had been erect, it now sagged nearly to the ground.

As they watched, the hatchet-faced man carefully stepped over the lowered wire. He found a metal post and pulled it up straight, raising the wire along with it. That done, he wheeled, dusted his hands, and headed up the slope in the direction of the Hall house. Darkness covered him as he moved into the jungle. His footsteps could be heard for a while longer, and then they faded into silence.

The Three Investigators waited and then slowly got to their feet. The salvage yard was quiet, as if closed down for the night. The beady-eyed man had disappeared from view, too. The boys started back up the hill.

Pete suddenly hissed a warning and they froze.

They heard a stealthy movement in the grass and, as their pulses quickened, the sound of soft footsteps. Peering into the darkness of the jungle, they backed off uncertainly.

A thick, shadowy shape detached itself from a tree and stepped towards them. With hearts leaping, the boys turned and ran. A hidden root caught Jupe's foot and he fell heavily to the ground. His hand struck something hard and cold. He heard a growl behind him and grasped the hard object as he jumped to his feet. It was a length of metal pipe.

Pete grabbed Jupiter's arm and started to pull him along. There was an angry bellow from the darkness, and they were suddenly caught in the gleam of a torch.

Heavy footsteps crashed through the undergrowth. Still holding on to his weapon, Jupe fled, propelled by Pete. Bob was just ahead of them, his feet flying across the slope. He lost his footing and as he fell, Jupe and Pete charged into him, carrying him up and along.

The torch beam stabbed at them again, and they heard a harsh voice yelling for them to stop. Instead, they ran faster.

Panting noisily, following Pete's unerring sense of direction, the boys cut across the hillside. They burst out of the jungle on to the road to the Hall house. Just ahead was the gleaming Rolls-

Royce. As they ran for it, its headlights flicked on.

Jupiter flung the door open and threw himself inside.

"Quick! Step on it, Worthington!"

Bob and Pete tumbled in beside him as the tall chauffeur calmly answered, "Very good, Master Jones." The motor was already purring smoothly, and deftly he wheeled the big car round.

As they headed back for the exit gate, a man broke out of the jungle and leaped for the car. Worthington swerved instantly, and they had a brief glance at the contorted face of the man. He raised his fist and ran after them.

"Wow!" breathed Pete. "That's Bo Jenkins, the new animal helper."

Looking back through the glass, they saw Jenkins stop and shake his huge fist in a threatening gesture. It carried so much menace that they instinctively slumped low in the back seat of the car, although they were already safely away from their pursuer.

Pete jumped out as Worthington slowed down at the gate. He opened it, and after the car glided through, swung it closed again. Then Pete leaped back in and sat back, slowly shaking his head.

"What was that all about?" he asked.

Jupe had no reply. He could only scowl, puzzled as he gripped the weapon he had not used.

Pete, Bob, and Jupiter stood by the gates to The Jones Salvage Yard. Worthington had brought them back safely and had been thanked and dismissed.

"It's late," Jupiter said, "but I suggest we have a quick meeting. We have to put down what happened this evening between that man Olsen and the other, Dobbsie. It might contain clues we will need for solving this mystery."

He led the way swiftly into Headquarters, tossing the metal bar he had found at Jungle Land on to his work-bench before stooping to enter Tunnel Two. Inside, the boys clustered around the office desk, and Bob drew out his notebook.

"I take it we can skip the last part with that big guy Jenkins chasing us," said Bob. "There wasn't any mystery about that—he was just plain mad."

"We'll omit Bo Jenkins for the time being," Jupe agreed. "I imagine he was merely patrolling the property. Perhaps he was within his rights to chase off trespassers who might disturb the animals."

"I don't know about that," Pete protested. "We weren't exactly strangers there. He saw us earlier at the cage when Mr Hall and Doc Dawson brought the escaped gorilla back. He could have acted a lot nicer about it, if you want my opinion."

"True," Jupe said, "but it was dark. Perhaps he didn't see us clearly, and thought we were just some kids who had broken in. I'm inclined to give Bo Jenkins the benefit of the doubt. I suggest we ignore him and get to the discussion between Mr Olsen and Mr Dobbsie."

While Bob scribbled furiously, the boys reconstructed the conversation they had overheard and discussed what it might mean.

"What could be right under their feet?" asked Bob.

"It must be small," Pete said. "Because he also said it was like looking for a needle in a haystack."

"Not necessarily small," Jupe said. "It would be difficult to find something that looked like all the other junk in that heap."

"Like what?" asked Bob.

"I don't know," Jupe said. "But we have clues. Read back that part about rocks and X's, Bob."

"Okay," Bob said. "It went something like this: 'The information from Dora's alarm tells us. DOX ROX NOX EX REX BOX.' I assume all those words end in X because of the next bit. 'Six X's. Could be the code or six hundred K's. That's half a million dollars, Dobbsie. That's a lot of rocks.' "

"More or less correct, I believe," said Jupe. "Olsen also used the word 'cable'. We don't know who Dora is or what her alarm is, but Dora's message sounds like a cable. It's typical of what is called cablese—all the words are short and only important words are included. And, like many cables, this one seems to be in code. As a rule, parties who want to keep their business transactions secret establish a private code or cipher. Usually there's a key letter or word that lets them decipher each other's messages easily."

"Well, we don't have the key to the code," said Pete.

"I don't think we need one," said Jupe. "All those words probably end in X, as Bob said. But

99

most of those words translate easily into plain English. The message can be read DOCKS ROCKS KNOCKS EX WRECKS BOX." He printed the decoded message for them on Bob's pad.

"Great," said Pete. "What's that supposed to mean?"

"I'm not sure," said Jupe, "but I'm getting an idea." He straightened up excitedly. "I think ROCKS is the important word. Olsen said something was half a million dollars, and then he said that was a lot of rocks. Does that suggest anything to you?"

"Half a million dollars worth of rocks?" asked Pete. "Rocks out of the ground? How's that possible? I mean, who'd want it?"

" 'Rocks' has another meaning, Pete," Jupe said. "It's also slang for 'money'. Olsen and Dobbsie are looking for money! Half a million dollars! My guess is that Olsen and Dobbsie are involved in some crooked scheme. They sound like gangsters, and that much money sounds like somebody's loot!"

"That's quite a guess," said Bob dubiously. "But even if that's true, what's the rest of the message supposed to mean?"

Jupe frowned. "I don't know, Bob. Apparently it tells where to find the money. Maybe the rest of the conversation will give us some clues."

"What about that part about wrapping them both up?" Pete asked. "Who's he talking about?"

Bob read from his notes. " 'If we can find the rocks first, we'll wrap them both up.' "

Jupe shook his head. "They spoke about one man first. They said, 'Why don't we move in on him?' Then later Hatchet-Face said, 'He'll give us an opening. Somebody got careless tonight.'"

"Who?" asked Pete.

Bob looked over his notes. "If being careless refers to letting the gorilla out, they think Eastland might have done it."

Jupe scowled. "I don't see why he would take such a risk. It's true that according to the agreement Jim Hall would have to pay Eastland fifty thousand dollars as forfeit for an accident. But I don't think Eastland would be foolish enough to take such a chance. That gorilla was dangerous! I'd sooner believe that Hank Morton was being spiteful again."

"Fine, but that has nothing to do with rocks," said Bob. "We're not getting anywhere."

Jupe tapped his fingers on the desk and thought awhile. "We're forgetting the first thing we ever learned about Olsen," he said finally. "He came here to the junkyard and wanted to buy cages. Then tonight he seemed to refer to me and the cages." Jupe winced as he remembered Olsen's calling him "the fat kid".

"Maybe he thinks he'll find his rocks in cages," said Pete sarcastically.

"Don't laugh," said Jupe. "Look! BOX in the cable might mean cage! WRECKS BOX means pull apart the cage and you'll find the money!"

"Your cages are already wrecked," objected Pete, "and Olsen didn't seem to think they were very valuable. He only offered you twenty dollars."

"True, true," said Jupe. "I can't explain that. But perhaps Olsen's really looking for another cage."

"Sure. In the scrap yard. Blending right in with the cars," said Pete. "I think we're all tired and just going round in circles."

Jupe stood up and stretched. "You're probably right, Pete. I suggest we quit for tonight. We haven't come to any definite conclusions—but at least we're sure of one thing."

"What's that?" asked Bob.

"We've got a mystery to solve," said Jupe with satisfaction.

14

Bob Makes a Discovery

THE next morning Bob came downstairs to breakfast more puzzled than ever. So much had happened the day before, and so little of it made any sense. He wondered if Jupiter wasn't grasping at straws in deducing the meaning of that crazy code.

Bob said good morning to his father, who grunted a reply from behind the morning newspaper. He was still on his first cup of coffee and obviously wasn't ready to talk to anyone yet. Bob looked around for something to read himself. He had read all the cereal boxes, so he turned to the stack of out-of-town newspapers lying on a nearby bookcase. His father, a newspaperman, frequently brought home papers from other parts of the country. He had explained to Bob that no one newspaper could carry all the news, and that he liked to see what stories other papers considered newsworthy.

Bob leafed idly through a paper, reading the comics and checking the headlines. He picked up another, and an article caught his eye. It was a UPI dispatch from Koster, South Africa. It read:

79-YEAR-OLD OPENS
AFRICA DIAMOND RUSH

With a whoop belying his 79 years, Pieter Bester leaped into the air, snatched his claim certificate, and took off running.

While 3,000 spectators cheered, he opened what could be the last official South African diamond rush, as 165 prospectors were turned loose Wednesday on the Swartrand alluvial diamond field.

Veteran prospector Hendrik Swanpoek, 72, who discovered the diamond field, had his usual luck. While staking out the first of his claims on the site, he unearthed a 48.12-carat diamond which he sold later for $42,000.

"I don't want to discourage anybody," Swanpoel said with a grin, "but I've already got most of the good stuff."

The article went on to give details of the government-sponsored diamond rush. The region was 75 miles northwest of Johannesburg, once known as the "Land of the Diamonds". In the uproarious boom days of 1927 and 1928, the article continued, 150,000 diggers scooped $28 million worth of high-quality gems from the Grasfontein and Bakerville diggings 50 miles west. The rules were, hopeful prospectors had their names put into a hat, and only the lucky ones whose names were drawn were permitted to the starting line. Each one was allowed three 45-square-yard claims. Veterans of earlier rushes hired local athletes for the sprint, or after careful coaching, had their sons run for them.

"Gosh!" breathed Bob. "Forty-two thousand dollars for one diamond! That's a lot of money!"

He turned the page and another news item caught his eye.

MAN INDICTED IN GEM CASE

Porto Ferraro, a former assistant to the Minister of Mines in Koster, South Africa, was indicted by a federal grand jury Tuesday on charges of smuggling diamonds into the United States last year. He was arrested at Los Angeles International Airport.

Customs agents found on his person five packages of cut and polished diamonds weighing a total of 659.14 carats, with a retail value of about $750,000. The two-count indictment charges Ferraro with smuggling and with failing to pay duty. Each count carries a possible sentence of two years in jail and a fine of $5,000.

"Wow!" said Bob. He'd never known diamonds were worth that much money.

"What's that?" said his father, putting down his newspaper and taking a sip of coffee.

"I was just reading about diamonds," explained Bob. "It says here that a 48-carat diamond sold for $42,000. That's a lot of money! What is a carat, anyway?"

"Well, it's a unit of weight used for gem stones. It's divided into 100 points, just the way a dollar is divided into 100 cents. A one-point diamond is very small. A 100-point, or one carat, diamond is a pretty good size."

"How big would that 48-carat diamond be, then?"

"Very large, for a diamond. Let's see, there was a famous Indian diamond called The Sancy. It was about the size and shape of a peach stone and weighed 55 carats. Your 48-carat diamond would be slightly smaller."

"How much would that weigh in pounds and ounces?"

"Here"—Mr Andrews pulled a reference book

out of the bookcase and handed it to Bob—"look up the table of weights and measures in this and see if you can figure it out."

Bob read that a carat was equal to 3.17 grains troy or 0.2 of a gram. A gram, the basic unit of weight in the metric system, equalled one twenty-eighth of an ounce. He scribbled some figures in his notebook and looked up in astonishment. "Forty-eight carats are only about one-third of an ounce."

His father nodded. "Yes, a carat is a very small unit of weight. You need a system with units that small when you're measuring such valuable things."

"Okay, how much is a carat worth?"

"No fixed amount. But for a diamond, you can figure roughly about a thousand dollars to a carat, depending upon the quality and brilliance of the stone. That 48-carat diamond sold for $42,000, you said. The gem was therefore not quite perfect, or a lot was lost in cutting."

"Cutting?"

Mr Andrews nodded. "Size and quality are important, but you can't evaluate a diamond until it's been cut into its usual 58 facets, and polished. Sometimes a lot is lost in the cutting process. You see, Bob, those found in diamond fields or mines are very rough stones, looking like ordinary rocks or pebbles—"

"Gosh!" Bob cried. "Excuse me, Dad! Thanks a lot—but I've got to make a phone call!"

Mr Andrews smiled as his son dashed off for the

phone. He was used to these abrupt endings to their conversations.

Bob quickly called Jupiter. "Hey, Jupe, did you know that uncut diamonds look like ordinary little rocks?" He went on to report what he'd learned from the newspaper and his father. "So maybe Olsen really is after rocks—diamonds!"

"Of course, of course!" said Jupiter. " 'Rocks' is also slang for 'jewels'." Jupiter was silent for a moment. "Good work, Records. Your information fits in very nicely with some further deductions I made this morning.

"Now, can you come right over here? Mike Hall called. George is acting a scene for Jay Eastland today and he'd like us to be there."

"Sure," said Bob, "but I thought you had to work today."

"Uncle Titus decided to stay home and work in the yard, so I'm not needed. Which is just as well. I have a strong feeling that things will continue to go wrong at Jungle Land until we solve its mystery. Meet me in Headquarters as soon as you can. Pete is already on his way."

"Konrad has offered to take us to Jungle Land today," Jupe was saying. "We've only a few minutes to discuss a serious problem that has come up. If my conclusions are correct, it may direct our actions when we get there."

Bob looked at Pete, mystified. "What's going on?"

Pete shrugged.

Jupiter announced importantly, "On the basis

of Bob's new information and my own deductions, I believe that the Hall brothers are involved in a smuggling racket!"

"What?" Bob protested.

Jupiter continued, "Cal Hall is shipping animals to his brother here. I think that under cover of those shipments he's also smuggling diamonds out of Africa."

Bob turned to Jupe. "But diamonds come from South Africa, and Cal Hall is operating in Central Africa. Aren't those two places a long way apart?"

"Mike told us that Cal Hall was in Rwanda for the mountain gorilla," Jupe said. "But for this kind of work, he would travel all over Africa. And there are a lot of other countries in Africa besides South Africa that produce diamonds. The Congo, Ghana, the Ivory Coast, Liberia, Sierra Leone, the Republic of Central Africa—all export diamonds."

He picked an atlas off a shelf and turned to a page showing Africa. "Here's a country in East Africa, not far from Rwanda. It used to be Tanganyika. See it? Right near Uganda and Kenya. It's called Tanzania now. It has diamond mines, too. Also, according to this atlas, the most abundant wild life is in East Africa. Cal has to get to the east coast to ship his animals, and he would naturally pass through Tanzania. If you note, there's a big coastal city. That's the capital, Dar es Salaam."

Pete whistled. "That sounds familiar. Get out your notes, Bob."

Bob whipped out his notebook and flipped to the page of the night before. " 'The information from Dora's alarm tells us,' " he read. He whistled. "Dora's alarm—Dar es Salaam—they sound pretty much the same."

"We don't yet know why Olsen should have that cable message," Jupe said. "But obviously Cal Hall sent it to his brother from the point of shipment, to let him know the diamonds were coming."

His eyes gleamed. "The first word of the cable makes sense now. DOX, spelled d-o-c-k-s, refers to a landing pier for ships. The diamonds and the animals are being shipped from the docks."

Bob printed out the two forms of the cable message on a clean piece of paper.

DOX ROX NOX EX REX BOX
DOCKS ROCKS KNOCKS EX WRECKS BOX

"We now think ROCKS means diamonds, and you think WRECKS BOX means to pull apart the cage," Bob said. "What about the other words?"

"I haven't figured out the third and fourth words yet," Jupe admitted. "But I think I was also incorrect about WRECKS. We should have left it as R-E-X, because that way everything falls into place!"

He paused significantly.

"C'mon, Jupe!" said Pete. "Out with it!"

"Rex is the Latin word for king. The lion is the king of beasts. REX BOX could mean, in this instance, George's cage! And George was shipped from Africa. I would say the message conclusively refers to smuggling diamonds into this country along with George and his cage. And, furthermore, I think the diamonds have become lost somehow, and whoever is looking for them is coming around too often—and making George nervous!"

Pete nodded. "Even an ordinary watchdog would be acting up if strangers were walking around at night near his house."

"But Jim Hall is no stranger," Bob protested. "And according to Jupe, he's part of the smuggling team."

"No, Jim Hall wouldn't make George nervous. It would have to be somebody else."

"Ja. :astland?" said Pete. "He'd get anybody upset."

"Well, I suppose he's a possibility," said Jupe. "But I can't see any connection at this point."

Pete snapped his fingers. "Hank Morton! I bet he's involved! Remember, he might have let George out the other day. He could have done it so that he could get a look at George's cage."

"You're forgetting George doesn't have his cage any more," said Jupe. "Remember Mike told us they got rid of it, and Jim allowed George to live in their house."

"What about Olsen and Dobbsie?" Bob asked. "Where do they fit in? They seem to know what they're looking for, and even where to look for it."

"Olsen and Dobbsie are definite suspects," Jupe said firmly. "They could be part of Jim's gang."

"Why are they looking in the scrap yard then?" Pete demanded.

"The diamonds could be lost there," Jupe said. "Remember what the man said—it was like looking for a needle in a haystack."

Bob flipped through his notes again and read, " 'They lost it and we'll wrap them up when we find it.' How do you explain that last part, Jupe? It doesn't sound like they're working with the Halls."

Jupe pondered. "I'd forgotten that part. According to that, Olsen and Dobbsie are against Cal Hall and Jim. The term 'wrap them up' suggests a threat, to me. Maybe Olsen and Dobbsie broke with the Hall brothers and are now trying to hijack the diamonds. Or perhaps they're a rival gang with no connection to the Halls."

"Gosh!" Bob said. "It all sounds complicated. I wonder if Mike knows anything about this."

"I doubt it," said Jupe. "And we must be careful not to accuse his Uncle Jim, whom he idolises, or his Uncle Cal, until we've made absolutely sure. Agreed?"

Bob and Pete nodded. Jupe got up and stretched.

"All right then. Konrad is waiting for us outside. Perhaps this trip will be the one in which we unravel the mystery at Jungle Land."

They walked to the exit glumly. They enjoyed solving mysteries, but solving this one seemed to entail making several people unhappy. Jupe bit his lip. He wondered how he would ever break the news to young Mike Hall.

15

Black Death

MIKE was waiting for The Three Investigators at his house when Konrad dropped them off. He guided them along a trail that served as a short cut to the location of the Jay Eastland movie set. It was a natural jungle setting, a flat clearing bordered by giant trees and thick undergrowth. Large rocks were scattered on the north side at the foot of a short but steep cliff. A ledge jutted out of the cliff a little way above the ground.

The movie set hummed with activity. The work crew was busy setting up cables and tall reflectors for the lights, which were set on huge iron tripods. Eastland was to one side, talking to a group of actors and checking their various positions while a few men pushed the camera into range.

Bob looked at the bustling workers. "Have they started yet?"

Mike shook his head. "It's been overcast all

morning. But the sun's coming out now and they'll start shooting any minute. George is in the first scene."

"Did he have a peaceful night?" Jupe asked. "Or was he nervous again?"

"He slept fine," Mike said. "He conked right out after Doc Dawson gave him the tranquilliser. A good thing, too, because that panther made a rumpus half the night."

"Oh, no," groaned Pete. "Don't tell me we have another mystery—a nervous panther!"

"I don't think so, Pete. He just needs to calm down from his trip and adjust to life here."

"How's George's wound, Mike?" asked Bob.

"Just about healed. You can barely even notice where he was cut."

Mike pointed to the edge of the set. Jim Hall stood alone with the big lion at his side. He saw them and waved them over. The Three Investigators walked up, cautiously watching George. The tawny beast sat quietly, its yellow eyes staring into the distance. Its long tail flicked as Hall rubbed its ears.

"Glad you could make it, boys," Jim Hall said. "As you can see, George is in great shape today. We've rehearsed his scene several times already, and he knows exactly what he's supposed to do." He glanced toward the busy producer-director. "I hope Eastland gets going soon while George is still nice and relaxed."

The big lion yawned, exposing long ivory teeth. A dull rumbling sound came from its throat.

As The Three Investigators looked up apprehensively, Jim Hall smiled. "He's purring, boys. That's a good sign. It means George is in a happy mood." He looked impatiently toward Eastland. "Come on, let's go," he muttered.

The fat producer moved across the set towards the cliff, giving instructions in a loud fretful, voice. "Over here with the camera," he ordered.

Eastland looked at a sheaf of notes. "We'll need to be on our toes for this scene. It's a quickie but we want to get it right the first time, understand?"

"No retakes makes it cheaper," Pete whispered in Jupe's ear.

Eastland waved an actress and an actor over. "Miss Stone, you and Rock Randall stand here." He pointed below the overhanging ledge. "The lion will be up on the ledge, looking down. You two will have a scuffle. When Randall has his back to the ledge, the lion jumps on him. Is that clear? Any questions, Sue? No? You, Rock? All right, then."

Eastland turned to the cameraman. "You hold on the scene as George jumps. Randall will try to fight him off, and they'll wrestle a few feet. Then Randall slumps to the ground, the lion paws him, and it's all over.

"We cut then to the next scene, which gives Hall a chance to come in and get his lion calmed down while we prepare the next setup with Sue. Hopefully, there won't be any trouble."

Jim Hall flushed. "George understands what

he's to do, Eastland. Just make sure Randall slumps to the ground and doesn't try to get up. If he does, George will knock him down again. There won't be any accidents."

The producer nodded with a smirk. "We all hope not." He turned to the actor. "I hope you've kept up your insurance policies, Rock."

The actor looked pale and frightened. "Come on, Jay. Cut the comedy."

He moved nervously away and lit a cigarette.

"Rock Randall looks awfully anxious," Jupe whispered to his friends. "And Eastland isn't helping him any by suggesting he can't trust George."

Pete looked at the big lion sitting placidly near its owner. "I don't blame Randall for looking nervous," he said. "How can you expect to be jumped by a big lion and not be nervous?"

"But he's trained," Mike said. "George won't hurt anybody. He'll only be pretending."

"I thought Rock Randall was in a fight yesterday," said Bob. "He doesn't look it."

"Make-up," said Pete knowledgeably.

Eastland walked across to the actress. "We'll shoot your scene with George right after that one, Sue. You'll be asleep in your tent. George pokes his head in the opening and goes in. He's just curious but you see him and wake up and scream. He opens his mouth and roars. That's it. Okay? You don't do anything silly like jumping out and hitting him. You just sit up, pull the covers up, and scream. You got it?"

The actress put her hand to her throat. "I've never worked with a lion before, Mr Eastland. Are you sure he's safe?"

Eastland smiled. He took a folded paper from his pocket and waved it. "That's what Jim Hall, his owner and trainer, says. I've got the guarantee down here in black and white."

The actress turned away, visibly upset.

Pete touched Jupe's shoulder and glanced away. Following his gaze Jupe saw the hatchet-faced man looking on from the edge of the set. He leaned forward to Mike. "That man over there, Mike—do you know him?"

"The thin-faced man—yeah—his name is Dunlop. He does some kind of work for Mr Eastland."

"Dunlop? Are you sure? Not Olsen?"

"It's Dunlop, all right. I've heard Eastland calling him that. I think he's some kind of technical expert on firearms."

Jupe glanced at Pete and Bob to see if they had overheard. They nodded. The man now identified as Dunlop walked casually away without looking back. Jupe frowned. He remembered that the night before the hatchet-faced man had threatened to return to The Jones Salvage Yard. Learning he was an expert on firearms made Jupe even less happy about it.

"How about Hank Morton?" Jupe asked. "Have you seen him around again?"

Mike grimaced. "He wouldn't dare to show his face around here again. We're just lucky Doc

Dawson got George in shape so fast for today's shooting."

"Say, Mike," said Jupiter, "what ever happened to George's cage? Where did you get rid of it?"

"I don't know. I suppose it was thrown over the fence into the scrap yard. That's where we throw most of our junk, and that cage was pretty old. Why?"

"Just curious," said Jupe.

Eastland suddenly snapped his fingers at Jim Hall. "Okay, Hall. We're all set. Get your lion up there and ready for action."

Jim Hall nodded and tugged gently at George's ear. "Come on, boy," he said softly. "We're putting you to work."

With George at his heels, he walked to the big rock formation. He stopped, leaned down, whispered, snapped his fingers, and pointed up to the ledge. George obeyed instantly and bounded lithely to the top. The lion stood there a moment, looking down majestically. It looked every bit its role of lord of the jungle, and Jupe and his friends gazed up at the animal admiringly.

Jim Hall whistled softly and gestured with his hand. The lion made a purring sound, then looked off into the distance, its long tail flicking restlessly.

Rock Randall and Sue Stone took their positions beneath the ledge. Eastland nodded. A man leaped forward. "Ready for action," he shouted. "Quiet on the set."

As all eyes focused on the impending action, Jupe caught his companions' attention and jerked his head to the side. He moved off quietly. Bob and Pete hesitated a moment, and then reluctantly followed.

"You picked a fine time to leave the set," Pete muttered when they were out of sight of the movie company. "Just when we finally had a chance to watch George act."

Jupe shrugged. "George's act is what I am depending on. I hope he has everybody's attention. That gives us a chance to do some investigating on our own."

"Where?" asked Bob.

Jupe pointed ahead in the direction of Jim Hall's house. "Diamond country," he said.

Cautiously, the boys approached the white house. "The new cages are around the other side," Jupe whispered. "I want to look them over first. It's quite likely that other cages besides George's are used for smuggling. We'll have to move quietly and make certain that we're not observed."

Bob looked surprised. "Observed by whom, Jupe? Everybody was around the movie set."

"Not everybody," Jupe said mysteriously.

Following Jupiter's example, Bob and Pete waited at the corner of the Hall house, listening. Then, they quickly moved round to the side, crouching low under the windows.

The two cages were separated by the length of the house. They approached the first one and peered in. "We're in luck," Bob said. "The gorilla's asleep."

The dark, shaggy form was huddled in a corner.

"What's so great about it?" Pete asked. "Are we going into its cage to look for smuggled diamonds?"

Jupiter moved slowly around the cage, examining it closely. "If diamonds are being smuggled in with these cages from Africa, how would it be done? Creating a false top or bottom seems a logical way, doesn't it?"

"Well, yes—" Bob agreed. "But can you tell just by looking?"

"No, it wouldn't be that obvious. The outside of this cage looks normal, the usual wood-frame roofing over the bars. But that seems too easy to get at. I've an idea the inside would be the more likely place. But for us to examine that thoroughly, the gorilla would have to be out of its cage."

Pete sighed with relief. "Thank goodness! I was afraid you'd want us to get in there with him."

Jupiter had already turned away. "Let's check the panther's cage," the stocky boy murmured. "Possibly we can detect someth—" He stopped suddenly and caught his breath.

Bob turned, puzzled. "What's wrong, Jupe?"

"Stay still!" Jupe hissed. "Don't make any sudden moves, and don't run!"

"What's going on?" asked Pete.

"Look straight ahead," Jupe said shakily. "The black panther's cage is open—and he's not in it!"

The boys stared at the empty cage. Prickly chills went down their spines and turned their legs to jelly. Then, horrified, they heard the sound they were dreading. A savage, spitting snarl behind them!

Jupiter gulped. He stood at a slight angle from Bob and Pete, and his quick sideways glance was enough to shake him further.

"H-he's up in the tree about twenty feet behind us," he whispered. "We may have to take a chance and separate. Now when I count three—"

Jupe's voice faltered as he saw the tall grass ahead of him ripple. He gasped as it parted and he caught the glint of a rifle barrel. Incredibly, he saw the rifle slowly rise.

A harsh voice directed, "Don't anybody move!"

The boys held their breath as a man stepped slowly out. They recognised the grizzled vet, Doc Dawson.

The grey eyes of the vet squinted. He took a slow step forward, his finger tightening on the trigger.

Suddenly there was an unearthly, ear-splitting scream behind them. In the same instant, the gun went off.

The boys ducked as a great, soaring shape smacked to the ground with a sickening thud a few feet past them. The black body twitched once and was still.

Doc Dawson stepped forward, looking both angry and discouraged. His dusty boot kicked at the long, outstretched claws of the panther.

"Lucky for all concerned I'm a pretty good shot," he said.

Pete let his breath out. "Is he—is he—?"

"Yep, he's dead as nails, sonny. That was a real

bullet. Never thought I'd have to kill one of Jim's animals." The vet shook his head ruefully.

Jupe tried to take his eyes off the spreading red stain. "Thanks, Dr Dawson," he said, swallowing hard. Then, "How did he get out?"

The vet shook his head. "It's my fault, I reckon. I needed to check him over, so I gave him a tranquillising shot. I stepped away for a few minutes while I was waiting for the drug to take effect. Next thing I knew he was on his feet and out of his cage. For some reason, the drug didn't work. I ran back to the jeep to get my gun—the one I use for killer hawks."

"Do you think somebody let the panther out?" asked Jupe.

"Who'd do a crazy fool thing like that?" countered the vet. "Anybody who tried that'd likely get mauled. No, I expect the cage door just wasn't locked properly."

"Might that drug you used have been tampered with? Weakened somehow by somebody?"

The vet looked shrewdly at Jupiter. "It could have happened that way, son. I leave my medical kit around a lot. Never saw no reason to distrust anybody here." He shook his head. "It sure beats me. Appears as if somebody sure has it in for Jim Hall. The shame of it is he's such a real nice fellow."

Pete leaned over the panther. "I guess you had to shoot to kill then, didn't you?"

"That's right, son. That baby might look like an overgrown pussy cat to you boys, but take it from me he was a real mean killer. If he'd got away, there's no telling what might have happened." He cocked his head and addressed the boys in a sharper tone. "What are you boys doing up this way, anyhow? Jim told me you'd be over at the movie set today watching George acting in the movie."

"We were there," Jupe started lamely, "but then —we thought we'd look around."

Dawson eyed Jupe and Bob and Pete in turn. "Jim told me you fellers were investigators." He smiled thinly. "Find out anything yet?"

Jupe shook his head. "No, sir. We're still confused."

"Can't say I blame you," the vet said. "Lots of confusing things happening round here lately. Things that don't make no sense at all. Want to hear one of the most confusing things about it?"

The boys looked at him questioningly.

Doc Dawson put a small cigar in his mouth, spat, put a match to it, inhaled smoke, and spat again. Then he levelled the thin cigar at them. "I'll tell you, then," he said. "Every time you kids show up here, another animal breaks loose. Think it over. Am I right?"

The boys looked at one another.

Dawson broke the spell by laughing sourly. "I'm right," he said.

He kicked at the body of the black panther. "I'll be right back for this baby," he said. "In the meantime, boys, I got some good advice for you—"

"What's that, sir?" asked Bob.

"Watch yourselves at all times," the vet said curtly.

He turned on his heels and walked away. In a moment he had disappeared into the tall, waving grass.

16

Iron Bars

As soon as Doc Dawson walked away from the dead panther, Jupiter led the other investigators down the hill to the fence by the salvage yard. The boys looked over at the huge spread of scrap iron, covering several acres. Workmen could be seen here and there.

"What are we doing here?" Pete asked.

"We're looking for the smuggled diamonds," Jupe replied. "And we're looking for George's old cage."

"You think those diamonds are still in George's cage?" asked Bob.

"I doubt it," said Jupe. "That cage has been around a long time. But we might get some ideas if we could find it."

"But, Jupe," complained Pete, "if the diamonds

123

aren't in the cage, what are they in? What do we look for? A little paper bag?"

Jupe scowled. "Frankly, Pete, I don't know what the diamonds would be in. I don't think Olsen or Dobbsie know either, or they would have found them by now."

"Olsen and Dobbsie looked all over this place last night and didn't find anything," said Bob. "What makes you think we'll have better luck?"

"It's daylight," said Jupe. "That should give us an advantage."

"Craziest thing I ever heard of," muttered Pete.

A workman who had been near the fence moved away, leaving the area clear. "Let's go," said Jupe.

The boys found the section of fence that had been pulled out of line the night before. It was an easy matter to loosen the metal upright again, and the wire netting with it. Seconds later, they had crawled into the middle of a junk pile that seemed to contain all the abandoned automobiles in the state.

Heavy clanking noises began on the other side of the salvage yard, punctuated by shrill whining sounds.

"Let's see how that metal shredder works," Jupe said.

He pointed to a huge crane. It was several hundred yards away, operating at the opposite end of the yard. As they watched, they saw a tiny figure in the cranehouse shift a gear. There was a complaining whine. A huge metal claw came up from behind a mound holding an old car.

The operator shifted a lever and the cranehouse swivelled to one side. Whining, the metal claw swung over the assorted debris of the yard. It stopped, causing the car to sway dangerously, and then lowered abruptly. The claw opened and the car dropped, landing with a heavy clank. Immediately there was a whup-whup-whup sound and the car jolted crazily forward.

"Conveyor belt," Pete said, standing on a pile of junk. "It's taking the car right into that shed."

The conveyor belt was a series of flat cars moving forward in steady jerks. When the old car disappeared into the mouth of the shed, the belt halted temporarily.

There was a shrill, screaming sound from the shed, a rising whine that blasted the air and threatened their eardrums with its intensity.

"Metal shredder at work," observed Jupe.

"Ugh!" said Pete. "It sounds as if the car is being eaten alive!"

The crane had swivelled again. Once more the huge claw rose in the air, swaying until it had seemingly found its prey. Then, with a whine, it pounced on another derelict car. Once more it fed the car into the shed.

Jupe turned away. "Okay. Now we know how it works. Let's get back to our own mystery."

The boys poked around for a while, without any luck.

"Maybe I'd do a better job if I knew what to look for," said Pete, kicking a piece of junk.

"Hold it, Pete," Jupe cried. "What's that?"

He ran over and picked it up carefully.

"It looks like a cage," Bob said. "Or maybe something that once was a cage."

"How can you call it a cage?" Pete demanded. "It doesn't have any bars. It looks like a broken old box."

"Perhaps the metal shredder has already processed it," said Jupe. "If you recall, the shredder selects metal from objects and discards the rest."

"Uh-Uh," Pete said as he dived off the pile. He came up grinning, holding a long, black iron bar. "That metal shredder is a fake," he said. "It can't tell iron from anything. What do you call this?"

Jupe was so pleased, he almost shouted with joy. "Good work, Pete! That might be what we're looking for. Let me see it, please."

Pete handed the bar over and Jupe promptly dropped it.

"Butterfingers!" Pete scoffed.

"No, I didn't expect—" Jupe bent to pick up the bar again. "That's odd," he said. "It feels heavy."

"Of course it's heavy," Pete said. "Why do you think I was complaining the other day when we had to unload a ton of these from your uncle's truck?"

Jupe stared down at the bar, his eyes gleaming thoughtfully. "I didn't notice. I'm certain the other one I had was—"

He stopped, his mouth open.

"What's wrong, Jupe?" asked Bob.

"N-nothing," Jupe said. He slung the bar across

his shoulder. "Quick! We've got to get back to our junkyard at once!"

"But why?" Pete protested. "If you're so happy with one iron bar, how do you know I can't find more?"

"Because," Jupiter stated as he moved away, "there aren't too many that bear the specifications I have in mind."

"Such as what?" Pete demanded.

"Such as containing smuggled diamonds," Jupiter answered, heading rapidly for the wire fence.

They didn't have too long to wait for Konrad to pick them up on his return trip from nearby Chatwick. On the ride home, Jupiter refused to be drawn into conversation. Instead, pinching his lower lip, he stared out of the window, nodding to himself several times as if to confirm certain inner convictions. Bob and Pete were accustomed to their leader's temporary fits of silence and knew he wouldn't explain himself until he was ready.

Once at the yard, Jupe hurried to his workshop. He stopped at the workbench—and cried out in dismay.

"It's gone!"

"What's gone?" asked Bob.

"The iron bar I picked up last night when Bo Jenkins chased us." He ran over to the junk pile hiding Headquarters and returned, looking puzzled. "The first bar I had has disappeared, too."

"What's this all about?" asked Pete.

Jupe shook his head impatiently. "I'll tell you later. Come on, I have to find Uncle Titus. Maybe he knows something."

Uncle Titus was across the street at the Jones' house, sitting and smoking his pipe. He nodded contentedly as the three boys approached.

"Howdy, boys," he said pleasantly. "Have a good time today?"

"Pretty good, Uncle Titus," Jupe began. "I wanted to ask—"

"We did pretty good here, too," interrupted his uncle. "Yes, sirree, had a good spell of business."

"What did you sell, Uncle Titus—some iron bars?"

His uncle rocked and nodded. "Right smart of you to guess, Jupe. Yes, sir, we did just that. Hans and your aunt scoured the yard for all we had. We needed them, you see," he added with a wink.

"What for, Mr Jones?" asked Bob.

"What for? To make cages, of course. Told you the other day we were going to, didn't I, Jupiter? Well, today Hans and me started to work on them, and then this feller comes in. His problem is he needs some big animal cages—and he needs 'em bad. Some kind of an emergency, I figure, where you suddenly need a lot of cages.

"Well, sir, I had to think fast. Y'see, we meant to fix 'em all up but we were still a few bars shy."

Jupe felt sick inside. "Was it that man who was here the other day? The one called Olsen?"

"Not that feller. Another chap. Very likeable sort of man. Truth is, Jupe, even though I had my mind made up to save those cages for a circus, this chap's work was close enough to help me change my mind."

"It was?" Jupe repeated dully.

Titus Jones nodded, drew deeply on his pipe, and blew smoke. He finally went on. "Well, on account of him being such a nice chap and worried so, needing 'em so bad, I decided to co-operate. We all worked like the dickens fixing the cages and hunting for bars. Now your aunt saw you drop a bar near your workshop—that was the other day—and she picked that one up."

"Oh, Aunt Mathilda did?" Jupiter groaned.

His uncle nodded. "A good thing, too. We were still one bar too little even with that, until Hans found another one on your workbench, Jupe. We figured you had no earthly use for it. Bars and junk like that come in here all the time, you know, and you're always welcome to what you want—providing we don't need it for a customer. Right?"

Jupe nodded dumbly.

His uncle smacked the dottle from his pipe. "Well, that feller couldn't believe his eyes when we showed him we had the four cages all ready to go. Paid me a hundred dollars apiece, without my even painting 'em up. Said his animals would feel at home in 'em just like they were."

"You got those cages over in the Chatwick Valley, didn't you, Uncle Titus."

"Yep. At a big scrap yard. They didn't care about cages. Their main business was in junked cars. Had a teriffic machine to eat 'em up. Made a racket, it did."

Jupe gestured helplessly, his worst suspicions confirmed.

As Mr Jones stretched and stood up to leave, Jupiter had only one more question. "This man with the animals, Uncle Titus—the one you sold the cages to—did you get his name?"

His uncle smiled benevolently. "Of course I did. Easy one to remember, too." He squinted into the distance to remember the easy name. "It was, lemme see—yep, Hall. That was his name, all right. Jim Hall."

Jupiter stared at his friends.

17

Jupiter Explains

A CALL to the Rent-'n-Ride Auto Agency found Worthington available soon for another trip to Jungle Land. While waiting for him to arrive, the boys gobbled some lunch in Aunt Mathilda's kitchen.

"All right, Jupe," said Bob as the boys settled into the back seat of the Rolls-Royce. "It's about time you explained what's going on."

"It's very simple," said Jupe. "The diamonds are being smuggled by the Hall brothers in iron bars."

"Are you feeling all right, Jupe?" Pete asked. "That iron bar I picked up at the scrap yard and handed you—are you talking about that kind of bar?"

Jupe nodded.

"But that bar was solid iron," Pete said. "How can you smuggle diamonds in something like that?"

"You can't," Jupe said. "But you can smuggle diamonds in a hollow bar. Remember I told you that your iron bar felt different? Well, it was. It was a lot heavier than the one I picked up last night when Bo Jenkins was after us. And it was a lot heavier than the bar I put aside when we were unloading Uncle Titus's truck. It was so much heavier that suddenly everything clicked.

"I knew that I had hollow cage bars, and that Uncle Titus must have bought his bars and cages at the scrap yard where Jim Hall had tossed George's cage and probably others, too."

"But how did you know that the two bars you had contained diamonds?" asked Bob.

"Well, I didn't know for sure," said Jupe, "until I heard that Jim Hall had bought the cages from Uncle Titus. He never would have returned for them if the smuggled diamonds weren't still in them. It's just my bad luck that I had the bars and then lost them. I still don't know why he waited so long."

Pete looked puzzled. "I don't get it. If he knew

the diamonds were in the cages, why did he discard them in the first place?"

"Perhaps the heat was on," Jupe said. "He couldn't afford to have them traced to his property. My guess is he dumped them over the fence at the scrap yard as a temporary measure, thinking they'd be safe there and he could pick them apart later. But somehow they got mixed up with a lot of other junk there, and my Uncle Titus bought them from the yard owners, along with all the long bars and railings."

"That's possible," said Bob. "Mr Hall could have then asked the yard owners who bought the junk and traced it to your uncle's junkyard. Olsen and Dobbsie must have known about the bars, too. Now that I think of it, Olsen first asked for bars when he came to your uncle's yard. Remember?"

Jupe nodded.

"I wonder if one of those men was the mystery buyer," added Bob.

"Mystery buyer?" asked Pete.

"Yes, the customer who bought the pile of bars and railings from Mrs Jones when we were making our first visit to Jungle Land. Those bars might have had diamonds in them, too."

"Naw," said Pete. "Those bars were awfully heavy—don't forget I was the one who carried them. And they were much longer than all the cage bars we've ever seen."

"I'm inclined to agree with Pete," said Jupe. "I don't think it matters who bought those bars. It was probably an innocent customer. And, if it wasn't—well, Olsen and Jim Hall both showed up at our yard later, so they couldn't have found the diamonds earlier."

"Hey, Jupe," said Pete. "What about that bar you found last night? Where did that come from?"

"That one could have got loose and fallen out of a cage when Jim Hall was dumping it into the scrap yard. I wish I knew how many cages were involved here. We know what to look for now, but we don't know how much to look for."

"All those bars look alike," Bob put in. "How can anybody tell which is which? When the cages arrive, they're all in place. How would Jim Hall know which bars have the diamonds his brother Cal inserted?"

Jupe smiled mysteriously. "There's a way of knowing."

Bob and Pete looked at him sourly. They knew from past experience that Jupiter would never divulge the last remaining secret to a mystery until the last possible moment.

Bob frowned. "We still haven't solved the mystery we were called in to investigate," he said. "Who is making Jim Hall's lion nervous? And if Mr Hall is tied in with the diamond smuggling, who's letting his wild animals escape from their cages? He might lose Jungle Land if there's an accident."

"We'll know the answer to that when we put all the loose ends together," Jupe said. "It's possible Jim Hall himself let George out when we got there the first time, as a diversion. He might have let the gorilla loose, too, and pretended to go off looking for him. If you recall, he came right back to where the gorilla really was pretty fast."

"Bringing Doc Dawson and his stun gun and saving our lives!" Pete said. "I won't hold that against him."

"What about this morning?" Bob asked. "Jim Hall was on the movie set with George. He couldn't have slipped away to let the black panther out, could he? And have Doc Dawson cover up for him and say it was his own fault?"

"It's possible," Jupe said thoughtfully. "Doc Dawson might have an idea of what Jim Hall is up to. He might be trying to cover up for him and maybe to protect Mike, as well. Doc Dawson always seems to turn up when he's needed. That suggests to me that he is aware of the situation, and able to anticipate just what is going to happen next."

Soon the Rolls-Royce was entering Jungle Land.

"Drop us at the foot of the hill leading to the Halls' house, Worthington," ordered Jupe. "I think that we should arrive discreetly."

The boys walked up to the quiet white house on the hill. As they came close, they stopped to listen.

"Not a sound," Pete whispered. "Maybe he's already found the diamonds and cleared out."

Jupe pushed his lower lip out. "We'll have to go in, anyway. We owe it to Mike to explain."

Bob and Pete nodded agreement. Jupe took a step forward and stopped.

"What's wrong?" whispered Bob.

"I thought I heard something," Jupe said. "Maybe we'd better check the cage area before we go in."

He turned and the others followed him into the shadows of the clearing.

"Seems quiet," Jupe said. "I don't see—"

He was interrupted as something heavy was thrown over his head. Bob and Pete were caught the same way. The boys were grasped by strong hands. Their cries were muffled, and although they struggled and kicked, they could not get away from their surprise attackers. Helpless, they were carried along in total darkness.

18

Trapped!

COVERED by a heavy blanket, The Three Investigators were unable to make out the voices of their abductors. They were bouncing as if they were being carried over rough terrain. One of their carriers stumbled and complained loudly. Another voice curtly cut him off.

The caravan halted. Ropes were lashed round them. They felt themselves being lifted again and then heaved headlong on to a springy surface. A heavy door thunked shut.

"That oughta keep 'em out of the way," a voice said.

They heard receding footsteps and then silence. They struggled to straighten themselves, pausing as they heard another sound.

Whup-whup-whup---pp!

They felt themselves being jerked forward, then rocked back abruptly. There was a whining sound and a heavy crunch as if something had grabbed them from both sides. The whining sound became a groan. Suddenly they felt the odd sensation of being lifted.

"Goodness!" Bob exclaimed. "Are we riding in something?"

"Apparently," Jupe said. "And I don't like the sound of it. We'd better work fast. Try to slip the blanket off first. That way we won't suffocate, and we may be able to see where we are—and be heard!"

Following Jupe's directions, they pushed and pulled in turn. Gradually the heavy blanket over them was tugged down.

"Use your fingers," Jupe urged. "Keep pulling down and rolling the blanket under you."

They struggled to get free, their hearts thumping wildly as they heard the menacing sounds all around them. Something chattered and roared beneath them, and from above they heard groaning, creaking sounds that sent chills down their spines.

Suddenly they were rocking in a wide swinging arc.

"It's the claw!" Pete yelled.

In a last convulsive movement the boys jerked the blanket down from their heads.

They gasped.

Straight ahead they saw nothing but the sky.

Far below was the spread of junked cars in the scrap yard.

At either side were the huge metal talons of the giant claw, gripping the old car that they rode in. They were trapped in the air—and headed for the metal shredder! They began to yell for help, but the huge machine in the shed below started to chatter and scream, roaring out a series of deafening sounds.

Pete shook his head. "No chance! We can't compete with that monster. Not even if we yell our heads off!"

"Apparently the crane operator can't see us either," Jupe cried. "We've got to get out of these ropes so we can attract his attention!"

They struggled and rocked but the ropes held tight.

They heard a shrill whistle. Abruptly the giant claw dropped. Then, with a sickening lurch, they were falling to the ground.

They bounced as they hit. Almost immediately, they were jerked forward. They stopped, rocked, and were jerked forward again.

"We're on the conveyor belt now!" Jupe said. "We don't have much time. Come on—the metal shredding process takes place right ahead!"

Again they struggled, but it was to no avail.

Relentlessly the conveyor belt advanced.

They yelled again, but their voices sounded puny in the yard's roar. "Kick the doors!" Jupe yelled. "Maybe we can knock them open."

They tried to obey but their efforts were futile. The ropes lashed around them were too tight. Tied together as they were, they were unable to use their legs. They thrashed about uselessly, and fell back, exhausted.

"It's no use!" Pete gasped. "Our only hope is that somebody working the metal shredder inside sees us in time."

"I doubt that," Jupe said. "A processing machine like this is usually run by a computer. It's not a question of our not being metal. The car we're in *is!* The selective scanner couldn't possibly reject us until it was too late!"

"You're not kidding," a voice said.

They stared incredulously into the cold eyes of the hatchet-faced man!

"Get the door on the other side, Dobbsie," Hatchet-Face said.

Surprisingly, his touch was gentle, although they felt the strength in his hands as he lifted them out. As they rolled on the ground, the car they had been riding in jerked forward.

Staring wide-eyed, the saw it disappear into the shed, to be lost in a cloud of steam. Heavy clanking sounds reverberated and the machine inside screamed.

Jupe turned with a tremendous sigh of relief to

the two men. His expression changed suddenly.

Dobbsie was holding a long-bladed knife!

"Be reasonable!" Hatchet-Face said cajolingly. "We have to cut those ropes off you kids, don't we?"

Jupe nodded dumbly. He looked at Bob and Pete. They returned his mystified glance.

The beady-eyed man bent and slashed deftly with his knife. In a moment they were free.

As they rubbed their arms and legs to regain circulation, the hatchet-faced man looked down coldly at them. "Looks as if we got here just in time," he rasped. "What happened?"

"Somebody threw a blanket over us, tied us up, and threw us in a car," said Jupe. "I don't know if we were intended for the metal shredder, or not. We're grateful to you for preventing us having to find out."

"Any idea who did it?"

Jupe shook his head. "It happened too fast. We were rounding the corner of Jim Hall's house—" He stopped abruptly and glanced at the men. "How did you know we were trapped in the car?"

The hatchet-faced man sighed and looked over Jupe's head at the other man. "We happened to be in the yard. Dobbsie here thought he saw a moving kicking bundle being thrown into a car at the far end. That's a bit unusual, so we went to investigate. Whoever did it ran off before we could get over. Then the claw got you and dumped you on the conveyor track. We couldn't get the crane operator's attention or stop the belt moving. So we had to do it the hard way and drag you out ourselves."

Pete shivered. "I can't believe he would have done that to us. I just can't believe it!"

"Who, kid?" asked the hatchet-faced man. "And what do you kids know that's so dangerous somebody nearly had you killed because of it?"

Jupe lifted his head. "We're conducting an investigation," he said. "We have our suspicions but we're not at liberty yet to divulge any names."

The hatchet-faced man grinned. "Oh, you're not, eh? Maybe we should have kept out of it and let you continue your investigations—" he pointed to the throbbing shed "—in there!"

Jupe cocked his head. "As a matter of fact," he said, "both the actions of you and your friend have aroused our suspicions, too. But I don't suppose you have anything to do with the diamond smuggling, or else you wouldn't have rescued us."

Hatchet-Face looked at Dobbsie. "What'd I tell you? The kid is wise to the operation!" He looked down and laughed at Jupe. "I suppose you can tell us where they are, too."

"I suppose I can," Jupe said slowly. "But I won't."

Hatchet-Face jerked his head at the other man. "Come on, Dobbsie. We're wasting time. While we're here yakking, they could be getting away."

The beady-eyed man with the mashed nose came close to Jupe and raised a warning finger. "This is big time stuff, feller—not for kids. Watch your-selves!"

The menace in his powerful frame was unmistakable. He wheeled away to join his swift-moving companion, leaving The Three Investigators with a warning they could not afford to ignore!

19

In the Bag

YOUNG Mike Hall looked surprised when he threw the door open. "Jupe! Hi, fellows! C'mon in. We didn't expect you back today."

"I know," Jupe said as he entered the house. "Have Mr Olsen—the man you called Dunlop—and another man been here?"

Mike shook his head. "No, why?"

Jupe frowned. He wondered where they were. "I suppose your Uncle Jim is out, isn't he?"

Mike shook his head again. "What gave you that idea? He's in the back room with George, resting. Wait a second. I'll call him."

As he walked off, Jupe looked at Bob and Pete.

"It beats me, too," Pete said. "I was sure they were heading here."

"Maybe they're off looking for the cages," Bob said.

A cheery voice interrupted. "What cages?"

"Your old cages, Mr Hall," Jupe said.

Jim Hall looked surprised. "What are you driving at?"

"You ought to know, Mr Hall," Jupe said. "You're the one who bought back George's old cage, along with the other three, from my Uncle Titus."

Hall's face looked blank. "I—what?"

"You bought back the cages, and took them away," Bob put in. "The ones with the bars that hold the smuggled diamonds."

Jim Hall looked from one boy to the other with a dumbfounded expression. "Okay," he said. "Now you tell me. Maybe I'm not hearing so well today."

Pete shuffled his feet and look uncomfortable. "But I guess you didn't have anything to do with shanghaiing us and dropping us off at the metal shredder?"

Hall shook his head dumbly and turned to Mike. "What are your friends talking about?"

"I don't know," Mike said.

"You told us you had a problem," Bob said. "It was a mystery and you wanted our help. Who was making George nervous? Or what? But it turns out the mystery is how your brother Cal ships you diamonds from Africa, along with some animals. Some of the cage bars with the diamonds in them got lost somehow and that's why you had to buy the cages back from Jupe's Uncle Titus earlier today."

"You're crazy!" Mike burst in. "I've been with Jim every minute since early this morning. He hasn't stepped out of Jungle Land once today!"

Jupe looked up at Jim Hall. "You didn't?"

Hall shook his head.

"My Uncle Titus said he sold the cages to a man named Jim Hall. I'm sorry I didn't ask him to describe the man. I think I can guess now who it was—"

"Dobbsie?" asked Bob.

"It's possible," Jupe said. "Uncle Titus said it wasn't Olsen-Dunlop. It could have been Dobbsie." He looked up at Jim Hall again. "You don't know anything about any diamonds?"

"I don't even know what you're talking about," said Hall.

"Why did you get rid of George's cage?"

Hall shrugged. "It seemed wrong to keep him locked up in a cage when I was trying to train him with love and kindness. I felt we were losing touch every time I had to lock him inside again. Once Mike came to stay with us, I decided George had to be proven trustworthy. I got rid of the cage, had it thrown over the fence into the scrap yard, and that was the end of it. George became a regular member of the household, just like Mike and myself."

"But you kept the cage outside your house for a while after George moved in, didn't you?" Jupe persisted.

"Yes, until recently. I made up my mind to get rid of it completely when Jay Eastland came along and wanted to hire George for his movie. I didn't want him to get the idea George was still a wild animal. From that point on, Jay Eastland saw George only as a well-trained housepet."

Jupe looked rueful. "I owe you an apology, Mr Hall. It appears all my deductions and assumptions have proven false."

"We all make mistakes, Jupe. Maybe it's time you told me what this is all about."

Jupe explained from the beginning, starting with the arrival of the cages in The Jones Salvage Yard, and then the man named Olsen. "Mike says he works for Mr Eastland and is called Dunlop. But he told us his name was Olsen. A thin, hatchet-faced, light-haired man."

"I don't know him but I think I've seen him around the set," said Hall.

"He was looking over the scrap heap last night," Bob said. "Along with a man he called Dobbsie. They talked a lot about the smuggled diamonds. We couldn't figure out if they were part of a gang or what. They're the same two who rescued us a while ago when we were on our way into the metal shredder!"

Jim Hall listened carefully. When they had finished telling all they knew, he shook his head. "I'm sorry, boys, but I don't understand a single part of what you've said. Maybe it's true that these goings on made George upset and nervous. Maybe it's true that somehow diamonds are being smuggled in here. But I'll tell you one thing you can bet on," he added, his eyes flashing. "My brother Cal wouldn't have a thing to do with anything crooked!"

Jupe nodded and thought a minute. "Can you tell us what other cages you've discarded over the past few months?" he asked.

"We threw out two or three old cages a year ago," Jim Hall said. "But the only one lately was George's."

"Apparently that was the start of it, then," Jupe said thoughtfully. Abruptly he asked, "How is George feeling today?"

Jim Hall smiled.. "First rate. He did a good job on the movie set this morning and he's been fine ever since. He's inside snoozing now. Doc Dawson was here and gave him a tranquilliser."

Jupe motioned to his companions. "Well, we'd better be going. We still have some work to do, fellows."

Mike Hall opened the door. "Come on back again when you can," he said. "I'm sure Jim doesn't blame you—"

"He should," Jupe said severely. "I had no business making an accusation before I had sufficient evidence. I owe you both an apology, Mike."

As Jupe went out, his foot caught on the threshold of the door and he stumbled across the porch. He grabbed for the porch post, yelled, and yanked his hand away.

"Oww!" he cried. He looked down at the drop of blood on his finger. "I just caught my finger on a splinter."

"Gosh, I'm sorry, Jupe," Mike said. "Come on inside. We'll find a Band-Aid for you."

"It's okay," Jupe said sheepishly as he went back in the door. He sucked his finger. "Just a little cut."

Mike snapped his fingers suddenly and pointed. "I was about to say it's too bad Doc Dawson isn't around to fix you up. Look—he forgot his medical kit."

Jupe looked at the worn, black leather bag sitting on a chair. "Would he mind if I helped myself to a bandage?"

"Are you kidding?" Mike said. "That's what it's for—emergencies. Help yourself."

Jupe opened the bag and reached inside for a roll of gauze wrapped neatly in blue paper. Holding it awkwardly, he fumbled with the protective cover. A small yellow piece of paper fluttered out.

Mike picked it up. "Looks like you dropped one of Doc's prescriptions, Jupe. Here, better put it back."

Jupe glanced at it automatically as it was handed to him. His lips moved wordlessly and he stared at it pop-eyed.

"What is it, Jupe?" asked Bob.

Jupe shook his head and looked at the scrap of paper again. "I can't believe it," he said slowly. Then he sighed a long sigh. "But, of course. Now the whole thing begins to make sense."

"What can't you believe?" asked Pete. "What makes sense?"

Jupe held out the scrap of torn paper. "Read it yourself."

They stared at the paper in Jupe's hand. It read:

DOX ROX NOX EX REX BOX

Mike looked mystified. "What does it mean?"

"It means a man we never suspected is behind it all," Jupe said. He shook his head ruefully. "It's all perfectly clear now."

"What are you trying to tell us now, Jupe?" asked Jim Hall.

"You won't like it," Jupe said. "It's Doc Dawson."

Jim Hall smiled thinly. "I don't think you know what you're talking about, son. Doc's an old friend. Let me see that piece of paper."

As he held out his hand, the front door opened.

A burly figure stood there. Head close-shaven, arm tattooed. "I came to pick up Doc's bag," he said. "He forgot it here."

His eyes narrowed as he saw the open medical bag, and then the small slip of yellow paper in Jupe's hand. His lips twisted angrily. "I'll take that, you snooping kid!" he roared.

Before Jupe could move, Bo Jenkins had snatched the paper from his hand. He crumpled it in his huge fist and reached for the leather bag.

Jim Hall spoke up mildly. "Hold it just a second, Bo. There's something going on here and—"

Jenkins made a sudden movement and pulled out a gun. "Stay out of it, Hall, if you know what's good for you. We got it all now and nothin's stopping us."

Jupe gulped. "You're the man who bought all the cages from my uncle—and gave Jim Hall's name!"

Jenkins grinned. "Wise apple, huh?"

Jim Hall whistled softly as the animal handler grabbed the black bag.

Heavy, padding steps sounded across the room. An ominous rumbling made Jenkins turn and stare. His jaw sagged and he paled.

A large, yellow-eyed lion stood there, head down and long tail twitching restlessly. The growling continued.

Instantly Jupe leaned against the door, closing it.

Jenkins whirled again at the sound, his gun jerking.

"Forget it, Jenkins," Jim Hall said calmly. "You're not going anyplace. One more step and George will have you for dinner." Hall turned to the lion. "Won't you, George?"

The lion slowly opened its cavernous mouth and moved forward.

There was a clattering sound as the gun fell from Bo Jenkins's fingers.

"That's better," Jim Hall said. He bent forward to retrieve the gun and waved the frightened man to a chair. The lion came forward and stopped at Bo's side, opening its mouth in a huge yawn.

"Now then, Bo," Jim Hall said pleasantly. "What can you tell us about some smuggled diamonds?"

20

End of the Puzzle

As they rounded a turn in the trail, Mike pointed ahead to a small house next to a barn. "That's Doc Dawson's place," he said. "The dispensary is in the back."

Sounds of hammering came from the barn.

Jupe smiled. "That's one thing he never figured on. When my Uncle Titus has something fixed, he does a very thorough job."

"What do you mean, Jupe?" asked Mike.

"You'll see in a minute," Jupe said mysteriously.

A small pickup truck stood in the driveway by the barn. Alongside it four cages lay tumbled on the ground. The grizzled vet stood next to one with a hammer raised in one hand. In the other he held a long pair of pliers.

He paused as Jim Hall strode up, flanked by the boys. His eyes flicked past them and narrowed.

"Howdy, Jim," he said. "Anything wrong?"

Jim Hall shook his head. He tossed the black leather bag at the vet's feet. "Heard you were looking for your bag, Doc. You left it at the house."

"Thanks, Jim," Dawson said. He gazed beyond them and frowned. "I sent Bo Jenkins—I thought—" He looked at the cages, scowling. "I need him to help—"

Hall nodded. "Bo's all tied up at the moment, Doc. Maybe we can give you a hand. What's the trouble?"

The vet looked at the hammer in his hand. "No trouble, Jim. Just wanted to make sure the bars are good and tight. Don't want any more accidents. That fellow Eastland will have every nickel of yours if one more animal gets away."

Hall smiled. "Thanks, Doc. I appreciate your concern." He looked at Jupe. "Can you tell which bars?"

"I think so, sir," Jupiter said. "But I'd need to borrow his hammer."

"No problem," Hall said. "Can you loan this young fellow your hammer for a moment, Doc?"

Dawson hesitated, then handed it to Jupe. "Guess so. What's up?"

"These young fellows are The Three Investigators. I hired them, you recall, to find out what's been making old George nervous. They've come up with some cock-eyed notion that it's all because of some smuggled diamonds."

Dawson grinned. "No kidding? Cock-eyed is right." He looked at Jupe. "Any idea where they might be?"

"Yes, sir," Jupe said. "If you would just step aside for a moment, please."

"Why, sure," Dawson said easily, moving away. "Only go easy with that hammer, son. I wouldn't want those bars loosened after all the trouble I've been to tightening them up."

"You didn't tighten them up," said Jupe. "Hans and Uncle Titus did, back at our junkyard."

Doc looked surprised.

"You'll notice," Jupe continued, "they didn't put back the bars the way they were. Uncle Titus is very fussy about giving a customer no reason for complaint. So he and Hans bolted and screwed the bars in this way so they wouldn't work loose as they did before."

"Very interesting," Dawson said.

"So you can't hammer them off," Jupe said. "All you can use the hammer for is this, really." He walked around the cage beating at the bars with the heavy hammer. He stopped at the fourth one from the end, then continued through the others, pausing once more. He returned to the fourth one again.

"There are two on this cage," he said.

Dawson glanced at Jim Hall. "Any idea what he's talking about?"

Hall frowned. "I'd rather wait and see, Doc."

"Most of these bars are rusted," Jupe said, "indicating they've been outside and exposed to the weather a long time. They could belong to any of the cages Mr Hall discarded. But this rusty one gives off a different sound—it's hollow, you see. So my deduction is this one could have come from George's cage.

"This one here," Jupe continued, striding to the opposite end of the cage, "is hollow, too." He struck it with his hammer. "It's still in good condition because it just came in recently. It's from the gorilla's cage. Bo Jenkins took it off the night the gorilla arrived. The gorilla twisted the other bars apart and broke out. I believe the gorilla went after Bo and he became frightened and ran, tossing the bar away in his panic. I happened to come across it by accident."

"But how did Bo Jenkins know you had it?" Mike asked.

"He was out looking for it later that night," Jupe said. "He heard us and pointed his torch at us and saw me holding it. He'd seen us before and probably Doc Dawson told him who we were and where we came from. He came to the yard and found my uncle working on the cages. He must have been delighted when he heard they'd have to search the yard for extra bars. He couldn't be sure, but there was a good chance the gorilla bar would turn up. Of course, he had no idea that George's bar was around, too."

"How can you be sure you've found the right bars here?" asked Mike.

"I can't, until we take the bars off," said Jupe. "But I expect we'll find the diamonds in them, since I used the smugglers' own method of locating them."

"How do you know that?" asked Mike.

"The cable told me, and Doc Dawson confirmed it. The cable said, 'DOX ROX NOX EX REX BOX.' Which means, knock on the bars of the lion's cage and you'll find the diamonds inserted at the docks. EX, I would guess, stands for 'out of'—take the lion out first. A wise precaution, considering what happened with the gorilla.

"Now, do you recall what Doc did last night when the gorilla was brought back? Doc tested all the bars on its cage with the hammer. He did the same thing with the panther cage. At the time it merely seemed an odd way to test the strength of bars. But Doc was actually testing for diamonds— probably trying to make sure Jenkins had picked the right bar, or possibly making sure there were no others. Once they had the manner of smuggling arranged and the cable informing them how to look for the hollow bars—it was easy. Any bar that sounded hollow would contain diamonds."

Jupiter turned to Doc Dawson. "May I have the pliers, please?" Doc silently handed them over.

Jupe clamped the long pliers to the top bolt on the rusty bar he'd singled out. A few hard turns and the bolt came off. Jupe stooped and repeated the action with the bottom bolt. He took the hammer and knocked the bar through the drilled slots in the boards. As it came out, Hall and the boys crowded around.

Jupe knocked the top cap off the bar, then turned it over and struck it with the hammer. A thin trickle of greasy yellow stones came out.

"Those are diamonds?" Pete asked.

Jupe nodded. "Rough, uncut diamonds, Pete. They look like ordinary rocks and pebbles when they're found."

"Gosh!" exclaimed Bob. "There's a ton of them there."

Jupe smiled, looking down at the pile of dull stones. "Well, not a ton exactly, Records. Mr Olsen-Dunlop mentioned six hundred K's. He was talking about carats, I believe. A carat is worth approximately one thousand dollars. Allowing for some loss in cutting, we have a good half-million here. And with those in the gorilla bar, perhaps a million dollars' worth of diamonds altogether."

Jim Hall stared at the pile of stones and shook his head. "I'm sorry, Doc," he said. "I'm afraid you have some explaining to do."

There was no answer.

Jim Hall looked up, and twisted his head in surprise. Dawson was gone. They heard the sound of the truck engine starting up.

"He's getting away!" cried Pete.

The truck backed off with a roar as the boys started for it. Almost immediately two cars came from the trees and braked to a quick stop behind it, blocking the driveway. Two men leaped out.

"Hatchet-Face and Dobbsie!" cried Bob.

They grabbed Dawson as he jumped from the cab, and brought him forward to the barn.

"What's going on? Who are you two?" demanded Jim Hall.

Jupe pointed. "That one's Mr Olsen—he's been after the bars from the beginning."

"No," said Mike. "His name is Dunlop. He works for Jay Eastland."

The hatchet-faced man shook his head. "Sorry, boys—but you're both wrong. Stevenson's the name."

He flipped open his wallet and held it out.

Jupe's face reddened. "His card says Stevenson, all right." He looked up at the grinning man. "We thought you were part of the gang."

"Customs agents have to act mysterious, son," the man explained. "Dobbs here is with the Treasury Department. We're both working for the same firm—the United States Government. And we've been trying to break up this smuggling ring for a long time."

Dobbs gestured to the pile of stones lying on the ground. "Looks like the kid saved us a lot of trouble. We knew Dawson was getting diamonds, but we couldn't move in until they actually showed up. We didn't know exactly where they were and that's the kind of evidence that's needed."

"You'll find some more in another bar," Jupe said.

The Treasury agent kicked at the pile of stones. "Now all we have to do is find the other man—Bo Jenkins. He seems to have disappeared."

"You'll find him back at my house," said Jim Hall. "He'll be waiting for us."

The two men looked startled.

"He's not going anywhere," Jim Hall stated. "George is looking after him."

Dobbs looked at him wide-eyed. "George—the lion?"

Jim Hall nodded.

Stevenson grinned. He clapped Jupe on the shoulder. "Okay, Investigator—you already found half a million. Would you like to try for another?"

Jupe stepped forward to the cage. Pointing to the second bar he had selected, he said dramatically, "You will note, gentlemen, that this bar is not as rusted as the first one that was extracted from the lion's cage. The gorilla was a recent arrival and therefore—"

Bob and Pete exchanged grins. They knew how their leader loved to make the most out of a situation.

Doc Dawson laughed harshly. His shoulders sagged. He looked like a man who had bet a lot of money and lost.

"Hurry it up," he said. "I'd like to see how much I lost before I tell you everything."

21

Some Questions from Mr Hitchcock

A WEEK later, The Three Investigators sat in Mr Hitchcock's office, being congratulated.

"Thank you, sir!" chorused the boys.

"There are a few small points I should like to have cleared up," Mr Hitchcock told them. "This barbarous device—the metal shredder—am I to assume that your nearly fatal engagement with it was accidental?"

"Yes, sir," Bob said. "Bo Jenkins and Doc

Dawson tied us up and tossed us into an old junked car. They did it merely to get us out of the way. They never expected that the crane would drop the car on the conveyor belt."

Alfred Hitchcock nodded. "I would hope they would be more careful next time, if indeed there should ever be one, about the process they select for discouraging interlopers." He laced his fingers together. "This Hank Morton person—where does he fit in? Did he let George out deliberately and then wound him? And why was he running away the night the gorilla escaped? Was he involved in that, too?"

"No, sir," Bob said. "No to all of those questions. He came back to Jungle Land after being fired because he was suspicious of Doc Dawson. According to Hank Morton, Dawson made it look as if he had mistreated the animals, and Jim Hall took his word for everything. Dawson, of course, was trying to replace him with Bo Jenkins. When Morton came back, Doc decided to fix him for good. He let George out himself, planning to blame it on Morton.

"George cut himself accidentally out in the jungle. I guess he didn't know how to take care of himself out there, since he grew up in captivity. When Morton led us out to him, he was only teasing us. He knew George and could handle him. But when he stepped away for a minute, Bo Jenkins found him and hit him over the head. So Morton was blamed for that, too.

"That night when the gorilla broke loose,

Morton was trying to find Bo Jenkins. Instead he ran into the gorilla and was frightened away, just as Bo Jenkins was."

"What about the panther's escape?" asked Mr Hitchcock. "Did Doc Dawson engineer that?"

"No, sir," replied Pete. "At least, he said he didn't. We think it was a real accident. We're just grateful that Doc saved our lives. Mr Stevenson said that might be a point in Doc's favour when his case comes to trial."

Alfred Hitchcock glanced down at the papers on which Bob had summarised the adventure. "Ah, yes, Mr Stevenson, the government agent, also known as Olsen and Dunlop. You say he was planted with the Jay Eastland movie company by the authorities, to watch the smugglers?"

"Yes, sir," Jupe said. "He happens to be an expert on firearms and was available to Jay Eastland in that capacity. Eastland was acting so violently against Jim Hall, however, that he aroused Stevenson's suspicions. As it turned out, Eastland had nothing to do with the smuggling itself. But he was trying to take advantage of the contract Jim Hall had agreed to. He could have used an extra fifty thousand dollars and was hoping to pin something on Hall. But he couldn't, and since filming is over, Jungle Land is safe."

"Now as to the smuggling itself," said Mr Hitchcock. "Doc Dawson enlisted the aid of this Bo Jenkins to help retrieve the hollow bars. The diamond shipments originated in Africa, taking advantage of Cal Hall's deliveries of animals to his brother here. Was Dawson the ringleader? Did he plan the entire operation or was he merely an accessory? Exactly how did he fit in?"

"Doc Dawson planned it all," answered Jupe. "The diamonds were stolen from the surface portion of a deposit at Mwadui in the Shinyanga district of Tanzania. The smugglers followed Cal Hall to the port of Dar es Salaam and there switched the cage bars, first on George's cage, then on the gorilla's. When George left Africa, they alerted Doc Dawson with that coded cable."

"And why didn't Doc Dawson take the diamonds from the lion's cage as soon as it arrived?" Mr Hitchcock asked Jupe.

"Because he was expecting a gorilla to arrive with more diamonds soon afterwards. Only two shipments were planned. I guess he figured that the first lot were safe where they were, hidden in the cage bar, so he could wait till the second lot came and then clear out with a million dollars' worth of gems. But the gorilla didn't come for a long time. Meanwhile, Doc Dawson came down with the flu. While he was sick, Jim Hall threw out the lion's cage. It got broken up in the scrap yard and the bars misplaced. By the time Doc caught up with it, it was too late.

"It was also too late because by then the authorities were on to the smuggling operation. Stevenson wouldn't tell us how they learned about it—said he was sorry but he couldn't divulge his sources. When he and Dobbs got Dawson with the evidence, his confederates in Africa were rounded up."

The director tapped Bob's report again. "You surmised that George was being made nervous by the various attempts to get at the bar with the diamonds. Were you correct in that assumption?"

"Yes, sir. At first, I think, George was only restless because he was cooped up in the house at night. But then Stevenson and Dobbs started prowling around, which upset George."

"I still do not understand," rumbled Alfred Hitchcock, "why Doc Dawson, a respectable veterinarian, would become a diamond smuggler."

"That's easy," offered Pete. "He was a smuggler *before* he came to Jungle Land. He'd been through Africa and pulled various small jobs there years before. When he found out about Cal and Jim Hall's operation, it seemed perfect for his plans. So he joined up with them, using his skill with animals to get by, while he planned the entire diamond operation in Tanzania. He really did love animals, but he also loved the excitement of getting rich quick and dangerously."

"Not to mention criminally," added Mr Hitchcock. "I believe we are well rid of the fellow. He failed in his biggest attempt, the always tempting million-dollar haul. And you boys thwarted him by dint of clever deductions and perseverance. I'm proud of you all. You solved a most perplexing mystery."

"Mystery is our business!" said Jupiter Jones.

The Three Investigators
in

THE SINGING
SERPENT

by Nick West

Based on characters created by
Robert Arthur

The Mystery of the Singing Serpent was first published
in the UK in a single volume in 1973 by
William Collins Sons & Co. Ltd.

A Short Preview
by Alfred Hitchcock

Welcome, mystery lovers! We are gathered together again for another stimulating case of The Three Investigators, whose official motto is "We Investigate Anything". If they had known what they were getting into when they tackled the curious case of the singing serpent, they might have changed their motto!

Be that as it may, they find themselves this time drawn into the dark world of witchcraft, where mystery and intrigue lead them from one enigma to another until—but I am not a blabbermouth. I promised faithfully not to tell too much, and I shall keep my promise.

Indeed, I shall only say that The Three Investigators are Jupiter Jones, Pete Crenshaw and Bob Andrews, who all make their home in Rocky Beach, a small municipality in California a few miles from Hollywood. Their Headquarters is a mobile home trailer in The Jones Salvage Yard, a super-junkyard owned by Jupiter's aunt and uncle.

The boys make an excellent team. Jupiter has a quick mind and is adept at deductions. Pete is less intellectual but sturdy and courageous. Bob is somewhat studious and an excellent researcher. Together they have solved some very unusual mysteries indeed.

Which is all I shall say at this time, for I know you are eager to dispense with this preview and get to the main feature!

ALFRED HITCHCOCK

I

The Girl on the Appaloosa

"I WOULD BE HAPPIER, Jupiter, if you didn't come to breakfast in your swimming trunks," said Aunt Mathilda Jones.

Jupiter Jones pushed back the sleeves of his sports shirt and reached for his orange juice. "I'm going swimming with Bob and Pete," he said. "They'll be here any minute."

Across the table, Uncle Titus Jones brushed a crumb from his big black moustache. "Don't eat too much," he warned Jupiter. "You're not supposed to swim on a full stomach."

"You don't want to get cramp," said Aunt Mathilda. She then moved her coffee cup to one side and began to look through the *Los Angeles Times*.

Jupiter took a single slice of toast.

"Well, my gracious to Betsy!" said Aunt Mathilda. Then she sighed.

Jupiter looked up in interest. Aunt Mathilda was not much given to sighing.

"I was seventeen the year that movie came out," said Aunt Mathilda. "I saw it at the Odeon."

Uncle Titus looked blank.

"I don't think I slept for a week after," said Aunt Mathilda. She passed the paper across the table to

9

Uncle Titus. Jupiter stood up and looked over his uncle's shoulder at the picture of a thin man with high cheekbones, pinched nostrils and piercing, dark eyes. In the photograph, the man stared intently into a glowing crystal ball.

"Ramon Castillo in *The Vampire's Lair*," said Jupiter. "He was a great master of make-up."

Aunt Mathilda shuddered. "You should have seen him in *Cry of the Werewolf*."

"I did," said Jupiter. "It was on television last month."

Uncle Titus finished reading the news story that accompanied the photograph of the late great character actor. "It says here that the auction of Castillo's estate will be held on the twenty-first," said Uncle Titus. "I think I'll go."

Aunt Mathilda pondered this, frowning slightly. She knew that Uncle Titus dearly loved auctions. She also knew that The Jones Salvage Yard, which she and Uncle Titus owned, was famous for its stock of hard-to-find items. People came to the yard seeking everything from steel beams and old bathtubs to antique sundials. Nevertheless, some of Uncle Titus's more unusual purchases had been difficult to sell. Aunt Mathilda was a firm believer in making a profit.

"They're selling the entire Castillo collection," said Uncle Titus. "All of his costumes and even the crystal ball he used in *The Vampire's Lair*."

"There are dealers who specialise in that sort of thing," Aunt Mathilda said. "Besides, the bidding will be high."

"I suppose so." Uncle Titus put the paper aside. "The collectors will be out in droves."

"I'm sure they will." Aunt Mathilda stood up and began to clear the table. Halfway to the sink she paused and listened. From the street outside came the clip-clop of hoofs. "The little Jamison girl," decided Aunt Mathilda.

Jupiter went to the window. It was the Jamison girl, and as usual she was astride her Appaloosa. The horse stepped along with its head high. It was a magnificent mare, brown with white markings on its hindquarters. "Beautiful horse," said Jupiter. "Typical of the Appaloosa breed."

He did not comment on the rider—the girl who sat straight in the saddle and looked neither to left nor right.

"Going for a gallop on the beach, I guess," said Aunt Mathilda. "That must be a lonely child. Marie told me her parents are in Europe."

"I know," said Jupe. Marie was the Jamison maid, and she and Aunt Mathilda were friends. On her afternoons off, Marie often came to have tea with Aunt Mathilda and to tell of the doings of the Jamison family.

Thanks to Marie, Jupe knew that when Mr Jamison bought the old Littlefield mansion some months before, he spared no expense in having the place restored. He knew that the chandelier in the dining-room had once graced a palace in Vienna, and that Mrs Jamison had a diamond necklace which had once graced the throat of the Empress Eugénie. He knew that the girl on the Appaloosa was Allie, the Jamison daughter, and that the mare was her personal property. Jupe even knew that at the moment an aunt of Allie's from Los Angeles was presiding over the grand household, and in Marie's opinion, the aunt was very odd.

The girl and the horse disappeared round the corner, and Aunt Mathilda put the dishes she was holding on the draining board. "You could try being nice to that girl," she told Jupe. "The Jamisons only live a short distance down the street. We're practically neighbours."

"She doesn't seem especially neighbourly," said Jupe. "I think she only talks to horses."

"Perhaps she's shy," said Aunt Mathilda.

Jupe did not reply, for Bob Andrews and Pete Crenshaw had come swooping down the street on their bikes. Like Jupe, Bob and Pete wore scuffed sneakers, swimming trunks and sports shirts.

"See you later," said Jupe to his aunt, and he hurried out to meet the other boys.

The three were off then, with Jupiter pedalling furiously at his bicycle. Jupe had once been a child actor, and had been called Baby Fatso. It was still easy to see why. In spite of his extra weight, however, he was ahead of Bob and Pete when they reached the corner of the street and turned down the short hill towards the Coast Highway.

Suddenly, "Watch out!" Pete shouted.

A horse screamed in terror. Jupe saw a huge shape rear in front of him. He threw his arms over his head, and as he fell he wrenched himself to one side. His bike clattered away.

There was another scream. It was thinner and higher —not an animal scream.

An instant later, hoofs struck the tarmac very close to Jupe's head.

Jupe rolled away, then sat up. The Appaloosa was backing and prancing, ears flat against its head. The Jamison girl was lying on the road.

Bob and Pete dropped their bikes and Jupe scrambled up. All three hurried to the girl. Pete bent and touched her on the shoulder.

The girl was gasping, struggling to catch her breath. With a convulsive effort, she managed to get her lungs full of air. Then she shouted, "Take your hands off me!"

"Hey!" said Bob gently. "Take it easy, huh?"

She came to a sitting position and clutched at her knee, where blood streamed through a rip in her faded jeans. Her eyes were dry, but she was panting, almost sobbing.

"You really got the wind knocked out of you," said Pete.

She ignored him and glared at Jupiter. "Don't you know horses have the right of way?" she demanded.

"I'm sorry," said Jupe. "I didn't see you."

The girl stood up slowly. She looked at her mare and then back at Jupiter. Her eyes were pale—the same tawny colour as her long hair—but at that instant they were cold with rage. "If you've hurt my mare . . ." she began.

"I don't believe the horse is damaged in any way," said Jupiter stiffly.

The girl limped towards the Appaloosa. "Easy, girl!" she called. "Here, girl! Easy!"

The mare came to her and put its big head down on her shoulder.

"Did they scare you?" asked the girl. Her hands went up to stroke the horse's mane.

Aunt Mathilda appeared at the top of the road. "Jupiter? Pete? Bob? What's going on?"

The Jamison girl patted the horse again, reached up to grasp the saddle and tried to mount. The horse took a step backward.

"Hold it for her, Pete," said Jupe. "I'll give her a hand."

"I don't need a hand!" snapped the girl.

Aunt Mathilda came down the road. She stared at Allie Jamison—at the tangle of hair, the torn jeans, the bleeding knee. "What happened?"

"They scared my horse," said the girl.

"And she fell off," added Pete.

"It was an accident," said Jupe.

"I see. Jupiter, go and tell your Uncle Titus to bring one of the trucks. I'll drive Miss Jamison home so she can have that knee attended to."

"I don't need anyone to drive me home," said Allie Jamison.

"The truck, Jupiter," said Aunt Mathilda. "And Pete, you hold the reins on that horse."

"Does it bite?" asked Pete.

"Certainly not," declared Aunt Mathilda, who really knew very little about the subject. "Horses don't bite. They kick."

"Oh, great!" groaned Pete.

2

The Night Visitor

WHEN BOB, PETE AND JUPITER led the Appaloosa up to the Jamison house, the truck from the salvage yard was standing in the driveway. Aunt Mathilda and the Jamison girl were nowhere to be seen.

Pete looked at the massive pillars that supported the roof over the veranda. "Too bad Aunt Mathilda didn't wear her hoop skirt today," he said.

Jupiter chuckled. "It does look like an old Southern mansion," he conceded.

"A big old Southern mansion," said Bob. "Where do you suppose we find the horse department?"

Pete pointed towards the rear of the property. "There's a field with a fence round it."

"Fine," said Jupe. They led the mare up the drive, past a flagstone patio which was shaded by a wistaria vine.

Behind the house, the driveway fanned out to become a courtyard. Next to the fenced field was a triple garage. One double door stood open, and inside there was a stall. Pieces of tack hung from pegs on the walls.

The back door of the house opened and Marie, the maid, looked out. "Boys, would you take the saddle off Indian Queen and let her into the field? Then come in. Miss Osborne wants to see you."

Marie disappeared into the house, closing the door behind her.

Pete looked at the mare. " Indian Queen?"

" I believe Allie Jamison calls her Queenie," said Jupe. " That's what Marie told Aunt Mathilda."

" Who's Miss Osborne?" asked Bob.

" She's the aunt who's staying here while Mr and Mrs Jamison are in Europe," Jupe told him. " According to Marie, she's rather peculiar."

" Peculiar how?"

" I don't know exactly, but Marie thinks there's something odd about her. If we're going to meet her, we can judge for ourselves."

Jupe removed the mare's saddle. Bob opened the gate to the field, and the horse trotted into the grass beyond the fence. Jupe found a stand in the garage for the saddle and a peg for the bridle. Then the boys opened the back door of the house and stepped directly into a huge, sunny kitchen.

They went through the kitchen to a wide central hall with a staircase. To the left was the dining-room, and the boys looked out past the crystal drops of the famous chandelier to the wistaria-shaded patio. To the right of the hall was the living-room which was all green-gold paleness. Beyond the living-room, a door opened on to a panelled room lined with books.

Allie Jamison was in the living-room stretched out on a sofa with a towel under her leg. Beside her sat a woman who might have been Aunt Mathilda's age, or perhaps a bit older. She wore a long gown of purple velvet, trimmed at the throat with a band of silver. Her hair was a delicate shade of lavender.

"Aunt Pat, Mum will kill me if I bleed on the sofa," said Allie. "Look, I'll go upstairs and . . ."

"Now dear, just lie still. You've had a shock." The woman did not look up at the boys, and Jupe saw that her hands shook as she cut the leg of the girl's jeans up from the ankle. "Oh, my. It's still bleeding," she said.

"A nasty scrape," said Aunt Mathilda, who had established herself in a chair near the fireplace. "Still, children do survive these things."

"I'll need some cobwebs," said the woman.

"Cobwebs?" echoed Aunt Mathilda.

"Cobwebs?" said Marie, who stood by holding a basin of water.

Bob and Pete shifted uneasily, and Pete looked questioningly at Jupe. Jupe smiled. "Cobwebs," he said to Marie. "Spiders make them."

Marie went pink with outrage. "There are no cobwebs in this house. I dust every week."

"Oh, how unfortunate," said the lady in purple. "Well, in that case, bring the gold jar from my medicine cabinet."

Marie went, and for the first time the woman in purple focused on the boys. "Thank you for helping my niece," she said. "Of course, this whole thing could have been prevented if she'd worn her purple scarf. Purple is for protection, you know."

"Of course," said Jupiter.

Marie returned with a small gilt jar.

"This should do it," said Allie's aunt. "It's not quite as good as cobwebs, but it *is* good. I made it myself." She took the lid from the jar and applied a clear ointment to Allie's knee.

"Would the Medical Association approve?" asked Allie.

"Now, dear, it's sure to work," said Miss Osborne. "I gathered the herbs in the dark of the moon. Look. The bleeding's stopped."

"I hate to say so, Aunt Pat," said the girl, "but it stopped before you put that rubbish on. What now? Do we order a wheelchair?"

"I think a bandage . . ." began Miss Osborne.

"I'll take care of it. It's no big deal." Allie got up and headed for the hall. She passed the boys as if they were invisible, then paused at the foot of the stairs. "Thanks," she said. "I mean, thanks for bringing Indian Queen home."

"No trouble," said Pete, who had stayed as far away from the horse as possible.

Allie went upstairs.

"I'm sure Allie is really grateful," said Miss Osborne. "She's a bit upset now, and you've been so kind and . . . and I'm afraid I didn't get your names."

Aunt Mathilda stood up. "I am Mrs Titus Jones and this is my nephew, Jupiter Jones. And Pete Cranshaw and Bob Andrews."

Miss Osborne stared at Jupe, her violet eyes wide. "Jupiter Jones! Why, you're Baby Fatso!"

Jupiter did not care to be reminded of his stage name. He felt his face getting hot.

"The world's youngest has-been," said Pete with a smile.

"Ah, but to have been part of the wonderful world of cinema!" exclaimed Miss Osborne. Her eyes went past Jupiter to the window. "It's Mr Ariel!" she cried.

Aunt Mathilda and the boys turned to look. Out on the street, a man dressed in a black suit was getting out of a taxi. He had, thought Jupiter, the palest face ever seen on a human being. He looked as if he spent all his days in some deep cave.

Carrying a suitcase, the man headed up the drive to the path leading to the front door.

"He *is* coming to stay after all!" Miss Osborne was obviously thrilled. "I was so hoping."

"We won't intrude," said Aunt Mathilda. "We must be going anyway." And before Miss Osborne could say one more word, she was shepherding the boys out the front door and across the verandah. They passed the black-clad man on the path.

Aunt Mathilda paused before she climbed into the cab of the pickup truck. "If you boys are going swimming, you'd better go," she said. "Do you want a ride back to your bikes?"

"No thanks," said Jupe. "We'll walk."

Aunt Mathilda shook her head. "Never in all my life! Cobwebs on a wound! What an idea!" She climbed into the truck and slammed the door.

"It's an old folk remedy for bleeding," said Jupiter, who read a great deal and had a head crammed with odd bits of information.

"Dreadful!" announced Aunt Mathilda, and she backed the truck out of the drive.

"And peculiar," said Pete. "Marie is right. Allie Jamison's aunt is one very peculiar lady."

"She is, at least, very superstitious," said Jupiter.

He dismissed the subject of Allie Jamison from his mind then. Not until late that night, as he was falling asleep, did he think again of the Jamison house and the jar of ointment—herbs gathered in the dark of the moon. He smiled and pulled the bedclothes up to his chin. He was almost asleep when the pounding began at the door.

"Mrs Jones! Mrs Jones, let me in!"

Jupiter sprang out of bed, snatched his dressing-gown and charged into the hall. Aunt Mathilda was halfway down the stairs, with Uncle Titus behind her. Jupe followed and saw his aunt unlock the door.

Marie, the Jamison maid, almost fell into the house. "Oh, Mrs Jones!" she wailed. She was in her dressing-gown and slippers.

"Marie, what is it?" asked Aunt Mathilda.

"Can I stay here tonight?" pleaded Marie. She collapsed into a chair and began to weep.

"Marie, what *is* the matter?"

"The singing!"

"What?" said Aunt Mathilda.

"The singing." Marie twisted her hands. "There's something in that house and it's singing." She grasped Aunt Mathilda's arm. "It was horrible. Not like anything I ever heard. I can't go back there!"

3

The Insistent Client

As GENTLY AS SHE COULD, Aunt Mathilda released herself from Marie's grip. "I'm going to call the Jamison house," she announced.

Marie sniffled. "Call if you want," she said. "But I'm not going back!"

Aunt Mathilda dialled the Jamisons' number and reached Miss Patricia Osborne. The conversation was brief. "Miss Osborne says she didn't hear anything strange," Aunt Mathilda reported when she hung up the telephone

"Miss Osborne *would* say that!" exclaimed Marie.

"What do you mean?" asked Aunt Mathilda

"I mean . . . I mean she's peculiar and there's peculiar things going on in that house and I'm never going back. Not for anything!"

Marie would talk of it no more, and she did not go back. She spent the night in the spare bedroom. In the morning Uncle Titus went to the Jamison house and collected her suitcases, which Allie Jamison had packed. Uncle Titus then drove Marie to her mother's home in Los Angeles.

"I wonder what Marie heard," said Jupiter Jones after she had departed.

Aunt Mathilda only shrugged.

Jupiter was still wondering several days later when he walked across the street from his house to the salvage yard in the middle of the morning. Hans and Konrad, the two Bavarian brothers who helped out at the yard, were cleaning a marble mantelpiece. Uncle Titus had bought it from the demolition contractors who were dismantling a burned-out house in the Hollywood Hills.

"Pete is in your workshop," said Hans.

"He want to use the printing press," added Konrad.

Jupe nodded. He did not need to be told that the press was in operation. He had assembled the press himself, out of old parts, and while the machine was efficient enough, it was noisy. He had recognised the familiar clanking and groaning the moment he came in the gate of The Jones Salvage Yard.

Jupe went quickly past piles of old timber and stacks of steel beams to his outdoor workshop. It occupied a corner of the yard out of sight of the main area, which was Aunt Mathilda's special domain. The shop was sheltered from the street by the tall wooden fence that enclosed the entire yard, and it was partially sheltered from the weather by a six-foot-wide roof which ran all the way round the inside of the fence. Uncle Titus had built the roof to protect his most valuable junk.

In the workshop, Jupiter found Pete Crenshaw bent over the press, running off a stack of business cards. Jupe picked up one of the cards and examined it. It read:

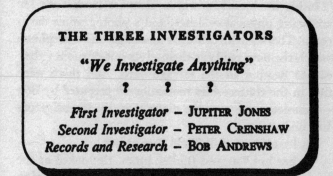

THE THREE INVESTIGATORS

"We Investigate Anything"

? ? ?

First Investigator – JUPITER JONES
Second Investigator – PETER CRENSHAW
Records and Research – BOB ANDREWS

Pete stopped the press. "Satisfied, First Investigator?" he asked.

Jupiter nodded. "Very neat," he said. "And it's gratifying to know that the firm of The Three Investigators has been so successful. I wasn't sure, when we started, that we would ever need an additional supply of business cards."

Pete did not comment. He had been somewhat less than confident when he had joined with Jupiter Jones and Bob Andrews to found The Three Investigators. But Jupe's superior powers of deduction, Bob's talent for detailed research and his own athletic abilities had proved a powerful combination. The three young sleuths had been able to unravel mysteries which had seemed unsolvable to many of their elders.

The Investigators made their headquarters in a thirty-foot mobile home trailer which was hidden away behind piles of junk, not far from the workshop. Uncle Titus had given the trailer to the boys when he found it was too damaged to sell. They had since fixed it up to suit themselves.

Inside headquarters was a compact laboratory for analysing physical evidence, and a photographic darkroom. There was an office for meetings, and a telephone which the boys paid for themselves out of money they earned helping in the salvage yard. And there were files in the trailer—files meticulously prepared by Bob —complete reports on the many cases the Investigators had undertaken.

"It hasn't been dull," said Pete at last.

"It has not," agreed Jupiter Jones. He looked at the business card in his hand, with its three question marks. "The universal symbol of the unknown," he said. "The question mark is always intriguing. Mystery is always intriguing. I wonder, for example, about Marie."

"The Jamison maid?" questioned Pete.

"Yes. What did she hear in that house that frightened her? Was it something really strange, or did she let her imagination get the better of her? She said that Miss Osborne is peculiar, but she never explained why she thought so."

"Miss Osborne puts cobwebs on cuts," said Pete.

Jupiter suddenly held up a warning hand. There was a rustle beyond the heap of junk that separated the workshop area from the rest of the yard.

Pete strode quickly out of the workshop. An instant later, Jupe heard him exclaim mildly, "I thought I smelt a horse."

Allie Jamison stamped into the workshop area with Pete trailing her. "Very funny!" she said.

"How long have you been standing out there eavesdropping?" asked Jupe.

"Long enough," said the girl. Without waiting for an invitation, she sat down in an old chair near the press.

"Long enough for what?" said Jupe evenly.

The girl took a card from the stack on the printing press and looked at it. "My allowance will not stretch to cover a professional detective," she said. "What are your rates?"

"You want to retain The Three Investigators?" asked Jupe.

"Beginning right now."

"I'm afraid we'll have to know more about what's involved before we decide whether or not we're interested," said Jupiter Jones.

"You're interested, all right," Allie shot back. "I've been listening to you two, and I know you're interested. You're dying to know what happened at our place the night Marie ran away. Besides, you don't have any choice."

"What's that supposed to mean?" asked Pete.

"You guys are getting careless," said Allie. "On the back fence of this place there's a painting of the San Francisco fire of 1905."

"It occurred in 1906," Jupiter informed her.

"Who cares? The important thing is that there's a little dog in that picture. I've been watching that fence. When you poke your finger through the knothole in the dog's eye, you can open a gate in the fence. You've got a secret entrance to this place. Does your aunt know?"

"Blackmail!" cried Pete.

"It is not blackmail," declared the girl. "I don't want

money. I'll pay you. What I want is help, and I hear you're the best talent in town—not that that's saying much."

"Thanks a lot!" said Pete.

"You're welcome. Now, do you help me, or do I go and see your aunt?"

Jupiter sat down on an empty crate. "Exactly what do you have in mind?"

"I want to get that creep Hugo Ariel out of the house," said Allie quickly.

"Ariel? Isn't he the man who arrived the day you fell off the horse? A pale man dressed in black?"

"That's the one. The reason he's pale is that he never goes out in the daytime. His father must have been a mole."

"He arrived at your house the morning you fell. That night, Marie ran away." Jupiter pulled at his lower lip. "She did hear something strange," he suggested. "It wasn't her imagination."

"It sure wasn't." Allie Jamison suddenly seemed less confident. She was folding the business card in her hand, creasing it nervously, then unfolding it again. "It had something to do with Ariel," she said slowly. "He's making that noise somehow, some way. I never heard that sound before he came."

"He's still there at your house?" asked Pete.

"He is, and my Aunt Pat seems to think he's wonderful. But then, Aunt Pat is totally off her rocker. Even before Ariel showed up, she used to draw a circle round her bed every night with a knife. That was to keep away evil influences. Now she's taken to lighting candles—lots of candles. They're very special candles.

They're delivered from a shop in Hollywood and they're all different colours. Purple is for protection and blue means something else and orange is good and red is very powerful. Every night Aunt Pat and Ariel go into the library and light candles and lock the door."

"And then?" prompted Jupiter.

"And then, sometimes, I hear that sound." Allie shuddered slightly. "I can hear it even if I'm upstairs, but I can hear it best if I'm in the living-room. It comes out of the library."

"Marie said it was a singing noise," said Jupe.

Allie looked down at her hands. "I suppose you could call it singing, only ... only I never heard any singing like it before. It's really eerie."

Jupiter frowned. "Marie said something was singing. She didn't say it was *someone*, she said it was *something*. She made it sound as if the noise wasn't made by a person."

Allie pulled herself erect in the chair and looked squarely at Jupiter. "Look, it doesn't matter. Ariel's doing it somehow and I can't stand it. It's got to stop!"

"Is it so bad?"

"It's bad. It's so bad we can't keep any help. The agency's sent two maids since Marie left. They won't stay. The place is knee-deep in dust and I'm starving to death, since I happen to be a rotten cook and Aunt Pat is worse. And I'm not allowed to make any noise because Ariel sleeps all day and wanders round the house all night. I don't like it and I want him out!"

"Getting rid of unwelcome house guests isn't

exactly in our line," said Jupe. "I should think that if you had a talk with Miss Osborne . . . ?"

"I have talked with Aunt Pat until my throat hurts," said Allie. "She just smiles at me as if I had butterflies in my brain and changes the subject and talks about her old film junk."

"Film junk?" echoed Pete.

"She collects stuff from old films," explained Allie. "She has everything from the fake eyelashes Della LaFonte wore in *Spring Fever* to the sword John Maybanks used in *Marko's Revenge*. Every time some film star pops off or decides to move and get rid of his stuff, Aunt Pat is right there at the auction. That's where all her money goes."

"It sounds like a harmless hobby," said Jupe.

"So does lighting candles," Allie pointed out. "Only if Ariel comes with the candles, I draw the line. He's too much. He's got to go—him and his horrible noise!"

Pete leaned back against the printing press. "You know, Jupe, it could be kind of fun," he said. "We could apple-pie Ariel's bed and put frogs in his bathtub and snakes in his shoes."

Allie snorted. "Ariel would just love snakes. What I want to do is get something on him!"

"Blackmail again?" said Jupe quietly.

"He asked for it, butting in in *my* house. Only I can't find out anything about him. He doesn't talk to me—he doesn't even seem to see me. And Aunt Pat won't tell me anything. There's something funny about him, and she doesn't want me to know what it is."

"But if she already knows—" began Pete.

"What she knows can't be really bad," interrupted Allie, "or she wouldn't have him around. She's kind of a dimwit, but she's not bad. What I want is some information I can clout him with. I need to know where he came from and what he's up to. That's where you come in.

"Now listen, tonight, Aunt Pat's giving a party. She's been on the telephone inviting people and Ariel has been stirring up some brew for a punch. If there's going to be a party there will be other people in the house and maybe they'll give us some lead to Ariel. So since it *is* my house, you're invited to the party."

"Do we taste the punch?" asked Pete.

"No. You don't mingle. You observe. Then you track the guests to their lairs, or whatever we decide is best. I'll meet you at eight o'clock out by the garage. Cut across the back so no one sees you from the house." She stood up. "You'd better be there," she warned, "or I'll have a talk with Mrs Jones about that secret gate."

Jupe and Pete listened to her footsteps going away across the salvage yard. "We have a new client whether we want one or not," said Jupe.

He pushed aside a piece of grating behind the printing press, revealing a large corrugated pipe which was padded with odd scraps of carpeting. This was Tunnel Two, another of the secret passageways in the salvage yard. It led under the piles of junk that concealed the mobile home trailer of The Three Investigators. At the far end of the pipe, a trap door opened directly into Headquarters.

"What are you going to do?" asked Pete.

"I don't think Bob is working at the library this

morning. I'll call him and tell him we're all invited to a party."

"I'll go with you," said Pete. "I want to nail down those loose boards in the back fence. I hate to give up Red Gate Rover, but with Allie Jamison in the neighbourhood, I don't think we have much choice."

4

The Singing Serpent

IT WAS DUSK when Jupiter Jones, Pete Crenshaw and
Bob Andrews strolled past the Jamison house.

"Not a large party," said Jupiter.

There were three cars parked in front of the house—
an orange sports car, a green estate car and a dusty, tan
saloon.

Beyond the house, The Three Investigators cut across
some open ground to get to the garage behind the
Jamison mansion. Allie Jamison was waiting for them.
"The group has gathered," she announced. "They're
in the dining-room and the patio doors are open. Don't
make any noise and follow me."

They stole across the bricked courtyard and down
the drive to the patio, with its shadowing Wistaria. At
the edge of the patio, Allie stopped.

Jupiter held a branch of Wistaria aside and looked
past Allie's shoulder into the dining-room.

What he saw was unlike any party he had ever seen.
There were five people in the room, and they stood in a
silent circle round the table. Miss Osborne wore a long
purple garment with wide sleeves and a high neck.
Opposite her was the man called Hugo Ariel. He was
dressed all in black, as he had been when the boys first
saw him. His pale face gleamed in the light from two

tall red candles which had been inserted into heavy silver candlesticks. His black hair was cropped short, but it had been brushed forward so that little tendrils reached towards his heavy eyebrows.

To Ariel's left was a thin woman in an orange gown. Like Miss Osborne, she had tinted her hair, but she had chosen an unfortunate colour. The harsh red clashed with her orange robe.

Opposite the red-haired woman was a blonde lady fairly bursting out of a pale green gown. And next to her was the fifth member of the party. He looked out of place. The others stood straight, waiting expectantly for something. He slumped. The others had obviously dressed carefully for the party. He had not. His jacket looked weary and worn, and the inch of T-shirt that showed above his sports shirt would have been better for a trip to the laundry. His sparse, greying hair needed cutting.

Allie beckoned to the boys to follow her up the drive. When they were a little distance from the patio she stopped. "Cosy bunch, huh?"

"Are they going to just stand there?" asked Pete.

"Beats me," said Allie. "I wandered around among the guests until Ariel started giving me his special fishy stare. The guy with the messy clothes owns a delicatessen and his name's Noxworth. The skinny freak in the orange dress is Madelyn Enderby, Aunt Pat's hairdresser. She says she vibrates well in orange. I guess she does. At least she twitches a lot. The blonde owns a health food store."

Faintly, from the direction of the patio, came the sound of hands clapping.

"Something's up," whispered Allie. "Let's go."

The Three Investigators and Allie returned to the patio and peered in past the Wistaria in time to see Miss Osborne hand Ariel a crystal goblet filled with an almost colourless liquid. Ariel took the goblet without looking at her and held it out towards the burning candles. His face was like a mask, as white as plaster and without expression. Only his eyes moved; they glinted darkly in the candlelight.

"We can begin," said Ariel.

The people gathered round the table shifted slightly, and Jupe thought he heard someone sigh.

"We are not the full fellowship tonight," said Ariel. "It may be that we can do nothing, or it may be that Dr Shaitan will send us his spirits. The voice of the serpent may speak to us across the miles. We can try."

He touched the goblet to his lips, then passed the drink on to the woman in orange.

"The fellowship won't fail!" croaked the woman in orange. She sipped from the cup. "Why, when I had that trouble with my landlady, I—"

"Silence!" said Ariel. "You interrupt the rites."

She subsided and handed the cup to Miss Osborne, who sipped and passed it to the seedy Mr Noxworth. He tasted it, gave it to the blonde in green, and she returned it to Hugo Ariel.

"We will be seated," said Ariel.

Each member of the party took a chair.

"Miss Osborne, state your intention," commanded Ariel.

Aunt Pat bowed her head. "I wish for the crystal

ball. I wish that Margaret Compton will be called away so she can't get it."

"Shall we invoke the power of Belial?"

"I ask that this be done," said Aunt Pat.

Ariel looked round the table. "What do you say?" he asked the others.

"I've got problems of my own," said Noxworth.

"The problems of one are the problems of all the fellowship," Ariel reproved him.

"Let's ask Belial to send the Compton woman on a nice long trip," twittered the woman in orange. "A trip beginning . . . when was it, honey?"

"The week of the twenty-first," said Aunt Pat.

Ariel's dark eyes went from Aunt Pat to the blonde, and then to Noxworth. "Then we are agreed," he decided.

He leaned back in his chair and closed his eyes. The others sat, staring at the dancing flames of the candles. For some minutes, nothing happened. The figures in the dining-room might have been painted on canvas, they were so still.

Then Allie and the boys heard it. In the night, through darkness which was now almost complete, they heard the sound. It was faint at first, a soft throbbing. It was a pulsing that seemed to stir the air. It was a singing sound, and yet it was in no way a song. There were no words. There were no syllables. There was only a rising and falling of notes that were no true notes. It was shrill, then gentle. It was high and piercing, then a low murmur. It wavered and stopped for an instant, then burst forth again in hideous gurgling waves.

The Three Investigators listened in mounting panic. The awful song was like nothing on earth. It threatened them with evil and terror and deep, dark power. It enticed them to join its own mindless agony. Bob swallowed noisily, and Pete drew a deep breath and held it.

Only Jupiter remained calm enough to concentrate on the scene before them. He noticed that no one had moved in the dining-room. Hugo Ariel's face was turned towards the ceiling. He had not stirred.

At last Allie backed away from the patio. The boys went with her, retreating rapidly up the drive, the weird singing following them like some evil, living thing.

When they reached the back court, Allie leaned against the house. The boys felt the fear slowly drain from them.

"That was what Marie heard?" asked Jupe.

Allie did not speak. She only nodded.

Pete ran his hand through his hair. "I'd leave, too," he said.

Allie breathed deeply. "I can't leave," she said finally. "It's my house, and it's my aunt. That Ariel has to go!"

"But it couldn't be Ariel," said Jupe quickly. "He couldn't make a noise like that without moving a muscle!"

"He couldn't make a noise like that at all, but he did it," said Allie flatly.

In the garage, the Appaloosa kicked against its stall and whinnied.

"Queenie!" cried Allie. "Someone's in there!"

Jupiter leaped to the garage door, threw it wide and was knocked flat on his back by someone who rushed out, struck wildly in the dark and fled, crashing through the open ground next door.

"Jupe?" Pete knelt down.

"I'm all right." Jupe got up slowly. "Did you see who that was?"

"Chunky guy," said Bob. "Not too tall. Had a bushy moustache. Maybe a walrus moustache."

Allie regarded them with some respect. "You don't miss much. How could you tell in the dark?"

"There is a moon," Jupiter pointed out. "And investigators must have quick powers of observation," he added pompously. "For instance, have you noticed that the singing has stopped?"

A light came on in the kitchen, and the boys slid into the shadows beside the garage.

The kitchen door opened. "Who's out there?" called Pat Osborne.

"It's only me, Aunt Pat," said Allie. "I was checking on Queenie."

"You do fuss about that horse," said Miss Osborne. "Come in, right away." The kitchen door closed.

From the front of the house came the sound of a car starting.

"The party's breaking up," whispered Bob.

"Come back in the morning," said Allie softly.

"We will," promised Jupe, and Allie's sneakered feet whispered off across the bricks to the house.

"Let's scram," said Pete. "And if I never hear that sound again, it will be okay with me!"

5

The Mysterious Fellowship

THE NEXT MORNING, The Three Investigators leaned on the fence and watched Allie Jamison's Appaloosa browse in its private meadow. "Some people don't have it that good," remarked Pete.

"Most people don't eat grass," said a voice behind them.

The boys turned to see Allie, clad in her usual faded jeans, but wearing a freshly ironed shirt. If she had been frightened the night before, she had recovered. The look she sent them was challenging. "Well?" she said. "Any bright ideas?"

Jupiter Jones glanced at the Jamison house. "Did anything happen after we left last night?"

"Nope," said Allie. "No crazy singing. No mysterious intruders with moustaches. Nothing." Allie climbed up to straddle the fence. "What about that man who was hiding in the garage? What do you think he was up to?"

Bob smiled at her and shook his head. "We don't know a thing about him, and without any facts, we can only guess. He might be an ordinary sneak thief looking for a way to get into the house, or he might be a tramp looking for a place to bed down for the night."

"Or he might have something to do with that weird

sound," suggested Jupiter Jones. "Hugo Ariel spoke of the voice of the serpent coming across the miles."

"But serpents don't sing," said Allie. "They hiss."

"You never heard the noise before Ariel came to the house," reasoned Jupe, "so Ariel must be responsible for it in some way. Yet last night, when the singing began, he was sitting in your dining-room in plain view and he wasn't making a move. In fact, he seemed to be in some sort of trance. He couldn't be the singer. The noise must be produced in some other fashion."

"How about a tape recording?" put in Pete. "They're doing terrific things with sound now. If Ariel's using taped sound, the man in the garage could be an accomplice. He could have planted the equipment near the dining-room. He could have been waiting until the session was over, planning to get it back, only we scared him off."

"That's possible," said Jupe, "but we'd better not leap to any conclusions. Ariel may have no connection with the moustached intruder. He wouldn't really need an accomplice if he was using tape."

Allie hunched her shoulders. "So we're back where we started, and Ariel continues to get free room and board here. I don't care much for some of Aunt Pat's other friends, either."

"The other guests last night?" said Jupe. "That man Noxworth looked like an odd character."

"You might say that. How can he possibly run a delicatessen? He ought to be exterminated by the Board of Health!"

"He is slovenly," said Jupiter in his precise way. "Yet from what Ariel said last night, he and your aunt are members of the same fellowship, whatever it may be. And last night the guests were all united in wishing that someone named Compton would be called away during the week of the twenty-first so that your aunt could obtain a crystal ball."

"Crazy!" exclaimed Allie. "Absolutely crazy!"

Jupiter permitted himself a somewhat superior smile. "I think I know which crystal ball it is."

"You do?"

"On the twenty-first, there will be an auction of the estate of the late Ramon Castillo, the movie star. Among the things to be sold is the crystal ball he used as a prop in the film *The Vampire's Lair*. My aunt and uncle were discussing it the other day. Your aunt collects items used in famous films. Wouldn't she want that crystal ball?"

"Her mouth must be watering at the idea!" said Allie.

"And she wants a person named Compton to be away from the city at the time of the auction."

"Aunt Pat and Margaret Compton hate each other's guts," said Allie.

"Is Margaret Compton also a collector?"

"She's a collector, all right, a very successful one. She's a rich widow and has much more money than Aunt Pat. If she wants that thing, she can bid it up so high that Aunt Pat won't be able to touch it."

"And Hugo Ariel, by lighting candles and making strange sounds, is going to prevent the Compton woman from attending the auction."

"Nice of him," said Allie, "but why is he doing it? It can't be for money. Aunt Pat has a little income from shares, but that's all. If she has to fuss about a high bid on a crystal ball, she isn't going to have much to give Ariel, is she?"

"So we don't know the motive," said Bob.

"But we do have an objective," countered Jupiter. "We want to get Hugo Ariel out of Allie's house. We can't be sure that Ariel has an accomplice, so let's assume that he doesn't. If we could search the house, we might find the equipment he uses to produce his night songs. We could then demonstrate this to your aunt, Allie. I think this should cause her to lose faith in him."

Allie grinned wickedly. "She'd toss him out on his ear. Great idea! And searching the house will be a cinch, because today Ariel got a phone call."

"Is that unusual?" asked Jupiter.

"It is. He never gets any calls. He never goes anywhere. But this morning the phone rang and a man asked for Ariel. I had to bang on his door to get him up."

"I'm sure you got to an extension and listened," said Pete slyly.

"No time," said Allie. "He was only on the phone for a couple of seconds. He said, 'Very good,' and hung up, and he told Aunt Pat that tonight there will be a meeting of the entire fellowship.

"Haven't you asked your aunt anything about this fellowship?" said Bob.

"Of course I asked her, and a fat lot of good it did. She says it's a nice club she belongs to. She says it's sweet of me to take such an interest in her social life. And she's all excited. She's going out tonight, and

Ariel's going with her. So if we want to search the house for the gadget Ariel used to make that sound, we won't have any interruptions."

Jupiter mused, pulling at his lip. "He might carry the thing on his person," he said. "In that case, we'd find nothing."

"Aren't you even going to try?" demanded Allie. "It could be under the rugs or in the curtains or . . ."

"Yes, it could," admitted Jupe. "How are you at searching houses?"

"Well, I've never done it," admitted the girl, "but it isn't the kind of thing you have to take courses for."

"Fine. Tonight, you search. Don't forget the garage, in case there is an accomplice. Look for anything unfamiliar—a fine piece of machinery, a miniature tape recorder, anything like that."

"I'm so glad I hired you," said Allie. "I get to do all the work."

"Look everywhere," Jupe instructed her. "It could be under the table or the sideboard or . . ."

"In the Wistaria, maybe?" suggested Allie.

"Yes, in the Wistaria. Don't fall off the trellis."

"Don't worry. And while I'm climbing around on that trellis, what are you going to be doing?"

"We will be following your aunt and Ariel to the meeting of the fellowship."

6

The House at Torrente Canyon

"It was nice of you to bring your own car, Worthington," said Pete warmly.

Worthington smiled. He was piloting his trim Ford saloon down the Coast Highway, several hundred yards behind the purple Corvette that belonged to Pat Osborne. "A gold-plated Rolls-Royce is not the ideal automobile in which to tail anyone," said Worthington.

Some time before, Jupiter had entered a contest sponsored by the Rent-'n-Ride Auto Rental Company and had won the use for thirty days of an antique Rolls-Royce with gold-plated trim. With the car had come Worthington, the perfect English chauffeur. He had driven The Three Investigators during several of their cases. After the thirty days had elapsed, a grateful client had arranged for the boys to have unlimited use of the Rolls-Royce. By now, Worthington had become so interested in the work of Jupiter Jones, Pete Crenshaw and Bob Andrews that he considered himself a part of the firm—an unofficial Fourth Investigator. When Jupiter had called the car rental agency that morning, the chauffeur had gladly offered to use his own car to follow Miss Osborne and Hugo Ariel to the meeting of their mysterious fellowship.

"She's turning on to Sunset Boulevard now," said Worthington.

"Don't get caught at those traffic lights," warned Jupiter Jones, who sat next to Worthington.

"I shan't." Worthington switched on the indicator and slid through the intersection just as the light changed to amber. "I hope she reaches her destination before it gets too dark," he said, and he guided the Ford up the steep hill away from the ocean. Sunset Boulevard wound ahead, past trim homes and gardens bright with geraniums. The boys lost sight of the Corvette from time to time when the road curved, but it always came into view again. At last, the little car slowed down.

"Torrente Canyon," murmured Worthington. "We can't lose her now. That's a dead-end road."

The Corvette turned into the canyon road, and an orange sports car spurted down Sunset and followed it. "Aunt Pat's hairdresser," said Jupiter.

"Just follow her red hair, Worthington," said Pete. "It probably glows in the dark."

Worthington chuckled and turned into Torrente Canyon Road. He followed the orange car until it pulled over and stopped on the grassy bank beside a high brick wall. There were other cars parked beside the road. The boys crouched low in the Ford as Worthington drove past the purple Corvette. Miss Osborne and Hugo Ariel were getting out.

Worthington looked into his rear-view mirror. "The woman in orange is waving to Miss Osborne."

Bob and Pete twisted round to look out of the back window. "I see the tan car that was parked in

43

front of Allie's house last night," said Bob excitedly.

"The delicatessen man," guessed Pete. "There sure are a lot of people here tonight."

Worthington let the Ford drift to the right and brought it to a stop on the unpaved shoulder of the road. "I counted eleven cars," he said.

The boys looked back and saw the red-haired woman join Ariel and Pat Osborne outside a huge iron gate with spikes on the top. Ariel spoke briefly to the two women, then stepped to the wall near the gate. He reached up and took something from a niche in the wall.

"I think that's a telephone," said Bob.

It was a telephone. Ariel held the receiver to his ear, listened, then said a few words and replaced it in the niche. Seconds later, the watchers in the car heard a strident buzz. Hugo Ariel leaned on the gate and it swung open. The two women followed him through and the gate closed behind them.

Worthington and the boys waited, not speaking. No more cars appeared on Torrente Canyon Road. No one else approached the big gate. After fifteen minutes, Jupiter opened the door of the Ford. "The gathering of the fellowship must be complete," he announced. "It now remains for us to discover what kind of fellowship it is."

The others got out of the car and followed Jupe to the gate in the brick wall. "Your Uncle Titus would love to have this," said Bob admiringly, touching one of the scrolls which decorated the gate.

"I doubt if it's for sale," said Jupiter. He took hold of the polished brass handle and tried to force it down, then up. It would not budge. "Locked," he said. "I expected as much."

Pete was investigating the niche near the gate. "Shall we try the phone?" he said. "No dial. It must connect directly with the house."

"I say, Master Pete," warned Worthington.

Pete grinned and took the phone off its hook. He heard a clicking noise, and then, "The night is dark," said a voice on the telephone.

"Ah . . . well, yes, it soon will be," said Pete. "Sir, I represent the United Biscuit Company, and this week we're offering a special on chocolate—"

The phone clicked and went dead.

"They aren't interested in biscuits?" asked Jupe.

"They sure aren't." Pete replaced the receiver. "Darnedest way to answer a phone I ever heard. You know what he said? He said, 'The night is dark.' "

"Part of a password, no doubt," said Jupiter. "If we were members of this fellowship, we would know what to answer."

Bob looked in through the gate. "It *is* getting dark," he said, "and look at that house. You can just make it out up at the end of the drive. There isn't a single light in the place."

It was true. No windows glowed in the house. It appeared only as a hulking mass against the evening sky.

"There are eleven cars parked on the road," said Jupe. "Two of the cars brought three people—the three we saw go in through the gate. That means there are at least nine more people visiting that house. Twelve in all."

"What are they doing?" asked Worthington. "There should be *some* light."

"There may be heavy curtains," said Jupiter.

"And they could be using candles," Bob pointed out. "Candles seem to be important to these people, and they wouldn't show through curtains."

The Three Investigators stood in the darkening road and thought of the group that had gathered at the Jamison house the night before, of the candles glowing in the dining-room and the goblet that had been passed from one person to another. And they thought of the sound they had heard—the terrible, tuneless singing.

"I wonder if we'll hear it tonight," said Pete, almost to himself.

"Hear what?" asked Worthington.

"We aren't sure, Worthington," said Jupiter. "We think it's what Ariel calls the voice of the serpent. However, we'll never learn anything standing here."

"There might be another gate," said Bob.

"There might," agreed Jupe, "and it might even be unlocked. Most people are very particular about the locks on their front doors, but very few bother about their back doors. It's a thing that causes the police no end of work."

"All right," said Pete. "Let's go and see."

"Worthington, why don't you stay in the car and keep the engine running?" said Jupe. "We don't know anything about this fellowship. It's possible that we may have to leave, and leave quickly."

The chauffeur hesitated. "Very well," he said. "I'll turn the car round and keep the engine running." He walked away up the road, and the boys heard the door of the Ford open and close and the engine start. Headlights blinked on, and Worthington made his U-turn and coasted down past the gate. He went on for about fifty feet, then pulled to the side of the road. The headlights went out, and the road was suddenly very, very dark.

"I wish we'd brought a flashlight," said Pete.

"We're better off without one," Jupe told him. "We don't want to attract attention. Let's go."

The Three Investigators began a careful circuit of the brick wall. They walked slowly, stopping from time to time to listen. They heard no sound from beyond the wall. Once Bob jumped and almost cried out when some small creature scuttled across his feet and dashed away.

"A fox," said Pete quickly.

"Did you see it?" asked Bob.

"No, but let's just say it was a fox."

"Quiet!" warned Jupe.

But then they were back on the paved road. They passed Worthington and his softly purring car. They arrived at the big gate again. Their tour was finished and they had found nothing. There was no second gate. They knew only that the property was large, that there were no near neighbours and that the house at the head of the drive was still dark.

"We must get over that wall," decided Jupiter. "Pete, you're the athlete. I can lean on the wall and you can climb on my back."

"You're out of your mind!" declared Pete.

"I see no other way," said Jupe. "If you won't do it, I must, but it seems to me that you're the logical one.

Once you get on top of the wall, you can help me up and we can help Bob. It's the only way we can get in to see what's happening in that house."

Pete sighed, as he had many times since joining Jupiter Jones and Bob Andrews. "I'm not sure I want to see," he muttered. But when Jupe bent, put his arms over his head and braced himself against the wall, Pete came through. He put one knee on Jupe's back, touched the wall with his hands, placed a sneakered foot on Jupe's shoulder and stood. "Here goes," he said, planting both hands on the top of the wall. He pulled himself up.

He sat on the wall a moment to survey the dark grounds around the darker house. Then it happened.

The alarm bell rang first—an ear-shattering, persistent clanging.

"Get down!" cried Jupe from the roadway.

Floodlights blazed suddenly. There were eight of them, two at each corner of the wall. Pete clutched at the bricks, caught and blinded by the blue-white glare.

"Jump!" shouted Jupiter.

Pete tried. He swung himself round and let his legs drop outside the wall. But then, under his hand, a brick slipped, gave way and fell. And Pete fell, too. Backwards, inside the wall!

7

Caught!

PETE LANDED ON HIS BACK on soft turf. He rolled a bit and brought himself to his knees. The alarm bell stopped clanging. Pete blinked and turned his head away from the glare of the floodlights.

A thickset man stood between Pete and the wall.

"You little sneak," said the man. He did not move, but his voice chilled Pete. "Just what do you think you're doing here?"

Pete opened his mouth to say something and found that his throat was suddenly very dry. He began to get up, and the man took a single menacing step towards him. Pete froze, half-crouching.

"Pete?" called Jupiter Jones from the other side of the wall. "Pete, did you find him?"

The man shifted and looked around. "Who's that?" There were quick footsteps beyond the wall, and Jupe appeared at the gate. "Hey, mister," he said to the man who stood over Pete, "did you see him?"

Pete felt himself begin to relax. Jupiter Jones was putting on an act, and whatever act it was, Pete knew it would be a good one.

"See who?" asked the man.

"The cat," replied Jupiter brightly. "I'm going to get

it if I don't find him. He's a seal point Siamese, and my mother doesn't know he's out. I saw him go over your wall."

"Tough!" said the man.

"He's probably up a tree someplace," said Jupe.

"Too bad." The man turned away from Jupe, pushed back a mane of grey hair with one hand, then scowled at Pete. "You, kid," he said. "Out!"

Pete stood up.

"Hey, please!" called Jupe. "Let me in and I'll help my friend look for the cat."

"Help him look my foot!" The man took Pete by the elbow and pushed him towards the gate.

"My mother will murder me!" protested Jupe.

"We've all got problems," snarled the man. "Beat it or I'll call the cops."

Jupiter retreated a step and watched. As the man neared the gate, his hand went out to touch something in the ivy that grew up the inside of the wall. The gate clicked.

"You come over that wall again and you're going to have more to worry about than a lost cat," said the man. He opened the gate and thrust Pete out on to the road, then slammed the gate shut.

"If you should see the cat . . ." began Jupe.

"Scram!" shouted the man.

Jupe and Pete turned and walked a few paces down the road to the place where Bob waited. The floodlights at the corners of the property blinked out, leaving them in darkness.

"Whew!" said Pete.

"Good thinking, Jupe," murmured Bob.

The boys heard the man go a few paces up the drive and then stop.

"He's waiting to make sure we leave," whispered Jupiter. "We'd better walk away, and Worthington can follow with the car. That man is already suspicious. If he sees us get into a car, he'll know we weren't simply looking for a stray cat."

"Let's go," said Pete quickly.

The boys straggled towards Sunset Boulevard, talking loudly of the elusiveness of cats, the value of Siamese in particular, and the dreadful fate that awaited boys who allowed their parents' pets to escape. As they came abreast of the Ford, Jupe whispered to Worthington to follow them in a few minutes.

The Investigators halted at Sunset and Torrente, well out of sight and hearing of the big house.

"Interesting household," said Jupiter. "There is a gathering there with at least twelve people present, but we saw no lights. There is an alarm system which I imagine is activated by an electronic device on top of that wall. And one needs a password to enter the gate."

The Ford came gliding down the road and stopped. The boys opened the doors and got in.

"A thoroughly obnoxious person!" exclaimed Worthington, waving his hand in the direction of the house.

"Could you hear him?" asked Pete.

"He was loud enough," said Worthington. "I was tempted to take steps. Did he hurt you, Master Pete?"

Pete slumped back in his seat. "No, but I don't think it would have bothered him if he had."

Worthington started to edge out into the traffic on

Sunset Boulevard. There was a truck approaching from the left, and as Worthington waited for it to pass, a car spurted down Torrente Canyon Road and shuddered to a stop next to the Ford. The driver of the car revved the engine impatiently.

"That's the orange sports car," said Bob. "The twitchy hairdresser is on her way."

"Then the group must be leaving," surmised Jupe. "We'd better get to a telephone right away. Allie is supposed to be searching her house for evidence against Hugo Ariel. We don't want Ariel and her aunt to find her at it."

Worthington turned on to Sunset. "There's a telephone booth at a petrol station less than half a mile from here," he announced.

At the petrol station, Jupe called the Jamison house. Allie answered before the phone could ring twice.

"The meeting of the fellowship is breaking up," said Jupe. "We found out almost nothing. Have you finished your search?"

"Yes, and I didn't find a thing."

"You looked everywhere?"

"I went over this place with a fine-tooth comb. I also used a magnet. There's nothing except the dust that's piled up since Marie took off."

"Then if Ariel uses some device to make that noise, he carries it with him," said Jupe. "Or perhaps he does have an accomplice."

"Which brings up an interesting point," said Allie brightly. "We have a new houseman."

"Oh?" said Jupe.

"Yes. Not a maid this time. A houseman. Tonight

this man called and said he'd been in Rocky Beach and he heard we lost our maid and might need help, which we certainly do. He wanted to make an appointment to come and see the lady of the house."

"So?"

"So I figured, with my mum in Europe, I'm the lady of the house. Aunt Pat hardly takes a big interest, after all."

"Allie, you didn't make an appointment with a total stranger who called up without even—"

"I did better than that," said Allie proudly. "I asked him to come here and I hired him."

Jupe waited, feeling that there was more to come.

"Aren't you going to ask me why I hired him?" said Allie.

"Why did you hire him?"

"Because he has a walrus moustache," said Allie. "You said the man who was hiding in the garage last night had a walrus moustache. Now I don't know if this is the same man. I didn't get a good look at that guy last night. But if he *is* the same man, he must have some special interest in what goes on here. He could be an accomplice. So let's get him where we can keep an eye on him, huh? He reports to work at eight tomorrow morning, and I hope he gets eggshells into Ariel's morning coffee."

"What will your aunt say?" demanded Jupiter.

"I'll think of something clever to tell her. See you tomorrow out by the old corral."

She hung up and Jupe returned to the car.

"Allie okay?" asked Pete.

"I don't know," said Jupe. "Either she's the smartest

girl I ever met, or she's an idiot, or maybe she's both."

"How can you be a smart idiot?" asked Pete.

"Somehow, I believe Allie Jamison could manage it," said Jupiter Jones.

8

The Serpent Strikes

When The Three Investigators arrived at the Jamison house the next morning, Allie was sitting on the front steps, grinning like a Cheshire cat.

"A dream of a man!" she announced. "Listen!"

Jupiter, Bob and Pete listened. From inside the house came the drone of a vacuum cleaner.

"I didn't even mention it to him," said Allie. "He stowed his suitcase in Marie's room, took one look round the house, went for the broom copboard and got busy. So much for Aunt Pat's cobwebs."

"Then he'll be living here?" asked Bob.

"Isn't that nice?" said Allie. "We can really watch him."

"Let's hope it will be nice," replied Jupe. "What did your aunt say when you told her you'd hired a man for the house?"

"Whose house is it, anyway?" demanded Allie. "I told her I'd asked around and this man seemed okay, and she said that was nice of me, dear, and went to bed. She's fuzzy about details."

"Where has he worked before?" asked Jupiter.

"He didn't say and I never pry," said Allie, virtuously.

"The heck you don't!" exclaimed Pete.

"Want to see him?" asked Allie. " Do you think you

can tell if he's the same man who was in the garage?"

"I doubt if I could," said Jupe. "I hardly saw him. Bob had the best look at him."

Bob nodded.

"If he is the man," said Jupe, "don't accuse him, Bob. Pretend not to recognise him."

Allie yanked open the screen door and the boys followed her into the house. The new houseman was labouring over the green-gold carpet in the living-room. He looked up, saw the boys standing in the hall with Allie and switched off the vacuum.

"Was there something you wanted, Miss Jamison?" he asked.

"Not a thing, Bentley," said Allie. "We're going to get some lemonade."

"Very well, Miss Jamison." The man clicked the vacuum on again and continued with his work.

In the kitchen, Allie took four bottles of lemonade from the refrigerator. "Is it him?" she asked.

"I couldn't be sure," admitted Bob. "He's about the same size and the moustache looks right. But it was dark when that man knocked Jupe down and it all happened so quickly."

"He doesn't look like the kind who knocks people down," said Pete. "He's sort of ... well, sort of neutral."

"Beige," said Allie. "He's a beige person. Not too tall and not too short and not too thin and not too fat. Sandy hair and eyes that aren't any particular colour. He'd be invisible if he didn't have that moustache." She took a bottle opener from a drawer and began to remove the caps from the lemonade bottles. "And what have you three to report?"

Jupiter quickly outlined the events of the evening before. When he finished, Allie said, "I think I'm way ahead of you. All you managed to do last night was fall off a wall, while I found a genuine, one-hundred-per-cent mystery man."

"You came to us to get rid of a mystery man," Pete reminded her. "By the way, aren't you afraid that vacuuming is going to wake your house guest?"

"Ariel went out," said Allie, and swallowed some of her drink.

"I thought he never went out in the day time."

"This morning he went out. He took Aunt Pat's car and departed for points unknown."

Aunt Pat appeared in the kitchen doorway.

"Allie, who is that man in the living-room?" asked Miss Osborne. She was dressed in a lavender housecoat with a purple sash, and her lavender hair was perfectly arranged.

"It's the new houseman, Aunt Pat," said Allie. "We hired him last night, remember?"

"Oh, yes. How nice. What did you say his name was, dear?"

"I didn't," said Allie, "but it's Bentley."

"Bentley. Bentley. Like the car. I'll remember that." She smiled in an absent-minded way at the boys, who murmured good-morning to her.

"Can he cook?" Miss Osborne asked Allie.

"He said he could cook."

"Then I'll go and talk to him about dinner." Miss Osborne wandered out of the kitchen.

Allie leaned against the sink. "I don't care if he runs off with the silverware, just so we get one decent meal out of him. There's more to this pots and pans stuff than meets the eye." She turned her head and glanced out into the back courtyard. "Speaking of things meeting the eye," she remarked, "if you'll look to the east, you'll see that creep Ariel fighting his way out of Aunt Pat's car."

The boys had to smile. It was a struggle for Ariel to get his long legs out of the purple Corvette. He wriggled sideways, slid out and pulled his black shirt straight about his thin waist.

"I'd love to know what he's been up to," said Allie.

Ariel opened the back door and came in. He let his flat, dark eyes rest on Allie for a moment, then started past her without speaking.

Allie promptly stood in his way. "Mr Ariel, I don't think you've met my friends," she said.

Ariel looked intensely annoyed, but he stopped and permitted Allie to introduce the boys. When Bob cheerfully held out his hand, Ariel allowed his own limp hand to be shaken. He said absolutely nothing. When the introductions were completed he stepped round Allie as if she were a post and went on into the hall, pulling the kitchen door shut after him.

"How'd you like that?" demanded Allie. "I get it from him all the time. He acts like I'm some kind of a . . . a thing! I'd want him out of here even if he didn't make that horrible singing."

"Mr Ariel!" Aunt Pat's voice, high and excited, carried to the group in the kitchen "Has it been accomplished?"

Allie went to the door, leaned on it slightly and applied her ear to the resulting crack.

"There is no need for anxiety," said Ariel from the front hall. "The wishes of the fellowship—your wishes —will be carried out. The serpent has been delivered. All is in the hands of Belial. You have only to wait."

"But the twenty-first isn't far off," protested Aunt Pat. "Are you sure there's time? Oh, perhaps it is a silly whim, but I do want it, and if Margaret Compton gets there first . . ."

"Your faith wavers?" demanded Ariel. There was an edge to his voice.

"Of course not!" said Aunt Pat quickly. "I have the most profound trust."

"Then you will excuse me," said Ariel. "I must rest now. These affairs are demanding."

"I understand," said Miss Osborne.

Ariel went up the stairs.

"Sounds like he's turning in for another day," said Allie. "What a slug!"

"The serpent has been delivered," said Jupe. "Now what did he mean by that?"

"Is somebody mailing out snakes?" asked Pete.

Allie shook her head. "Aunt Pat can't abide snakes. That's just the way they talk. They say something and it means something else. The other night they talked about the voice of the serpent coming across the miles, remember?"

"And we heard it, didn't we?" Jupiter reminded her. "We heard the singing."

"Whatever that was, it was no snake," insisted Allie. "Snakes do not sing."

"But something is going on," said Jupe. "It has to do with Hugo Ariel and the house on Torrente Canyon and that strange singing. And it may have some connection with your new houseman. There's nothing we can do at the moment except watch and wait. Let us know if something odd happens. I have to get back to the salvage yard."

"And I'm due at my job in the library," said Bob.

"And I've got to mow the lawn," said Pete.

"What a bunch of private eyes!" complained Allie. "You've all got other jobs on the side. Okay. Go do whatever it is you do when you're not falling off walls and I'll call you if anything happens here."

The boys finished their lemonade and went their separate ways. When Jupiter reported at The Jones Salvage Yard, Aunt Mathilda was directing Hans and Konrad, who were unloading the larger of the two trucks.

"Jupiter, I need you," said Aunt Mathilda.

"Yes, Aunt Mathilda."

"Your Uncle Titus has lost his mind. Look what he bought!"

Jupiter looked. The truck was loaded with old cast-iron stoves.

"Wood-burning stoves!" said Aunt Mathilda. "In this day and age! They were in an old warehouse in East Los Angeles, and it was going to be torn down. Your uncle said they were so inexpensive he couldn't pass them up. Jupiter, however will we sell them?"

"We'll find a way," said Jupe.

"Well, help Hans and Konrad get them off the truck and put them someplace where I can't see them. The very idea!"

Aunt Mathilda stormed away, and Jupiter set to

work helping Hans and Konrad unload the stoves and store them in a spot towards the back of the yard. It was slow work, since the stoves were heavy and had doors which kept dropping off. After lunch there were more chores. Jupe worked until three and then crossed the street to the Jones house to take a shower. He found his Uncle Titus glaring at a newscast on television.

"Terrible!" exclaimed Uncle Titus.

"What's terrible?" asked Jupiter.

"The things people do on the motorways. Look at that!"

On the television screen, Jupe saw a scene which was all too familiar. A saloon had crashed into a bridge abutment on the Hollywood Freeway. Traffic was being directed past the crashed car.

The voice of the announcer came on over the picture. "The driver of the car, Mrs Margaret Compton, was taken to Angel of Mercy Hospital where her condition was reported as fair."

"Mrs Margaret Compton!" cried Jupe.

"You know her?" asked Uncle Titus.

"I've heard the name, Uncle Titus," said Jupe. "Excuse me. I have to call a client!"

9

A Secret Meeting

AT SEVEN THAT NIGHT, Jupiter left the house and went to The Jones Salvage Yard. He had told his aunt that he had unfinished work in his workshop, and that he might be late. However, when he reached his workshop, Bob and Pete were waiting for him with their bikes.

"We're to meet Allie at Swanson's Cove," said Jupe quickly.

"We exit through Green Gate One?" asked Bob.

Jupe nodded. "We'd better. It's far enough from the house so Aunt Mathilda won't see us."

Pete went to a place in the fence close to the workshop and inserted two fingers into a crack. He pulled, and two boards swung up. Pete put his head out, looked up and down the street, and reported that the coast was clear. Jupe grabbed his bike, which had been leaning against the printing press, and the three boys slipped out through the opening in the fence.

When the boards had swung closed behind them, Bob stopped to stare thoughtfully at the fence. Like the back fence of the yard, the front fence had been decorated by artists of Rocky Beach. Here along the front was a stormy ocean scene, with a sailing ship struggling through huge waves. In the foreground, almost under Bob's eyes, a fish lifted its head from the sea to stare at the ship.

"Allie caught on to Red Gate Rover," said Bob sadly. "I hope she hasn't been snooping around the front of this place. I'd hate to have her know that that fish marks the spot where Green Gate One opens."

"If she's discovered that," said Jupiter Jones, "we'll have to abandon Green Gate One and construct another entrance. Let's not worry about it now. This is an emergency."

"Right," said Pete. "Let's go."

The boys got on to their bikes and pedalled down the street, away from the Jones house and the salvage yard, and then down to the Coast Highway. A five-minute ride brought them to Swanson's Cove. Allie Jamison was already there, leaning against a boulder that jutted out of the sand. Allie's horse stood nearby, its reins dangling.

"Margaret Compton was hurt in a car accident today," said Allie.

"I told Bob and Pete about it," said Jupe. He sat down facing Allie. "How is your aunt? What's happened since I talked to you?"

"She's all upset," said Allie. "She's crying. She hasn't stopped crying since we caught the report on the news."

Bob leaned against the rock. "Things are moving, aren't they?" he said.

"And rather quickly," said Jupe. "Only this morning Hugo Ariel told Miss Osborne that a serpent had been delivered, and that Miss Osborne's wishes would be carried out. Tonight Mrs Compton is in the hospital with more serious things to worry about than the auction of the Castillo estate. She won't be around to outbid Miss Osborne for Ramon Castillo's crystal ball."

"This isn't the way Aunt Pat wanted it," declared Allie. "When she saw the newscast she yelled, 'She might have been killed, and it would be my fault!' Ariel helped her up to her room. They closed the door, but I was out in the hall and I listened."

"Naturally," said Pete.

Allie ignored him. "She said something about how she didn't know it would turn out like this," Allie went on. "He said it was her desire, and now it was time for her to do something. I couldn't get it all, but whatever he wants, she doesn't want to do it. He said he'd wait, but not forever. After a while he came out and went downstairs.

"I went in after he left, but she wouldn't talk to me. She told me to run along, so I did, only I didn't run far."

"You stayed in the hall," said Pete.

"You bet I did, and I heard her making a telephone call. She asked to speak to Mr Van Storen."

"How long did it take you to get to another telephone?" asked Jupiter Jones.

"Too long," confessed Allie. "By the time I picked up the receiver downstairs, she was telling someone she'd send in her houseman with a letter of authorisation, and a man said, 'Certainly, Miss Osborne,' and everybody hung up."

"So then?" asked Bob.

"So then I heard Aunt Pat moving around upstairs. She called Bentley and he went up, and when he came down he was tucking a package all wrapped in brown paper into his pocket. He went out in Aunt Pat's car. Said she'd given him an errand to do."

"Did that interest Mr Ariel?" questioned Jupe.

"It interested him plenty," said Allie. "He went up those stairs like a shot out of a cannon. Aunt Pat was ready for him. I could hear him yelling at her and she yelled back. She said she'd sent Bentley to Beverly Hills to pick up some special face cream for her, and that's all."

"Do you believe her?"

"No, and Ariel didn't either. Only Bentley came back later with the face cream, so what could Ariel say? But it was a lie. Aunt Pat doesn't buy face cream. She makes her own out of rose petals and glycerine and stuff."

"Did you question your aunt?" asked Jupe. "Or did you speak to Bentley?"

"I didn't need to question either of them," said Allie. "I know where Bentley really went. Mr Van Storen is one half of the firm of Van Storen and Chatsworth in Beverly Hills. He's a jeweller and a very good one. I also happen to know the combination of the safe in my mother's room, so I opened the safe. My mother's necklace was gone."

The boys sat silently on the sand for a moment, letting this news sink in.

Jupiter spoke up at last. "Do you mean that your aunt gave a necklace which once belonged to the Empress Eugénie to a man whom she scarcely knows and sent him to the jewellers with it?"

"I never said she was very bright," said Allie. "She's an adult, so she's supposed to be responsible. So I guess that's why my mother gave her the combination of the safe—so she could get the necklace out in case the house burned down or something."

"Does she know that you know the necklace is gone?" asked Bob.

"She sure does. I tackled her the second I got her alone. She claims my mother asked her to have the necklace cleaned while she was away."

"Not a likely story?" asked Jupiter.

Allie made a wry face. "There's no emergency about having a necklace cleaned," she pointed out. "And she didn't need to send Bentley. Van Storen and Chatsworth would have come for it."

"So she went to some trouble to get the necklace to the jewellers without Ariel's knowledge," said Jupiter. "I think we can come to several conclusions."

"Such as?"

"First, from what your aunt said about the Compton woman's accident, it was caused—or she believes it was caused—because she wished the Compton woman out of the way. She invoked the power of the fellowship. She feels guilty.

"Second, Ariel is putting some pressure on her. He has stopped playing the role of an honoured guest and is trying to bully her. Did he see the housemán with the package?"

"No," said Allie. "He only saw Bentley get into the car and drive away."

"Does he know the necklace was in the safe?"

"I don't know. I don't think so. He didn't try to go near the safe. He only wanted to know why Aunt Pat sent Bentley out."

"Which brings us back to the mysterious Bentley," said Jupiter. "Is he the man who was hiding near your house the night your aunt entertained her friends from the fellowship? Or is he a stranger who happened to learn that you needed household help? If he is the man who knocked me down that night, what is he doing in the house? At least we know he can't be an accomplice of Ariel's, or Ariel would not need to be suspicious of him." Jupe sat brooding, pulling on his lip as he did when he was thinking with special intensity.

"There are several things we must find out immediately," he decided. "We must find out, first of all, whether the necklace was actually delivered to the jewellers."

"Oh, blast!" cried Allie. "Oh, why didn't I think of that this afternoon? I could have called Van Storen and Chatsworth right away!"

"In the morning," advised Jupiter. "You can call from the salvage yard, if you want, so no one will overhear. And in the morning we must find out whether Margaret Compton's accident was truly connected with the fellowship. Did Ariel deliver a live snake to her, for instance?"

"But Aunt Pat wouldn't send anybody a snake!" protested Allie. "She doesn't like Margaret Compton, but she wouldn't wish a thing like that on her. She wouldn't want her worst enemy to open a box and see a snake!"

"Then what was delivered?" said Jupe.

"I don't know."

Bob spoke up. "Ariel said that your aunt didn't need

to worry because it was all in the hands of Belial. I looked that up in the library. Belial is the name of a demon. And Ariel mentioned a Dr Shaitan the other night. I checked that, too, in the library. Shaitan is another name for Satan."

Pete shivered. "Demons and snakes! Some combination!"

Allie sat, picking up handfuls of sand and then letting the sand run through her fingers. "What is Aunt Pat mixed up in?" she said at last.

"We don't know," said Jupe, "but it could be something very nasty."

10

The Golden Cobra

ALLIE APPEARED at the salvage yard early the next morning, looking as if she had not slept at all. The Three Investigators were waiting for her near the office in the yard.

"Aunt Pat is crying," she reported. "Ariel is sleeping, just for a change. Bentley is washing the windows."

"And Aunt Mathilda is washing the breakfast dishes," said Jupe, "so you can use the telephone in the office to call the jewellers'."

Allie didn't hesitate. She settled herself at the desk in the office, dialled Van Storen and Chatsworth, and gave an excellent imitation of Miss Patricia Osborne asking when the Empress Eugénie necklace would be ready. She listened for a few moments, then said, "Very good. Thank you," and hung up.

"They have the necklace," she told the boys. "They said it will take several days, and they'll hold it until they're notified to deliver it. What a relief!"

"Then it's safe," said Jupiter, "and whatever your new houseman is, he isn't a jewel thief. Now to find out whether a serpent figured in Mrs Compton's life in any way yesterday."

"You don't suppose Ariel planted a snake in Mrs Compton's car, do you?" asked Pete.

Allie shuddered.

"That would be enough to cause almost anyone to drive into a bridge abutment," said Jupiter Jones. "However, we shall see."

"What are you going to do?" asked Allie.

"I'm going to the library to look up serpents and demons and strange cults," reported Bob.

"Pete and I will go to the hospital to see Mrs Compton," Jupiter told Allie. "Hans is taking the small truck into Los Angeles, and we can ride with him."

Allie got up and went to the door of the office. "I'll go home and keep an eye on everyone there," she said.

"We'll call you," promised Jupiter.

She nodded and went out, and Hans rattled up to the door of the office in the truck. "Ready?" he called.

Jupe and Pete climbed into the cab of the truck next to Hans. On the drive into Los Angeles they were silent, each thinking his own thoughts. When they reached Vermont Boulevard, Jupe asked Hans to stop outside a small flower shop. He bought an African violet with several blooms and wrote a card to go with the plant. Hans then drove the boys to Angel of Mercy Hospital.

Outside the hospital, Hans stopped the truck. "You want me to wait?" he said. "What you doing, anyway?"

"We need to talk to a lady about a snake," said Pete. Hans gulped.

"Never mind, Hans," said Pete. "Don't ask any questions. You'll be happier if you never know."

Jupe got out of the cab. "I think I'd better do this alone," he said. "We don't want to attract too much attention."

"Okay," said Pete. "I'll wait with Hans."

Jupe went up the steps into the hospital carrying his plant.

"Mrs Margaret Compton?" said Jupiter to the woman at the reception desk. "Is she receiving visitors?"

The woman fingered her way through a box of file cards. "Room 203, East Wing," she said. "The elevator's down the corridor and to your right."

Jupiter thanked her, carried his African violet down the corridor and went up one floor in the elevator. The elevator opened in front of an office, a bustle of activity with a doctor making a telephone call, an orderly depositing a tray loaded with tiny glasses, and a nurse who ignored Jupiter.

Jupiter cleared his throat. "Mrs Margaret Compton Room 203," he said. "Is she able to have visitors?"

The nurse looked up from her charts. "She's just had a sedative," she said sternly.

"Oh." Jupiter Jones allowed his round, cheerful face to droop. "I could come back," he said in a woebegone tone, "but I'd like to see Aunt Margaret and I'm supposed to work this afternoon. They take it out of your pay if you don't show up on time."

"Oh, all right! Just wait a second. Let me check and see if she's okay."

The nurse strode down the hall with a rustle of nylon skirt. She was back in half a minute. "She's awake. You can go in, but don't stay too long. She needs to get some sleep."

Jupe assured her that he would not stay long, and hurried down the hall to Room 203. The door stood open. In the single bed inside was a woman with a round, ruddy face, sleepy eyes and a quantity of white hair. She was firmly anchored by a cast which bulked high under the covers and reached from her foot to her waist.

"Mrs Compton?" said Jupiter Jones.

The grey, heavy-lidded eyes fell on the African violet in Jupe's hands. "How nice," said the woman.

"It's an especially fine violet," Jupe told her. "It's from the Western Flower Mart, and the customer who purchased it was anxious that it be delivered directly to you."

The woman reached under her pillow and drew out a spectacle case. "The card," she said. "Hand me the card, please."

Jupiter put the plant on the table beside the bed and handed the card to her. She squinted at it, managed to focus and read, "With best wishes for your quick recovery." She looked puzzled and turned the card over. "It's not signed," she said.

Jupiter knew this perfectly well.

"Like that thing yesterday," said Margaret Compton. "There was a card on that, too, and it wasn't signed. So careless, not signing cards."

"Perhaps I can help," said Jupiter Jones. "The man who bought the plant was tall and very thin. He had black hair and he was very pale."

"Hmmn," said Mrs Compton. She seemed on the point of going to sleep.

Jupiter cast about in his mind for some way to introduce serpents into the conversation. Suddenly Margaret Compton roused herself slightly. "Funny! The man who delivered the cobra thing yesterday looked like that. Wonder who . . . who could . . . ?"

"Cobra thing?" echoed Jupiter Jones.

"Yes. Nice little . . . nice . . ."

Again Mrs Compton looked as if she might go to sleep. Jupiter spoke up quickly. "A cobra? How unusual. Do you collect reptiles?"

The grey eyes opened. "No, no! Not really a cobra! It was a bracelet. I don't usually like . . ." She drifted off for a second.

"You don't usually like snake objects?" prompted Jupe.

"No. Awful things, snakes. Only this was kind of . . kind of pretty. I put it on. Wish I knew who sent it." The woman's hand reached towards the drawer in the bedside table. "Show you," she murmured. "In my handbag."

Jupiter opened the drawer and handed her the small handbag that he found inside. She fumbled with the clasp, got the bag open and groped inside. "Look. Isn't that . . . ?"

"Very interesting," said Jupiter Jones. He took the bracelet and turned it in his hand. It was indeed interesting—a circlet of gold-coloured metal with an opening that would allow the wearer to slip it over her wrist. Next to the opening, the gilded band was decorated with the head of a cobra. Tiny specks of precious or semi-precious stones were set into the eyes of the snake. Behind the head the metal band flattened out into the cobra's hood, which was delicately orna-mented with green and blue enamel.

Jupiter ran his finger round the inside of the bracelet. It was perfectly smooth. "You had it with you yesterday when you were driving your car?"

"Yes. Wearing it. Was it yesterday? It seems so long now." She turned her head, her eyes closing. "Stupid thing," she complained. "Wheel coming off like that!"

"A wheel came off the car," said Jupiter. "Nothing else disturbed you? Nothing in the car?"

She opened her eyes again. "Nothing in the car? No. But the wheel. It came off. I saw it rolling ahead on the road and then, the bridge and . . . and . . ."

There was a rustle in the doorway behind Jupe. He turned to see the nurse glaring at him.

"I'm going," he told the nurse. He handed the bracelet back to Mrs Compton. "I hope you'll enjoy your plant," he said softly, and he left the room.

"I told you not to stay long," scolded the nurse.

"I'm sorry," said Jupiter. "I only wanted to talk with her for a minute."

He went down the corridor to the elevator, descended to the ground floor and hurried out of the hospital.

"Any luck?" asked Pete when Jupe reached the truck. "Was she any help?"

"She was a great deal of help." Jupe climbed into the truck next to Pete. "She had the serpent with her."

"A snake?" Hans was astonished. "You mean she got a snake with her in hospital?"

"Not a real snake, Hans," said Jupiter. "It was a bracelet with a cobra's head on it."

"Maybe there's some kind of trick," suggested Pete. "The Borgias had rings with secret compartments for poison, and a needle would shoot out and stab the enemy."

Jupiter shook his head. "I examined it closely. There

are no gimmicks. It is only a bracelet, but Hugo Ariel
delivered it to her personally. Aside from that bracelet,
there were no snakes in Mrs Compton's car when it
crashed yesterday. A wheel came off and the car hit a
fly-over. Now if anyone can tell me how a bracelet can
cause a wheel to come off a car, I will cheerfully eat
those cast-iron stoves Uncle Titus just bought!"

11

Bentley's Secret Papers

WHEN JUPE AND PETE returned to the salvage yard and entered Jupe's workshop, the light over the printing press was flashing. This signalled that the telephone was ringing in Headquarters.

"That may be Allie," said Jupe. "I gave her our private number."

Pete pulled aside the grating that concealed Tunnel Two and scrambled through the corrugated pipe to Headquarters. When Jupe followed him and climbed up through the trap door into the trailer, he was already on the telephone.

"She did have a serpent, but it's only a bracelet," Pete was saying. "It couldn't have hurt her."

Pete listened. Allie's voice came to Jupe as an excited chatter.

"The wheel came off her car," said Pete. "That's all there was to it. It was an accident."

Allie was silent for a few seconds, but then she said something that caused Pete to scowl. "But we've just got back!" he protested.

The telephone chattered again, at some length. Pete sighed and pulled a pad towards himself and wrote an address on it. Finally he said, "All right. After dinner," and hung up.

"What now?" asked Jupiter Jones.

"Allie was calling from the kitchen phone," said Pete. "She said Ariel and her aunt are locked up in the library and Bentley is doing some shopping. Bentley gave her letters of reference. One was from a woman in Brentwood who had to leave town when her husband was transferred to Kansas City, and the other was from a professor in Arcadia. She tried to call Kansas City and there's no listing for the woman. She tried to call the professor in Arcadia. His telephone has been disconnected."

"Not reassuring," said Jupe. "She should have checked on Bentley before she hired him."

"Well she didn't, and now she wants us to do it," said Pete. "She told Bentley she needed to file an official form so she could pay tax on his salary, and he gave her his home address. It's 1854 North Tennyson in Santa Monica. She wants us to go there right now and find out if Bentley really has a place there and any other stray information we can dig up."

"And you told her we'd go after dinner?" said Jupe.

"Darn right. If I don't show up at home soon, my mother's going to brain me!"

"Aunt Mathilda is also becoming a bit impatient," said Jupiter. "I think you're right. After dinner would be the best time to go to Santa Monica."

"Allie says frog and we jump," observed Pete.

"She *is* our client," Jupiter pointed out. "She shouldn't have hired Bentley on a whim, but she did. Now she wants to know more about him. I think she should. I'll call Bob and ask him to meet us on the road in front of the supermarket at seven. Is that okay with you?"

"I can make it," said Pete.

"Then seven it is," said Jupiter.

And at seven, The Three Investigators were riding their bikes down the Coast Highway towards Santa Monica. North Tennyson Place, when they located it with the aid of a street map, turned out to be a small court opening off an avenue. At 1856 there was a large stucco house with a red tile roof. A sign on the lawn indicated that number 1854, the address which Allie had given Pete, was in the rear.

"A garage apartment," decided Jupiter. He went a short way down the drive, then returned, nodding. "An upstairs apartment over a double garage."

"So how do we find out if Bentley really lives there?" asked Pete. "He's at the Jamison house now."

"We ask for him at the big house," said Jupiter. "We could be—let's see—we could be friends of his nephew Freddie. We just rode over from Westwood and decided to drop in on him."

"That's enough to get a conversation started," said Bob.

Jupiter marched to the front door of the stucco house and rang the bell. He waited for almost a minute, then rang again. No one came to the door.

"So much for that great idea," said Pete.

Jupiter picked up his bike, wheeled it to the pavement and looked back at the garage. "Let's assume that Bentley does live here," he said. "It's often possible to tell a great deal about a person simply by observing the place he has chosen for his home."

"So we snoop?" said Pete.

"We can look in the window," replied Jupiter.

Looking in the window of the garage apartment proved to be extremely easy. A flight of stairs went up the outside of the garage and ended in a small landing. There, next to the door of the apartment, was a window with the blinds up.

"How fortunate." Jupiter Jones pressed his nose against the glass.

Pete crowded in beside him and looked, too, and Bob stood on tiptoe to peer over Pete's shoulder.

The last light of the setting sun gleamed in through a window in the front of the apartment. It fell on the opposite wall, where there were shelves crammed with books. The boys could see a work table stacked with file folders and more books, a typewriter on a smaller table, a swivel chair and a floor lamp. There was also a studio couch covered with tan corduroy.

"Looks more like an office than a home," said Pete.

Jupiter stepped back from the window. "Our mysterious houseman likes to read," he decided. "He also likes to write."

Bob whistled. "Get a load of those titles!" he said. "The books on the table. He's got *Witchcraft*, *Folk Medicine and Magic*. That's a new one. We got it at the library this week and it cost $10.95. He's also got *Voodoo—Ritual and Reality*."

"Anything on snakes?" asked Pete.

Jupe tried the doorknob, which would not turn. He then examined the window. "It's not locked," he announced. He looked at his two friends. Pete scanned the empty yard around the garage and Bob stared across at the stucco house.

"We'll get into real trouble if we get caught," said Pete.

"We mustn't get caught." Jupe pushed the window sash up. The window opened almost without noise. A second later, Jupe was inside the apartment, with Bob and Pete close behind him.

In addition to the books on magic that Bob had spotted on the table, the boys saw shelves loaded with accounts of the rituals of primitive peoples, learned tomes on folklore and several works on black magic as it is practised in modern cities.

"That guy must feel right at home with Aunt Pat Osborne and Hugo Ariel," said Pete.

"If he's read all these books, he's got my respect," said Bob. "I got into some of them today, and they can be tough going."

"An authority on the occult," said Jupe. "One wouldn't expect to find an authority on the occult acting as a houseman."

Jupiter bent over the work table and began to read the tags on the files that were piled there. There was a file called "Mara's Clients," and one marked "The Green Triangle." There was also a file—a thick one—tagged "The Fellowship of the Lower Circle."

"Now I wonder if that could be *our* fellowship." Jupe opened the file. "Oh, yes!" he said.

"What is it?" asked Bob.

Jupe picked up two sheets of paper. "Here is a set of notes on Miss Patricia Osborne. Bentley finds her interesting. For instance, he indicates on this sheet that she has belonged to more than five unusual sects in the past ten years, that she subscribes to two astrology magazines, and that she once travelled to India to study under a philosopher there. The Indian trip did not last long. Miss Osborne did not find the plumbing adequate. There is also a note here that Miss Osborne moved to the house in Rocky Beach in May, and that Hugo Ariel arrived not long ago."

"Anything else?" asked Pete.

Jupiter pulled out another sheet of paper. "Here's a report listing Miss Osborne's assets, which are adequate. She would not be considered wealthy."

"Bentley is interested in money?" asked Pete.

Jupiter turned over other papers in the file. "It seems so. There's a similar report on Noxworth, the man who owns a delicatessen. He also owns property in East Los Angeles. He's worth a lot more than his appearance indicates."

"The lady in orange?" asked Pete.

"Madelyn Enderby, the hairdresser?" Jupe thumbed through the file. "She has belonged to a number of odd associations. She owns her own business and her income runs to five figures a year. She has an active account with a stockbroker in the San Fernando Valley."

"Anyone else we know?" asked Bob.

"The lady with the health food shop," said Jupe. "Health food must be quite lucrative. She has applied for a loan to open a second shop in another location. And there are a number of reports here on people we don't know."

"Magic and witchcraft." Bob touched the books on the table. "And also money."

"Perhaps they all go together," said Jupe.

Pete slid open a drawer in the table. It was empty except for a few paper clips and a miniature tape recorder. There was a tape on the spool of the recorder. "I wouldn't mind having that," said Pete. "You could carry it in your pocket."

Bob picked up the instrument. "Nice," he said. "Runs on batteries. No wires to plug in." He pressed a button on one end of the recorder, and a little compartment opened. Inside was a tiny microphone. "Perfect," said Bob. "A little recorder that can be hidden anywhere, with a sensitive microphone. The Secret Service probably doesn't have anything better."

"I wonder what's on that tape," said Jupiter. "How does the rewind mechanism work?"

Bob fumbled with the recorder for a second and watched the tape rewind. Then he reversed the switch. The recorder gave out a few preliminary cracks and rustles, and then The Three Investigators heard someone say, "We can begin."

"That's Ariel's voice!" exclaimed Bob.

"We are not the full fellowship tonight," the voice continued on the recorder. "It may be that we can do nothing. Or it may be that Dr Shaitan will send us his spirits. The voice of the serpent may speak to us across the miles."

"He bugged Allie's house!" said Pete.

"Must have hidden this near the dining-room door," deduced Bob.

The boys heard the hoarse voice of Madelyn Enderby and the grumbling complaint of Noxworth, the delicatessen man. They heard again Pat Osborne's wish that Margaret Compton be called away.

Then, frightfully clear in the quiet of that small room, they heard the sound. They heard the singing which had frightened Marie out of the Jamison house, and which had driven Allie to ask for help.

"The voice of the serpent," said Jupe.

Bob shuddered and put the tape recorder quickly down on the table, but the dreadful, wordless song went on and on.

The tape turned slowly to its end. The terrible singing faded to a low sob and died. When the little machine emitted only a soft hum, Jupiter Jones realised that he felt cold. The sunlight that had streamed into the apartment was gone, and it was growing dark.

And there was a man standing in the doorway. Bentley!

12

The Houseman's Sudden Move

"OH MY GOSH!" exclaimed Pete.

Bob jumped, and quickly turned off the little tape recorder.

Jupiter Jones stood still and considered several possible explanations that he could offer Bentley. He decided that none would do. "We were just leaving," he said.

The man with the walrus moustache remained in the doorway. "Were you planning to go out the way you came in?" he asked. "You used the window, didn't you?" Bentley's voice was angry. There was no bluster in it, and no fright. Jupe saw that Bentley was no longer the meek houseman. It might take dynamite to move him out of the doorway.

Jupiter thought quickly. "Bob," he said, "give me that tape."

Bob lifted the spool of tape off the little recorder and handed it to Jupe.

"That tape is my property!" said Bentley.

Jupe held up the tape. "Tell us, Bentley, how did you record this? Did you hide the machine on the patio the night Miss Osborne had guests?"

The houseman moved then. He lunged across the darkening room and gripped Jupe's wrist.

"Run for it!" shouted Jupe to his friends.

Bob and Peter rushed for the open door. Jupe let go of the tape suddenly and hooked his right leg behind Bentley's left knee.

The houseman floundered backwards, cursing. The spool of tape flew across the room. Jupe let it go and ran.

As Jupe shot out of the door, Bentley grabbed the back of his shirt. Jupe tore free and bounded down the stairs.

Bentley did not try to follow. He stood on the landing holding a piece of Jupe's shirt and watched the boys snatch up their bikes and pedal rapidly away.

The Three Investigators were blocks from Tennyson Place before they stopped.

"Are we in trouble, or is Bentley?" wondered Pete. "If he calls the police, we can tell them about that tape and those files."

"The tape and the files can easily be hidden or destroyed," Jupe pointed out. "We *are* guilty of housebreaking, and Bentley has seen us with Allie. He knows where to find us if he wants to."

"What do we do now?" asked Bob.

"We go back to the salvage yard, report to our client and wait. We may not have any trouble. We know that Bentley had to be trespassing on the Jamison property to get that recording of the meeting with Ariel and the others. We know that he has a finance report on Miss Osborne. Wouldn't it be embarrassing if Bentley had to explain why he has that report?"

"Blackmail?" asked Pete.

"Possibly," admitted Jupe. "Let's get back to Headquarters and call Allie."

"She could have warned us that Bentley would be at that apartment tonight," said Pete bitterly.

"She may not have known," said Jupe.

At Headquarters, Jupe's guess was proved correct. The telephone was ringing when the boys made their way up through the trap door into the mobile home trailer. The caller was Allie Jamison.

"Oh, you guys, I'm sorry!" she began. Jupiter put the telephone down on a loudspeaker system he had rigged up so that the other Investigators could hear the conversation.

"Bentley caught us," said Jupiter tersely.

"I'm sorry," she repeated. "I tried to reach you, but you'd already left. He said he'd forgotten something he needed. I couldn't tell him he had to stay in nights, could I?"

"I wish you had tried," Jupiter told her. "I have a torn shirt and he now knows we are spying on him. You may have lost one houseman."

"You don't think he'll come back here?"

Jupe hesitated. "He might be brazen enough to try," he told Allie, "but we got into his apartment and we saw enough to make us suspect that Bentley might be trying to blackmail your aunt. He has a report on her financial position. Also, it was Bentley who was hiding in the garage the night your aunt and Ariel met with the members of the fellowship. He has a tape recording of that meeting."

"That doesn't figure," said Allie. "You couldn't blackmail Aunt Pat. She's clean."

86

"If she's clean, why is she so upset about Mrs Compton's accident?"

Allie did not answer.

"Where is your aunt, by the way?" asked Jupe.

"She's upstairs crying."

"And Hugo Ariel?"

"He's in the library, doing whatever he does."

"Have you heard that singing again?"

"No. It's peaceful as a tomb here, and just about as cheery," said Allie.

"Well, keep your eyes open," called Pete, "and let us know if Bentley shows up."

But Bentley did not show up. Allie called the Jones house first thing in the morning to report the non-appearance of her houseman. Later in the day, Jupiter and Bob rode down to Santa Monica, to Tennyson Place. The windows in the little building behind the stucco house looked blank, and again Jupe rang the bell at the main house. A wispy woman answered the door and told Jupe that it would not be possible for him to deliver a prescription from the chemist to her tenant in the garage, since he was no longer there. He had moved out that morning and had left no forwarding address.

"Do you recall what removal company he used?" asked Jupe. "There's an unpaid bill at the store."

"He moved himself," said the woman. "He went someplace and got a car and a trailer and moved himself. He didn't have that much to move."

Jupe thanked her and rejoined Bob on the sidewalk. "I think we'll hear nothing at present from Bentley," he told Bob. "I don't know whether I'm glad or sorry."

13

The Empress Diamonds

"I'M BEGINNING to miss Bentley," Allie told Jupiter on the third day after the houseman's disappearance. "He at least moved around. Aunt Pat sits in her room and broods, or she sits on the patio and broods. Ariel hovers. He hardly lets her out of his sight."

"Is he hovering this morning?"

"No. He's having his hair cut."

"What do they talk about?" asked Jupe. He and Allie were leaning on the fence in back of the Jamison house, watching Allie's horse.

"They don't."

"I'm afraid your aunt is involved in something sinister," said Jupe. "Bob has been researching witchcraft, and many of the things your aunt has been doing are mentioned in the witchcraft books. Drawing a circle around her bed with a knife is one. There are also many formulae for invoking spirits or casting spells which involve lighted candles."

"We haven't lit any candles for days," said Allie.

"The auction of the Castillo estate takes place next week," Jupiter told her. "Does your aunt plan to attend? Mrs Compton won't be there to bid on that crystal ball."

"No, Mrs Compton won't go any place for months.

Her leg was broken in two places. But I don't think Aunt Pat plans anything," said Allie. "She's numb. The only thing she does is call the hospital every day to check and see how Mrs Compton is doing, and even then she doesn't talk to Mrs Compton. She talks to the nurse."

Allie looked towards the front of the house. A black limousine had pulled into the drive. A chauffeur got out and opened the back door, and an elegant man dressed in striped trousers and a morning coat emerged from the car holding a package in his gloved hands. Jupe goggled. Such glory was seldom seen in Rocky Beach, and never at eleven in the morning.

Allie's eyes narrowed. "Van Storen and Chatsworth!" she announced. "Everything they do is a major production. They can't make a plain old delivery. I think my mother's necklace is home again. Suppose we meander inside and watch what happens?"

Jupe followed her in through the kitchen. Aunt Pat Osborne was in the hall in the act of accepting the package from the messenger. Jupe noticed that her purple gown was wrinkled and slightly soiled, as if she had worn it for several days—or as if she had given up thinking about what she wore. Her hands shook slightly as she handed a receipt to the man from Van Storen and Chatsworth.

"Allie dear!" she cried, and her voice was high and a bit shrill. "Jupiter. Good morning!"

The jewellers' man departed for his car.

"Your mother's necklace, dear," said Miss Osborne to Allie. "Open the package, won't you, and see if they did a good job?"

Allie silently tore away white wrappings and opened a dark green leather box. Inside, arranged on white satin, was a necklace that was inches wide. It held more than a hundred diamonds, all blazing with cold, white light.

"Gaudy, isn't it?" said Allie to Jupe.

"My dear, it's most historic," Aunt Pat said.

"It is also heavy as lead," Allie told her. "My mother practically gets a neckache every time she wears it." She closed the box. "I like pearls better. You don't need an armed guard following you around when you wear them."

Miss Osborne turned away from Allie. "Is that a car in the drive?" she asked.

"It's the werewolf of Rocky Beach, returning from the barber," Allie told her.

"Allie, put the necklace in your mother's safe," said Miss Osborne quickly.

A car door slammed in the back court. Aunt Pat looked towards the rear of the house, and she hid her hands in the folds of her robe. "Right away, dear."

"Okay, Aunt Pat," said Allie. She went up the stairs with the box and just missed Hugo Ariel, who came in reeking of hair tonic.

Allie, without the box, reappeared at the top of the stairs. "I'll talk to you later, huh?" she called down to Jupiter.

"I'll be waiting," promised Jupe, and he left.

Jupiter busied himself in the salvage yard for the rest of the day. He was never far from his workshop, however, where he could check to see if the telephone in Headquarters was ringing. At five, Allie called.

"What did you think of Aunt Pat's performance this morning?" asked Allie.

"I thought it was almost professional," said Jupe. "But it was clear she didn't want Hugo Ariel to know that the necklace was delivered today."

"She must have called the jewellers after Ariel made his appointment with the barber," said Allie. "I think the delivery was timed so that Ariel wouldn't be there to see it. But if it's so blasted important to keep Ariel away from that necklace, why did Aunt Pat have it returned? She could have ordered Van Storen and Chatsworth to hold it until my mother got home."

"Unless she needs it," said Jupiter.

"She'd better *not* need it!" cried Allie. "It's my mother's."

"True," said Jupiter. "And since it is your mother's, and since you do know the combination of the wall safe, it would be no trouble for you to remove the necklace. Would you let The Three Investigators have it for a short time? There's something I'd like to confirm. Could you get the necklace out of the house without its being seen?"

Allie did not hesitate. "I've got a poncho that I wear sometimes when I'm riding. You could almost hide a live rooster under that."

"Very good," said Jupiter. "Bring the necklace to the salvage yard the first minute you can. It's probably going to be safer here, anyway. I'll wait for you in my workshop. Now, if you'll hang up, I'll call our friend Worthington. We'll need him tomorrow."

Allie was at the salvage yard before six with the

green leather box containing the necklace. Jupe took it from her, and after she left he stowed it away in the desk in Headquarters. Early in the morning Worthington appeared with the Rolls-Royce.

"This is a great responsibility, Master Jupiter," said Worthington, when Jupe gave him the box. "A necklace that once belonged to an empress!"

"You're the only one who can do it," Jupe told him. "It would look very peculiar if I tried, or if Bob or Pete had the necklace."

Worthington nodded. "I'll be extremely careful," he promised. "I should be back here by about two."

"We'll all be waiting," promised Jupe.

It was almost exactly two when Worthington returned to the salvage yard. Jupe met him at the gate and led him to the workshop. Bob and Pete were waiting there with Allie, who sat hunched on an up-ended box.

"Miss Jamison," said Worthington, and he sat down in Jupiter's chair. Opening the green leather box, he took out the necklace and draped it across one knee. "It's beautiful," he said, "but it's worthless."

"Worthless!" Allie jumped up. "It's my mother's necklace! It belonged to the Empress Eugénie. It's priceless!"

Worthington was distressed. "I'm sorry, Miss Jamison, but it is *not* the Empress Eugénie necklace. It's an imitation. I called upon three valuers, saying that I found the necklace among the effects of a recently deceased relative. I was told not to try to obtain insurance on it, since one does not insure costume jewellery."

"Costume jewellery?" Allie looked ready to choke. "Give it to me!"

Worthington handed the necklace over.

"Are you going to discuss this with your aunt?" asked Jupiter mildly.

"Discuss it with her? I'm going home and ram this junk down her throat, and then I'm going to make her tell what she did with the real necklace."

"We can guess what she did with it," said Jupe. "You yourself suggested the safest course. She had an imitation made by Van Storen and Chatsworth, and she directed that the real necklace remain with the jewellers until your parents return."

Allie sat down again on the box. "That's like finding out that the class dunce is really Albert Einstein. So the necklace is safe."

"But why would she have an imitation necklace made?" asked Pete. "What's she going to do with it?"

Allie frowned. "All this hocus-pocus must have something to do with Ariel. Aunt Pat has been so careful not to let him see the necklace."

"Maybe she's afraid he'll steal it?" guessed Bob.

"Fine! Let him! He can steal this fake and get lost!"

"I don't think this is a simple matter of theft," said Jupiter. "Somehow this necklace business is all mixed up with Mrs Compton's accident and the fellowship and the power of the singing serpent."

"Is that serpent still singing at your house?" Bob asked Allie.

"No," said Allie. "No one sings at our house."

"Scared?" asked Pete.

"Yes, a little."

"I don't think you're in any danger," Jupiter told her. "As long as Ariel doesn't suspect you of being a threat to him, he won't bother you. Bentley is involved in some way and may show up again, but he doesn't seem violent."

"It isn't me I'm scared for," said Allie. "Why should I be scared for me? They think I'm only a pesky kid. I'm scared for Aunt Pat. Tonight she and Ariel are going to another meeting of that creepy fellowship. I heard them talking about it this morning. Ariel said Dr Shaitan was assembling the others at Torrente Canyon and Aunt Pat had to go. She doesn't want to. She cried a lot. But she's going."

"Excellent!" said Jupiter.

"It isn't excellent!" shouted Allie. "It's horrible. I hate to see her like this."

"I'm afraid until we discover the secret of the fellowship, you won't see her any other way," said Jupiter. "Worthington, could you . . ."

"I'd be delighted to pay another visit to the house in Torrente Canyon," said Worthington.

"I'm coming, too," announced Allie.

"Allie, please!" said Pete.

"It's *my* aunt," she pointed out. "It's also my mother's necklace that's involved, and Ariel is living in my house. I'm going. Worthington, where will I meet you this evening?"

"I had thought," said Worthington, "that the car park in front of the Rocky Beach supermarket—"

"Fine. What time?"

"Would half-past seven be agreeable, miss?"

"Perfectly. See you at seven-thirty." Allie strode out, hiding the necklace under her poncho.

"A strong-minded young lady," said Worthington. The Three Investigators did not disagree.

14

Dr Shaitan's Spirits

WORTHINGTON had no cause to change his mind that evening. Allie was waiting with The Three Investigators when he appeared at the Rocky Beach supermarket driving his grey Ford. She was calm enough, but her jaw was set in a way that meant she planned to see some action. "I'm going to get into that house," she told Worthington as he held the car door for her.

"Yes, miss," said Worthington.

"We'll get into the house," Jupiter Jones assured her. "We have a plan."

"What is it?"

"Wait and see," advised Jupe.

Allie had a long wait. They reached Torrente Canyon to find the road outside the walled house empty and deserted. "Good!" exclaimed Pete. "We're the first ones here."

Worthington parked up the road beyond the house and Bob got out of the car. "I'll keep watch from that bunch of oleanders across from the gate."

Bob nodded and walked back towards the big house.

"Good," said Jupe.

He was hidden in the oleanders, watching, when the first car came up the road.

It was Madelyn Enderby who got out, crossed to the

gate and reached for the telephone set into the wall. Bob was about to leave his hiding-place when the purple Corvette appeared. Hugo Ariel was at the wheel. In the twilight, Bob could barely see Miss Patricia Osborne. Her head was bowed and she dabbed at her eyes with a handkerchief. Ariel helped her out of the car. The buzzer on the gate rasped, and Ariel and Miss Osborne joined Madelyn Enderby and went in.

A few minutes later, a pale blue Cadillac rolled to a stop. Bob saw a thin, brown-haired man go to the telephone in the wall. Careful not to make a sound, Bob slipped out from behind the oleanders and crossed over to the gate.

The man was holding the telephone receiver to his ear, listening. Then he said, "I will descend to the lower circle."

He hung up and turned.

"Good evening," said Bob. "I'm looking for 1483 Torrente Circle."

"This isn't Torrente Circle," said the man. "It's Torrente Canyon Drive. You're on the wrong street."

The buzzer on the gate sounded. The man stepped past Bob, opened the gate and went through.

Bob returned to Worthington's Ford. "I will descend to the lower circle," he said. "The guy on the phone says, 'The night is dark,' and then you have to answer, 'I will descend to the lower circle.' "

"The password!" Allie leaped from the car.

"Keep alert," Jupe told Worthington.

"I'll be waiting for you," promised the chauffeur.

The Three Investigators followed Allie down the

road to the gate. Jupiter lifted the telephone receiver from the niche and put it to his ear.

"The night is dark," said a husky voice.

"I will descend to the lower circle," answered Jupe. His tone was as deep as he could manage.

The telephone clicked and Jupe hung up. A moment later the gate buzzed. Pete turned the handle and pushed, and the huge portal swung easily in.

The Three Investigators and Allie slipped inside. The gate shut behind them. When Bob tried the handle on the inside, it would not move.

"There's a switch hidden in the ivy to the right of the gate," said Pete. "The night I fell off the wall, that thug used it to open the gate before he tossed me out."

Bob peered at the ivy. "I see it. Looks like a circuit breaker."

"Don't touch it," warned Jupe. "It might set off some kind of alarm. We know where it is. We can use it if we need to get out fast."

"Now for the house," said Allie.

"No. Now we wait," Jupe told her. "If this meeting of the fellowship is anything like the one we saw before, there are more people to come."

Jupiter was right. From a shadowy corner of the grounds, the boys and Allie watched the gate open again and again to admit visitors. After fifteen minutes, eight more people had walked up the long drive to the house.

"Eight, plus Madelyn Enderby, Miss Osborne and Ariel and that one I overheard on the telephone," said Bob. "That makes twelve, the same as the other night. I wonder if that's all."

It was. When ten minutes had passed without a sound from the gate, they decided to move.

"Now let's watch it," warned Pete. "I don't want to meet that guy who guards this place."

They moved slowly and noiselessly across the grass. When they were quite close to the house, they saw that one tiny chink of light showed through curtains which had been drawn over a long window. They edged away from this and circled to the back of the building.

"There's a door," said Jupe softly. He crept forward in the darkness, careful not to stumble on an unexpected doorstep. He felt for the doorknob and found it. But the door was locked.

Allie backed away and looked up at the rear of the house. "Up there," she whispered. "A window, and if anything's open anywhere, it's that. It's so high they wouldn't bother with it."

"Probably a pantry or a storeroom," guessed Jupe. He looked at the opening doubtfully. "It's very small."

"I can get through," said Allie quickly.

"No, you can't," put in Bob. "You're not thin enough."

"You are, Bob," said Jupe. "Be careful."

"Don't worry," said Bob.

Pete braced himself against the house, and Bob clambered up on to his shoulders.

"Is it open?" asked Allie.

Jupe shushed her and listened to wood sliding on wood. Bob grunted, pulled himself up, slipped in through the window and disappeared. Perhaps a minute ticked by. Then the lock turned softly on the back door and the door opened.

"Come on," whispered Bob. "They're all out front someplace."

The Investigators and Allie crept across a kitchen, guided by a faint glow from the front of the house. At the kitchen doorway they stopped and looked into a wide hall. To the left they saw a broad staircase, and to the right, opposite the staircase, they saw an arched doorway. The light came from that door.

Jupe drew back into the kitchen. Outside the uncurtained windows, the moon shone dimly through the tree-tops. Jupe could barely make out the shape of a stove. He heard a tap drip, and he saw that there was a second door leading out of the kitchen. It showed as a black, gaping hole in the wall, to the left of the first door.

Jupe tapped Bob and pointed. Bob nodded. Jupe took Allie's arm and guided her through the second door into inky blackness. Pete and Bob followed.

They had to feel their way. They went forward, inch by inch. Strange objects got in their path. Pete touched one and felt velvet. It was a sofa.

At last there was a hairline of light. It had to be coming through a crack under a door. Jupe let go of Allie's arm, took two slow steps forward and let his fingers slide over wooden panels until he touched a knob. It turned without a sound. Jupe pulled the knob towards him and opened the door a few inches.

He was looking out across the broad hall and in through the lighted archway.

"The fellowship is assembled," said a familiar voice from across the hall. Hugo Ariel was speaking.

Jupe opened the door a few more inches, and the

others crowded round him. They stared into a chamber where tall, black candles burned in silver candlesticks. In the middle of the room was a large, round table, covered with a black cloth. Twelve people were grouped around it, standing behind chairs. Hugo Ariel seemed to be at the head of the table, facing the hall. Before him was a chair that looked more like a throne. Gilded wooden cobras twisted around the arms and up over the back of the thing. Next to it stood Pat Osborne, looking forlorn.

The fellowship waited, not moving, in a room that seemed filled with motion. Jupe realised that the group was surrounded by a shifting, billowing darkness. Black hangings covered walls and windows and swayed with every draft.

Ariel shifted his weight behind the throne. "The fellowship is assembled," he said again.

The boys and Allie heard footsteps on the stairs. A shape came between them and the candlelit room. Someone wearing a long, black cloak paused in the archway, then swept into the room and went to the far side of the table. He sat down in the serpent throne and, for the first time, Jupiter and the others could really see him. Jupe heard Pete let out a faint gasp.

If Hugo Ariel was pale, this man was ashen. His face was so white that it seemed to glow and float against the blackness of his own garb—for he was swathed from head to toe in the colour of night. Even his hair was hidden by a close-fitting black cap.

The man drew his cape around him with gleaming white hands and bowed his head slightly.

The assembled company sat down.

The man on the throne clapped his hands twice. Hugo Ariel glided away from the table, then returned with a tray. On it was a silver cup, which Ariel offered to the man in the chair.

"Belial favour all those here!" said the man. He took the cup and put it to his lips.

"Moloch hear us!" It was a chorus of voices.

The man handed the cup to Pat Osborne. She took it, looking as if she might weep. "Belial favour all those here," she said shakily. She drank and passed the cup as the others intoned the prayer to Moloch.

Again and again the favour of Belial was asked. Again and again the group called upon Moloch to hear them. The cup came back at last to the person in the serpent chair, who returned it to Ariel.

Next Ariel produced a small charcoal brazier with four legs. He put this on the table in front of the caped one, who then stood and extended his hands over the live coals. "Asmodeus, Abaddon and Eblis, look upon us!" he cried.

Ariel offered a silver dish. The man in black sprinkled something from it on to the brazier. A column of smoke sprang up and a thick, sweet smell drifted to the watchers across the hall.

"Belial hear us!" pleaded the caped man. "Send the power of the serpent to guard us. Let us see your countenance. Let us hear your voice!"

The man was still then. Everyone was still, and in that stillness Allie and the boys heard the beginning of a dreaded sound. Someone or something was singing.

Allie started, as if she wanted to run. Jupe grasped her arm and held her still.

The sound grew louder. It rose, wordless, until it stung at the bone and shrivelled the flesh.

Again the man in the cape dipped into the dish. Again incense was thrown into the brazier. And in the seething mass of smoke, something moved!

Bob took a sudden, deep breath.

"Belial has favoured us!" proclaimed the caped man. "The serpent that never dies is among us!"

The silent watchers trembled when they saw the thing that writhed in the smoke. It was a huge cobra, a shimmer of green and blue, a spread of hood, a red-eyed glitter.

The song went on and on until it was a fearful, shrill pulse of noise that made Jupe want to cover his ears. At last, mercifully, it began to dwindle. The smoke thinned. The terrible serpent paled and faded. The singing ceased. The thing was gone.

The caped man seated himself. "The good of one of our fellowship is the good of all," he said. "We will join hands."

Pat Osborne stared straight ahead, but she put her hand on the table. The man in black took it.

Jupiter nudged Pete. Footsteps came softly down the stairs, and a dark shape blocked the watchers' view of the fellowship. It was the muscular man who had been patrolling the grounds the night Pete fell off the wall. He stood in the hall, surveying the room where the caped man presided over his brazier and his disciples. After a moment, he went into the ritual room, walked to the far side of the table and bent to whisper into the ear of the man on the throne.

"Impossible!" said the caped man. "We are all present."

"There should be thirteen," insisted the other. "Miss Enderby, Mr Ariel and Miss Osborne came in together. Everyone else came separately. But I opened the gate eleven times. There should be a thirteenth member!"

The man in the cape stood up. "It seems that we may have an intruder nearby," he told his followers. "The fellowship is dismissed. I will summon you again when the time is right."

The Investigators drew back from the door, and Jupiter closed it silently.

"They're on to us," whispered Pete.

There was a scraping of chairs from the ritual room, and a babble of voices.

"Very thorough," said Jupiter softly. "That man who tends the gate can count."

"Let's go!" urged Bob. "In two seconds they'll be searching this place."

"You go," said Jupiter Jones.

"You're kidding!"

"I'm not." Jupiter's voice was so low that the others could scarcely hear him over the bustle of the departing fellowship. "Go out the back, the way we came in. Make a disturbance. Climb the wall. Set off the alarm. Make them think they've scared everybody off. Then get to the car and tell Worthington I'll meet you at Sunset and Torrente as soon as I can."

"Okay, Jupe, but watch it," said Bob.

"I will," promised Jupiter.

He heard his friends slip back to the kitchen. Then the kitchen door opened and slammed shut. He heard shouts from the grounds outside. Allie yelled, and he heard the clamour of the alarm bell. Flood-lights blazed in the yard, and from the road came the sound of cars starting.

Jupe waited. Soon there was quiet—the quiet of an empty house. Jupiter opened the door, looked around the hall, then hurried across to the ritual room, where he hid behind the black curtains. After a time there were steps on the drive outside. The inhabitants of the house on Torrente Canyon came into the hall and closed the door.

"Just kids," said one voice. "Kids get curious."

"You have to hand it to them, Max," said a second voice. It was the voice of the man who had occupied the throne. "They sure moved going over that wall."

Jupiter Jones smiled to himself. Bob, Pete and Allie had got clean away—and he now intended to find out whatever he could!

15

The High Priest's Scheme

JUPITER FOUND a small tear in the black hangings that shrouded the ritual room. He stood stock still, so that he would not reveal his presence to the men in the room, but his fingers worked at the little tear, making it bigger. Soon he could look out into the room, and he saw the man named Max touch a switch near the door. An overhead light clicked on.

Jupiter almost sighed. By flickering candlelight, the ritual room had had a dark fascination. Now that fascination was gone. Jupe saw that the covering on the table was dusty, and that the hangings in the room were cheap and sagging. The silver candlesticks were dented and flecked with tarnish.

If the room was shabby, the two men in it were equally worn. The man with the grey hair—the man who had thrown Pete off the grounds—was going from one tall candle to another, snuffing out the flames. Deep lines ran from his eyes down to the corners of his mouth. He was beginning to run to fat, and a double chin drooped over the top of his dark shirt.

His companion lolled on the throne, absently stroking the carved cobra on one of the arms. He had pushed the chair back to put his feet on the table. In the full light, Jupiter saw that his ghastly paleness was not natural. Some greenish, chalky substance was caked in the creases round his mouth and beside his nose.

"That telephone system at the gate is a total loss," said the man in the chair.

The man named Max snuffed out the last of the candles and sat down wearily. "Look," he said, "I could go down and stand at that gate and check everybody who comes through, but that won't work either. You can't fight kids. They'll get in somehow, and they talk. We've made a bundle here. Why don't we fold the operation and move? You can have a fine time being Dr Shaitan in San Francisco or San Diego or Chicago. Let's go before things hot up for us."

"But Max, the best is yet to come," said the man called Dr Shaitan. He reached up and pulled off his black cap. Jupe wanted to laugh. The high priest of the sinister fellowship had flaming red hair. An instant later, the black cape was unfastened and thrown aside. The man took a crumpled tissue from his pocket and dabbed at his chalky face. The greenish powder came off in streaks, revealing pink skin.

"Do you have to do that here?" complained Max. "You're getting that stuff all over the place."

"I'm thinking." Dr Shaitan rolled the stained tissue between his hands. "It's taken us a long time to set up this bunch of pigeons. The Enderby woman came through like clockwork when her landlady went to Dubuque, and old man Robertson made a beautiful donation when the power of the singing serpent was invoked to keep that building contractor from putting up a high rise next to his house. Pat Osborne hasn't paid off yet, but she will and it will be juicy. Hugo Ariel will see to it."

"It may be so juicy that we won't be able to handle it," said Max.

"We can handle anything," declared Shaitan. "You just have to know where the market is." He smiled. "Ellis did a good job with the Compton woman. No one suspected a thing. Did you notice Pat Osborne tonight?"

"Scared," said Max.

"Very much so," said Shaitan with grim satisfaction. "She'll be even more scared if she doesn't make her offering. Now Noxworth isn't going to scare easily, but he won't have all these pangs of conscience, either, and he's got real dough. No hot stuff there. We'll get cold, hard cash. We see to it that his competition folds up and he'll be duly grateful. It'll be worth hanging in here for that."

Max snorted. "The things that these nuts get upset about floor me," he declared. "The Osborne dame wants a crystal ball that once belonged to a movie star, and Noxworth can't stand it when the place across the street draws more customers than his own lousy delicatessen. Noxworth's got money he hasn't even counted yet. Why should he care?"

"It isn't the money," said Shaitan. "It's the power. These people want to believe they've got power, so we convince them that they do."

"How are you planning to convince Noxworth?" asked Max. "Is his competition going to have a motor accident, too?"

The man who enjoyed being Dr Shaitan put his

fingertips together and stared at them dreamily. "You lack imagination, Max. No, the singing serpent will perform in a different key for Noxworth. It will be a bit riskier, but it may work. Even if it doesn't, Noxworth won't get off the hook because we'll see to it that he, personally, delivers the serpent. And we'll see to it that he witnesses the result. He'll come through, just the way Pat Osborne will come through."

Dr Shaitan yawned. "I'm beat," he said. "I'm going to bed." He got up and started for the doorway.

"You left your cape," said Max.

"I'll get it in the morning." Shaitan's footsteps went away up the stairs.

"Slob!" snarled Max. He pushed back his chair and went to the doorway. The light switch clicked and the lower floor of the house on Torrente Canyon went dark. Jupe heard Max follow the high priest of the fellowship up the stairs. A door slammed. Water gurgled in the pipes at the back of the house.

Jupiter slipped out from behind the black curtains and tiptoed out of the ritual room into the hall. He stole to the back of the house, and was pleased to find that Dr Shaitan and his assistant had neglected to lock the kitchen door after they returned to the house. Jupe slipped out without making a sound and started for the gate. He looked back once to see lights in several of the upper windows. The shadow of a man showed clearly on one drawn blind. Jupiter grinned. Dr Shaitan had his head thrown back. He was gargling.

Jupe wished he had a photograph of the demonic high priest at his bedtime ritual. Then he was at the wall, searching in the moonlight for the switch hidden in the ivy—the switch that would open the gate and release him. When his fingers touched it, he took a deep breath and flipped the plastic lever. The alarm did not clang. The floodlights did not blaze. There was a faint sound from the house. It might have been something triggered by the switch, but Jupe did not pause to wonder. He stepped to the gate, turned the handle and tugged. The gate opened.

At that, stunningly, the floodlights did glare.

"Hey! Hey, you kid! Hold it right there!"

Jupiter did not turn round. He did not have to. He knew instantly that the voice belonged to the muscular Max. He began to run.

"Hold it, I said!" shouted Max.

Something hit Jupiter—something large. He felt himself tumbling over and over, rolling in the road. And someone was rolling with him.

"Keep down, you idiot!" said a voice in his ear.

There was a roar, and buckshot whined overhead and crackled through the oleanders beside the road.

"Don't move," cautioned the person who was holding Jupe down.

Jupiter winced as another roar came from the driveway of the walled house and more shot whistled above him.

"Now!" cried Jupe's captor. He flung himself away from Jupe. Jupe lunged to his feet and saw a man sprint towards the place where Torrente Canyon Road came to a dead end. The man looked back at Jupe for a bare second. "Run!" he shouted.

Jupe ran in the opposite direction. He ran as fast as his trembling legs would carry him.

Worthington's Ford was parked at the corner of Sunset and Torrente, and the engine was running. The back door popped open. "Okay?" asked Bob.

Jupiter scrambled into the car. "Go!" he shouted.

Worthington went so quickly that Jupe was thrown to the floor.

"What happened?" asked Allie from the front seat.

Jupiter pulled himself up. "There was a man outside that gate tonight with a large moustache and fair hair. Does that sound like anyone you know?"

"Bentley?"

"I think so," said Jupe. "I'm almost positive it was Bentley. And I wish I could talk to him now. I'd like to thank him."

"For what?" asked Allie.

"If it hadn't been for Bentley, I might now be punctured in several places. Dr Shaitan's friend lost his patience with juvenile intruders, and Dr Shaitan's friend has a double-barrelled shotgun."

16

Trouble for Aunt Pat

"IT's WITCHCRAFT, but it isn't," declared Bob.

The Three Investigators were in Headquarters, reviewing the events of the night before. Bob had his file on the case of the singing serpent. He also had several books. One was *Witchcraft, Folk Medicine and Magic*, the book that the boys had seen in Bentley's apartment. Bob tapped the volume. "Those men are going by the book," he said. "It could be this book, or any book on witchcraft. They're all pretty much the same, whether the author is writing about voodoo in the West Indies or what happens among the aborigines in Australia. It works the same way, only what those guys in Torrente Canyon are doing can't possibly work."

"Because the victim doesn't believe?" asked Jupiter Jones.

"Right. Because the victim doesn't believe."

"You care to explain that?" asked Pete.

"It's simple." Bob held up the book on magic. "This one's by Dr Henry W. Barrister, who's a professor of anthropology at Ruxton University. He's been to Africa and South America and Mexico and Australia and he keeps finding about the same thing. When a witch doctor wants to put a curse on someone, he can use different methods. With voodoo, he sticks pins in a doll. In Mexico, the witch goes to a nice dark cave and lights candles and says spells. Then he cuts a thread. That thread is the victim's life. The witch doctor has cut his life short. Pretty soon the victim learns that his life has been cut, and he gets sick and dies."

"I don't get it."

"The victim believes," put in Jupiter. "He knows a spell has been cast and he believes that he'll die, so he does."

"You mean just believing in a thing like that can hurt you?" Pete looked a bit green.

"If you believe strongly enough," said Bob. Again he tapped the book by the anthropology professor. "The man who wrote this has seen people get sick and die of terror because someone put a curse on them."

"Then Ariel and Shaitan are doing the same thing," decided Pete, "only they're using a serpent. The serpent is delivered and bang! Big trouble for whoever gets the snake."

"That's what has happened," agreed Jupe, "but, as Bob says, it can't be magic. The victims don't believe. Margaret Compton wasn't afraid of the singing serpent. To her, it was only an odd bracelet. It's Allie's aunt who believes that the accident happened because the serpent was delivered to Mrs Compton. She blames herself and she's afraid. It's natural. She isn't a malicious woman and she wasn't expecting anything so drastic.

"But of course we know that the accident was no accident at all. I heard that much last night. The man who calls himself Shaitan arranged with someone named Ellis for the wheel to come off Mrs Compton's car."

"And now Shaitan and his pal are dreaming up something to eliminate Noxworth's competition," said Bob gloomily.

Jupiter rubbed his forehead. "It's the place across the street," he said. "Those were the words Max used. The place across the street has more customers than Noxworth."

"Another delicatessen?" said Pete. "That's nuts!"

"It is to us," agreed Jupiter, "but remember, Miss Osborne wanted the crystal ball which had belonged to Ramon Castillo. Miss Enderby had a quarrel with her landlady and invoked the power of the serpent. Some very silly things can stir up strong feelings.

"And there is the desire for power. Shaitan said it—these people want power. Shaitan wants money. I wonder what Bentley wants. He's the big question mark. He goes to work as a houseman, then disappears when his interest in magic and in the fellowship is discovered. What is his interest?"

"Maybe it's money, too," said Bob. "Maybe he is a blackmailer. Whatever it is, be glad. He kept you from getting peppered with buckshot."

"I am glad. He must have seen the gun in Max's hands. He jumped on me and knocked me out of the line of fire and kept me down until Max had used up both his charges of shot."

"So he's still the mystery man," said Bob, "but we know what the score is on The Fellowship of the Lower Circle. They're a bunch of con men milking superstitious people like Allie's Aunt Pat. What do we do now?"

"Tell the police?" suggested Pete.

"Would they believe us?" asked Jupe quietly.

"Mrs Compton *was* hurt," Pete insisted.

"An accident. A wheel comes off a car. Who knows why? If it was done cleverly enough, it could be impossible to detect. And even if we could persuade the police to visit the house in Torrente Canyon, what would they find? Two men and some black candles. We can't go to the police. Not now, at any rate. We need proof."

"Ariel?" said Bob. "He's putting the screws on Aunt Pat for sure."

"He'd never admit it, and she'd never testify against him," decided Jupe. "She's terrified of him. Whatever the fellowship wants from her, she will eventually give them. She's afraid not to."

"We can all guess what they want," said Pete.

Jupe nodded. "Something that might be too hot to handle, unless you know the right people. They don't want money from Miss Osborne. She hasn't much. They want the Empress Eugénie necklace."

"Which is safe in the vault at the jewellers'," said Bob.

"Jupe! Jupiter, where are you?" The cry came to the boys through the air vent of the mobile home trailer. "Jupiter Jones!"

Jupe leaped up. "That's Allie!"

Pete snatched open the trap door that led to Tunnel Two. "Never a dull moment when that kid's around," he said.

Bob and Jupe followed Pete through Tunnel Two to Jupiter's workshop, then ran towards the driveway of the salvage yard. Allie was there, near the office. She was almost in tears, and there was an ugly red mark on one cheek.

"Dr Shaitan!" she said. "He's at the house!"

Pete whistled. "Did he do that?" he asked.

"What?" demanded Allie.

"Your face. It looks as if someone hit you."

Allie pushed her hair back with both hands. "Aunt Pat," she said.

"You're kidding! Your aunt socked you?"

"She didn't mean it," said Allie hastily. "She was scared, that's all. She looked out and saw this big car pull up, see, and it was Shaitan with his black cape and his cap and the whole bit. The other creep who lives in that house was dressed as a chauffeur. Aunt Pat told me to get out. I wasn't going to do that, so she got angry and hit me, then shoved me out of the back door just as the front doorbell was ringing. And she locked the door." Allie gave a gasping little laugh. "I didn't know she had it in her."

"*Now* we call the cops!" declared Pete.

"No, we can't. Don't you see? She's alone there with those men. They might hurt her."

"Then we must get to your house," exclaimed Jupe. "Quickly!"

They raced up the street to the Jamison house, but they were only in time to see a black car pull away. Max was at the wheel and Ariel sat beside him. Shaitan, capped and caped, sat in the rear.

The front door of the house was unlocked. Allie

rushed through and let it bang against the wall. "Aunt Pat!" she shouted.

Miss Osborne was a lavender shadow in the green-gold living-room. "Allie? Allie, I'm so sorry. I didn't mean to strike you."

Allie ran towards her aunt. "Are you all right?"

"Yes, I'm all right." A single tear ran down Miss Osborne's cheek and trembled, unnoticed, on her chin. "Mr Ariel and . . . and . . ."

"Dr Shaitan?" said Jupiter Jones.

Miss Osborne reached out blindly, touched a chair and sat down.

"Did they want the necklace?" asked Jupiter. "Did you give them the imitation?"

Miss Osborne stared at him, at the other two boys and at Allie. "You knew?"

"We've known for some time that there was an imitation. We guessed that Shaitan wanted the Empress Eugénie diamonds, and that that's why Hugo Ariel stayed in this house. Did they threaten you, Miss Osborne?"

She began to sob. "It was horrible! Horrible! They said I had to make an offering." She took a handkerchief from a pocket in her gown and wiped her eyes. Then she blew her nose in a determined manner.

"But I fooled them," she said proudly. "I pretended to hold out. I made them wait. Wasn't that clever? Because the thing they have is paste, and the real necklace is safe!"

"In the vault at the jewellers'?" asked Jupe.

"At the jewellers'? Why, no. It was delivered when they brought the imitation. The real one was in a bag

—an ordinary paper bag. I put it in the pocket of my dress and then later I hid it."

Allie sighed. "It's still in this house?"

"Of course it's in this house. Where else would it be? But it's safe. No one will ever find it. I'll never tell. I won't even tell *you*."

Allie knelt beside her aunt. "All right, Aunt Pat. You don't have to tell me. But we must call the police." Her voice was very gentle.

"No!"

"Now we have proof," said Jupiter. "What they did to you is extortion. You must speak to Chief Reynolds."

"No!"

"Miss Osborne, those are dangerous men, and they are by no means finished with their business in Los Angeles. Unless you talk to the police, innocent people may be hurt."

"An innocent person *has* been hurt, and it's my fault. I can't! I won't! You don't know what you're asking! You don't know what it would mean!"

"All right, Miss Osborne," said Jupiter. "Only think about this: How long will it take Dr Shaitan to discover that the necklace is an imitation? What will happen then?"

Pat Osborne was silent.

"Think about it, Miss Osborne," said Jupe, "and don't wait too long."

17

A Warning from Pete

MISS OSBORNE was still sitting in the living-room, dazed, when The Three Investigators left.

"That woman is really, really dumb!" said Pete.

"Is she ever!" agreed Bob. "And we can't do anything if she won't talk to the police."

"There is one thing we can do," said Jupiter. "We know what Shaitan plans. He's going to eliminate the delicatessen that's across the street from Noxworth's store. We'd better locate that delicatessen and warn the owner. He'll be the next one to receive the serpent."

"But will he believe us?" asked Bob.

"Probably not," said Jupiter. "However, we can give him one of our cards and ask him to call us if a serpent object suddenly appears in his life. When the serpent *is* delivered, he'll be curious. I think he will call us."

The boys reached The Jones Salvage Yard and went into the office, where Jupiter consulted the Los Angeles telephone directory. "Noxworth's Mini Market is at Beverly and Third Street," he said.

"There couldn't be two of them," said Bob. "Do we call Worthington?"

Jupiter frowned. "Let's not run Worthington ragged. We can get into Los Angeles on the bus. Once we see

Noxworth's store, we can easily spot the opposition. Only, I have a feeling we'd better not all go. If Shaitan shows up at Allie's house again, she'll call here. I want to be here if that call comes."

Bob leaned against a filing cabinet. "I'd like to stay here, too," he said.

"Okay. I'll go," said Pete. "But if that call comes from Allie, you guys had better yell for Chief Reynolds and the Rocky Beach Police Department. No telling what those crooks will do when they find out the necklace is a fake."

Pete went off then to catch the bus into Santa Monica. In Santa Monica he transferred to a Los Angeles bus, and by noon he was standing at the corner of Beverly and Third Street.

Pete spotted Noxworth's Mini Market immediately. It was directly across the street from the bus stop, and Pete decided that the store matched the man. The windows, like Mr Noxworth's undershirt, would have been better for a good washing. Tatters of newspaper decorated the parking space, and someone had dropped a lemonade bottle near the door. Shards of green glass lay there undisturbed.

Pete scanned his side of the street. A television repair shop shared the block with another food store. Gleaming chrome letters on the wall of the delicatessen proclaimed that H. Hendricks supplied gourmet foods. Inside the shop, a large man with dark, curly hair scooped potato salad into a carton, while a plump lady consulted her shopping list. The white formica counter was spotless and uncluttered. There was no other food store in sight.

Satisfied that he had located Noxworth's competition, Pete waited until the plump lady left the store. Then he went in.

"Mr Hendricks?" said Pete.

"Yes?" said the man behind the counter.

"You *are* Mr Hendricks?" asked Pete. "I mean, you own this store, don't you?"

The man looked Pete over. Pete saw that he had more than his fair share of muscles. There was no trace of grey in his dark hair, and the brown eyes were steady and clear. In short, Mr Hendricks looked well able to take care of himself.

"You need a job, son?" he asked. "I hired a boy to deliver for me last week, but if—"

"I don't need a job," said Pete. "I only need to be sure you own this shop."

"You fussy about who sells you your pickles? Okay, I'm Hendricks and I own this place. Now what's on your mind?"

"I came to warn you, Mr Hendricks. I know this is going to sound crazy, but something bad will happen to you. I don't know exactly what, but it'll be bad."

Pete put one of the cards of The Three Investigators on the counter and wrote the private number of Headquarters on it. After a moment's thought, he added the number of The Jones Salvage Yard.

"If you should see a snake—" began Pete.

"I'll call the zoo," said Hendricks.

"I don't mean that kind of snake," protested Pete. "It won't be a live snake. It might be a statue of a snake, or a pin or something like that. It will be a cobra. If someone delivers a cobra to you, call either of these numbers. If one doesn't answer, the other will."

Hendricks did not touch the card. He looked as if he were waiting for the punch line to a joke.

"We think we can help you," Pete said quickly. "It's very serious. Someone's out to get you. When you see the snake, you'll know that something bad is going to happen. Now if you'll co-operate with us, we can—"

"Beat it," said Hendricks.

"Mr Hendricks, we want to help."

"I said beat it!" The brown eyes had gone hard.

"Maybe when you see the snake, you'll change your mind," said Pete.

Hendricks started round the counter and Pete fled to the door. "Call any time," he said.

"Scram!" shouted Hendricks.

Pete scrammed. On the bus ride back to Rocky Beach he decided, unhappily, that he had not been at all successful in delivering the warning. He felt that Jupiter Jones might have done a better job. Jupe could be very convincing.

It was afternoon when Pete reached The Jones Salvage Yard. Bob and Jupe were there. Bob was looking on as Jupe hosed down a sundial which Uncle Titus Jones had recently acquired.

"Noxworth's competition is a man named Hendricks," said Pete. "He is one heck of a tough guy."

"Did you warn him?" asked Bob.

"I warned him, and I left our card and the telephone number of the yard and the telephone number of Headquarters. He chased me out of his store."

"He didn't believe you." Jupiter turned off the hose.

"We expected that. But if he does receive a snake object, he may call."

"I don't think we should wait for that call," said Bob. "We should go to the police now. How can we protect a man who won't listen to us?"

Jupiter turned towards the gate of the salvage yard. A patrol car was pulling in, and Chief Reynolds was at the wheel. "It looks," said Jupe, "as if the police have come to us."

The head of the Rocky Beach Police Department stopped his car and got out. He approached The Three Investigators with the air of a man who is both weary and irritated. "Would you hot shots please tell me what you're doing now?" he asked.

"Have you had a complaint about us?" asked Jupe.

"I've had a call from the Los Angeles Police Department, Juvenile Division. They asked me if I knew you, and I had to admit that I did." The chief pointed a finger at Pete. "You paid a call on a shop-keeper named Hendricks today," he accused.

Pete gulped.

"You left your calling card and the telephone number of this place," said the chief, "which is why the LAPD called me. They think that you're trying to threaten Mr Hendricks."

"Threaten him?" cried Pete. "I wasn't trying to threaten him. I was trying to warn him."

"It didn't sound that way to Hendricks. It sounded more like a threat. Care to explain?"

"We'd be glad to," said Jupiter quickly.

"Fine," said Chief Reynolds. "I'm listening."

Jupiter decided that professional ethics would not

permit him to mention Allie and her aunt, but otherwise he told the chief everything. He told of finding a mysterious house in Torrente Canyon, and of the peculiar brand of magic being practised there. He admitted entering the house. He related the conversation he had overheard between Shaitan and his confederate. "We believe that Mr Hendricks is in danger," he finished. "When the power of the singing serpent is invoked—"

Chief Reynolds held up his hand. "That's enough. Don't get so carried away. Los Angeles is full of weirdos who burn candles and chant to the moon. If they arrested everyone who thinks he's got some kind of pipeline to super power, there wouldn't be standing room in the city jail. Now I will explain about you three to the Los Angeles police, and that won't be easy. But please do me a favour. Keep out of other people's houses, or you'll really collect a load of buckshot some day."

When he had gone, Pete said, "You should have told him about Miss Osborne and that necklace."

"I couldn't," said Jupiter. "Allie is our client and we have to protect her. And Miss Osborne would deny our story, anyway."

In the office of the salvage yard, the telephone rang. Jupiter went to answer it. He was back outside in seconds. "That was Allie," he said. "The power of the singing serpent has been invoked against her aunt! The cobra was just delivered!"

18

Living Terror

ALLIE WAS WAITING in the doorway when the boys arrived at the Jamison house. She had the cobra in her hands. It was not a piece of jewellery, like the serpent which Margaret Compton had received. It was a gilt statue about six inches tall. The body of the snake was a heap of shining coils. The hooded head reared out of this. Red eyes sparkled as Allie held the thing up.

"Who was the messenger?" asked Jupiter Jones.

Allie led the way to the living-room and put the statue down on the coffee table. "I don't know," she said. "Someone rang the bell and left the box on the front porch and took off."

"I don't suppose it matters," said Pete.

"No, I don't think it does. What does matter is that Aunt Pat got to the box before I did. Even before she unwrapped it, she was shaking. She knew."

"And then?" asked Bob.

"She saw the snake and she read the card."

Jupe bent over the white square of cardboard on the table. " 'Belial will claim his own. A soul is more precious than diamonds,' " he read aloud.

"They printed it nice and big, so she'd be sure to get the message," said Allie.

"And she got the message?" said Bob.

"Well, she fainted. I never saw anybody faint before. I didn't know what to do. After a while she opened her eyes and began to moan. I got her upstairs and put her to bed."

"Will she talk with the police now?" asked Bob.

"No. I told her she had to. I told her we had real evidence—the wrappings and the card and all. She said it wouldn't do any good. She said it might be too late, and the only thing that might help would be to give Shaitan the real necklace."

Jupiter started. "She isn't going to do that?"

"She can't," Allie told him. "She hasn't got it. I found it."

The Three Investigators looked at her, waiting.

"We saw a film on television a while back," Allie explained. "It was a spy picture, and the lady spy hid some microfilm in a box of bath powder. Aunt Pat doesn't have a lot of real original ideas. After you left this morning, I went into her bathroom and there it was in the powder box."

"I hope you found a good place to hide it," said Pete.

"In case I get run over by a bulldozer before my folks come home, look in the oat bin in the garage," Allie told him.

"Not bad," said Pete.

"No. Except that now I'm the one who's got to decide, and it's rough. Aunt Pat just lies there in bed and looks at the wall. I'm afraid she's really sick. I mean really, truly sick."

"She may get worse," warned Jupe. "She hasn't been well for some time, has she?"

"No. Not since Mrs Compton's accident."

"I don't think you should be alone with her," said Jupe. "I'll call Aunt Mathilda and ask her to come and help you."

Allie brightened suddenly. "Jupe, your aunt's a strong character, isn't she? Do you think if we told her the whole story, she could make Aunt Pat talk?"

"Aunt Mathilda is made of iron," said Jupe, "but in this case, I don't think she could help. Your aunt is too terrified of Shaitan and Ariel. No, it will be better if we just tell Aunt Mathilda that your aunt is having an attack of nerves and you can't handle it alone."

"I can't," said Allie.

"Okay," said Jupe, and he went to the telephone and called the Jones house. Within fifteen minutes Aunt Mathilda was in the house. She surveyed the situation, frowned fiercely at the sight of Pat Osborne huddled in her bed, decided that Allie needed a nap and that the boys would have to leave.

"You and your uncle can eat dinner out," she told Jupiter. "I'll stay here tonight and we'll see how things are in the morning." Aunt Mathilda then disappeared into the kitchen to explore the Jamison refrigerator and the cupboards. Jupe heard a pot clang down on the stove.

"You'll have a good meal tonight," he told Allie.

"I don't like to leave," said Pete. "I mean. shouldn't we go on guard duty here to make sure nothing else happens?"

"Disaster has already struck," said Jupiter. "I don't think anyone will try anything more now. Besides, Aunt Mathilda will cope, and she isn't afraid of singing serpents or anything else that I know of."

He turned to Allie. "Even if your aunt won't talk," he said, "you can. You can call the police. You said yourself you have to decide."

Allie shook her head. "It would be a nightmare. What could I say? That my aunt's being victimised by witches? And she's so ashamed. She thinks she's the one who hurt Margaret Compton."

The kitchen door opened. "Jupiter!" said Aunt Mathilda sharply. "Pete! Bob! You boys go on now and let that child get some rest."

The boys went, and when Jupe called the Jamison house late that evening it was a snappish Aunt Mathilda who answered the telephone. She told Jupe that Allie was sleeping and that Pat Osborne was not, and that she had the situation well in hand. She then told Jupe to go to bed and not to call again.

Jupe went to bed and lay for a long time staring at the ceiling. He finally slept, and dreamed dark dreams in which he followed a flickering candle down damp and mouldy corridors while unseen things slithered at his heels. He woke in the silent hour before dawn and thought of the little serpent on the table in the Jamison living-room. He thought of Pat Osborne, wasted and sickened by fear.

In his mind's eye, Jupe saw Shaitan again, with his dark cloak and his ghastly, pallid face. Two nights before, Shaitan had lounged amid his seedy black trappings and plotted leisurely plots. Now the man was in a hurry. He had come openly to the Jamison house to threaten Pat Osborne. Why?

Jupiter decided that he knew why. In the blaze of floodlights at Torrente Canyon, Shaitan and his accomplice had seen Jupiter Jones—a curious boy snooping on unusual householders. But Shaitan must also have seen the man with the moustache, Bentley. And Bentley had acted quickly to save Jupe and to defy Shaitan. In some way Bentley had frightened Shaitan.

Jupe twisted and turned in his bed. If only he could find Bentley. But there seemed no way. The mysterious houseman might be the key to the entire affair, but Jupe could think of no strategy that would lure Bentley into the open. Meanwhile, Pat Osborne was growing more and more ill. Was her terror of Shaitan strong enough to kill her? And Hendricks, the unsuspecting owner of a delicatessen on Beverly Boulevard. What would happen to Hendricks?

Then Jupe remembered the book Bob had taken from the library—the book on witchcraft. It had been written by a professor at Ruxton University, and Ruxton was not ten miles from Rocky Beach. Jupiter suddenly smiled. Even without Bentley, he might find a way to help Pat Osborne. And if Shaitan was in a hurry now so much the better. The Three Investigators had to fight a defensive battle, and before he dropped off again, Jupe knew what the next move would be.

19

The Serpent Strikes Again

THE Three Investigators were at the Jamison house bright and early. When they arrived, Aunt Mathilda was going upstairs with a breakfast tray for Pat Osborne, and Allie was in the kitchen gulping orange juice.

"I've decided what to do about the necklace," Allie told the boys. "I'm going to return it to Van Storen and Chatsworth. Let them worry about it."

"Good!" applauded Bob.

"And you?" asked Allie. "What will you be doing?"

"There's a man in Los Angeles named Hendricks," said Jupe. "He owns a delicatessen and we think he will be next to receive the serpent. I believe it will happen quickly—perhaps today. Shaitan wants to finish up his operation. Hendricks is Noxworth's competitor, and Noxworth is due to pay tribute to Belial. We're going to Los Angeles."

"But what about Aunt Pat? She's in awful shape."

"Aunt Mathilda is here," Jupe reminded her. "You can stay. You can send for the man to come from Van Storen and Chatsworth, can't you?"

"Yes, I can. But what if Shaitan shows up?"

"He won't," Jupe predicted. "Allie, your aunt believes in the power of the serpent, and it has made her very ill. Shaitan knows her so he knows this. He won't come here. He'll wait for her to send for him."

"I don't think she can send for him," said Allie. "She can hardly move. She's almost paralysed."

"There is a way we can help your aunt, Allie, but first we have to think of Hendricks. What we have in mind for Miss Osborne will take time, but she has some time. Hendricks may not."

"What are you going to do?" asked Allie.

"We're going to stake out Hendricks' store," said Bob.

"Then I'm going, too," declared Allie.

"You are not," said Pete. "Shaitan might get rough. That Hendricks is no weakling."

"I am going!" snapped Allie. "Listen, if Aunt Pat has time and Shaitan won't come here, the necklace is safe where it is. I will not sit here and stew while you catch the nuts who've made all this trouble. I'm going!"

Aunt Mathilda came in with the breakfast tray.

"Mrs Jones, I'm going into Los Angeles," said Allie quickly. "I want to talk to Aunt Pat's doctor. Can Jupiter come with me?"

Aunt Mathilda looked puzzled. "I think you should get her doctor," she said. "Your aunt isn't a bit better this morning and she won't eat a thing. But why can't you telephone? Why go all the way to Los Angeles?"

"I can't remember his name," said Allie, "and the number isn't in Aunt Pat's book. But I do remember where his office is. It's in a building on Wilshire next to a church. It's near Western. Once I get there, I can find him."

"There surely must be an easier way," said Aunt Mathilda. "Why don't we just ask Miss Osborne?"

"Haven't you noticed?" said Allie. "She won't talk. I asked but she wouldn't tell me."

"All right," said Aunt Mathilda, "but don't dilly-dally. Jupiter, get Hans to drive you in the truck. It would take all day by bus, and your uncle doesn't have time."

Allie hugged her. "Thanks, Mrs Jones!"

The boys said nothing. They followed Allie out, leaving Aunt Mathilda to scrape Miss Osborne's untouched breakfast into the waste bin.

Hans gladly got out one of the salvage yard trucks for the drive into the city. "Beverly and Third Street," directed Pete, and he climbed into the back of the truck along with Bob and Jupe. Allie rode in the cab with Hans.

At Beverly and Third Street, Jupe asked Hans to drive round a corner and park on a side street. Hans did so, then reached across the seat to open the door for Allie. "You want me to come with you?" he asked the boys.

"No," said Jupe. "You wait here and relax. We may be gone for quite a while."

"Okay." Hans took a newspaper from under the seat and prepared to relax.

Allie and the boys rounded the corner and cut across the Hendricks parking area. "That's Noxworth's store over there," said Pete, pointing to the untidy place across the street.

Allie's nose wrinkled with distaste.

The door of the Hendricks store opened and a small boy scooted out. Hendricks was just behind him.

"Don't come back today," Hendricks told the child.

Jupiter reached the door just as Hendricks was putting a key into the lock.

"Sorry," said Hendricks. "I'm closed."

"You received the serpent," said Jupiter.

Hendricks straightened up, looked round and saw Pete. "You again!"

"Mr Hendricks, we want to help," said Pete.

"You do, do you? Okay, the cops filled me in on you. You kids are a bunch of amateur private eyes and you think you're on to some big witch doctor thing. Now I think you're nuts, but I can't chance any lawsuits so I'm closing. Beat it."

"You received the serpent," said Jupe again.

Hendricks reached out and gathered up a fistful of Jupe's shirt. "Did you bring that thing?" he asked. "If you did, I'll wring your neck!"

Jupe did not try to break away. "We didn't bring the serpent, but we know it must be a cobra with jewelled eyes. How did it arrive?"

Hendricks studied Jupe's face, then let go of his shirt. He opened the door and pointed towards his counter. There was a gilded cobra, a duplicate of the one that had been sent to Pat Osborne.

"I went in the back room for a couple of minutes," said Hendricks. "When I came back, that thing was on the counter."

"I see," said Jupiter.

"So you see. I'm glad. Now go. I've called the cops, but I don't want anyone around just in case something does happen. So blow! Scram!"

A little girl scudded up to the store. Hendricks

grabbed her by the shoulder and spun her around. "Go home to your mother and stay there," he ordered.

She gaped at him.

"Home!" shouted the delicatessen man.

The little girl went.

"Customers!" complained Hendricks. "They're like termites. You can't get rid of them."

A man wearing stained blue trousers and an over-sized, ragged coat made his unsteady way round the corner of the building. "Coffee?" he pleaded.

Allie examined the newcomer with interest. She had seen few panhandlers in her life, and this one was especially seedy. He must not have owned a shirt, for pink, wrinkled skin showed at the neck where his shabby coat was open. His grey hair had gone uncut for many a month, and the stubble on his cheeks was days old.

"Coffee?" he said again. "Say, mister, maybe a sandwich? I haven't eaten for two days."

Hendricks dug into his pocket and pulled out a roll of notes. He peeled off one without even looking at it and thrust it at the tramp. "I'm closed. The guy across the street will sell you a sandwich."

"You're a good man," said the tramp warmly. He took the money, turned, stumbled and fell into the rack of newspapers that stood beside the shop door.

"Blast!" cried Hendricks.

The tramp thrashed about, a jumble of arms, legs and newsprint. "S'okay!" he said. He untangled himself, lurched to his feet and ambled away.

"Hey, mister!" called Allie. "Wait a second!" She

darted forward to pick up a small, square black object from amid the pile of papers that now blocked Hendricks' entrance. "You dropped your radio."

The tramp began to run.

"Allie." Jupe kept his voice very calm. "Allie, give that to me."

"Good lord!" said Hendricks.

Allie looked at the little black box in her hand. "What is it? What's the matter?"

Hendricks snatched the object and threw it. He threw blindly. It arched high in the air, landed on the sidewalk across the street, bounced twice and hit the wall of Noxworth's little shop.

There was a flash and a roar, and the windows of Noxworth's Mini Market collapsed inward!

Jupe had a glimpse of Noxworth's face, white with terror, peering from behind a counter. Then Hendricks was racing down the street after the fleeing tramp.

"It was a bomb!" said Allie. "I thought it was a radio."

"Allie, my girl, you've led a sheltered life," declared Pete. "Hardly any real tramps own transistor radios."

20

Wanted: One Witch Doctor

ON THE RETURN TRIP from Los Angeles, Allie sat in the back of the truck with the boys.

"Now the police will question Aunt Pat, won't they?" she asked.

"I'm sure they'll be gentle with her," said Jupe. "After all, she isn't a criminal."

"I wanted to keep her out of this."

"There wasn't any way," Bob told her. "Once the police knew how dangerous Shaitan was, we had to tell them everything."

"Allie, you were great," said Pete. "If you hadn't picked up that bomb, Hendricks' store would have been blown up." He chuckled. "I'd hate to see anything happen to Hendricks. What a guy! How'd you like the flying tackle when he caught up with that bogus tramp? And the way he sat on the crook until the cops got there?"

"I enjoyed the look on Noxworth's face more," said Jupe. "The last thing he expected was to have *his* windows blown in."

The truck stopped in front of Allie's house. Aunt Mathilda must have been watching for them, because the front door opened immediately.

"Where have you been?" called Aunt Mathilda.

"Miss Osborne is much worse. Dr Peters is with her now. I had to call him. Did you find her own doctor?"

"No, we didn't." Jupe hurried up the path. He looked past Aunt Mathilda and saw Dr Peters.

"Does she have any close relations here?" asked the doctor.

Allie skidded past Jupe and Aunt Mathilda. "I'm it, at the moment," she said.

"I want to move her to a hospital," Dr Peters said. "She won't consent."

Allie went up the stairs two at a time. Jupe followed her.

Miss Patricia Osborne looked like a shrunken doll under the covers of her big tester bed. She turned away when Allie came into the room.

"Aunt Pat, you've got to snap out of this," scolded Allie. "It's all over. Shaitan is a con man and the cops are going to grab him."

Pat Osborne did not stir.

Allie seized her arm and shook her. "You've got to help yourself now. Come on! You need to be in the hospital."

Miss Osborne touched Allie's hand. "The necklace," she whispered. "Get it, Allie, please?"

Allie pulled away. "No. You can't give the necklace to Shaitan. Didn't you hear what I've been telling you? By this time, Shaitan's in jail where he can't hurt anyone."

"You betrayed him?" Fresh horror showed in Pat Osborne's face. "Allie, he'll blame me!"

"Nonsense!" Allie tugged at one of her wrists. "Come on, now, Aunt Pat."

Jupe took Allie's elbow. "Let her alone," he coun-selled. He led Allie into the hall. "She can't help her-self," he said. "Don't you see? She's more afraid of Shaitan in jail than out. There's only one thing to do. We fight fire with fire."

"How?" asked Allie.

"She's been bewitched."

"Jupiter Jones, you know that's hogwash!"

"But your aunt believes it, and it's killing her. We have to take off the curse. We have to find another witch doctor. It's in all the anthropology books. When someone's been cursed, you find another witch doctor to send back the curse."

Allie sagged against the wall. "Where do we get a witch doctor?"

"I think I know." Jupiter started downstairs.

In the lower hall, Bob and Pete milled around a worried Aunt Mathilda. The doctor was pacing in the living-room.

"That professor at Ruxton University," said Jupe to Bob. "The one who wrote the book on magic. Do you remember his name?"

"Bannister, I think. No. No, it's Barrister. Henry Barrister."

"That sounds right. And Ruxton is just over the hills in the valley." Jupe started for the kitchen, and the two other boys trailed him.

"Are you going to do what I think you're going to do?" asked Bob.

"I am," said Jupe. "We've had black magic, and now we need a white witch. It could be Barrister. He cer-tainly knows the subject."

Jupe took the telephone from the wall and dialled directory enquiries. "Have you a number for a Henry Barrister in Ruxton?" he asked.

Bob put a pad on the counter in front of Jupe and handed him a pencil. Jupe wrote down a number the operator gave him and hung up. "If only he's at home," he said.

He dialled the Ruxton number. At the other end of the line, a telephone rang and rang. Then there was a click as someone lifted the receiver.

"Is this Dr Barrister of Ruxton University?" asked Jupiter.

After a pause, the other boys heard Jupiter say, "Good! My name is Jupiter Jones, Dr Barrister, and I need your help. It's difficult to explain over the telephone, but there's a woman here who has had a curse put on her, and we—"

Jupiter stopped talking and listened.

"Yes, she's very ill," he said.

Again Jupiter listened.

"Yesterday," he said. "A package was delivered to her. It contained a statue of a serpent."

After a few moments, Jupiter said, "I'm calling from Rocky Beach. The woman's name is Miss Patricia Osborne."

There was another pause, and Jupe said, "That's very kind of you." He gave the address of the Jamison house and hung up.

"He's coming," he told Pete and Bob. "He said he'll bring someone who can take off the curse."

"Great stuff!" crowed Pete. "A voodoo priest, maybe?"

"We'll see," said Jupiter.

The kitchen door opened and Aunt Mathilda put her head in. "Jupiter, what are you doing?"

"I found a doctor, Aunt Mathilda. Dr Barrister."

"Thank heavens! Dr Peters isn't able to get any-where with Miss Osborne. Maybe she'll listen to her own doctor."

"Let's hope so. He's on his way."

"Good. I'll go and sit with her in the meantime. And one of you boys should see to that horse."

Allie drifted into the kitchen. "I'll take care of Queenie," she told Aunt Mathilda.

"The doctor's coming," said Jupe to Allie.

"You found one? That's great!"

Aunt Mathilda went upstairs and Dr Peters took his leave, fussing and promising to return later. The boys wandered out to the veranda and sat down on the steps. Allie joined them presently. "How long will it be?" she asked.

"Very soon now," said Jupe.

And very soon a car turned on to the street and came at a rapid clip towards the Jamison house. It swerved into the driveway and the engine died. The driver got out and rushed up the path.

"Jupiter Jones!" said the man.

Jupe started, and so did the others.

"Miss Jamison, I'm very sorry," said the man to Allie. "I had no idea things would go so far."

Jupe stood up. "Just who are you?" he demanded.

"I'm Dr Barrister, and I should have known better. I thought they were the usual harmless dabblers in magic."

Allie gasped. "You . . . you shaved off your moustache!" she managed at last.

The man who had been known as Bentley touched his upper lip and smiled. "It wasn't real. I thought if I was going to be an investigator, I'd need a disguise."

21

Mara's White Magic

DR BARRISTER sat in the Jamison living-room and
turned the little figure of the cobra in his hands. "An
intricate bit of work," he said, "but then, they weren't
playing to a primitive audience. A wax doll wouldn't
have been convincing."

"Does it matter what the witch uses?" asked Pete.

Barrister put the serpent down. "Not at all, so long
as the victim knows he's been cursed. The power of
suggestion takes over. The victim is terrified, and the
terror doesn't end."

"Can you help?" asked Allie. "Can you make Aunt
Pat believe you're taking the curse off?"

"Not I. Do I look like a witch doctor?"

Allie and the boys had to admit that he did not.
Whether you called him Bentley or Barrister, he was
the same calm, inoffensive person.

"Your aunt has seen me pushing a vacuum cleaner
in this house," he said. "She wouldn't believe in me,
but I think she'll believe in Mara. Mara is very convincing. She's waiting in the car. I've explained the
entire affair to her and she knows what to do."

"Is she a witch doctor?" asked Bob.

"She's a gypsy, and she does seem to have certain
gifts," said Barrister. "She can cure warts, for example,
and she has had some success as a fortune teller. She's

also mastered a ritual which is guaranteed to send the most stubborn curse back to the one who inflicted it. You'll have to help her, but you may enjoy that. I'll go and get her."

He went out of the room and returned shortly, bringing with him a wrinkled woman whose hair was bound up with a number of scarfs. Mara's blouse was a faded pink, and her wide green skirt reached to the toes of her scuffed shoes. There was an air about her of dust and old clothing, but there was also a brightness. Her black eyes sparkled under shaggy brows.

She picked up the serpent. "Is this it?"

"That's it," said Dr Barrister.

"Hah!" said Mara. The gypsy nodded to Allie and the boys. "We will work together," she told them. "You do what I say and you say nothing. Do you understand?"

"We understand," said Jupe.

"Is the woman upstairs?"

"Yes," said Allie.

"Then we will go." Mara made for the stairs, carrying the serpent.

"Merciful gracious to heavens!" At the foot of the stairs, Aunt Mathilda came face to face with Mara and seemed about to go into shock.

"It's all right, Aunt Mathilda," Jupe assured her. "Why don't you wait with Dr Barrister?"

"Dr Barrister? Is Miss Osborne's doctor here? Why didn't you call me? What are you up to?"

"Dr Barrister will explain." Jupiter turned to the professor. "This is my aunt, Mrs Jones. She's been taking care of Miss Osborne."

"Delighted to meet you, Mrs Jones," said Barrister. "Come and sit down and I'll explain. You won't believe me, but I'll explain it all."

Aunt Mathilda stood firm. "Jupiter," she said, "I want you to tell me here and now—"

"Woman, you are in my way!" said Mara.

"What?" cried Aunt Mathilda.

"I have important work to do," said Mara. "If you stand in my way, you will regret it."

The gypsy's bold eyes locked into Aunt Mathilda's stern gaze. For a few seconds, Aunt Mathilda glared at Mara. Then, to Jupe's amazement, his aunt stepped aside. Mara did have gifts.

The gypsy went up the stairs and let Allie lead her to Pat Osborne's room. The Three Investigators followed.

Pat Osborne did not see Mara until the gypsy stood at the foot of the bed and called out.

"Oh, cursed one!" cried Mara. "Listen to me so you may live!"

Under the covers, Pat Osborne shuddered.

"More pillows," said Mara to Allie. "Put pillows under her head so she may see."

Allie scooted out and got three pillows. She coaxed her aunt to a half-sitting position and propped her up with the pillows.

"Look!" Mara held up the golden cobra. "This is the bringer of evil!"

Pat Osborne winced. "Belial!" she whispered. "The serpent is the messenger of Belial!"

"Hah!" said the gypsy. "Ten spirits I have, each more powerful than Belial. But he who summoned Belial will feel the curse."

The gypsy came around the bed and thrust the shining cobra towards Pat Osborne. "You must take this into your hands."

"No! No, I can't."

"You must hold it, woman," ordered Mara. She took Aunt Pat's hand in her own and closed the trembling fingers around the snake. "Hold it firm if you would save yourself!"

For the first time, a spark of hope seemed to liven Pat Osborne. She grasped the serpent.

From some fold in her wide skirt, Mara took a green cloth bag. "Green is the colour of spring," she told Aunt Pat. "It is the colour of life. You will put the evil thing into this green bag."

Without taking her eyes from Mara's face, Aunt Pat did as she was told.

"Good." Mara pulled the drawstrings at the top of the bag, closing the snake inside.

"Lock the door," she said to Allie. "Then light a candle."

There was no shortage of candles in the room. They stood about on every surface—green ones and purple, red ones and white. "A red candle," said Mara. "Red has power."

Allie lit a red candle.

"Now, no one may speak," said Mara.

No one did. No one but Mara herself, and when she spoke it was in a high, reedy voice, in a language that none of them understood. She held the green bag containing the little cobra. She addressed it, chanting and crooning. Sometimes her words were a gentle lullaby, sometimes a harsh and terrible threat.

Suddenly the gypsy clutched the green bag close to her faded blouse, threw back her head, let her eyes roll wildly and fell to the floor.

Aunt Pat stared. Mara's mouth was open, and from her throat came a dreadful, gurgling sound, and then a series of high, keening notes.

Mara the gypsy was singing, and she was singing the song of the serpent.

As the frightful sound went on, Mara twitched. Her back arched so that she touched the floor only with her head and her heels. Then she began to roll, thrashing from one side to another, cradling the bag in her arms, her open eyes sightless.

The scarfs which bound her head came undone, one after another. They slipped away and long, grey hair streamed over her face.

Still the song went on, louder and louder, higher and higher, piercing, chilling.

Pat Osborne sat up straight in the bed.

Mara gave a mighty shudder. She screamed, and her body went limp.

Allie and the boys waited. Pat Osborne watched. The gypsy woman seemed to sleep.

"Jupiter!" Aunt Mathilda's voice was loud in the hall. "Jupiter, what's going on in there? Open this door!"

Mara moaned and sat up. She groped at the green bag which somehow had remained in her grasp. She smiled. "I saw him," she said. "There is a man in black. His face is very white. He struggles. He is in the coils of the serpent."

"Jupiter, open the door this minute!" called Aunt Mathilda.

Mara got up from the floor. She went to Pat Osborne with the bag. "It is as I promised."

Miss Osborne's shaking hands tore at the drawstrings that closed the bag. She peered inside, felt the bag, shook it. It was empty.

"My spirits are strong," said Mara. "The serpent has returned to sting the one who sent it. The power of Belial has been broken, and Belial has turned on his master. You have nothing to fear."

She went to the door and opened it. "You can come in," she told Aunt Mathilda. "The woman in bed— she is well again."

22

The Last of the Snakes

"IT'S LIKE A MIRACLE," Allie told The Three Investigators. "Aunt Pat had soup last night and milk and biscuits at bedtime and two eggs this morning. Now she's hungry again."

Allie took two slices of toast from the toaster and began to spread them with butter. "I don't know what I would have done without your Aunt Mathilda," she said to Jupe.

"She's always there when you need her," Jupe informed her. "However, by this morning she has convinced herself that the entire affair of the singing serpent never happened. No matter how Dr Barrister explained it, she can't believe it. She is now down at the salvage yard, attending to business as usual and seeing that Hans and Konrad are not idle."

Allie put the toast on a tray and poured a glass of milk. "How come you're not at the salvage yard?" she asked. "I had an idea your aunt liked to keep you busy, too."

"Chief Reynolds came to the salvage yard this morning," said Jupe. "The Los Angeles police want to see us again. We're just on our way in."

"Did the Chief have any news?" asked Allie.

"That phoney tramp named Ellis is in jail, of course," said Bob.

"That's the place for a bomber," said Allie.

"Chief Reynolds said he talked his head off," Pete told Allie. "Noxworth talked, too. The police collected Hugo Ariel and the man called Max. They were at Torrente Canyon. Noxworth didn't know they'd paid Ellis to bomb Hendricks' store. He only thought something would happen to lay Hendricks low."

"That accounts for everybody," said Allie. "All except one."

"Dr Shaitan," said Jupiter.

Allie sat down at the table. "They didn't get Shaitan?"

"He wasn't at Torrente Canyon," said Jupe. "He disappeared, leaving everything behind, including his car. Chief Reynolds thinks he's probably in Canada by now."

Allie tucked her feet up on the rungs of her chair. "And what do you think?" she asked.

"You're still our client," said Jupiter Jones. "We can't consider the case closed until Shaitan is safely in custody."

"You'll have a long, long wait," said a voice from the doorway.

Allie spun about in the chair. The boys froze where they were.

The man called Shaitan stood facing them, his back to the hall. He looked very much as he had the night they witnessed the ritual in the black-draped room. However, his cloak was streaked with dust and matted with burrs. In one slender hand there was a gun.

"I've become awfully careless about locking the doors," said Allie bitterly. "Anyone could wander in here."

"Many people have wandered in in the past day," said Shaitan. "They're all gone now, aren't they? All except you brats and that fool of a woman."

"You're very well informed," said Jupiter Jones. "Have you been watching the house from the hill beyond the meadow?"

The man bowed to Jupe. "It was tiring," he said. "It was also tiring to walk the mountain trails to Rocky Beach. However, I decided it would be safer to abandon my car when I saw the police drive up to my front gate."

"Just for curiosity's sake, how'd you get out of that house on Torrente Canyon?" asked Pete. "The police got Ariel and Max."

"Fortunately, I was in the back garden when they came."

"So you went over the wall and left your buddies to take the rap," said Bob.

"Who wouldn't?" snapped Shaitan. "Now that stupid woman is upstairs, I suppose." He gestured with the gun. "You four will go up ahead of me. When I've had my little talk with Miss Osborne, I'll make sure that no one leaves this house for some time."

"You will not see my aunt," said Allie evenly.

"Allie, he's got a gun!" warned Pete.

"I don't care. He's done enough. He's not going to see her!"

Very deliberately, she put her hands on her hips and looked straight into Shaitan's weary face. "I know what you want," she said. "You want the Empress Eugénie necklace. Well, it isn't here and Aunt Pat doesn't know where it is, so get lost. You've had all you're going to get."

"If it's in a bank or at the jewellers', it can be retrieved," said Shaitan calmly. "Miss Osborne will telephone. And if it's hidden here, it can be found."

"It isn't in a—"

"Allie!" cried Jupe.

Shaitan's eyes went from Allie to Jupe, then back to Allie.

"You were going to say it isn't in a bank," he said. "Is it at the jewellers'? No. Somehow I think it isn't at the jewellers'. And not in this house? Now where would one hide a priceless necklace like that?" He waved the boys back and came close to Allie. "You know. You'll tell me."

Allie drew back. "I don't know."

"Of course you know. You know all the places it isn't, so you know the place where it is." His right hand still held the gun, but his left hand flashed out. His fingers closed on Allie's shoulder. "Where is it?"

"Take your hands off her!" yelled Pete.

"I won't tell," shouted Allie. "You can go jump!"

"You'll tell." The hand tightened on Allie's shoulder and Shaitan began to shake the girl.

"Stop that!" yelled Bob.

Out beyond the back court, Allie's Appaloosa mare stomped in her stall. Her excited neigh came clearly to them.

"What's that?" demanded Shaitan.

"Only Queenie," said Allie. "My mare."

"Oh, the Appaloosa," said Shaitan. "Yes, I know about her. You care a great deal about that horse and she . . . she has a stall in the garage."

No one spoke.

"Not in the house," said Shaitan. "In the garage. Yes, the necklace is hidden in the garage, where no one can get to it without disturbing the horse. That's what you did, isn't it?"

Allie pulled away from him.

"Out, all of you!" ordered Shaitan.

The horse whinnied again.

"Go on!" commanded Shaitan. "Out to that garage and show me the necklace!"

"I won't!" Allie was almost in tears.

"Do as he says, Allie," said Jupe. "You're not bullet-proof."

"He won't get far," Bob predicted.

"We'll see about that," said Shaitan. He herded them out of the back door and across the courtyard. The garage door stood partly open. Jupe swung it wide and they went in.

"Now where is it?" demanded Shaitan.

Queenie bobbed her big head up and down and whinnied at the sight of Allie.

Shaitan looked at the horse. "You wouldn't hide it in the stall," he decided. "It might get stepped on or eaten. Let me see. The hay? Perhaps. Or the oat bin?"

Allie stiffened ever so slightly.

"It's the oat bin!" cried Shaitan. "You put it in the oat bin!"

He curtly ordered the boys to stand next to the stall. He then shoved Allie towards the feed bin. "Get it!" he said. His voice was very cold. "Get your hands in that thing and dig out the necklace or I'll break your arm."

Cautiously, without looking round at the horse, Pete undid the latch on Queenie's stall.

"Get it!" said Shaitan again. He grabbed Allie's wrist and twisted her arm behind her back.

"You're hurting me!" cried Allie.

Pete stepped to one side and looked at the Appaloosa. The mare's ears were flat against her head.

"Go, Queenie!" shouted Pete, and he swung open the door of the stall.

Queenie moved like a dappled fury. Her hoofs beat briefly on the cement floor of the garage, and then she reared over Shaitan, flailing at the air and screaming as only a furious or terrified horse can scream.

Shaitan let go of Allie. "Get away!" he yelled. His gun swung to take aim at the horse.

"No!" Allie struck at his arm.

The gun went off. The sound of the shot seemed to fill the garage almost to bursting, yet the boys distinctly heard the bullet whine off the floor and splatter into the wall.

Queenie's hoofs struck the floor. Her big head lunged forward. Her big mouth opened and her teeth clamped down on Shaitan's arm.

Shaitan screamed and dropped the gun. It skidded across the cement. Jupe crouched without taking his eyes from Shaitan, who was trying to pull away from the horse. He picked up the gun.

"It's all right, Allie!" shouted Jupe. "Get the mare away."

Allie ran and threw her arms around Queenie's neck. "Easy, girl," she said. "Let go! Easy!"

The Appaloosa released Shaitan, and the sinister high

priest sagged back into a corner of the garage, holding his injured arm close to his body.

Jupe put himself between Shaitan and the door. "Don't try to leave," he said quietly. "I'm not an excellent shot and I might do you some serious damage without intending it."

Shaitan saw the gun in Jupe's hand. He said nothing. He sat there, holding his arm, panting.

Bob stepped behind Jupe. "I'll call Chief Reynolds," he said. "It won't take him five minutes to get here."

"No hurry," said Jupiter Jones cheerfully.

Pete grinned at Queenie. Allie was coaxing the mare back into her stall. "I always had an idea that that animal might bite," declared Pete. "Only I never expected it would come in so handy."

23

Mr Hitchcock Asks Some Questions

"I SENT FOR YOU," said Alfred Hitchcock, "because my curiosity is aroused."

The famous film director tapped a heap of newspapers which were on his desk and looked searchingly at The Three Investigators. "I read of a bombing in Los Angeles. The crime was witnessed by three boys from Rocky Beach, and by a girl about your age. The names of the minors were not published."

Bob handed a file across the desk to Mr Hitchcock.

"We were there," he said.

"On a case, eh?" said Mr Hitchcock. "I had an idea that might be it." He opened the file and read Bob's notes on the Mystery of the Singing Serpent.

It was quiet in the office then, except for the rustle of papers. Finally Mr Hitchcock looked up from the file. "It's not complete."

"I'm still working on it," said Bob.

Mr Hitchcock sniffed. "Astounding what people will believe," he said. "I suppose the cobra you saw at that house in Torrente Canyon was some sort of special effect?"

"They had projectors in the ceiling to throw images of the serpent on the column of smoke," said Pete. "You'd think it wouldn't work. You'd think they'd need special glasses to convince people they were seeing a real snake, but with all that movement in the smoke, it did work. It looked like a real, live, three-dimensional snake."

"Even we were fooled," said Jupiter, "and those people wanted to believe in the serpent. Of course, the serpent *had* to sing. They had to cover up the noise from the projectors."

"There's usually a reason for everything," said Mr Hitchcock. "How did the serpent sing?"

"It was Ariel," said Jupe. "We thought he made the noise with some device. He did not. He used to be a ventriloquist, and he could make that noise without showing any strain whatever. With Mara, we could see who the singer was."

"Mara has talents, doesn't she?"

"Many," admitted Jupe. "She's a quick mimic. Dr Barrister played his tape of that session in Allie's dining-room as they were driving to Rocky Beach. She could sing like a serpent before they even turned in the drive.

"Mara also did something clever with the green bag in which Miss Osborne placed the serpent statue. She won't admit it, but Dr Barrister is sure she had a second bag hidden in her skirt. She switched bags while she was rolling around on the floor, gave the empty bag to Miss Osborne and walked off with the serpent."

"That's a very old trick," said Mr Hitchcock. "Has Dr Barrister told you why he was so interested in Miss Osborne and the fellowship?"

"He's writing a book on the psychology of super-stition," said Jupiter Jones. "He knows most of the strange cults that exist in Los Angeles because that's his subject. He's even joined many of them. And Miss Osborne had joined many of them. He'd seen her often —many times before he became Bentley the houseman. Then she dropped out of all of them. She and Madelyn Enderby."

"This intrigued him?" asked Mr Hitchcock.

"Yes, because it didn't seem in character. Miss Osborne was obviously looking for something special in these strange groups, and so was the Enderby woman. He wondered if they'd found it somewhere else, so he asked his wife to have her hair done at Miss Enderby's shop. Fortunately, Madelyn Enderby likes to talk, and she talked a great deal about the fellowship. Dr Barrister got actual names and places. He checked on the members and discovered that all of them were people of means."

"He was suspicious?" asked Mr Hitchcock.

"Not at first. He thought they were merely a group of well-off individuals who were probably paying good money to sit in that house in the canyon and listen to a serpent sing. This isn't so odd. But he himself couldn't get into that house. Membership was by invitation only, and no one invited him—or his wife. Shaitan probably checked on him and decided he was dangerous.

"So Dr Barrister took to watching, and when Hugo Ariel moved to Rocky Beach, he took to snooping. And he was very much interested in Pat Osborne. She's a marvellous subject for a man who wants to write a book on the psychology of superstition, and she was different from the other members who went to Torrente Canyon in that she did not have a great deal of money. Shaitan, of course, knew about her wealthy relatives."

"Was it Madelyn Enderby who passed along the word that the Jamison maid had left?" asked Mr Hitchcock.

"Yes, it was. And that's when he got the idea of putting on a walrus moustache and infiltrating the house to observe Miss Osborne. Then Mrs Compton had her accident and Miss Osborne sent the necklace out and he became uneasy."

"That's when he really started hanging around that house in Torrente Canyon," put in Bob. "He was there when Allie and Pete and I went over that wall. He saw the floodlights and heard the alarm. And he was there, luckily, when Jupe ran out."

"A good man to have on your side," said the director. "Too bad you frightened him out of the Jamison house when you searched his apartment in Santa Monica. But why did he have that apartment? You said he makes his home in Ruxton."

"It was a blind," said Pete. "He wanted a place near Rocky Beach in case anyone checked on him. Also, he said it was peaceful there and he could get a lot of work done. He has four children."

Mr Hitchcock chuckled. "Part of the disguise, like the moustache," he said.

"He didn't really need it," said Jupe. "I don't think Pat Osborne would have noticed him, moustache or not. He has the kind of face everyone forgets."

"And when you wanted a white witch, you happened to call him," said Mr Hitchcock.

"It was like a miracle," said Jupe. "We had no

explaining to do, and he had a tape of the serpent singing and could coach Mara. The police used his files to contact members of the fellowship and invite them to an identification parade."

"You should have been there!" exclaimed Pete. "You should have seen their faces when they saw Shaitan without his cape or his cap. He looked like a lost leprechaun. His real name's Henry Longstreet, but he's also known as Harry the Dip because he used to be a pickpocket. Ariel started life as Johnny Boye and once got arrested for peddling fake chrome polish in a car park. The man called Max is an ex-burglar and Ellis, who did the actual bombing and sabotaged Mrs Compton's car, has quite a record. He'll do anything for money."

"Allie told her aunt all about it," said Jupe. "It didn't help much. She's sitting on the patio now, wondering how soon she'll be able to go into Hollywood to consult with Mara."

"A hopeless case," said Mr Hitchcock. "But what did happen to Miss Enderby's landlady?"

"Nothing," said Bob. "She went to Dubuque because her sister invited her. Probably lucky for her, but Miss Enderby thought Belial engineered the trip and no one told her anything different."

"What about the man who was worried about a high rise building going up next to his property?"

"The land wasn't stable enough for a high rise," said Jupe, "and they credited that to Belial."

"One nice thing," said Pete. "That crystal ball that started the trouble? Allie bought it. Her aunt didn't want it, after what had happened, so Allie took it to the hospital to Mrs Compton."

Mr Hitchcock nodded. "A nice gesture."

"It was," said Pete. "Allie's okay, I guess, but I think I'll be glad when she goes to boarding school in the autumn. We'll get to use Red Gate Rover again—and besides, she's kind of a strain to have around. Like, she can think up lies quicker than anybody I ever met, and she has this thing about getting her own way."

"It appears so," said Mr Hitchcock, "but there could be compensations. For example, if you treat her nicely, she might let you ride her horse."

"Thanks a lot," said Pete, "but if I have to go by Appaloosa, I'll stay home!"